CORAL BEACH CASEFILES

• RADICALLY BOTH •

ENGEN
BOOKS

Published in Canada by Engen Books, St. John's, NL.

ISBN: 978-1-77478-161-6

Reprinting material originally presented in: *Inner Child, Gang War,* and *Chains.*

Distributed by:
Engen Books
www.engenbooks.com
submissions@engenbooks.com

First hardcover printing: April 2024

Cover Image: Liz LeDrew
Cover Design: Matthew LeDrew

Praise for the
CORAL BEACH CASEFILES
Series

"It is the writing of it's generation: visual, to-the-point and in-the-moment." - *The Northeast Avalon Times*

"This is an amazing start to the dark paranormal thriller series, the Coral Beach Casefiles. Make no mistake, even though this is YA, it is dark and gory. It holds nothing back. The descriptions are wonderfully done. The visuals are powerful and brought the nightmare to life." - Christine Rains, author of *The 13th Floor*

"It has more depth and mystery than I first expected. The race to stay ahead of the killer made it a hard book to put down." - Peter J Foote, author of *Stowaway's Luck*

"Is unrelenting and full of surprises. You will never want to leave Coral Beach." - Paul Carberry, author of *Carcharodon*

"An unabashedly entertaining romp into the macabre, Black Womb is a delightful homage to 80's/90's slasher movies and delivers on its promise keep you guessing at every turn of the page." - Nicole Little, author of *Roxy Buckles and the Flight of the Sparrow*

"Black Womb is an exciting horror story full of action and introducing a bunch of interesting characters. The story flows quickly and is a great read for a first-time novelist." - Lisa M Daly, author of *Their Sturdy Pride*

"Matthew has a way of drawing you in and keeping you engaged to the point where you don't realize how long you've been reading until the book is finished." -- Kelly Rose, author of *Undead Rebirth*

"The Black Womb lives, thanks to Smoke and Mirrors, Matthew LeDrew's third novel in his saga. Released by Engen Books in 2009, it is a mature and complex tale with many twists and turns that is sure to please fans of action, drama, horror and mystery. If not for a dip in the middle portion, this would easily be the best book – thus far – in the series. As it stands, it may be the most entertaining." - Jay Paulin, author of *Emma Awesome*

CONTENTS

Introduction
by Matthew LeDrew

This trilogy serves as an end to the Coral Beach Casefiles series, but that was not always to be the case. Originally, there was no "series break" between *Chains* and *The Long Road*, or between *The Long Road* and *Cinders*: it was to be *all one series*.

Nowadays, that seems insane. Like, properly nuts. The tone difference between the series, the location, the supporting cast, *everything* is drastically different. In fact, the *only* thing to remain the same is the main character and his plight, and even that alters over time. These are different series, and it's silly to think that they could ever have been anything but.

But that means that when these books were *planned* and even first written, they weren't planned to be an *end*. And that's interesting looking back, because that forms one of my favorite endings to a story I've told yet. No spoilers, but the series ends in a way you would not expect, and I love it for that.

There's a quietness to this ending. It's an ending that comes not from plot but from character, that comes from these young characters ceasing to think childishly.

Other things changed with the transition from *Coral Beach Casefiles* to *The Xander Drew* series. I met Ellen Curtis, the woman who would become my wife, while writing *Cinders*. It was the first book to be edited by Erin Vance, the woman who would become my best friend, editor-in-chief, and business partner. I didn't know it when writing these books in my late twenties nor when we published them in my early thirties, but everything was about to be different. Engen Books was about to go from what was essentially self-publishing into one of the top publishers in its region in a few short years. I'd soon have oversight in a way I didn't on these first ten books: an editor to look over my shoulder and call balls and strikes, to curb my worst impulses. My life was about to become more stable, and so suddenly I was writing about the troubles of youth not from the point-of-view of someone in it, but from the point-of-view of someone looking back on it. And that's a different book. I couldn't write these books today, for good or ill.

But I look back on them, and they're still a part of me. I've grown past the rage that fuelled them, but it's still there. When I wrote these books, I was a young man angry at the injustice he saw in the world and wishing he could grow claws and rip it all down. Now I'm still angry at that injustice, but I feel like I can do something about it. Now those same feelings fuel action, not rage.

But the rage is still there. And so, unable to be either the solely the young man who wrote the Coral Beach Casefiles nor solely the older one who wrote The Xander Drew series... I'll settle for being radically both.

Matthew LeDrew
April 4, 2024

BOOK EIGHT

INNER CHILD

PROLOGUE

"Ashes, to ashes..." said Reverend Gallagher, as Mandy's casket was lowered into the ground. His arms were raised and a few flakes of snow were falling from the sky, getting caught in the same breeze that made the robes under his arms billow. He was bald except for clumps of white hair that clung stubbornly behind his ears. "And dust, to dust..."

Mandy had always loved the snow, or so Xander had recalled her once saying. Now she would never get to see it again.

"Nobody's here..." Cathy mumbled, looking around at the surprisingly small crowd gathered.

"Julie's still in the hospital," Xander said coldly, not turning away from the coffin as it landed in its hole with a dull thud. "Tommy wanted to stay with her, since her whole family was going to be here. Mike doesn't go to funerals anymore."

Cathy nodded, remembering her boyfriend's stance on the rituals of the dead.

"She was special," he said, mostly to himself.

Tears started to stream down Cathy's face. "You did everything you could."

"Sure I did," he responded, trying to hide the sarcasm in his voice.

School would start up again soon, and everything would get back to normal. Without her.

Once again, they were forced to leave someone behind and to press forward. To commit to continuing to live, if only to honor the memories of those who could not make such commitments.

Once again, good people had died when the bad continue to live.

"It should have been me," Xander said finally, drawing Cathy's attention.

"What?"

"It should have been me. I should have been faster, smarter... or just plain ignored O'Toole. I made every wrong choice that day."

"Xander..." she sighed, crying, unable to think of a way to finish the sentence that would make him feel better.

"I have been asked by a shared friend of Mandy Peterson and I..." Reverend Gallagher continued, reaching down into his robe. "...to read a passage from the journal of Miss. Peterson."

Xander raised his head, eyes blank as he listened.

Reverend Gallagher opened the book, flipped a few pages ahead, and then went back.

Tears started to flow down Xander's cheeks.

Though she wasn't quite sure why, when Cathy saw it she cried too.

Reverend Gallagher coughed.

"There is only one passage," he said, his lower lip shaking as he, too, started to cry. "It... It is dated the night before her death. It reads simply: 'I love my life. I can't wait to live it.'"

Cathy broke down, her tears absorbed by the earth.

Reverend Gallagher stepped down, wiping his eyes in his sleeve as the rest of those gathered broke down as well.

Xander just stared down at the grave, as stone-faced as the headstone. He turned, looking up at Sara's grave on the hill, and listened.

CHAPTER ONE: AWAKENINGS

"In the darkness it followed them, just enough light for them to see. It chased them through the brush and the woods, the tree limbs scraping past them, tearing at their limbs, cutting deep, deep, everything cut deep. The wind whistled through the branches as they ran past, singing the songs of their deaths, and it was beautiful.

"It was not an evil thing that pursued them, for its need to kill went far deeper than what we mere mortals define as right and wrong. It was simply a need to be, an urge to sate the growing hunger for flesh. It did not hate them, nor they it, because they knew that it was its instinct to give chase, as much as it was theirs to run.

"The ground beneath its feet stuck to it, keeping it moist and warm; a loud sucking sound accompanying every powerful stride as it broke the twigs that sliced at its prey, its eyes never batting for fear of being prodded. It thought only of the hunt, of the taste of victory.

"The moon overhead and the ground beneath, it chased as they were chased. It ran as they did run. And as it caught them, their flesh biding mercy to its claw, they became one under a common need, a common goal, and came to know and understand each other in the hour of their passing.

"The need to go on."

Alexander "Xander" Drew sat on the edge of his bed and stared down at the soft, carpeted floor of his bedroom. It was five-thirty in the morning and he had yet to shut his eyes, other than to blink when necessary.

He watched his hands, clasped loosely in front of him. They were shaking. They had been for the better part of an hour now, all of which he had spent looking at them and willing them not to shake. And yet, they refused to do so.

His palms were cold and sweaty, beads of moisture dripping off them down onto the floor. They were covered in scars and gaping wounds that only he could see, long since healed. In his mind's eye his wrists bled and the liquid dripping from them was a dark crimson, splashing down upon the carpet in great bursts and staining it forever. But like all things, it would heal in time. Everything here healed.

He was bare from the waist, covered in goosebumps from the harsh winter winds that made it in through his windowsill, and yet he was not cold. His body was covered in scars, too, but some of them were actually there. One was deep, still throbbing with pain every now and again, over his right side. Some that did not know him often asked if that was where his appendix had been taken out. In fact, it was where his life had been taken out, and exposed for all to see.

Other marks were invisible, like the one over his heart. He often wondered how many times a heart could be ripped out and yet still be there, still feel, still beat. Alone in the darkness, he often wished that it was gone.

His square jaw was set, his teeth clenched in determination. Every breath made his cheeks quiver and shake with frustration. His molars ground together, making a sound that even he found unpleasant, his ear lobes twitching around uncut swatches of auburn hair wet and sticky with sweat.

His eyes twitched, their blue irises fixated on his quaking fingertips. Veins had begun to form in their sclera from stress and lack of sleep. His brow furrowed, eyebrows slanting as he tried even harder to stop, and they only seemed to convulse more.

His mouth was dry and tasted of copper. He kept clacking his tongue against the roof of it and expecting to find blood, but there was none. Yet the taste remained, just like the scars.

His long nose was red from the chill, a stray drop of mucus falling from it every now and again onto his checkered flannel pajama bottoms. He responded only with an exaggerated sniff, not wanting to move away or do anything that would move his disobedient hands from view.

"Guh," he gasped finally, realizing that he had been holding his breath, his chest heaving as oxygen burned at his aching lungs.

The gaping maw of a cut on his left wrist poured out blood just as water poured from a faucet, never ending, never bringing him peace. No, never peace.

He reached down slowly with his right hand, keeping one eye trained on them on the off chance that it stopped shaking. It had not stopped shaking all the while he was in the shower, no matter how hot he had made the water. It had not stopped long enough for him to suffer down his mother's meat loaf, the fork almost falling from his trembling hands.

But maybe it would stop shaking now.

He reached under his bed and pushed aside the box of old monster comics and an unopened set of computer disks, his hand finally finding a wooden box pushed deep beneath the mattress. He clasped it firmly and pulled it out.

Across from him, against the far wall of his room, his computer monitor stared blankly at him. He had not turned it on in days, and now it stared back at him in the dark like a never-ending void. Like the abyss.

He placed the box upon his lap and ran his fingers along its smooth surface, his thumbnail catching on the frayed and splintered corners. He looked at it silently for a long moment, then lifted the cover and revealed its red velvet interior.

The light that reflected off of its contents illuminated his face, gleaming off of his eyes. It was a knife, roughly a foot long from the tip of its blade to the end of its handle. A dagger then, to be precise. It was inside a metal sheath decorated by a carving of a long line of fire, which made light sparkle and dance off of it. The flames came from the mouth of the dragon that occupied the handle, its mouth gaping open toward the blade, tail swirling down to the bottom.

His eyes darted in their sockets toward the door, making sure that it was shut tight and locked.

He picked up the blade and pressed the locking mechanism near his thumb, shifting it to the right with ease and detaching the dagger from its hilt. He placed the case back into the box gently, and then closed the lid.

On the blade itself there were markings on it that looked Cantonese but weren't, weren't anything that he could find online or in the books at school. There was blood on it already, but it was not his. No, much worse. It was the blood of someone he could not save, and it could be seen by more than just him... but he saw it everywhere, especially on his hands.

Frowning at his reflection in the steel, he turned back toward his disobedient left hand, wrist facing up.

It was already bleeding in his mind's eye.

He pressed the tip of the dagger to where he saw the cut begin in his head, slowly applying pressure until it punctured through the flesh, a small pool of blood pushing up from around it. Slowly, methodically, he traced the cut he saw with his cold steel pen, sketching out what he knew in his damned heart was right.

The blood came now in a splash as he dropped the dagger to the floor. The sound woke him, made him know that this was real and not just another illusion that his mind had created for him. This was happening, and he was strangely glad.

Pain ruptured from the open wound as the blood squirted out. Slowly, painfully, his vein filled eyes rolled back into his head. All of the colour drained from his face until he was as white as the paper that was scattered around his floor.

He clenched his teeth even harder as his body threw itself backward, slamming his head against the sloping wall of his room and falling onto his bed where his hands finally stopped shaking. The flow of redness slowed to a weak dribble, and his lungs released their final breath.

There was nothing but silence for three long minutes, as the space heater in the corner struggled to kick in and fight against the raging storm outside.

Deep inside his chest, his heart let out a final, pitiful hum as it stopped beating.

Something stirred to life in his abdomen and began to beat the second that his heart failed to do so.

His left hand twitched, ever so slightly. Then again.

It twitched and blood started to come out of it. This time his blood was a deep, thick black, and instead of flowing down and staining his dark sheets like the rest it began to flow upward against the pull of gravity, toward his fingers.

Inching along like a million ebony earthworms, growing with every pump of Xander's black heart, it slowly made its way upward.

It trickled slowly, swirling around his pinky finger and enveloping it in darkness before moving on to the ring finger, picking up speed and confidence with every square centimetre of flesh that it took as its own.

All at once, the pinky started to twitch and bend, coming back to life and exercising its right to move. Slowly, a point poked its way out of its tip and grew into a long slender talon. The black bone gleamed against the dim light in the room the same way that the blade had, reflecting the pictures in their frames that lined his computer desk. Pictures of *her*. Pictures of *them*. Pictures of those that for all his effort he could not save. And the latest...

The blackness took his entire hand, the bones in his knuckles and the joints of his fingers snapping and crackling as they snapped in two and then healed themselves simultaneously, creating new tissue and marrow to fill the gaps, making his fingers longer. The darkness met with the cut where it had originally started, and for a moment looked like a thin leather glove covering his hand before the trail continued down his arm, swirling about and picking up steam.

His elbow cracked, bending in the opposite direction, then circled around until it was upright again, twisting and ruining flesh before it was taken over by the darkness, making it look smooth again.

The ooze on his hand began to dry, crackling like the ground over the desert as the moisture left it, turning it into small, square scales.

Xander's eyes snapped open with a barely audible click, his pupils rolling back into position, only now they were larger and darker. The blue irises had disappeared, taken over completely by the pupils that now refused to reflect light of any kind. The red veins in his eyes were gone, instead becoming the same deep black that was overcoming the rest of him.

"Guh," he managed to say again. He was trying to speak, to scream out the pain and fright that came over him along with the blood. Instead blackness erupted from his lips and vomited out onto his chest and stomach, joining with the first trail and hastening its decent downward.

All of the fat remaining on his abdomen was devoured, absorbed by the beast as it pressed on, seeming to only grow in hunger with every bite it took from his flesh. His rib cage (short one rib for months now) expanded outward as the cartilage grew, as if it were going to break free of the new flesh. The ooze piled into the puddle that had been Xander's stomach, churning about and forming muscles before working its way downward.

The blackness that Xander had spewed onto his chest dug into his flesh until it reached the breast plate, wedging itself into it and spreading it apart, opening his chest as wide as possible while rising, turning the fat and existing skin tissue into brawn and sinew.

It flowed down his legs, eliminating fat there as well, replacing it with thin, sleek tone. There was a gut-wrenching crack as his kneecap shattered and his bones broke, his entire leg shaking as it bent back the other way, like a horses hind legs, then back again, moving at will like the hinge of a door caught in the wind.

His ankles disappeared, the substance from which went toward expanding the mass of each respective foot, each gaining length and becoming more pointed, perfect for jumping and leaping long distances now.

His head thrashed back and forth as the blackness traveled up his neck, flattening his hair to his skull until it looked as though there was none, circling around his head to come at his face from all sides.

The organ deep inside his right side trashed and convulsed violently, pumping as hard as it could. It wanted to win, wanted to be free more than anything else.

His eyes darted back and forth as the blackness swallowed his face whole like a giant, gaping mouth until there was nothing but the white of his eyes left, and in a moment, his pupils finished expanding, relieving him of those as well.

He stopped twitching and all was silent and still and dead. There was a short snap as his nose broke, sinking down to form a curve all the way down his face. The ooze on his head dried into the bald shadow-figure it had so many times before.

Slowly, three curved red lines drew themselves on his face, as if someone were standing over him with a pencil. The top two diagonal lines opened, revealing themselves to be red, pupil-less eyes. They stared blankly and emotionlessly into the void before it, glowing and turning upward like a cat's.

The third line opened from the bottom down, showing off two long rows of serrated yellow teeth that went further back than any human set ever did. A pinkish tongue whipped around and about, saliva dripping from it.

When it spoke its words were course and rough, its throat ripped raw from blood and stomach acid.

"Black Womb lives."

It growled, bending its knees and standing up. It looked down with those large, opaque eyes at the pool of blood on the floor, sniffing twice. It closed its mouth, and when it did it seemed to disappear into a thin straight line across its face. It turned, first with its head and long neck and then with the rest of its body, toward the window. It still whistled cold air despite the noisy protests of the space heater. It walked to the window, clutched its release with its clawed fingers, and pushed upward. Snow billowed in, the entire blizzard seeming to want to enter the room all at once.

Feeling the wind but not the cold, the creature reached out the window, dug its claws into the side of the house and scaled its way down. The window slammed shut behind it.

Carefully, it leapt to the ground and walked into the thick Maine forest behind the house. Within seconds, it had sprinted across the yard and the yard next door and was hidden by the darkness of the brush, where nothing would see it even if it were directly in front of them.

"In the shadows it caught up with them, and they did not turn away, for they found that they could not bear to fight it any longer, and more than that, did not want to.

"They came to it willingly, tired from the hunt, and felt its tingle wash over their body as its breath hit them, and they were surprised at how good it felt. How freeing it was.

"They let the monster take them whole in its passion, biting their lips as they disobeyed all that their parents had instilled in them as children.

"All for that one moment of pure, unrelenting ecstasy.

"Their bodies throbbed and convulsed with pleasure as its tongue draped over them, and from their vantage point, naked and writhing in the shadows, it could see the world of the light out of the corner of their eyes, but the world could not see them, as the darkness sank snugly inside of them.

"And even as it filled them, clouding their thoughts and their actions, their hands going places they were told never to let them go, they could not help but remind themselves how wrong it was.

"That they were bad.

"Suddenly, it began to hurt. Then more and more, until the pleasure was gone, leaving only agony and death that wrenched at their hearts, the darkness enjoying it more and more with every swell of pain that surged through them, barring its massive teeth.

"And when they died it ate them, from the bottom up.

"And all they could think was how bad they were.

"And how much they deserved it.

"And how they could not wait to do it again.

"And how it had all been worth it."

Cathy Kennessy ran her brush through her long black hair, cringing as it ripped out yet another knot. Her eyes darted to the corner of her vanity where a bottle of conditioner sat, laughing at her with its false promise of silky smooth hair free of tangles.

She frowned, then turned back to her reflection in the mirror.

It was six-thirty in the morning and most people her age were still in bed asleep, not brushing their hair and waiting for the sun to come up. But her father had accidentally woken her while he was leaving the house to go to work, and then her little sister Trina got up to get a shower and made enough noise that their mother wouldn't notice her boyfriend leaving, and then when Trina was done Cathy got in the shower, new cream rinse in hand.

Again, she cursed inwardly.

The warm water had felt so good streaming over her body, beating the dirt and the dead skin off of it. But some things didn't come off with soap.

She sat on the wooden chair she'd picked up last month at a garage sale

7

wearing nothing but her yellow terrycloth bathrobe, gripping the handle of her brush as hard as she could. As she ripped another knot free, her robe fell open and revealed her breasts. She shut it quickly, although she was alone in the room and her door was locked tight.

She turned and looked around the room.

The only thing out of place was the bath towel she had used to wrap her hair in and the open closet door. She stared at the shadows inside the door for a long moment, then got up and walked over, retying her robe as she went. She scooped up the blue towel in one fluid motion, throwing it into the closet and slamming the door behind it.

She stopped and stared at it with her hazel eyes for a moment, one carefully plucked eyebrow arched upward, waiting for the door to respond to her gesture. Which of course, it did not.

One side of her mouth twitching in a slight frown, she forced a smile and turned back to her mirror.

Wiping the last few dabs of moisture off her pale round face, she picked up her red lipstick and pursed her small, perfect lips. Xander had given her that stick for her birthday a few months back. She remembered seeing him in the drug store looking through the wall of cosmetics with a confused look on his face, trying to pick out enough makeup to fill a small gift basket. When he finally picked out what he thought was the right shade he'd seemed so proud of himself, as though he'd accomplished something grand and spectacular. She applied it carefully, first to the bottom lip, then pressed the both of them together before leaning in and kissing the mirror, just for fun.

Slender fingers opened her jewelry box, fiddling through a jumbled mess of silver chains and charms collected from friends and relatives ever since she was old enough to wear them without strangling herself. Tapping one painted pink nail against the side of the case, she decided on a hair clip she'd gotten weeks ago while on a field trip to Los Angeles, smiling at the memory of the quirky little boutique clerk with the glasses that could have put the Hubble space telescope to shame. Parting her hair to her right side, she slid the silver clip in and snapped it tight.

She started to hum, though she did not know what or why. Music simply started flowing from her lips.

Her light, thin hands returned a few stray hairs to their rightful places. She turned, taking a quick, uncertain glance across the room again before she removed the robe, standing to let it fall to the floor before reaching over to her dresser to pick out underwear and socks.

She grunted as she slipped on her jeans, the tight ones with the frayed edges that the boys loved and her mother hated. She picked out a pink sleeveless top with frills, and as she pulled it on she could hear her boys commenting on her knack for wearing summer clothing in winter months.

She was thin and shaped like an hourglass in a way that made the opposite sex watch her intently, even those not of her age group, even when she didn't want it. Especially when she didn't want it, it seemed sometimes.

Her eyes were bright and full of zest as they turned back toward the mirror, her dark hair spinning around her as she did, accenting her facial features. Suddenly, with little to no work at all, she was beautiful.

She sighed, walking across her spacious room to her bed and letting herself fall upon it back first, looking up at the stars painted on her ceiling from the comfort of her pillows. Slowly, the smile faded from her lips. She sat up and looked around her room. The wind chimes hanging from her ceiling danced, although she didn't know where the breeze was coming from. Her dresser loomed over her, and her floor felt hot beneath her feet. It all felt so familiar, and yet something was different. Something had been made wrong that she could not make right until she knew just what it was.

Turning, she looked out her bedroom window. The snow and frost had piled up so much that she could barely even see to the street lamp on the corner. She could see only the motion, the snow blowing about outside.

She wondered if Xander or Mike were out there. If they were cold.

Sighing, she let the curtain fall back and turned back to lie down on the bed again. She closed her eyes, then let them shoot open again, looking around the room.

She did not close her eyes again until it was time to go to school.

"It came at them from inside the mirror, arms reaching out with tiny mouths at the end of each and every fingertip, devouring them like tiny cannibals, so hungry that they would eat even of their own flesh.

"And when they screamed it was neither piercing nor did it render any help as blood started to pour from their gaping, open wounds, for it was a silent scream, turned inward on themselves. As the scream pierced their very souls, they stopped feeling the thousands of razor sharp teeth, and eventually all they were was the tone of the scream.

"After time, the teeth were always there. The teeth had become a part of them, hard and sharp, covering their exterior so that no one ought see them, and no one would dare touch them for fear that they, too, would be devoured.

"And without the warmth of another the teeth sank deeper and the scream grew louder. It grew until they could no longer even hear it, becoming white noise, and they became deaf to all else.

"So great was their hunger for human contact that they turned on themselves, and became the teeth, both devouring until there was nothing left.

"With nothing left to feed on, the teeth on the tips of the fingers turned to their eyes, gouging them out.

"They heard nothing.

"They saw nothing.

"They felt nothing.

"They were nothing.

"And the teeth on the tips of the fingers went back into the mirror,

"To wait until tomorrow."

9

He lay on his bed, staring up at the walls around him.

The room was large, easily twice the size of the average room for a kid his age. It was lined with pictures that he had taken and that had been taken of him, of his life. That had always been a yearly ritual of Tommy Irons's. Every year, he'd change all of the pictures on his wall to those he'd taken the year before. His family had always used to call him "shutterbug" for it, back when they actually gave his actions any thought.

Most of the pictures on his wall now had been turned around, so that he would not be faced with their accusing eyes anymore.

First there was Jamie. He'd been killed. That wasn't something that happened every day back then, not like it was now. Still, that was always marked as the first. That was the point where everything turned on its head, and the simple became the sinister.

Then there was Grendel. He had betrayed all of them, but him most of all. Grendel did something horrible, then died before he ever got a chance to rectify it and make it right, as Tommy knew that he one day would have. Now he would be forever known by those that knew him best as a terrible person, which Tommy supposed was the way that it should be.

Phillips, then, for reasons that did not need explaining.

Derek, for turning on them all. For trying to kill Tommy and everyone he held dear, for no other reason than he felt like it.

Fred, his best friend, for dying.

Randy, for killing him.

Slowly, over the course of months, all of the pictures turned away from him, much in the way that the people captured upon them had.

Scattered across his bed were pins that he used to keep some of his pictures on the wall, like sensations that he used to hang his memories on.

Before him on his chest were the pictures of the newest person to have left him.

Tears dripped down his cheeks from his batting eyelids, soaking his goose down pillows as, one by one, he pinned the pictures up on the wall facing inward.

The first was of Cathy, Julie, and Mandy at the Factory. It was one of those pictures that he had taken for no occasion or reason other than the fact that he'd had his camera on him at the time and they hadn't noticed that he was standing there until it was too late. Those were the ones that he liked best, he found. Not the ones where everyone stood in a line like they were getting their driver's license photos, looking stone-drunk out of their minds with red eyes and pasty expressions, fake smiles plastered over dreary composers. No, he preferred the pictures that were natural, ones that he could look at and remember what people were like, not when they were all dressed up, but everyday normal, in case he ever forgot.

The three of them were sitting on one of the park benches that the Factory owners had bought from the city and fixed up, with an old-fashioned street lamp hanging overhead. Where they'd gotten that piece of nostalgia he'd never know, and never ask, either.

Cathy was sipping on her bottle of Cherry Coke via straw as per usual, her head turned slightly back to watch where, out of the camera's focus, Mike and James played pool. The angle made her hair drape down over a good portion of her face, turning it into something angular. She looked sexy and mysterious in an odd kind of way, wearing her tank top with the red and black vertical stripes (one shoulder strap fallen over and the other dangling) and tight jeans that left just enough to the imagination to make any man quiver.

Julie had actually managed to see him right before he pressed the shutter, but it wasn't a "deer-in-the-headlights" look. She'd been looking past him at Xander, who had just been coming in through the front doors behind him. There was a quirky smirk on her face, the one that appeared, only for a millisecond, whenever Xander walked into the room. He had been so happy when he'd developed the photos and found that he had captured it that he pinned it up while it was still wet, staining the bedspread beneath it with chemical dots that were still there now.

And Mandy. Amanda Peterson. She was doing something with her hair. Wasn't she always? She had both hands up, fixing her ponytails, inadvertently presenting her breasts through the sweater that she almost always wore, or some variation of it. There was nothing sexual about the pose, though. It was like looking at a portrait, a painting of a beautiful nude. If done right, there was nothing sexual about the nudity. That was the way this was. It was simply her in her element... her, simply being her, as no other person could. Her mouth was open to say something (most likely a sarcastic something) to Julie, who was completely oblivious to her.

Tommy had loved that picture for that exact reason. The fact that there she was, being perfect, and nobody was paying attention to her. Like a flower that bloomed only at night, when nobody could see.

Letting out a long, deep sigh, he tacked the picture back onto the wall, away from him.

He sniffed back a glob of mucus, wiping his nose in his sleeve as more tears poured down his face and shirt, tumbling to the surface until there was nothing left to them.

Hands trembling, he picked up another picture.

This one was of Cathy, Mike, Xander, and Mandy. It had been taken at the school dance just a few weeks ago, during the five minutes that Xander and Julie had been together. They were all sitting on a line of chairs against the wall. Usually he despised photo opportunities like this, but this one was natural enough.

Cathy wasn't herself, though. She was sitting three chairs away from everybody else, looking away from them, too. Still, there was that mystery about her, only accented by the fact that she wasn't part of the group in this shot. One of her hoop earrings had captured the light from the flash, giving her a movie star quality.

Mike just looked sad. Not upset per say, just plain not happy. His golden head of hair seemed a little less shiny, somehow. His head was down, tilted just slightly toward Cathy, who was not returning his gaze by any means. His hands were clasped in front of him, and even though it was a photo, you could just tell that he was twiddling his thumbs.

Xander was smiling.

Tommy had been very glad he had gotten a picture of it, for he was sure that he would need proof of this monumental event.

Xander was leaning side-on against the chair, his arm draped over the side as he talked with his hands to Mandy, as he was prone to doing when he was actually in a good mood. It was a rare occurrence.

And Mandy. Again, she looked so pretty. It was like she was trying hard to look plain and just couldn't do it. It made her shine all the more brightly in the darkened gymnasium. Her shoulder-length brown hair was pulled back behind her ears, revealing the m-shaped scar on her forehead that she was usually so self-conscious about, but now she was relaxed enough that she wasn't thinking about it enough to hide it. And those eyes. Those big, green eyes that always sparkled, even when there was no light for them to reflect.

A tear fell, plopping against the photo-paper with a tiny splash.

He pinned the picture back.

When he picked up the final picture, his lower lip started to tremble. This was the one he had been dreading, when there was nothing else to catch his eye, to distract his attention. It was Mandy Peterson. She'd been captured from the waist up, turning to look at him after he'd called out to her from behind. Her hair was dancing around her in swirls as she turned, her eyes wide with that sparkle he'd been talking about. He'd taken this just a few days before it had happened. Her lips were pale and he found a great deal of peace in them, just a little bit of her teeth showing. She'd gotten so mad at him for taking that picture, caught in a classic Peterson fury and nearly slapping the camera out of his hands before starting to laugh at the goofy, weak expression that had adorned his face.

Slowly, he turned, pinning that one on the wall, too.

Sniffing back hard, he turned into his pillow and closed his eyes, hoping to cry himself to sleep and get at least a few moments rest before his alarm went off.

He would not.

⋏⋋⋏

"They did not run, for they did not wish to. Instead they stayed there, bathed in light as the darkness swirled around them, taking each breath long and deep, just in case it was their last.

"The beast circled them, clacking its nails against the ground, making them twitch as the suspense rose to a nearly tactile level of unbearableness.

"It was maddening.

"At first, they did nothing. Then, all at once, they turned about and lashed out, pounding their fists into the creature, sending it scampering away, laughing at their attempts.

12

"That they would try to harm that which they simply did not understand, such being the plight of all mortals.

"But the blow missed, of course, and the arm traveled around the curvature of the earth, picking up speed as it went, until finally, they hit themselves.

"And the blow that would start to harm others

"Would cause their suicide."

"Argh!" Mike Harris screamed, punching the concrete wall in front of him. His knuckles were abound with an odd confluence of sensations, cold from the snow and wind that churned all around him, but at the same time warm thanks to the blood that flowed freely from them.

He heard the satisfying crack as something within his wrist popped free, smiling in contentment as it did. Blood from open wounds splattered in star shapes from the spot where he hit, while fresh ones were being torn open.

"Are you okay?" Came a voice from behind him.

He hit the wall once more, letting his hand linger there, using it to prop him up as he turned to look over his shoulder at whoever had spoken the kind words.

It was a short black man, bundled up in a parka with a hood, staring out at Mike from beneath its shadow. A scarf hung loosely around his neck, billowing in the stiff breeze that seemed as though it wanted to touch everything near it in some way, shape, or form. The man's hands were buried deep within his pockets, and he looked to be shivering. He took a step closer to Mike, taking a hand out of his pocket and reaching it out. "You're not hurt, are you?"

Mike stared at the man through squinted eyes for a long moment, the snow sticking to his hair and eyelashes, then he turned around to face the wall again, drawing back to punch. He grunted as saliva sprayed from his mouth and hit the ground, freezing there.

"Or something," he growled, deep in his throat.

The man shook his head and kept walking.

"They looked deep inside themselves,

"And they realized that the darkness had been inside of them the entire time.

"Following them like a shadow."

CHAPTER TWO: TEE YOU VEE

"Fuck," Cara cursed, as the Factory's heavy metal door caught a gust of wind and slammed her in the arm.

The Factory had always been a staple of life in Coral Beach, and in many ways it changed as society within the township changed. In recent years it had become a local arcade/club/pool hall where many of the town's teens went when they had nothing else to do, which was frequently, especially if they had a mind to stay out of trouble. When it came to legal fun in Coral Beach, the Factory had long been the be-all and end-all. It jutted up out of the otherwise calm Northeast landscape, always loud and exciting and neon.

Cara had been working there for three weeks now, even since Paul Russ had gotten sick with pneumonia and quit in a huff when he realized that he'd opted out of health benefits in order to help save up for a new car. In a town like this you didn't interview for a job. When Paul quit the owner called Cara and said that she knew that Cara had been without work for some time, and if she wanted to work there. Cara had hastily agreed.

The work was hard, but she didn't mind. Most nights she went home with her hands bleached white from the cleanser they used on the floor and her throat burning with the stuff, but one hot shower was all it ever took to reset her back to normal. Her husband liked having the extra money that her employment was bringing in, and they hadn't fought at all since she'd started. They'd even discussed taking a vacation together in the spring.

She only found two downsides so far: the stench of dope that she had to contend with every time Calla McFadden spent more than ten minutes in the bathroom, and the abuse that her left arm was taking.

Every day when she took the garbage out back to be picked up the next day, the back door managed to slam against her. With her arms full of trash bags filled to the brim with paper cups and soda cans, she never had any defense when it slammed against her full force, always into the meat of her forearm. It had happened so many times in the past few weeks that the flesh there was tender to the touch at all times, the large cluster of bruises there going beyond the normal colours of black and blue and delving into much scarier purples and reds and an odd, jaundice yellow that frightened her. Women began to look at her as though she'd been abused (even though Steve had never so much as raised a hand to her), and she felt that the more she protested this the more they thought it was true.

She threw the large black bag in her right hand over the guardrail and into the dumpster, grunting with exertion as she did. She heard something glass inside it break when it hit, but paid it no attention. Sweat dotted her brow just above her eyebrows and the undersides of her arms felt the chill of the cold Maine air as she grabbed the second bag and tried to lift it, failing the first time but succeeding the second.

He watched her from the trees just beyond the dumpster, his breathing picking up speed as he watched her sweat-laden bosom heave its way almost clean out of her shirt as she dropped the second bag into the dumpster.

Her apron got tangled in the guardrail and she pulled it free, spitting a large glob of saliva out onto the frozen concrete steps before heading back toward the door.

She stopped in the archway, her ears perking up as she swore she heard something behind her. She turned around and saw the same forest that was always there... same evergreens that had randomly grown all around the back wall of the building, each one weighted down with pounds upon pounds of fresh snow until they looked like they were about to crack off. The pure white of the virgin powder made the shadows between them seem even darker though, and she couldn't see anything that was going on between the branches.

He smiled as she looked right at him but didn't see him. She had green eyes... he loved women with green eyes.

She stared out into the trees, focusing in on one rock that stuck up out of the snow near the tree line (which was nowhere close to where he was watching her from) and could not shake the feeling that there were eyes on her... that same feeling that kept her from getting changed in public washrooms even where there was nobody around, or go swimming in anything more revealing than a one-piece.

-Chic.-

There was a sound, like something she'd heard before but could not quite place... almost like the way her dog's nails sounded against the hardwood floors when they needed to be cut. She paused once more, staring at a spot just to the left of where she had before... then turned to step back into the Factory.

He arose, emerging from the bushes with a thick scowl on his face and started forward.

Cara let the door to the Factory close behind her, careful not to let it slam into her behind when she left as it had on more than one occasion.

He bolted forward, making his way for the rusted green metal box that she'd thrown the trash into.

Sven Douglas was a small, middle-aged man with very little hair and buckteeth. What hair he did have left was graying in uneven clumps around his ears. He hadn't washed in days, and looked like it.

He'd been living on the streets for two days now, ever since he'd first gotten wind that somebody was hunting down all the Tees. At first he didn't believe it, and when he heard exactly what people said had been hunting them, he believed it less and less. Still, the first day after Mandy Peterson's funeral four of their senior members had been brought in by the police, and that wasn't something that he could just ignore, so he moved out onto the streets to give whoever was after him less of a chance of finding him.

-Chic.-

He'd managed to get two good meals out of his bank accounts before the police froze them, and then it had finally occurred to him: not only had most of his compatriots been brought into custody, but at least one of them must have rolled on him. He'd been hungry all day yesterday, and now it had finally come to this... feasting on trash when he would have much preferred to have been feasting on the trash lady.

Eyes glued to the door as he approached the dumpster, he turned toward the back of the building and stared out into the space beyond. There was a small sliver of street visible to him from here, and if he could see out than that meant others could see in.

-Cllus.-

Sweat began to pour down his brow and his throat started to ache with thirst as he remembered all of the times he'd seen kids finish half a bottle of Coke and then screw the top back on and throw it out. He could almost taste it even now, flat and warm but still so good.

Careful to avoid a sharp spike of metal along the dumpster's edge, he pried his thumb under the ledge and threw it open.

A shadow came out so quick and was so fast that Sven barely had enough time to scream before he was on the ground, pinned there at the shoulders with large, powerful hands. He shrieked, in such a high voice that he didn't recognize it as his own. He didn't know who that person screaming was, but he knew one thing for sure: whoever they were, they were going to die.

As he watched, horrified, the shadowman seemed to grow eyes and a long, slender mouth that glowed dark red. It came down so far that it was hard to tell where its mouth ended and its chest began, but somehow Sven knew that it didn't matter. This thing was all mouth.

Deep inside the skin of the Black Womb, Xander smirked to himself. What that contortion of muscle and tissue translated to on the face of the Womb was nothing short of horrific, a wide-angled grin with hundreds of sharpened teeth, pointed cheeks curving to block small sections of those large, triangular eyes. One of his arms was pulled back, the palm open and fingers outstretched; the claws at the tip of each extended to their fullest length.

Right then, that smile was all that Sven could see. The eyes, the black skin, the claws... that was fine. He'd been told about all of that before, although he'd never actually seen it. It was the smile that truly bothered him, making his sweat run and his blood boil over with fear as his heart raced within his chest.

The whole area smelled like cheap marijuana, and it only increased every time Sven exhaled. All of Xander's favourite land marks behind the building had been covered in snow to the point that he did not know one thing from another, and even in the fresh snow, the ground was littered profusely with cigarette butts.

Sven's eyes were bloodshot beyond comprehension, both from the fear and the drugs. His hands shook as they tried to pry away the Womb's arm to little effect, and his teeth rattled about inside his skull.

He was cold, too cold to have just come out. A few strong whiffs with his senses-heightened nose confirmed Xander's suspicion that Sven had been staying out here from quite a few days, trying to hide from the cops, the snow... and of course, from him.

"Do you have any idea how happy I am to see you?" Xander asked rhetorically. In his head, the words sounded enough like his own. But when they came out of the Womb's mouth, they became ridged and slurred and hoarse, like someone with the worst case of strep throat in history. He often wondered what the Womb sounded like when it was in complete control... but he could hardly ever remember those escapades, and even if he could, the Womb was ninety percent mute anyway.

Sven did not speak in return, even though Xander had given him pause in which to do so. He did, however, mutter a brief prayer to his mother, never once taking his eyes off that smile.

"A part of me blames myself for never trying this sooner. I guess I'll never know exactly how many lives I could have saved if I had actually put my all into hunting you guys down." He sighed, swiping his claws forward gently but accurately, stripping away the clothing on Sven's right arm until it was bare, save for a few strands of fabric. Exposed on the biceps was a broad, red letter T, though it was tattered by scar tissue and many recent removal attempts.

"I thought so," Xander sneered, the Womb's smile growing ever so slightly in its perturbed nature. "Looks like you tried to get rid of it. Naughty, naughty. You should have known I wouldn't forget a face like yours anyway."

He lashed out, rending his talons across Sven's face, loosening flesh from muscle and sending blood streaming down.

"Not anymore, in any case," he added, cocking his head to the side as he retracted the claws, punching Sven once in the central plexus and then again in the stomach. Sven bent over in pain and Xander ended the brief scuffle with a sharp blow to the back of his head, sending him face first into the snowdrift.

He sighed, turned to walk over to where he knew the Old Sitting Stone was located and brushed the snow off it. He sat down, leaned one arm against his knee, and let out a long breath that sent condensation billowing out in front of him.

Three days. That was all it had taken to round up the last of the living Tees and bring them to justice. For four months he had been fighting them, and now the last of them had finally gone down for the count.

He growled inwardly, turning and slamming on the back door to the Factory, hoping to get Cara's attention so that she would find the fugitive. He turned and began walking into the woods, slowly disappearing as morning light peeked over the hills.

CHAPTER THREE: FEAR ITSELF

-*BEEP*-
-*BEEP*-
-*BEEP*-
-*BEEP-BEEP*-
-*BEEP*-
-*BEEP*-
-*BEEP*-

That sound had kept Julie Peterson awake all night. She stared out of the window of her hospital room at the snow being blown off the roof, swirling gently to the ground, sparking in dawn's first light.

The room was mostly white and sterile, a stark difference from the clutter and colour that she was used to. There was one window in her single room that shone light in on her, its trim an off-white that was one of the more grabbing contrasts in shade in the place. The sheets that covered her looked and felt like paper. The only bit of colour in the room was a pegboard filled with get-well cards reserved for her well-wishers. There were precious few there, but a few homemade ones from her friends had brightened her demeanor ever so slightly. At some point during the night, a nurse had rearranged the machinery used to keep tabs on Julie's vital signs, and her heart monitor now completely blocked the pegboard.

She stared up at the slow drip of the IV with bloodshot eyes as each drop hung, suspended for an instant, before dropping into the tube that took it into her veins. Her eyes were bloodshot and watery, their pupils milky and unfocused, and her mouth had dry cracks at the corners.

Her usually carefully placed brunette hair was a tattered, static-filled mess. On any other day she might have been worried about it, even going into fits trying to tame the wilder strands, but today she could not care less.

There were dots of a white, vomit-like substance stuck to the corners of her mouth, and a bad taste had been growing exponentially in the back of her throat for the last two days.

Her tanned, freckled face had become pale and sickly, her infectious smile driven far away.

She had been dressed in a backless paper robe with two drawstrings on the back that became unbearably uncomfortable every ten minutes or so. As it was, fabric was bunched between the gown and the flesh on her back that threatened to pinch very soon, forcing her to move. She arched her backside ever so slightly to remove the discomfort, and pain immediately shot through her, starting from a burning hole in her chest and smoldering up her spine and into her brain, exploding there and sending tiny embers of agony sprinkling violently down through her body until her limbs twitched uncontrollably. Her teeth clenched as the heart monitor escalated its assault on her ears.

-BEEP - BEEP-

-BEEP - BEEP-

-BEEP - BEEP - BEEEP-

It punctuated her pain perfectly, like a tiny monosyllabic narrator, each tone marking the anguish that pumped throughout her via her veins. The agony slowly subsided as she settled back down into the bed, the pinch of her skin against the paper gown minuscule in comparison. Her lungs heaved in despair as the scar tissue around them stretched the bruises there, letting tiny slivers of fresh blood out of her body.

She quivered, trying for only a moment to halt the shaking of her lips and the batting of her eyelashes.

On the front of her gown, in nearly the center between her breasts, a small spot of blood wetted the paper. She noticed it immediately, worrying for a moment that it would continue to grow, but to her relief, it ceased.

Days ago, although in many ways it seemed like months, Julie Peterson had been shot trying to save her young cousin, Amanda.

Sven had managed to get his handgun out, and Julie was now wrestling with him for control of it, the both of them rolling around in the snow, biting and punching at one another for control over the weapon.

BANG!

All heads turned, wondering where the shot had come from.

Sven turned, the gun now visible in his hand, as well as the fountain of blood streaming out of the gaping maw in Julie's chest.

"No!" Tommy screamed.

Mike slammed Langley into the frozen ground and they both ran toward her. Cathy turned the corner and saw what was happening, and all three of them bolted toward Sven, who dropped the gun in fright as both men pounced on him. Cathy went to Julie's side.

"Julie!" Cathy screamed, pulling the girl's hair out of her face and being very careful not to touch the wound. "Julie, are you all right?"

"Don't..." she tried to say, as blood gurgled up from her throat. "Don't stop. You have to find her."

The bullet had managed to miss all her major organs, coming extremely close to her left lung. It hadn't gone through-and-through, but almost. It became lodged under the skin of her back, just to the left of her spine. Upon awakening from the operation, the doctor had told her that she was lucky.

If she had been able to speak or move at that time, she may have assaulted him.

Lucky would have been not getting shot.

Lucky would be Mandy still being alive.

Lucky would be not living in Coral Beach.

The pain subsided, and the scarring and stitches around her wound settled back into place. Slowly, the heart monitor regained its usual, annoying chime.

Something moved quickly in the corner of her eye.

She turned swiftly, her damp sweaty hair flailing about as she turned to face whatever it was. There was nothing but the corridors and the white walls.

She heard something squirm right beside her. As she turned to see, her chest objected to the motion by sending coarse pain through her fragile form. She stopped moving, letting her eyes dart about inside of her head again, looking for the source of the sound that now seemed to be coming from all around her... the floors, the walls, the curtains... it was even in the pine fresh scent that hung on the air. Suddenly, everything was quiet again, except for the steadily increasing tone of her heart monitor.

-BEEP-

-BEEP- BEEP- BEEP-

-BEEP- BEEP- BEEP - BEEP-

She looked around at every corner of the room that she could see from where she lay, inspecting every shadow until she was absolutely certain that she was alone in the room. She let out a long sigh of relief, her chest heaving once as she did. Grinning at her own insipid paranoia she turned onto her side, the pain only stinging for a moment as she did.

Her scream was heard in the nurse's quarters two floors down and seven rooms to the right, even before her heart monitor could alert them to the emergency.

CHAPTER FOUR: ETERNAL

The school bells chimed rhythmically, a hint of the tune that had once been apparent still lingering. Four years ago when it had gotten a wealth of new funding from the board after years of learning how to tighten their belts, the school had been faced with a surplus. At the end of the year they had been faced with two choices: either spend the surplus three thousand dollars by the last day of classes, or have that remaining money cut from the following year's budget. After a few hasty ideas were thrown around, the school administration finally decided on a digital bell to replace the old mechanical ones that still hung above the doorway to every classroom. For a few years the song they played (a midi riff of the school's theme, which itself was taken from an old Irish folk diddy) rang out at a lively tempo, but the speakers were old now and the sound mostly came out as one streaming blurb, like a tone-deaf man trying to sing in harmony with the birds outside his window.

"Damn," Xander cursed, craning his neck around the corner to see a gaggle of his classmates slowly drift their way into Coral Beach High. He sighed, then turned back quickly before one of the teachers noticed him.

"What have you got first period?" Mike asked, nursing his knuckles gingerly. He carefully peeled back a tiny strip of loosened flesh until it was almost off, then brought it to his mouth and bit it clean, spitting out the sour, copper-flavored remains.

"Tech. Barrett," Xander said glumly, taking a long haul of his cigarette and then throwing it to the ground with the rest of his growing collection. "You?"

"Physics. Mr. Calender," he replied. He was scuffing the dirty snow at his feet without really thinking about it, letting large piles of the fluffy white get onto his sneakers and soak in until his toes were freezing. "Any luck last night?"

"Finished off the last one outside the Factory in the wee hours."

"Oh." Mike nodded. "That's good, right?"

Xander's face twitched in disapproval. "Went down easy, didn't put up any fight at all. Sometimes I wish I could turn off the enhanced agility and all the other bullshit. I'd like to have had a real go at him."

"It's not all it's cracked up to be."

"So I'm told."

Mike again brought his hand to his mouth, sucking on the blood that was slowly ebbing out of the wound, his lips making an odd smacking sound as he did. "Any word?"

There was a sound emitting from deep within Xander's throat, as he reached for his pack of smokes, then decided against it, remembering the annoying chime of the homeroom bell.

"I'll take that as a no," Mike said.

"I'm going to go see her today, after class," Xander admitted, biting a stray end off one nail.

"Hmm. That's good, I'll bet she'll like that."

"They wouldn't let me in before now."

"Bastards. Is this a... private engagement?"

Xander turned toward his friend, making eye contact finally. "I was going to ask."

"Say no more," he offered, brushing it aside with his hand. "Me and Cathy are there, as long as you need us to be."

"Tommy, too," Xander added, getting up and brushing snow from his rear.

Mike shot him a look.

"Guy really proved himself back there. He deserves to be kept in the loop as much as we can afford."

Mike nodded slowly, then motioned for the both of them to start toward their classes.

Xander gave him a curt nod. He took one step and slipped in the snow, twirling as he tried to catch himself and twisting his ankle, landing on his back with his feet perched in the air. "Fuck!" He cursed loudly, attracting the attention of the few remaining students in the courtyard. "Fuck. Fuck, fuck, fuck."

Mike smiled, offering his friend a helpful hand. "Enhanced agility, huh?" He grinned, pulling Xander to his feet.

"It's been a long week."

"Right."

"Shut up."

"I agreed with you."

"Is this your idea of shutting up?"

"What did I say?"

"Because if it is... let me tell you, you do not have what is known as a firm grip on the idea."

"I said nothing."

"Keep it that way."

Mike snickered, as the two of them lumbered off to class, Xander limping a little as they did.

Chanelle McDonald's sky blue eyes darted over the colourful wall in front of her, a heart monitor beside her beeping silently. It was a special, noiseless model used only in the children's ward. The wall was a tapestry of colour and flavour, decals of various children's characters covering it, some of them with stethoscopes and blood pressure pumps. Mickey was there, and so were Bert,

Ernie, and Blue. They all smiled down upon her, the morning light reflecting off the whites of their eyes and teeth, making them eerie and creepy.

Her plump face was mushed against her paper pillow as she heard the sound again, a sick slithering sound that reminding her of the snake from the *Jungle Book* movie that her little brother always watched, over and over again, no matter how many times she begged him to put on one of the other dozens of movies that her parents had accumulated for them over the years. She shut her eyes as tightly as she could, praying that it would go away. That it wouldn't happen again, not to her, not to any of them. Not again.

Her brunette hair was in tangles, matted by sleepless nights in the stale, rough sheets.

Somebody started to scream, then stopped.

There was a muffled sound, and a high-pitched whine. It sounded like when her father's car wouldn't start.

The room got colder somehow, as Chanelle tried to find a way to close her eyes even tighter.

Bed sheets started to rustle, and there was the sound of kicking and pounding... then suddenly, there was nothing. After a moment of silence, she opened her eyes again. The eyes and smiles of the decals no longer were aglow with the evanescence of sunlight. She stared at Mickey, concentrating on the gold buttons of his overalls for a moment. There was a sneered laugh as the shadow moved, accompanied by the slithering sound again, slowly fading away until the door closed.

She shuddered deep within herself as she listened intently to the quiet that was wrapped all around her like a blanket.

༼ʎ༽

"D - E - A - T - H. Death," Miss Waller read aloud as she wrote each letter in big, bold letters across the chalkboard. The white chalk between her fingers scraped against the board and pierced the ears of every student in the classroom (including Cathy Kennessy, who was sat in the seat closest to the window).

Tabitha Waller had been the Family Education teacher at Coral Beach High for just over ten years now, ever since she'd transferred over from Kannibus regional. She was in her mid-forties but looked as though she were in her late sixties, with wrinkles that made either side of her face sag like melting wax and short hair that she had curled every Wednesday with the rest of the golden girls at the Luxury Discount Salon. She claimed to have moved to help take care of her brother who was ill with lupus, but she'd really been shunned out of town when the liberal core of Kannibus, Maine found out about her secret life. Tabitha Waller was a lesbian, one of only three she'd been able to detect within the limits of the town. The other two were a couple (the Forges) living as sisters. Tabitha hadn't had a date the entire time she'd lived there, and the Forges had begun to joke that if she didn't get one soon she'd be forced to turn in her "Rainbow Pass."

The change to Coral Beach had been sudden and jarring, but she'd gotten used to it here. After a few months she learned that Coral Beach, for all its right-wing sensibilities, had a prospering gay district, if one knew where to look. There was a bar near the center of town that held a ladies night on Tuesday evenings, and it hadn't taken her long to figure out that the ladies who frequented were of just her sort. She found that she could be happy here. No matter how bad the town had gotten in the past few months, she decided that neither hell nor high water was going to chase her out of another community... not while the students kept paying attention during her sex ed lectures and body shots on Tuesdays remained $3.99.

She turned toward her class, her features curling up into a smile. The wrinkles of her cheeks made deep shadows on either side of her lips, framing them there as if they were needed to hold her smile in place.

"Death. We deal with it every day," she said, turning around to face her class and finding that almost all of them had their eyes glued to her or what she'd written on the board. She allowed herself a smile, then swallowed and moved into the brunt of her lecture. "It can be found in literature as recent as the newest Stephen King novel or as far back as the first printed book, when Cain killed his brother Abel in Genesis. Shakespeare also used it more than his fair share, might I add. It is found in our newspapers, our plays, movies, and television... there has been a strong case made against its influence in the video game world on impressionable youth... and death is in our homes. Family, friends, loved ones... they all go eventually. But there are many ways to deal with death. Can anyone think of an example?"

The classroom was stone silent, as students tersely avoided eye contact with one another and fiddled with their erasers or tapped their pencils against their notebooks, waiting (if nothing else) for Miss Waller to answer her own question.

She looked out across her students, hands on her hips and her wrinkled face fighting the urge to curl at the corners. "I believe that there is no 'wrong' way to deal with death, that it is specific to each individual person. However, I think that death is also one of life's great learning tools. I think that if we do not get better at learning from death and learning from how we react to it, then we might as well resign ourselves to death as well."

There was a sound from the audience from the far wall.

Waller looked up and smiled, scanning the row for a student that would meet her eye. "Did someone have something to say?" she asked, in a voice that was neither encouraging nor stifling.

Nobody in the class spoke, only exchanged glances, many of them directed toward the middle window.

"If somebody has something to say..." the teacher trailed off, finally focusing the climax of many of the students' looks on one person in particular. "... Miss Kennessy?"

Cathy looked up from her notebook, suddenly aware that the majority of the waking eyes in the room were on her, including the teacher's. "Nothing," she said finally, her eyes immediately going back to her paper. "I didn't say anything."

"If it's worth saying at all, it's worth sharing with the rest of the class, Miss Kennessy." Waller smirked, leaning in as if to listen to what Cathy had to say.

Cathy slammed her pencil down on the desk, her eyes meeting the teacher's for the first time and revealing them to be so filled with anger that they were getting misty and lipid at the corners. "I said 'yeah, right,' okay?" She snapped, spittle flying from her lower lip. Stopping herself, she turned toward the window and tried to focus on the snow-covered elm sitting outside. She couldn't even really see it though, her mind tumbling with angry thoughts as her cheeks got redder and redder, unable to stop the onslaught of aggression.

Miss Waller stepped back a pace, her eyes widening. "Um..." she stammered, then finally composed herself. "If you don't agree with my lecture, then you are more than welcome to voice your own opinion on the matter, as all of my students are."

Cathy let out a heaving sigh and rolled her eyes.

"Miss Kennessy?"

"Okay," Cathy huffed, her voice almost giddy with rage as her arms flopped down onto her desk. "There are no wrong ways to deal with death? That is the biggest load of fucking shit I have ever heard."

"Now, Miss Kennessy..."

"No!" Cathy interjected. "Cursing at you is how I'm choosing to deal with death right now, so by your own philosophy, you can deal with it. And 'learn from death?' 'Oh, it all has a lesson?' Screw off! A week ago... *one week ago*... a thirteen year old girl was raped and shot! Not in New York, not in L.A., here! As in, down the street, here! And now you're standing around talking about what we can learn from it? Tell you what: as soon as people can start learning not to kill and maim each other, I'll get on finding out what I can learn from death, you fucking old 'tard."

"Miss Kennessy," Waller fumed, her nostrils flaring. "You can either apologize right now for your actions and tone, or you can see yourself to the--"

"I wouldn't stay another minute," she snapped, cutting off the teacher as she scooped up her notebook and headed for the door.

She paused at the doorframe for one final instant and shot a disgusted glare at Waller then slammed the door behind her, sending a plaque hung not far from it crashing to the floor.

ʎ˅ʎ

Mandy Peterson walked down the hall, her brown shoulder-length hair bobbing around her playfully as she did. Her big, green eyes lit up the hallway as her smooth, chubby cheeks grew wide in a grin as she caught sight of her friends.

"Hi guys!" She chimed musically as she waved high above her head, bouncing a little on the balls of her feet as she did. She was wearing a blue Coral Beach Cougars team sweater that flopped about aimlessly on her as she moved, making her look larger than she was.

Xander looked over at her and smiled, showing all of his teeth. His eyes lit up as she entered the room, coming over to join him, Cathy, Mike, and Julie around the cafeteria table.

"Hey, you!" He chirped.

"Hey yourself!" She replied, spreading out her arms and allowing herself to fall back onto the table with a big, dopey grin on her face.

Xander laughed.

"I think you get cuter every time I lay eyes on you," he said. He closed his eyes theatrically, and then opened them again with a shocked expression. "See? I was right! You're more beautiful than you were a moment ago!"

"Stop it!" She chuckled, slapping him on the arm with her notebook. "You're so corny, Xander!"

"That's Alex," Julie corrected, turning away from her conversation with Cathy and slowly putting her arm around him, giving him a kiss on the cheek as they spooned. "And I don't think he's corny at all. I think he's cute."

"Cute?" Xander said, raising an eyebrow.

"Dude..." Mike laughed out loud, punching his friend on the shoulder as he put his arms around his own girlfriend. "...You got the cute. You are officially lamer than you have ever been in your life."

"Shut up," Cathy groaned, grabbing his face with her thumb and forefinger so that his lips stuck out like a fishes. "I haven't heard you say stuff like that to me in months. Even if I did, you'd have to be *upgraded* to cute to get out of the doghouse you're in."

"Oh yeah?" He smiled, reaching out and tickling her furiously.

"Oh my God! Stop it, Mike! Stop it!" She squealed, laughter roaring out of her until her sides hurt.

Xander laughed at them, then turned back to Mandy. "So, what are you doing tonight? Anything?"

"Yeah, Mandy," Mike reciprocated, turning toward her while still tickling Cathy. "What are you doing tonight?"

"Well," she smiled, her rosy red cheeks blossoming with vibrancy. "I was think maybe I'd--"

"...cosign and tangent. These formulae give us what our chemical charts will be at both points C and F, respectively."

Xander looked around, realizing that he was, and had always been, in Mr. Howards' last period Chem class. He glanced around, making sure that nobody had noticed him as he had zoned out, then tried his best to catch up on his notes from Gwen Watson in front of him.

"The graph will always be the same at both points C and F when you are presenting chemicals with at least three sodium ions in its formulae, as you can see in the following three examples..."

Xander stopped, carefully placed his pen down on his desk, and watched his fingers as they moved.

Scars.

CHAPTER FIVE: REPRISE

"Hi! Sorry you got near-fatally shot in the chest! Here, have a fruit basket!" Mike said, holding the basket before him at the hospital gift shop. "Yeah, that's convincing."

"Well, sure, if you say it like that," Cathy groaned, taking a bite out of her chocolate bar. "How about... 'Here are some fruit, but I guess you had enough of that with Xander?'"

Mike shot her a look, then turned back to the pitiful fruit basket (consisting mostly of bananas) and placed it back on the shelf. "I swear to god, this is the most depressing room in this hospital."

"The gift shop?"

"Yeah. Full of cheesy things and useless junk. When I was sick that time, all the stuff my parents bought me just made it worse. It's like all the happy face balloons and shit have become symbols for sickness. Whenever I look at them now, I get all depressed."

"Hm," Cathy grunted, poking at a stuffed teddy bear with 'get well soon' sewn into its heart-shaped stomach. "I find it to be an interesting part of human subculture."

Again, Mike shot her a look.

"What?"

"No more Discovery Channel for you," he said flatly.

She rolled her eyes. "Come on, we have to find something."

"You pick. Girls are impossible to shop for anyway."

"Oh, really?" She smirked, placing a hand on one hip.

"Well, yeah," he said positively, picking up a fluffy heart pillow and waving it before him. "With girls there is so much to choose from, so many different tastes. With guys, it's simple: give him and comic book featuring women who have such big breasts and are so skinny that in real life their backs would be broken. That's all. You're done. He's happy... and you can read it before you even give it to him and he'll never know, so you're happy too."

Cathy stood, arms crossed, looking at him with one eyebrow cocked. "What girls?"

"Huh?"

"The comics. What girls in the comics?"

Mike chuckled to himself, putting down the heart pillow that he had, until this point, still been waving. "When you do this about regular girls it's weird enough. Fictional girls boarders on psychotic."

"What. Girls."

He sighed, hanging his head as low as it would without injuring his neck. "Rogue. I like Rogue, from X-Men. The comic, not the movies."

"There," she chimed, patting him twice on the head. "Now was that so hard?"

"More than you will ever know."

"I like Scarlet Witch from the Avengers."

Mike's head shot back up, looking at her bug-eyed.

"It's the tiara," she giggled, scrunching up the bridge of her nose.

Mike shook his head in amazement, turning back toward the shelves.

"Look at that!" He almost yelled, pointing with both hands at a small teddy bear wearing an eye patch, a cast and a crutch. There was even an adhesive strip across its bum. "Seriously, is that necessary? That's really depressing to me. 'Hey kids, your stuffed animals can get sick and die too!'"

"I'm sure that's the message they're trying to portray there, lover."

"Bears are stupid anyway," he grumbled.

"I like bears."

"You would."

"What's that?"

"Nothing, my sweet darling baby girl," he sang, smiling at her.

Rolling her eyes, she let her hands slump to her sides in frustration at the gift buying process, then turned to face Mike in her exasperation.

"Chocolates," they both said in unison.

Xander and Tommy both sat on the couch in the hallway outside Julie's room. Both men sat forward in their seats, elbows leaned against their knees and hands clasped together before them. Tommy looked at the wall opposite them, filled with pictures of children that had been lost and children that had been saved. The previous far outweighed the latter, a notion that made him want to look away, yet he did not.

Xander's head stayed turned in the direction of Julie's door without actually looking at it, his right knee shaking violently. He made no effort to stop or even control it.

"You know, you can go in," Tommy offered, motioning toward the door. "I'll stay here and wait for Mike and Cathy, if you want."

Xander smiled, turning his head down and away from the door. "Naw," he said, nodding at Tommy in appreciation. "I wouldn't know what to say if I went in there alone."

Tommy gave him a knowing look, nodding. "How about: 'how are you?' or 'I missed you?'"

Xander snorted. "Or, 'Hey, since you got shot not long after and I didn't have a chance to ask, are we still broken up?'"

"Right," Tommy agreed, pouting a lip. "Yeah, that one I'd leave out."

"You think? I thought it might make for an alright icebreaker. Maybe after I could bring up that zit that was coming out on her back the last time we made out. See if it got any bigger."

"More topics to steer away from," Tommy laughed, tapping Xander on the knee with his fist. "I think... I think maybe this is supposed to get easier."

"No," Xander whispered, looking down at his hands. For a moment, he could have sworn that there was blood on them. Drenching them. "It's supposed to get harder."

"Hey!" Cathy said, jogging up the hall with a shopping bag full of chocolates bouncing against her side as she went.

"Hey," Xander said, getting up and accepting her hug as she reached him, rubbing his hands soothingly over her back. He turned to Mike then, who gave him a nod as Cathy turned and gave Tommy a hug as he rose to greet her.

"What did you guys get?" Mike asked, holding up his own bag full of assorted chocolates.

Xander and Tommy both reached into their bags, each pulling out a small, stuffed bear with a broken arm and a crutch.

There was a long pause as Mike stared blankly at both of the bears, then at the faces of the men holding them.

"Looks cute," he said finally, dropping the chocolate back into the bag and turning toward the door.

Down the hall, a nurse wheeled a bed with a long cloth draped over it out of a room and down the hall toward them.

All four of them faced the door at different angles, each trying to look as casual as possible in their inability to open it.

"Are they giving her meds?" Cathy asked finally, taking a turn looking at all three of her men. "Does... does anybody know if they're giving her any meds?"

Xander bit his lip.

"Um, yeah," Tommy answered, coughing a little. "Yeah, her Mom... Sam?... She said they'd been giving her Morphine and stuff. For the pain."

"No, for the cookies," Mike said under his breath. No sooner were the words out of his mouth than he shot an apologetic look at Tommy.

Tommy forced a smile back.

The nurse continued to wheel the gurney down the hall toward them. One of the legs was loose and kept trying to pull the cart to the right, making a high-pitched squeaking noise as it did.

"No comments like that when we get in there, please," Xander said without looking at anyone in particular.

The three of them nodded, neither one looking at the other, as Xander took another step forward toward the door. Suddenly, his nostrils flared. He turned, a sickened look on his face as the nurse wheeled the bed past.

Cathy, Mike, and Tommy turned as well.

Hanging out from over the edge of the bed, barely uncovered by the sheet, was a small, chubby hand. It was as white as paper. The nails on the end of each finger were tiny and blue.

Cathy turned, burying her head into Mike's arms.

All of the colour drained from Tommy's face, and he brought a hand to his mouth.

Xander frowned as he turned back toward the door and sighed. He reached out, grasped the knob, and turned it.

CHAPTER SIX: VISITING HOURS

Xander opened the door and Mandy smiled up at him from beside Julie's bed, her lopsided grin slowly fading to an expression of worry and remorse. The look did not suit her face, making the whole scene appear wrong somehow.

"How is she?" Xander said, taking quick steps to be by her side as he took off his jacket and laid it over Julie's motionless feet. He took her hand and rubbed it softly as Mike, Cathy, and Tommy quietly came in behind him. Mike took an extra pace to give Mandy a simple kiss hello on the forehead, and then sat down next to Cathy.

"She's doing better," Mandy admitted, taking hold of Xander's hand as he held Julie's. "The doctors say that all the bleeding's stopped, finally. She could wake up any time, but... sometimes these things take awhile."

Xander nodded, giving her a quick smile. He reached up and pushed her hair back behind her ears.

"You've got such a pretty face," he chided, poking her softly on her nose. "I don't know why you'd ever want to hide it."

She rolled her eyes. "It's not my face I'm trying to hide. It's this big ugly scar."

Xander smiled, then he turned to Julie.

"Do you think she can hear us?" Tommy asked nervously, cracking his knuckles every few seconds. He never once took his eyes off Julie. "I mean, can she understand?"

"I think so," Mike smiled.

"Yeah, I read somewhere that talking to them can help." Cathy nodded. She tried to recall the magazine, then decided it was unimportant.

"Julie," Xander coaxed, squeezing his girlfriend's hand tighter. "Julie, you have to wake up, okay? We need you to wake up now." He paused.

Nothing.

"Jules, come on," Mandy coaxed, leaning in. "You gotta wake up. I love you, Cousin. You gotta wake up."

Julie's eyelids fluttered.

Xander smiled, large and bright.

"Julie!" He said louder, trying desperately to get a response. "Julie!"

Slowly, her eyelids opened, a smile prying around the corners of her mouth as she turned her head weakly to look at Xander.

"Alex..." she said, her voice painful to even hear. "...Alex, I love

Xander opened the door, revealing the cold, sterile room that seemed to have been sealed from within, like pickles inside an unopened jar. At first, all that was visible were dual lumps where Julie's feet poked up near the end of the bed; then, as each of them entered the room and came around the corner, she came fully into view.

She looked pale, almost as white as the walls that surrounded her. She stared straight up and the stucco ceiling until all four of them were almost on top of her. She jumped a little when she finally noticed them, clenching her chest as pain shot through it, then quickly faded.

"Hey," Xander said softly, sitting on the corner on the bed with both his hands on his lap.

"Hey," she replied, sniffling as she pressed a button on a remote that brought her bed into a sitting position. She winced a little when it stopped. "You guys came."

"Yeah," he said, reaching out and taking her hand finally, which she made no motion to stop. "Yeah, this is the soonest they'd let us in."

There was a long silence that was almost palpable.

"Um... I got you this," Tommy said finally, breaking the quiet as he reached into his bag and pulled out the stuffed bear with a broken arm.

"Oh, yeah," Xander said, having forgotten, pulling out his bear, with the crutch. "Me, too."

"Thanks," she said sweetly, putting one on each side of her, smiling at them both.

"We brought chocolate," Mike said between bites, motioning to both him and Cathy. Cathy grabbed the bag from him, putting it beside Julie.

"Thanks," she said honestly, staring down at the bag hungrily. "These are so gone the second they tell me I can eat solid foods."

Cathy smiled weirdly. "Sorry, didn't think."

"It's okay," she sighed, playing with a tuft of hair on the head of the bear Xander gave her. Her eyes turned away then, staring at the far corner of the room.

Again, Xander's nostrils flared and his brow furrowed. He turned to Cathy, who gave him a confused look, and he back.

"How... are you?" Tommy asked finally.

"The pain is less," she said, still looking at that spot in the corner for whatever reason. "The drugs they got me on make me kinda wonky, though."

She turned quickly, as if she had heard something behind her, hurting her chest again.

"How so?" Mike asked, tilting his head.

She laughed. "Earlier today I thought there was something in the room with me... It was horrible. A nurse had to come in and give me something to calm me down."

"If it's little pink elephants or Smurf porn, I know what you're talking about," Mike smirked, drawing glances from everyone. "What? You can't tell me I'm the only person here who's ever hallucinated about Smurfs getting busy?"

"No..." Julie interjected, shaking her head. "It was... I don't know what it was."

"Can you describe it?" Xander asked finally, squeezing her hand.

She took it away from him. "It was big. It was really big... tall, I mean. But it was really thin. And it didn't have any eyes... just big, black holes. It was wearing a suit..."

"A suit?" Xander questioned, raising an eyebrow.

"Yeah, but it didn't have any skin. It was all muscled, no skin anywhere that I could see. And it had this big bulge in its pants. It was grabbing itself and coming toward me and it said something, then I screamed and it went away."

"What did it say?" Cathy asked, cuddled into Mike now.

"It said... You have nothing to fear, but fear myself," she said distantly, shivering even though it had not gotten any colder in the room.

"Hn," Mike grunted.

Her brow wrinkled, sweat dotting along it and along the neckline of her blouse.

"It's okay," Xander said, in the softest voice he was capable of. "It's not important."

"Yeah. Yeah, I guess," she said faintly, then turned to the group as a whole. "Thank you guys so much for coming... but, would you mind leaving the two of us alone for a while, please?"

"Sure," Xander said respectfully, turning to the others. "Um, if you guys wanna stick around I'll probably only be a-"

"No, Alex," Julie said softly, cutting him off. "I meant... could you guys leave me and Tommy alone?"

Xander turned toward her as Tommy moved in and knelt down by her bed. She grasped his hand and squeezed it tightly.

"Yeah," he said finally, realizing that she hadn't even really heard his response, as he, Mike and Cathy walked out the door.

"Dr. Marx?" Nurse Williams called, opening the door to his office even as she knocked on it.

Dennis Marx dropped the notepad he was looking at, his knee coming up off the floor and slamming into one of the sharp corners of his desk. He cursed, frustrated, and ran his hands through his balding salt-and-pepper hair as Williams entered the room.

"Bad time?"

"What do you *want*, Debra?"

She swallowed. Her name was not Debra, but she was not about to correct him. He was a stubby little man that looked like a caricature of a mole, with large rimmed glasses and a small nose that came to a sharp point an inch or so in front of his face. There was an actual mole growing out the side of his neck, which was large with rough edges and hairs growing out of it that he refused to get looked at.

"The blue baby in room three eighty-one got dealt with, she's fine. Mr. Douglas is stable with non-life threatening wounds, and there was a code in Mr. Adams's room. We lost him."

"That's good," he said, already reabsorbed in his notepad.

She stared at him, tilting her head to one side.

"I mean, not *good*," he sighed, looking up from his papers. His hands were out in front of him as though he were pleading with her, his red Bic pen still clasped in his left one. "It's not good, it's... thank you for telling me."

Williams nodded, then turned to leave. The office was cluttered, with papers strewn everywhere containing mortician reports, medical journals and tox screens compiled over months and arranged in no particular order. There was a large stack of patient files on a love seat in the corner that had toppled over and intermingled with one another like a shuffled deck of cards, and she did not envy whoever had to rearrange them when it came time.

There was a mini-fridge in the corner with a padlock on it. It was the first time she'd ever seen it there, and her eyes lingered on it for a moment.

"Is there anything else?" Marx barked, looking up from his notebook and realizing she was still there.

"No..." she replied, shaking off her temporary daze and smiling at him. "Not at all, Doctor."

She let herself out and closed the door behind her.

He watched the door for a full minute, as though expecting it to do something else. When he felt secure that we was alone again, he walked over and locked it with the small latch near its knob, then fished his keys out of his pocket as he made his way over to his fridge.

He consulted his notes for a moment, then hunched over and pulled out a long tray full of glass vials, each one sealed tight with a taped-on label written in his own illegible hand. He lifted a few out, read their contents, then shoved them back in. On the fourth try he found the one he was looking for, smiled, and placed the rest of the tray back into his cooler.

It was labeled anthrax.

ᛉ

Xander sighed, flopping down on a chair one hall down from Julie's room.

"That's the last time I'm nice to that guy," he grumbled, slouching as far as he could without falling off the chair.

"Oh, stop whining," Cathy berated, giving him a little kick to the shin. "She just wants to thank him for saving her, is all."

"Oh, I'm sorry. Stopping Adam Genblade and defeating all of Circe doesn't qualify as saving anymore. I may have saved the whole town, which she is in, but does anybody say-"

"Are you done?"

"Very," he said, sucking in his lip and sitting up quickly.

"Good."

"So, what now?" Mike asked, frowning as he leaned up against the wall with his arm over his head.

Xander sighed, turning back to Julie's room and staring at it for a long moment.

"You guys can go on home," he said finally, dragging his hand through his hair. "I'm gonna stay here. Just in case she needs something."

Cathy stepped forward and hugged him, then she and Mike walked past him and out of sight.

Xander leaned his face forward onto the balls of his palms let out a deep, sorrowful sigh.

CHAPTER SEVEN: OMENS

Jillian was an Aegean cat, and there was absolutely nothing wrong with that.

That was what her master, Josie, had said to her often. Josie would rub her back or scratch behind her ears and say "Jillian is an Aegean cat, and there's nothing wrong with that with that," sometimes over and over again. Jillian, for her part, would close her eyes and purr ecstatically.

Three months ago Jillian had gotten out and had met a young stallion without a name, and now she was so plump that she could barely walk without waddling from side to side. Josie had been almost giddy when she'd discovered that there would soon be a litter of cute little kittens running around her home, and Jillian had taken to lounging about and enjoying herself in the sun while she waited for the big day (not that she had been opposed to doing that before she'd gotten pregnant). Then a week ago, she'd gotten the irresistible urge to get out... She wasn't running away, no, she'd definitely go back. She knew that Josie would worry without her. But she knew she had to find somewhere else to go to have her kittens.

She'd spent the last week in the hospital basement, curled up amongst a pile of old rags very near the furnace. Although she wasn't as good a mouser as she had been when Josie had adopted her from her previous home in the shelter, she'd still managed to make a good living for herself on the mice that lived in the ducts and walls leading to the hospital kitchen. The staff did not know who to thank for their pest control, but they were thankful all the same.

A door opened somewhere that shone a long stream of light over the basement. Her eyes went wide, glowing as they turned toward its source, but she did not move. There was an old janitor that came down here once every few hours, and although he'd never noticed her she'd become adjusted to his presence. The door closed again and the light vanished, but there was still something there... she could feel it even if she could not see it.

She listened hard, and for a moment all she could hear was the faint drips of the leaky pipes leading into the sewage system. After a moment she heard footsteps coming toward her. There was nothing sneaky or mysterious about them. They clambered and clunked on the cold concrete floor, and Jillian was convinced she could see them now, moving in and out of the little light offered from underneath the stairwell door.

Her ears flattened back and she hissed.

CHAPTER EIGHT: DOWN DEEP

Xander leaned forward on the hard green plastic chair because the curve of its lumbar support had been digging so far into his back that he was convinced no human spine could withstand it. The door to Julie's room remained at the far right of his field of vision. It had not budged since he left it over an hour ago. Nobody had gone in, and nobody had come out.

He sighed and ran his fingers through his hair, then slapped his hands down onto his jeans and rubbed along the ridges in the denim, letting out a long huff of air.

The nurse's station was at the end of the hall. There was a large, big breasted woman standing behind the counter there trying to complete some paperwork who stopped to say hello to every person that passed, even people that did not say hello to her or acknowledge her in any way. As more and more people passed she became more and more agitated, pressing down on her pen so hard that it started to cut through the paper.

A short, stumpy doctor passed by. She looked up from her work and said, "Hello."

He nodded in return.

She went back to her work, taking a moment to find her place again.

A patient walked by. She looked up from her work and said, "Hello."

The patient rolled his eyes and continued to the bathroom.

A young man wearing a striped shirt and carrying one of those bandaged bears walked by. She looked up from her work and said, "Hello."

He didn't even respond, or notice that she had spoken to him.

She went back to her work each time increasingly frustrated.

Xander shook his head and forced himself to look away. When he did, Julie's door came into view again, immediately coming into focus as though it had been waiting for him, like some trickster hiding behind a corner ready to leap out a yell boo at a moment's notice.

"Why don't you just go in?"

"It's not that simple," he replied. "She asked me to go."

"Then why don't you leave?"

He did not respond to that, keeping his eyes glued on the door.

Several long moments passed, and he felt a lump grow in his stomach. It was like his entire body was trying to collapse in on itself through a black hole in his chest. He felt every part of him slowly moving toward it, his shoulders slumping forward and his knees coming up. His head felt heavy, though he was not tired. Every part of him felt raw, and he wanted to claw at his chest with his fingers to try and dig the feeling out.

He heard something behind him, the solid *ticktack ticktack* of something crawling inside the wall or in an air duct. He felt like it was on him, whatever it was, and for a moment when he looked between his legs he could have sworn he saw a mouse scampering over his foot. He jumped slightly, realizing it was just his shoelace.

"Fuck," he breathed, reaching down and tying the errant lace. Sweat had begun to bead his face and all his joints felt stiff.

There was a loud rattling sound, and he got up from the chair and turned around. There was a large duct behind him spitting out air and sounds. Beyond the grate was dark, but he could see the edges of what looked to be a destroyed paper-wasp nest. He shivered, and then turned back toward the door.

"Fuck this," he huffed, patting his hands against his jeans again but this time coming back with a battered cigarette pack in his hand. He fumbled with the top and pulled one out. It was soggy and limp and he put it behind his ear and started down the hall toward the exit.

The big-breasted nurse looked up from her work as he passed by her station, a fake smile plastered on her chubby face. "Hell--"

"You have OCD," he snapped, continuing down the hall without even looking at her.

She stared, dumbfounded, then shrugged and went back to her work until the next person walked by.

⋏⋎⋏

Cathy sat in Mike's den on an old couch with holes in it, the sponge that poked up through them oddly comfortable. She'd been here before, but not often. The room had been limited to being his father's office for years while he'd been working from home, but now they were free to use it as they wished. His mother still never went in, not because there was anything sensitive inside, but simply because years of having to stay out had ingrained itself into her subconscious to the point that she often forgot the room was even there.

The room did not match any other in the home. A few years ago Mike's mother had gone on a redecorating and remodeling kick that had left most of the house open concept and in shades of bright greens and subtle yellow hues. This room (which had been all but forgotten in her projects) looked like the rest of the home used to: muted earth tones and hardwood everything. Hardwood floors, hardwood furniture, even the heavy curtains had been bought to be the colour of the hardwood, though they had since faded into a grayer version of it. Mike used the room a lot, much as he did now, sitting at the computer desk and staring into the screen.

She watched him intently for some time without even realizing it, her mind drifting from one thought to the next. "You know, until recently I didn't even realize your house had a computer."

He paused, then turned around and looked at her with a raised eyebrow. "Of course we have a computer. What house *doesn't* have a computer?"

"My house doesn't."

He paused and thought for a moment. "Huh."

35

He shrugged, then turned back to the monitor.

She sighed, then got up and moved over to the bookshelf and started going through the titles, running her fingers along the spines as she went and kicking up dust.

"Your dad sure does like James Patterson," she said, counting each book in her head.

"Nobody's perfect," he mumbled. The computer made a soft clicking sound as a new window opened.

"What're you doing over there, anyway?"

"I am looking up who the Mets are starting next season."

She turned around from the bookcase and shot him a weird look, one eyebrow arched and both lids bulging. It was wasted on his backside. Had he seen it he would have shot coffee out of his nose. "You like baseball?"

He turned in her direction only slightly, then motioned toward the wall that the desk was up against. It was filled with pictures of a young blonde boy in a baseball uniform resting a bat on his shoulder. Some were designed to look like large baseball cards (with actual stats and awards typed along the border) and others were black-and-white team shots in which the boy was clearly identifiable by his hair, which looked almost paper-white in them.

"Oh my god, that's you!" She smiled, walking over and tilting one of the frames to see it better.

"Of course it's me. Who did you think it was?"

"I don't know. Your cousin. I don't know."

"I don't have any cousins. You know I don't have any cousins."

"You're so *cute*," she said, ignoring him. Her tone was the same one that he'd noticed her using on children, her voice raising several octaves until it sounded like it could shatter glass. "Where's this one?"

He leaned back on his chair to see what she was referred to. It was a picture of him at about ten standing on a long row of bleachers. His father was towering over him, having to lean down so that his head could be in the shot and still get all of Mike. Mike was wearing a stripped Mets uniform and cap, and they were both holding up Mets flags. Mike's face was covered in freckles that were much darker than they were now.

"That is me and my Dad at a Mets game."

"You went to New York?"

"No," he laughed. "The Mets came to Boston to play the Red Sox... I've never been to New York. I wish."

She smirked. "You went to a Red Sox home game dressed like that? They must have loved you."

"I'm sure." He smiled, then turned back to the computer and clicked the mouse again.

The basement door closed behind Xander and he was in the dark again.

That was okay. He found that he'd always liked the dark, even as a child.

There was something about a black room that made him feel safe... as though he was curled up tight in a warm blanket so snug that no light could get in.

The basement was not warm though. It was so cold that gooseflesh covered his arms and made his hairs stand on end.

He stood at the top of the stairway that led down to the basement and waited for his eyes to adjust. After a moment when they did not, he sighed and reached deep into his pants pocket and withdrew a metal butane lighter. He popped the top and flicked the flint three times before it finally caught, illuminating the narrow stairwell in dull oranges and deep, black shadows. He held the flame back behind his head for a moment and tried to see where he was going. The shadows made the already narrow stairs look even thinner than they were. They seemed to sway back and forth as the light flickered in the slow breeze of the drafty basement, winding this way and that until they finally reached the concrete below.

He took his cigarette out from behind his ear, wet from sweat around its tip, and pinned it between his lips. Bringing the flame to his face he took three puffs in rapid succession, then pulled back and checked to make sure the cherry was lit. It ebbed at him like a dull red eye sticking out of the darkness, and did not fade. He put the butt between his lips and took a long drag, closing his eyes blissfully. He could feel the smoke in his neck and chest, the way the heat made him feel whole. He held it as long as he could and then let it go, the smoke playing and dancing with the flame and casting swirling shadows on the wall.

There was a sign on the wall next to him. He raised his lighter, and found it to be a No Smoking sign. He smirked, then turned his attention back down the stairwell.

It had stopped winding back and forth, although the flame still flickered about. There was a cool breeze coming from the cracks in the concrete that was still making him shiver. Every time he thought he was getting used to it the wind outside howled again and he heard it whistle through the cracks an instant before it touched his skin like a dead arm.

He narrowed his eyes, took another short puff of his smoke, and started down the stairs.

⁂

"So, that's everything?" Tommy asked, glancing at Julie then looking down at his hands again, rubbing his aching knuckles.

"Yeah, pretty much," she replied, her eyes dancing about in her head, as if searching her mind for any strands of information that she had forgotten. "Yeah, that's it."

He stopped for a second to mull things over.

"That's quite a bit."

"Yeah, pretty much," she repeated, trying hard to flatten the wrinkles out of her blankets.

Again, Tommy remained silent.

Julie's eyes shot downward, not knowing from his reaction whether or not to be ashamed by what she had told him.

37

"I had no idea that all of that happened," he admitted, almost sorely. "How come nobody tells me anything, anyway?"

She grinned. "It's not just you. Everyone's really secretive here. I think it's something that they put in the water, y'know?"

Tommy smiled a little at that. "Yes, actually. Everyone here has their own plans, their own little agenda. Julian, Derek..."

"Phillips, Randy..."

"Xander, Mike..."

"You." She grinned, raising her eyebrow at him.

He looked as though he were about to continue with another set of names, then stopped and smirked at her. "You catch a lot more than people give you credit for, don't you, Miss Peterson?"

"I try," she replied coyly. She turned from him to pound at her pillow, trying to get it comfortable.

"So, what about you?" He asked, leaning forward. "Hiding any other demons?"

"No," she said quietly, in a matter-of-fact tone of voice. "None of my demons are metaphorical."

⋏⟨⋎⟩⋏

The basement seemed to go on forever.

Xander took another puff of his cigarette and let the smoke curl around his head like a wreath. It stung at his eyes and made them water but he didn't care. With one hand holding the lighter high, he needed the other in case he fell.

The flame was almost useless. It seemed to get swallowed by the darkness just over a foot in either direction, devoured by the drafty cold of the hospital basement. He turned around just a few feet from the bottom of the staircase and found that he couldn't even see it anymore.

What was worse was the smell. He couldn't smell anything down here except the sterile stench of disinfectant and bleach that wafted down from the air ducts and was pooled in little puddles of chemicals that whoever spilled them thought would dry but never would down here. It blocked all his senses and made him helpless as he took one slow, deliberate step after another, making sure that he wasn't about to trip over a barrel or some stray tube.

Something sucked in the distance, like the last bit of water draining down a sink. Every few seconds there was a different sound of water gushing through one of the insulated copper pipes as somebody, somewhere in the hospital turned their faucets on and off. It never came from the same direction twice, sometimes so far and faint that he had to strain to hear it and sometimes right above his head. It shot fast as though it might burst, then slowed down to the barest dribble in an instant.

That tight feeling built in his chest again, like his body wanted him to try and touch his toes with his shoulders. He took another puff of his smoke and moved on.

There was a skittering in the darkness, like thousands of tiny legs all mov-

38

ing in unison along the floor. Without even thinking about it, his mind conjured up the image of a giant centipede with long pincers in the front crawling along the basement floor toward him, so big that it could wrap all around him like a boa constrictor before devouring him whole, all the while hearing that skittering clicking clacking as he went down the creature's gullet.

He shook the thought off.

"Nng," he snarled, as he took another puff and the ember reached his calloused fingertips. He brought the burn up into the light and watched as the blister slowly faded away until it was gone completely, like watching an artist erase a mistake he'd made on the page.

Holding the dwindling smoke between his lips, he reached into his pocket and pulled the pack out again. Of the two left he took the straighter one and clasped it between his lips on the other side of his mouth. Even though his lighter was already out, he lit the new smoke off the cherry of the old one (again puffing three times to make sure it was going) then flicked the old butt into the darkness.

It traveled far, much further than he would have thought he could flick it. It spun end over end long into the darkness, finally striking off a steel pipe and tailspinning its way down to the ground, casting a small circle of light around it as it went.

Right before it went out, there was something between Xander and the light... a black figure that stood tall and lanky, with its legs stretching out like poles. Its shoulders were hunched over, and although Xander could only see the outline of its form, he could tell that it was looking at him.

The ember went out, covering the distance in the blanket of darkness again.

Fear gripped at his gut, sticking into his stomach at all sides like a clawed hand.

"Hello?" He called, holding up his lighter and squinting into the darkness.

There was no reply, except the skittering of thousands of tiny feet again.

"Is somebody down there?"

Again, there was no response.

Casting a quick glance back in the direction of the stairwell (even though it had long since faded into the darkness), he started toward where he's shot the cigarette.

Several pipes gushed water overhead at once, and he heard at least one toilet flush. A furnace cut in somewhere to his right, and that slurping sound like water being sucked down a drain continued. So did the skittering. It got louder and louder the further into the basement he went.

Without touching it, he took a long drag from his smoke and shot the exhale out through both nostrils, traveling down behind either side of him like a dragon.

The flame still only allowed him to see a few feet in front of his face, and was dwindling.

He stepped in something cold and wet and knelt down, putting two fingers from his free hand down into it. He brought his hand into the view of the fire. At first he thought it was rusted water, but then the stench of ammonia (already prevalent here) shot into him and slammed harshly into his sinuses, and he realized it was urine.

He wiped his hand in his jeans feverishly.

The furnace cut in again and almost made him jump out of his skin. It was right behind him.

"Jesus," he cursed, holding out the flame as far as he could and seeing the tall metal sphere that seemed to go all the way up to the ceiling.

There was blood spattered across it in an upward arch.

Again he felt that pang deep inside his abdomen, almost like hunger or a nicotine fit but not either of those things. He stepped forward slowly and brought the lighter down until the soft orange glow found the carcass of a black-and-white Aegean cat.

Blood had matted into its soft fur and made it course and sticky, especially around its stomach. It was fat and looked as though it had been pregnant, and Xander found himself making a small, pitiful sound that he usually would have associated with something Cathy would do.

Her tiny face was bent upward, her eyes and mouth frozen open in fear and hatred. Her tiny, sharp teeth still had spit on them.

She had a long gash going from her pelvis to her neck, exposing her organs and her plump, full uterus. One of her legs was missing.

Xander shivered.

There was a collar around her neck, and he reached out carefully to turn its tag toward him.

It read: Jillian.

A pipe above him gushed water again, and there was that slow sucking sound... followed by a wet smacking.

His brow furrowed and he turned around, raising the lighter high again and taking several determined, brave steps into the darkness until the light found the wall.

There, huddled in the corner, was a man in a deep black suit.

His back was turned to Xander, but he could see the back of his bald head and the wisps of hair that clung to it in uneven clumps. The flesh on his skull was not smooth and round like his father's; it was scaly and segmented into long lines like stringy bits of muscle still clinging to the bone. It was huddled over something against the wall, completely oblivious to Xander and the light that now bathed it. He moved back and forth slightly, like a chair left to rock in the wind.

The suit looked pressed and clean, like the ones his grandfather had worn to church every Sunday until the day he'd died. It also looked like the suit they'd buried him in. It was too short on this fellow though, revealing thin legs and nonexistent ankles sticking out from underneath them.

The sucking sound was louder here, and consistently followed by the wet slap of flesh he'd heard a moment ago.

"What're you doing?" Xander asked finally, still standing a few feet from it.

It spun around quickly, and Xander froze in place.

It had no eyes. Just like Julie had said, it had no eyes... just black holes that seemed to go on forever like the basement. The light caught nothing in them. It had no flesh either, just malformed muscle that squirmed about like worms all over its face. It had a long nose and sharp, yellow teeth that could be seen right until they disappeared into his gums because it had no lips.

There was blood and flesh caught between its teeth.

It howled at Xander then disappeared, scurrying off into the darkness faster than even he could see. The scuttling centipede feet he'd heard all along was deafening now, skittering off along the wall away from him.

"Fuck!" Xander yelled, dropping the lighter.

It fell to the ground and snapped shut, leaving him in darkness.

He dove to the ground and patted for it, his cigarette falling from his lips and rolling along the floor.

His hand connected with something wet and slimy and he pulled it back, screaming. Finally he found the lighter and fumbled with it for a moment before realizing he had it upside down, turned it over, and lit it.

Light again invaded the basement, and he let out a long breath.

Holding the light forward, he saw what his hand had come to rest on.

It was Jillian's missing leg.

He shuddered, wiping his hand in his pants again and chasing along the wall after the creature.

It seemed as though he were jogging forever, much longer than he would have said the width of the hospital could have been. He'd lost all track of where the stairwell would be and didn't care.

Finally, he came up to the other wall and stopped. The skittering was gone, and so was the creature. He looked all around, but all he saw was darkness.

"Fuck!" He yelled, kicking the wall violently.

It rang. Like a bell.

He turned and saw an air duct near the corner, two feet wide and one foot high. There was a grate covering it that was screwed on, and the darkness inside was only made deeper by the flame in his hand, just like the one upstairs.

He stared at it for a long moment, the gong that his kick had made echoing down it until it disappeared.

Slowly, he bent down and lowered the flame to see inside.

He screamed louder than he ever had when its arm came through the grate and clawed at his face.

CHAPTER NINE: TIMOR

The phone rang in three different places in the Harris house: one in the kitchen, one in the living room, and one in the den. Each had their own separate and unique rings that were annoying enough on their own, but when they all combined together at different paces and volumes they instantly brought migraines with them.

RIIIING!

Doo doop doo doop doo doo doo doop!

Braaaaang!

It did this three times before Cathy tilted her head away from Mike's, forcing their lips apart. They were lying on the old couch in the den with one of Mike's feet caught in its sponge-stuffed holes and Cathy's legs wrapped around Mike's midsection.

"Are you going to get that?" She asked, even as he tried to lean into her lips again.

"I hadn't planned on it, no."

"Come on, it could be important."

"Not more important than this, I guarantee."

She shot him a look.

"Fine," he smiled. She opened her legs to let him go and he hopped on one foot over to his father's desk, snatching the cordless phone off its cradle and bringing it to his ear. "This had better be good."

"It's real," Xander said into the hospital payphone he held clutched between his cheek and his shoulder, dabbing white fluffy gauze against the other side of his face as he did. It stung violently, but he didn't flinch away.

Static roared in Mike's ear and he pulled back, wincing. "Who is this?"

"Shut up. It's real; I need you guys to look some stuff up for me. I'm going to stay here and try to see what's going on."

"Is that Xander?" Cathy asked, sitting up on the couch and adjusting her shirt.

"I think so, but he's being a douchebag," Mike grumbled, making no effort to block the receiver as he spoke. "What's real?"

"The thing Julie was talking about," Xander huffed, pulling the gauze back from his face and examining the level of fresh blood on it. He leaned to the side of the phone and examined himself in its metal back. There were still four white lines down right side of his face where its claws had run, but the wounds were closed. "The Fear thing. It's real."

"Real?"

"Real. I need you to find out what it is and what it can do, if you can. I'm hoping I can just cut it to bits and be done with it, but the fucker's fast. It's not human. It could be like me or Black Heart or something. Either way, we have to find it before it can do any damage to Julie or anyone else."

There was silence on the other end of the line.

Mike pressed the receiver against his chest and looked at Cathy. "He's finally lost it."

"I can hear you."

"I didn't say anything."

"I have superhuman senses. You can go fuck yourself. What's the problem?"

Mike frowned. "I'm sorry, I'd assumed we weren't going to be chasing after

42

figments of your ex-girlfriend's imagination today. But then again, I took my crazy pills this morning...did you?"

"It's real."

"One sec, I don't think Cathy believes me," Mike said, pressing the speaker button on the phone and then resting it on the cradle again. "Can you hear me?"

"Yes, I can hear you."

"Good. Now, be a dear and tell Cathy how batshit you've gone."

"It's real. The Fear demon thing Julie was talking about. It's real."

"Real how?" Cathy frowned, stepping a pace toward the speaker as though it were really Xander in front on her.

"Real as in I'm-looking-at-the-cuts-it-made-across-my-face-right-now real."

Mike stopped smiling. He turned white. "Did you fall asleep? It wouldn't be the first time someone in our group saw something otherworldly in a fever dream."

"Exactly," Cathy said. "Some of us relive past experiences, some of us dream up dead assassins, Julie's head makes up monsters... and some of us picture pornographic blue midgets."

Mike shot her a look.

"I wasn't dreaming. I was smoking."

"You said you'd quit!" Cathy huffed.

"Big picture, please," he barked into the phone, drawing the attention of the fat nurse at the station again. "You guys couldn't smell the fear on her, all right? Give me a little credit."

"That bad?"

"It was like the city dump at the town of fear. Whole room reeked of it."

There was a silence.

"What do we do?" Mike said finally, clearing his throat.

"Go to the library and see if you can find anything. I don't even know where you'd start. It eats animals, but something tells me humans are on the menu, too. I want to deal with this fast."

"Is it that you want to deal with this, or that you don't want to deal with anything else?" Cathy asked.

"Whatever. Same difference." He paused when he heard something behind him. A nurse (not the big one with OCD) wheeled another gurney out of the pediatric ward. The body on it was covered over with a sheet, but it was clear it was no more than three feet long. Xander turned and watched it in silence until it was around the corner and on its way down to the morgue. "Shit."

"What?" Mike asked, already pulling his coat on. "What is it?"

"It's the kids," he said, his voice almost a whisper. "It's killing the kids."

He hung up the phone without another word.

Mike and Cathy exchanged glances, then headed for the door.

43

CHAPTER TEN: CTPAX

Xander marched down the hall, trying hard to soften his clenched knuckles before he got to the pink and baby-blue door of the pediatric ward. His eyes squinted as the door got closer, the same stench he'd come across in the basement becoming more and more potent with each breath he took. It was the stench of death, and it was coming from a child's bed.

Fuming, he placed his palm flat against the door to shove it open, then stopped.

He sighed, stared at the back of his hand, and then hung his head.

"Not so easy, is it?" Mandy asked, walking up beside him holding her hands behind her back. She looked down from his hand to his shoes theatrically, mimicking his own actions.

"You shouldn't be here," he grunted, still staring at his boots.

"Why?" She asked, in a voice much like that of a child who was the only person not picked to play a game. "Just because you're a super-hero doesn't mean you're automatically in charge, you know."

"I know that, Amanda," he said curtly, choosing not to look at her with that particular scowl plastered across his lips. "I just... you shouldn't have to see this."

The smile faded from her lips, and she became serious. She reached out, touching her hand to his until both of them pressed against the door.

"Hey. It's me now," she said simply. "You don't have to be alone, because we both know you're not. And I won't have you talk to me like Julie and Cathy are the only women here that love you, okay?"

Smirking a little, Xander nodded, and the both of them opened the door together.

The walls were a plain off-white, coloured only in certain places, probably to the tastes of children that were forced to stay there long-term. They were, however, decorated with a variety of children's characters, like Mickey and Minnie, along with more masculine-definitive characters, like the Ninja Turtles and Spider-Man.

Three children were tucked into their beds. One was a young girl no more than seven, her hair vanished from chemo treatments and her head covered in lumps and scars. A boy looked to be asleep, but his eyes were open, a machine beside him helping him breathe. Another boy seemed to be sleeping peacefully at a weird angle to accommodate his various I.V.'s.

Mandy sighed, looking away from the little girl suffering from cancer.

"No child should have to go through this," she said, curling her lips in disgust.

Xander, still dripping Womb-blood but not caring, rushed to Mandy's side. He

44

propped her head up on his lap and he brushed the hair out of her broken face.

She tried to speak to him, but he shook his head.

"Shh..." he cautioned, hot tears streaming down his face as he held her close, her body... so cold. "Don't speak. It's gonna be okay. You're gonna be okay, I'm gonna get you help, love. Don't you -"

She raised a hand up to the side of his face and stroked it softly.

The last of the Womb's flesh dripped off him.

"So," she whispered hoarsely. "You're the guy everybody's been talking about..."

Her hand fell from his face to the ground with an unceremonious thud, leaving only the blood that had been on her hand behind. Several long moments passed, as Xander listened to her heart slow... then finally come to a stop.

His lower lip quivered as he reached up and closed her eyes for her, those beautiful, sparkling eyes that now seemed so dull and faded. Tears pitted against her cheeks, but she made no move to wipe them off. Slowly, he wrapped his arms around her and began rocking back and forth, cradling Mandy as the tears rushed from his eyes and nose.

"You're right," Xander said, shaking off the thought. "No child should."

"I don't understand. Why are we even down here? You can fight lots of things, Xander, but death isn't one of them."

"I know that," he said bluntly, never once turning to look at her. "Believe me, Mandy, more than you'll ever realize, I know that. But these kids didn't die. They were killed."

Mandy stopped walking, allowing him to get a pace or two ahead of her, before finally having to ask. "Kids? As in, plural?"

"Yeah," Xander whispered, touching the cold sheets of an empty bed. "Plural. My senses have been turned up to eleven ever since I stepped foot on this wing, and they haven't calmed down yet. Something's making them act up. Plus, that same smell that made my senses act up in the basement is here... I think at least three kids died here within the last week, not one."

"Oh..." Mandy drawled, unable to function enough to achieve a working response. "...I don't know what to say to that."

"I know," he said, finally glancing back at her from over his shoulder. "That's what makes you human."

"Who are you talking too?" Came a small voice from one of the corner beds.

Xander turned, noticing the child for the first time. He quickly turned back to Mandy but couldn't find her. He stared at where she had been for a moment before turning back to the child.

She was a beautiful young girl, no more than ten years old. Her hair was a very light brunette, probably just now turning from the blonde it must have been all though her early childhood. She was healthily plump. Her eyes were a deep sea green, like someone else he'd known not too long ago.

"Nobody," he said, realizing that he had yet to responded.

She shrugged, then turned back to her colouring book full of images of children playing safely. There was one image of a boy playing in the street, with a car coming toward him. The girl finished colouring the boy's hair blonde (inside

45

the lines for the most part), then turned the page to reveal the same boy with one foot in a cast sitting in a hospital bed. Again, she began to colour, this time starting with the blonde hair, as she already had that colour out.

Xander walked over to her, careful to keep a respectful distance from her. "What are you doing there?" he asked, trying to sound as nice as he could.

"Colouring. Duh," she said under her breath, as she picked up a cornflower blue crayon.

Xander laughed at himself a little. "Yeah. I guess that was a pretty silly question, huh?"

She did not respond, merely finished with the blue and picked up an orchid purple and started to scrawl away at the page.

"Man, you are really bad with kids," Mandy laughed, peeking over the girl's shoulder.

He ignored her, trying to think of something to say to the child.

"If you want her to pay attention to you, you're going to have to stop treating and thinking of her like a child, for starters," she said, righting herself and walking around the bed, strolling past him to look at some of the books on a shelf in the corner. "Ask the kid her name, at least."

Xander coughed, telling himself that he would have thought of that eventually. "Hey, I'm Xander. What's your name?"

"Chanelle Patricia McDonald," she said, not looking at him at first, then turning toward him with her nose scrunched up. "You have a really weird name."

"Yeah," Xander smiled. "It is kinda weird, isn't it? My real name is Alexander."

"Then why do people call you that?" She asked, turning back to her colouring book and grabbing a dark red from her crayon box.

He smirked, looking down for a moment. Across the room, Mandy turned to listen as well. "Well, when I was born my Mom died, and I don't know what happened to my Dad, so, I was given to some very nice ladies for them to take care of. They named all the little babies that they found after saints. I was named after Saint Alexander, but I was the third one, so instead of Alexander or Alex, they called me Xander."

The little girl looked up, and just as Mandy smiled at Xander so did she. "Did you get new parents?"

"Oh, yes," Xander said, sitting down on the corner of the child's bed. "I got new parents, and they loved me very much. And I have lots of friends, and I'm very happy now. And, at least I wasn't like the kid who must have come after me, because if I had been him I might have been called Lex, and that just would have had too many implications."

"What do you mean?"

"Nothing," he laughed, mostly to himself, but he heard Mandy giggle out of the corner of his ear.

There was a silence then, as the child continued to scribble away on her book.

"Can I... see what you're working on there?" Xander asked, rising up a little,

46

trying to catch a peek.

"No!" The child protested, shielding to picture with her body, glaring at him.

Xander stepped back a little, retracting the hand he had extended toward the child's activity book. "Okay. That's... that's okay," he said soothingly, crumpling his forehead. He glanced down at the girl's arms, seeing that they were bruised and swollen, her legs larger than normal as well. He sighed, then got up to walk away.

-Plip-

Chanelle laid the book down on the bed for him to see.

Xander's eyes went wide. His hand trembled as he picked up the book.

What had originally been a boy in a hospital bed with one leg in a cast and a doctor coming in through the nearby door had been turned into the same boy with dark red smears dripping from his eyes, mouth and ears. The doctor had been coloured in black, making him look shadowy and evil.

Xander coughed slightly, as Mandy came over next to him, shaking her head at the image.

"Chanelle, where did you get the idea for this?" He asked, trying not to sound as alarmed as he actually was.

"It's what happened to the others. Matthew, Darryl, and Justin. It came and it got them. And it killed them. Nobody else can see it, but we can. And it's going to kill me to. It's going to come and kill me tonight."

"Oh, really?" Mandy said, forcing a smile.

"And what makes you think that?" Xander added, trying not to sound mean.

"Because he told me so," Chanelle said, meeting Xander's stare with cold, hard desperation.

Xander just watched her for a minute as she turned to the next page in her book, featuring a little girl playing in her sandbox.

He turned, shot a glance at Mandy, then marched back out the door the way he'd come.

This time he made no effort to unclench his fists.

Mandy followed close behind him, trying to keep up.

CHAPTER ELEVEN: KNOWLEDGE

Mike opened the door to Coral Beach High and let Cathy in, then followed behind her. The hinge stuck for a moment, frozen at the half-closed mark, then slammed shut with a bang that echoed through the school.

The halls were empty, and carried the sounds of their footfalls all the way down the corridor. All of the students were gone now, and if the cars in the parking lot were any indication most of the staff was too. Principal Schneider was still there; he stayed late most days. Carter was still there, too. The building wouldn't be closed and locked completely for another few hours, whenever Mr. Larkin was done his cleaning rounds.

"Now that we're here, I'm not sure I totally get this," Cathy said. She was holding out her right hand as she walked and letting it brush along the combination locks on every locker they passed, the rattle it made echoing off the tiles and coming right back at her. "We're going to the library to look up people-killing monsters?"

"In this town you'd have to narrow your search a little more than that," Mike mumbled. He was looking in each classroom they passed as they walked by, and he paused briefly when he found one that actually had someone still inside it. Mrs. Carter was sitting at her desk correcting history papers. He looked at her for a moment, then moved on past. "But no, I don't think that will get us anywhere."

"What are we going to do then? Do we have a plan other than look stuff up?"

He opened the doors to the library, again letting her step in first before following her. "*Coral Beach Daily* is a small time newspaper with an idiot for an editor and an even worse tech staff. Their website is just purple font on a white background that tells people how to subscribe to the paper."

"And?"

"And if we were in any town *but* Coral Beach, we could do what I wanted to do online... but since we're in terminally-stuck-in-the-eighties-ville, we've got to do this the low-tech way."

He made his way to a long row of desks against the back wall that were covered in heavy blue tablecloths. He pulled up one cloth, saw there was nothing underneath, and dropped it.

"Still not sure I get it."

"Miles has a deal with the editor over at the *Daily*. Every year they get a big, hard-copy edition of all their issues printed for reference." He pulled up the next cloth and revealed a long row of tall bound books. "Last decade or so, they've gotten *two* printed."

She smiled at him as he reached down and withdrew three of the large books in one armload, slamming them down on a nearby desk. "I'm impressed. I had no idea you had knowledge."

"I don't have it. I just know where it's kept," he smirked.

They looked at each other for a moment, and became very aware of the fact that they were alone.

He coughed. "I was thinking that maybe we could go back and see just how many kids have died in that children's ward or at that hospital, and going back how far. I mean, if this thing is real, it didn't just appear, right? It must have been doing this for a while, either here or at towns close to here."

"Right..." Cathy nodded, grabbing one of the volumes. "I'll check the records for Coral Cove too. But like you said, around here you can't throw a stone without hitting a mysterious death."

"Only for the past year or so," Mike reminded her, taking back the volume she'd gotten and replacing it with an older one. "So disregard all information after that point as being biased, and concentrate on things before it."

She nodded, then opened the book as he disappeared below the table again, coming back with more volumes. Each book had roughly six months worth of papers in them, each paper ten pages long. She quickly started figuring out how many pages she had to skip in order to quickly reach the headline and obituary section of each issue.

"Can we talk about it yet?" She asked after a few minutes, turning the page and not looking at him.

He paused, and then laid the books down beside her with a hard thud.

"No," he said simply, then turned back to the shelves.

"How long do you think it'll be?"

"It was my fault, Cat. Xander trusted me to find her, and I couldn't. I should have followed my instincts. I didn't. So, you know what, it might be a while."

"It wasn't your fault. It wasn't anyone's fault except for Warren and Randy and the Tees," she yelled through clenched teeth, managing to make it into a whisper.

"I know that," he said, tapping his head. "Up here, I do know that. But there's no telling it to my heart."

She sighed, nodding in defeat as she realized that the conversation was over. She had already gotten more out of him than he had initially wanted to give.

He laid down three more volumes, then stopped and stared at the bookshelf along the adjacent wall.

It took her a moment to realize that he'd stopped, and when she did she looked up and watched him. "What's wrong?"

His mouth was dry as he stepped forward and ran his hand across a row of old books. They were arid and musty and smelled the way wood left out in the rain to rot smelled. Each one was a different colour, with their titles usually printed in tiny black ink at the top of the spine and then taped on again by the librarian at the bottom in much larger print.

She looked up and found that he was in the Classics section.

He ran his finger over *Alice in Wonderland, Beauty and the Beast,* and *Jekyll and Hyde* before finally coming to a rest of *Grimm's Fairy Tales.*

He turned and headed toward the door without a word.

"Where are you going?" She asked, flopping her hands onto the desk.

"I just realized."

"Realized what?"

"I *do* have knowledge," he said cryptically, leaving the room and letting the door close silently behind him.

Cheryl Carter ran her fingers through her curly gray hair, glaring down at the pile of papers before her, only half of which were done. She circled an "it's," used where there should have been an "its," mentally cursing the Language Arts teacher down the hall for not drilling proper grammar into the students' heads more thoroughly. Her eyes had grown red from staring at the tiny type (for which she had began to mark down for, as she had specifically requested twelve point double-spaced) and her trademark smile had slowly withered into a frown.

"Dammit," she said under her breath, clenching one of the papers until it began to wrinkle.

"Bad time?" Mike said from the doorway, making her jump.

She turned swiftly to see who it was, then smiled as she recognized him, her eyes automatically softening. "Not at all," she said warmly, motioning for the seat next to her desk. "Although I wonder what brings you here this late in the afternoon."

"Research," he answered half-truthfully, sitting down. "Actually, I was wondering if you could help me out with that."

"Not a problem," she smiled, pushing the papers away symbolically. "Anything to get me away from these. Nobody is passing this paper. I'm getting more and more annoyed with every single one. I am not kidding."

"Really? I did so good in History last year."

"Yes, well, maybe that's because you never said that America was founded by Christopher Christ."

"That might have had something to do with it, yes."

"Yes. Anyway, what can I help you with?" She said, resisting the urge to go on about the papers.

"Well, do you remember that chapter we did on urban legends? I'm doing a paper on one of them, I was wondering if you could help me out."

"No problem. Which one in particular?"

Mike smiled, laughing at himself even as he said the words. "The Boogey Man."

CHAPTER TWELVE: SWING SHIFT

Xander sat in the uncomfortable chair outside Julie's hospital room again, this time leaning back no matter what he feared it was doing to his spine. He had a newspaper opened in from of him, and was currently perusing the local section.

"I'd like to know what you're doing," Mandy said, leaning in between him and the paper to try and get his attention. And failing. "No wonder I thought Mike was the one with powers for so long. At least he does something."

He continued to sit, turning to page A5 to read about the staff changes at the Mayer, Summers, and Soul law firm.

"Seriously. Do something."

"I prefer to delegate," he replied dryly, scanning down over the page. "Work smart, not hard."

"That is bullshit!" She yelled, then turned to make sure she hadn't attracted the attention of the big-breasted nurse at her station. The nurse did not react at all, as if Mandy had never spoken. "That's bullshit," she said again, in a much lower tone.

Xander peeked over the tip of the paper at the nurse as well, then up at the clock on the wall. He watched it for a moment to make sure the second hand was still ticking away correctly, checked the time on his own watch, and then went back to his paper.

"Hey, crazy guy? That's my sister in there. You'd better get on saving her."

"It's not your sister, it's your cousin."

"She's *like* a sister."

"You fight constantly."

"That is how she's like a sister."

Xander frowned, then shrugged. He couldn't fault her logic.

The minute hand on the clock switched to the fifty-nine mark.

Mandy stared at him in stunned silence, then slapped her hands to her knees and stood up. She paced all the way to the wall, then turned around and pointed at him. "You talk and you talk about taking action... about *becoming* something you can stand to look at, but look at you! You're just sitting there! There is something in this hospital killing kids, and you're just sitting there! What the fuck is wrong with you?"

Xander reached into his breast pocket and pulled out his pack of cigarettes. There was one left, which he removed and placed behind his ear. He kept the pack in his hand.

"And now you're going to go have another smoke. That's just great. Because that worked *so well* the last time. You know what you are? I don't even know what you are. If I could come up with a word for what you are, it would be nasty. It would be like some kind of weird combination of cunt and bastard all rolled up into one and - -"

The minute hand on the clock switched over to zero.

The fat nurse got up and grabbed her lunch bag.

Xander stood up and let his paper fall to the chair behind him.

"Where are you going now?" Mandy demanded as he walked away. When he didn't stop she went after him. "I wasn't done."

"It's six o'clock," he said, not even really watching as the nurse turned around the corner to the elevators and out of sight. "Swing shift."

"Swing shift? What's that supposed to mean?"

He sat down in the nurse's chair and dumped the contents of his cigarette pack out. Flakes of nicotine sprinkled down onto the desk, followed by a small hunk of plastic and metal.

It was a thumb drive.

He plugged it in to the USB slot on the front of the nurse's computer tower, and watched as the logon screen on the monitor flashed away.

"What're you doing?" Mandy hissed, ducking down below the desk even though there was no one around.

"The day nurse has OCD," he replied softly as he opened the charts for the pediatric ward.

"And?"

"And she'd leave at six o'clock even if there was nobody there to relieve her. She'd leave at six o'clock if she were in the middle of trying to resuscitate a dead baby. She'd leave at six even if it meant she would fall down dead."

"And what makes you so sure the swing shift nurse is going to be late?"

He allowed himself a little smile. "I have it on good authority that her car has been impounded."

Mandy stared at him for a long moment. "You're evil."

"You have no idea," he said, moving deeper into the sub files. "I'm locked out of some."

"What does that mean?"

"It means I'm locked out of some," he frowned, moving quickly from one file to the next. "All of them living patients though. All of them under the care of a..." He made several loud clacks on the keyboard. "... Dennis Marx."

"I know him."

He turned to check the physical register next to him. "He's one of four peds supervisors here. Bit of a specialist. Did his internship at the Mayo Clinic and spent three years in Doctors Without Borders..."

"You're getting all that from the chart?"

"No, I'm down in records now. Trying to find a way around those folders locks."

Her eyebrows shot up, and she turned toward the screen.

"He was kicked out. For some kind of malpractice."

"That explains how he ended up at Coral Beach."

"I think it got overturned, but it's still in here... and most of the kids that have died in the ward in the past year have been under his care. A good chunk of them while he was on duty."

He got up and unplugged the drive from the front of the computer, which promptly returned to its logon screen. He took a look around, then stepped out from around the divider and back down the hall toward his seat.

"What about the locked files?" Mandy asked, hopping to catch up to him.

He patted his pants pocket.

"You copied them to the drive?"

"I copied *everything* to the drive," he drawled, sitting down and spreading his paper out in front of him again.

Mandy stared at him dumbfounded, then smiled.

Dr. Marx stepped into private room 1033 with his lab coat pulled tight around his waist. The light above the door shone down on his bald head and the few hairs that clung to it and made it look like a halo, but even that couldn't make him look angelic... the extra light just made the rest of his head look hollowed out and dark.

Billy Reynolds clutched the sheets on either side of his bed when he saw

Marx, his breathing picking up speed and fogging the inside of the oxygen mask he was wearing.

Billy had gotten HIV from a blood transfusion six years ago when he was ten. Even though all the proper procedures had been apparently followed, a bag of infected blood had gotten through the federal screening process and ended up in Coral Cove, where it stayed on ice and waited for someone to need a pint of AB+. That happened less than two months later, when Billy's father had hit a deer while driving drunk with Billy in the back seat. They gave him the blood, and for four years he'd been completely unaware of the time bomb coursing through his veins. He'd even lost his virginity to Karen King, something she herself has regretted ever since, even though they always wore a condom.

Then his cousin Wally had gotten sick with cancer, and Billy volunteered to give up his bone marrow. A routine blood test changed not only his life, but also the family's perceptions of which child was sick.

He only had the news three weeks when Karen broke up with him. He was on antiviral medications that made him vomit everything he put into his system for another year before the virus activated and became full-blown AIDS. Since then he'd spent more time at the hospital than he had at home. He'd lost almost a third of his body weight, his skin was a milky white, his teeth were falling out, and his lips were covered in lesions. At sixteen, Billy Reynolds was closer to death than most men of seventy. He had a lot to be scared of. Not only death, but also the process of dying... a process that would be longer and harder for him than for most.

Nothing scared him like Dr. Dennis Marx.

Marx came in and closed the door behind him, and immediately the heart monitor next to Billy picked up its pace, no longer a steady *BEEP BEEP BEEP* but a hurried, erratic *BEEP BEEBEEP BEEBEEEBEEP*. He hated the heart monitor. It was next to impossible to pretend you weren't scared with that thing strapped to your arm blaring at the top of its digital lungs.

Marx let his lab coat fall open. He was carrying a metal-and-glass syringe that was as big around as his thumb, but from Billy's point of view it was as big around as his leg.

BEEPBEEPBEEPBEEPBEEP

"Now there's no need to be frightened," Marx said, the light from the window glaring off his glasses and making them glow. He smiled that wide, funhouse smile of his as he leaned in over Billy's bed. "We're going to try and make everything all better."

Billy's eyes went wide as Marx held the needle up and flicked it twice, sending all the air to the top. He pushed the plunger and forced all the air out, the excess liquid squirting up and then back down onto his sheets. It smelled like feet.

Billy couldn't speak, couldn't move, couldn't do anything. His vision blurred as he started to cry.

Marx leaned down and inserted the needle into Billy's IV and pushed the plunger until it was empty.

The whole world went sideways as Billy's head lolled to the side, and after a moment his heart monitor slowed back to its steady *BEEP BEEP, BEEP BEEP*.

He couldn't shut his eyes but he could still see. Could still see everything as Marx leaned over him with that damned penlight and shone it in both his eyes, then ducked out of his field of vision again, revealing the air duct on the ceiling above him.

As Billy watched, horrified and unable to even say anything about it, eight long fingers made their way down from the darkness beyond the duct grate and gripped it.

Marx reached over and shut Billy's eyes.

All he could hear was the skitter scamper of thousands of little legs crawling around the metal tube.

CHAPTER THIRTEEN: BAIT

"What do you mean you haven't found anything yet?" Xander asked, leaning in as close to the payphone as he could. "It's been hours. Whatever that thing is, it could go after Julie tonight. Or Chanelle. Or both! What's taking you so long?"

"Considering that all I had to work on was: it's big and looks spooky, I think I'm doing all right," Cathy replied, trying her best to stay calm as she continued to flip through the pages, scribbling notes down into a steno book next to her as she did.

Xander sighed, pinning the phone between his ear and his shoulder. He used his free hand to wipe sweat from his brow. His other hand was busy propping him against the wall.

"Sorry," he breathed, lowering his voice as a nurse walked by. "But this place is starting to drive me around the bend. And Tommy is still in there with Julie. Seriously, doesn't that guy know the meaning of the term visiting hours?"

Cathy raised an eyebrow, shooting him a look that she hoped the silence portrayed through the phone lines.

"You have issues," she said finally.

Mike came in without a word, marching past her to the bookshelf. She turned to look at him and mouthed the word "what?"

It was ignored.

"Wait, what?" She said into the phone, grunting as she turned away from her boyfriend.

"I asked what you had so far," Xander repeated, rubbing the bridge of his nose.

"Um," Cathy replied, flipping back a page in her notebook. "There have been weird child and preteen deaths going on at this hospital and the ones in Coral Cove and other places around for almost... um, two... two decades now. But, I mean, all of the kids were sick. Most of them really sick, so I guess nobody really noticed. And there probably aren't as many as I'm seeing here, most of these probably are actually natural causes."

Mike came back from the shelf and shoved an open book in front of Cathy. Her eyes went wide. On the one page there was text, but on the adjacent page was an etched picture of a child in its bed, screaming as a creature came out of the closet at it. The monster wore overalls in this picture, along with a straw hat and a stem of wheat propped in its mouth. It had no skin, just contorted muscle tissue clinging to its bones, and it had no eyes... just a large, bulging erection in its pants as it came toward the child.

"Do you have anything else?" Xander asked, trying his best to sound patient.

"Oh, god," Cathy gasped, bringing a hand to her mouth as she read the inscription.

"What?"

"The Boogey Man, also called Fear, also called the Ok' La' Zarr... although it doesn't say in what language. It looks *exactly* like you and Julie said, Xander. Exactly. Oh." Her voice was almost a whimper.

"What?" Xander said again, paying perfect attention now. "What is it, Cat?"

"Oh, gawd, Xander. They must be so scared..."

"What? Why?"

"It... it sits on their chest and it grabs at them and cuts them and hurts them until they die, Xander. It just keeps torturing them, first mentally, then violently, until the child dies. It feeds off their fear, so it tries to keep the child alive as long as possible. Oh, gawd, Xander..."

"Okay," Xander said, clenching a fist until it bled. "Okay, it's okay. Fear... yeah, that makes sense. Is there anything else?"

"Yeah," she said, fighting back tears. "It says it's some kind of culler. That it culls the weak, traditionally. Whatever that means."

"Sick people," Mike relayed, touching her on the shoulder as he put more books in front of her.

"Sick people," she repeated into the phone, her hand rising to meet with his.

"Makes sense, as much as any of this does," Xander sighed, turning to see Tommy walking down the hall toward him.

"I don't know if it's part of what it needs or if it's just because sick kids are scared or what, but... oh, you've got to find this thing, Xander. You've got to stop it."

"I gotta go. Tommy's here."

"But what are you going to..."

"I'll handle it," he snapped, hanging up the phone and turning to Tommy.

"Hey, man," Tommy smiled, nodding politely.

"Hey," Xander reciprocated. "How is she?"

"Tired now. A nurse came in and gave her some painkillers. She sad that they'd knock her out, so I got scarce."

Xander nodded.

"You didn't have to stick around, y'know."

Xander smiled. "I got other people here."

"We all do," Tommy groaned. "Where's everyone else?"

"Home. Where I'm going," he said as a way of terminating the conversation, turning and walking away. "You should too, man. This place'll kill you after a while."

"Yeah," Tommy agreed, turning toward the exit. "I know exactly what you mean."

⋀⋎⋏

"Hello?" Cathy said into the phone, tapping on the receiver a few times. "Hello? Is anybody there?"

"Is he there?" Mike asked, taking the phone away and checking it himself.

"No! Bastard!" She growled, pushing the books away from her.

"What did he say?"

"He said he'd take care of it," she yelled, running her hands through her hair. "That stubborn idiot! How's he going to fight something like that?"

Mike stopped and thought for a moment, staring down at the etching in the fairy tales book. The child in the picture looked mortified.

"By baiting it," he said simply.

He got up and motioned for her to do the same, not even taking the time to pick up his coat as he headed for the door. She followed, scooping it off the desk as she went.

⋀⋎⋏

Marx leaned over his desk, scribbling away at his calculations as the sun finished dipping below the horizon. Not that he'd noticed. He hadn't looked up from his folders since dealing with Billy Reynolds, not even to finish eating his dinner, instead leaving it to grow bad on his desk with one bite taken out of it. It was a tuna fish sandwich that his wife had made with too much mayonnaise and a healthy chunk of diced onions for some reason he couldn't fathom, so it wasn't as though he would have devoured it even under the best of circumstances.

He stared at the number eight he had just made, his lip shaking a little. The number was important somehow, he knew it. If his data was right then this wasn't the last equation by far, and yet still, it seemed very important.

"What's up, Doc?" Came a voice from beside him, where previously there had been no sound. It was thick a raspy, like a person with a cancerous throat trying to talk while chugging a glass of water. He turned, only to be hit square in the face with a powerful fist. He spun around from the force of the impact, slamming his chin against the desk before hitting the ground with an unceremonious thud.

"Always wanted to say that," Xander said through the Black Womb's mouth, his eyes glowing a bright red, reflecting the fluorescent lights back to the ceiling. His skin was black and scaly, and he nearly blended in with the deep shadows that the furniture around him cast.

He took the shopping bag off his shoulder and plopped it onto the floor, then took a look around the room. He took his thumb drive out of the bag and shoved it into the slot on the front of Marx's computer, watching as the screen hummed to life again.

"What was the point of that?" Mandy yelled, staring down at Marx. There was blood coming out of a gash on his head. "He could be hurt."

"He could also be a Mormon," Xander snarled, double-clicking on the three encrypted files he'd transferred to the drive and then stepping out from around the desk. "I couldn't really give a shit about either fact right now."

"The files? Is that what all this was about?" She asked, leaning in and watching as the progress bar sped across the screen. "Couldn't you have just broken in at home?"

"Could have. Didn't want to. Several reasons," he said, but did not elaborate as to what those reasons were. His long tongue made him lisp on the *ess* sound at the beginning of several, but she didn't call him on it.

She watched as he scanned the room with those big red eyes of his, then finally found the fridge and walked toward it.

"What's in there?"

"What we came here for," he said, picking up the lock.

"You got some sort of fancy spy-thing for picking that too?"

"Yep," he said, pulling down on the lock hard and snapping it off.

Mandy's eyes widened.

He opened the refrigerator door and saw the long case of vials on top. He grabbed it by both sides and let it fall to the floor, all the vials shaking violently in their holsters.

"Watch it," Mandy said, jumping a little.

He pulled one of the vials out and looked at the label. It said anthrax. He put it to one side.

"Anthrax? What's he doing with anthrax?"

"No idea," he growled, shooting a look at Marx's unconscious form.

"Wait, what are you doing with anthrax?"

"Thing feeds on fear," he said, even as he picked up another vial marked Ebola and laid it down with the first. "That's why it's been hanging out in hospitals the last twenty years or so. Kids are easy to make afraid, even easier when they're sick. Even easier for parents to pass it off when you can write it off as fever dreams."

"And?"

"And now it's in Coral Beach... and thanks to me, this whole town is jumping scared. Fucking thing has an all-you-can-eat buffet." He picked up a vial of red liquid marked REYNOLDS - HIV, stared at it a moment, then put it back down.

"I'm following you. I am. *Why do you have Ebola and anthrax?*"

He took out a third vial and laid it with the other two, then grabbed all three and got to his feet.

"*And* influenza?"

"When the thing came at me the first time I was scared... scared about what was going to happen with me and Julie, more scared than I think I've ever been."

"Okay."

He frowned. "Not scared now. I like having something to hit, something to fight."

He sighed, then popped the tops off of all three of the vials and grabbed the half-filled coffee mug off of Marx's desk.

He turned to Mandy, who looked at him in horror.

"Gotta get scared," he whispered, pouring all three into the mug. He watched as the liquids seemed to disappear amidst the black caffeine.

"Here's to my health," he said sarcastically, shooting the liquid down his throat as fast as possible, then throwing the cup against the far wall and smashing it to pieces.

Mandy cringed, backing away from him a pace and almost tripping over the remaining vials.

He stood there for a moment, wondering if the drink would do anything to him, or if his healing factor would dispose of the toxins before they made their way into his system. He got his answer suddenly as he bent over, pain erupting from his gut as if it were on fire. The room started to spin in three directions at once, making him want to vomit. Blood started to dribble out of his mouth, and his hands and feet felt like jelly. It seemed impossible for him to stand or even crawl toward the door.

"Come on," he said angrily, clenching his jagged teeth as he stared at the open doorway in front of him, just a few feet away a moment ago, now miles and miles distant. "Come on, Drew."

The blackness ebbed off his body, losing its consistency until it was like dark water, pouring off onto the floor around him, revealing Xander. He was naked and covered in a thin layer of congealed blood. Slowly, every second aching, he reached for the bag he had dropped next to the desk and took his shoes out, along with his socks, shirt, and pants.

Every motion killing him, feeling like swords made out of fire were slashing through him, he pulled on his clothes and took his thumb drive out of the computer, then started his way down the hall, hugging the wall to try to keep himself from falling over and passing out.

"Black... Womb lives," he said half-jokingly, letting the smile fade quickly as it hurt his face to wear it. He made his way down toward the children's ward.

"This was a really bad idea," Mandy stated, walking along next to him with her hands clasped firmly behind her back.

"Than... ku. F'input," Xander said, shooting her a look. The words had made perfect sense to him, but took a second for her to translate.

"You're welcome," she frowned. "Stutter much? It was probably that anthrax... or maybe it was the Ebola?"

"Didn saw u comin up wit anie bright deias," he mumbled, stumbling and banging his knee against the wall. He grunted, then continued staggering forward, only pulling it together enough to stand when a nurse passed by him.

58

"You know, I think there was a strand or two of the AIDS virus in that fridge back there. Maybe you should take that with some Jack Daniels, just for good measure."

"Ew could help, y'know."

"I could... but this was your brilliant plan. Kill yourself and save this thing the trouble. A time saver, granted, but otherwise not your best work."

He paused, his eyes growing distant. "Ben making a lot of bad mistakes eight Lee."

"Yea. Well, no argument here," she groaned. "Trying to kill yourself is one thing, now you wanna make yourself suffer, too? You're going for the gold."

"No more children will die because of this thing, or because I failed to act," he said, turning angrily toward her. But again, she wasn't there. Sighing, he turned and continued staggering down the hall toward the children's ward.

Mike and Cathy ran down the street that they had come up just a few hours ago, their chests aching for them to stop, for them to let their lungs rest.

"I don't understand," Cathy gasped, stopping for a moment. She rested her hands against her kneecaps, took a deep breath, then started again. "What's he going to do? How's he going to fight it?"

"He's going to make himself scared," Mike replied grimly, still moving forward in the direction of the hospital. "He's going to negate the Womb and make himself scared. He's going to fight that thing without his powers, and sick to boot."

Cathy wrinkled her brow at him. "But he'd be as helpless as one of those children. That'd be suicide!"

"Exactly," Mike said, his voice deep and dark.

Cathy's eyes grew wide.

Chanelle McDonald pulled the covers high around her head, not letting any light into her private little cave she had created for herself.

She shivered, even though it was very warm in the room and even warmer curled up the way she was. She whined a bit, no matter how much she tried to stop herself from doing so. Fresh tears joined the old ones as they tumbled down her cheeks, making sudden plopping noises as they fell onto the paper sheets.

The room got colder all of a sudden, although it was still very warm. It was a different sort of cold. A frost that did not attack the skin or the muscles, instead bypassing all of this and chilling you in your bones, making them ache in pain with the cold.

There was a slithering sound, moving quickly from one part of the room to another, scattered all about, as if even the noise itself wasn't quite sure where it was coming from.

Another child, one of the boys, started to cry.

The slithering went close to him for a moment, then started frolicking about the room again... like a child in a candy store, unable to chose which treat it wanted first.

There was an odor, a sickly sweet stench like sugar water and vomit. It filled the air all around her, attacking from all sides and forcing itself into her nostrils until it was all she could smell, all she could taste.

She felt something run over her, like light fingers over her sheets.

Suddenly, something ripped the blankets off her, as quick as a flash. She turned to face it and started to scream, but it shoved its hand over her throat before she had a chance, muffling the sound of her voice. Its hand felt too soft... slimy and sticky. It was only when it came into the light that Chanelle realized that it had no flesh, just muscles and strips of twine holding them to the bone.

"Shh," the creature soothed, as the sweet smell turned into a taste, one that dripped off its hands in long globs and traveled down her throat. "Nothing to fear..." it said, revealing a mouth full of gums, no teeth to speak of, just rotting, decayed gums that smelled like a dead skunk. Its other hand was grabbing at its own crotch, feeling itself through the folds of its pressed suit, grunting ever so slightly as it did so, sending bursts of rot and bile onto Chanelle's face with each sound.

"Nothing to fear..." it said again, almost musical in its tone. It smiled, although without skin it was hard to tell it from the twitching muscles of its face.

It opened its eyes at her, revealing them to be nothing but gaping black holes, voids of nothing that seemed to go on forever...

... like the abyss.

She tried to scream again, but the sound was still muffled by the demon's hand, and she only got herself a mouthful of the goo that covered his body for her trouble.

"...Nothing to fear..." it repeated again, chanting it now as if it were a mantra, calm in its voice even as he struggled with the child. The fear in her escalated, and the creature absorbed it all, getting every last drop that it could out of her.

It drew back and slapped her across the face, sending her tumbling to the floor, splattering a trail of its slime across the wall. She tried to get up and run, but it was on her much too fast, grabbing her by her tiny hips and slamming her against her bedside table, again knocking her to the floor.

"Help!" She screamed as loud as she could, making it remember to cover her mouth. She tried again, but it muffled her voice.

It smiled broadly with its toothless, skinless mouth as it unbuttoned its pants and began to pull them down.

"Nothing to fear... but fear itself." It almost giggled, revealing itself not to have a penis or anything resembling one, but rather two great red eyes that stared at her, burning with eternal flame, hungering for more of her. One last time, she tried to scream.

"Hey," came a weak voice from the doorway, drawing both the girl and the creature's attention. There, slumped against the doorway just to keep himself from falling face first to the ground, mucus and blood running from his nose, his guts on fire... was Xander.

"Keep it in your pants," he glowered, staggering toward the villain.

The demon hissed, grabbing Chanelle by the arm and rising to its feet, holding her out. She dangled about a foot from the floor, tears streaming down her face.

It looked from Xander to Chanelle, then back again. Something deep inside those hollowed out eyes sparkled.

"Yeah, I'm a much nummier treat, aren't I?" He smiled, coughing up a great mound of blood. "Why don't you give up the girl and come on over to man land? I'll give you a nice treat of big dirty fear."

It squirmed its toes, and that scuttling sound of thousands of legs filled the room again. It was happy, Xander realized.

He squinted, both out of confusion and because from his point of view there were three demons and three girls, and he wasn't sure if he could fight all of them at once.

It crouched and dug the sharp edges of its fingers into the bruised fat of Chanelle's arm.

"Ooh, scary," Xander said, wobbling a little, waving his fingers in front of his face for effect. "Hey, you wanna know what's even scarier than that?" he poised, stopping shy of the tall, skinny creature, looking up at it so that they were almost nose-to-nose.

The creature opened its mouth, a long string of clicks coming out of it, as it tilted its head to the side, as if to ask: *What?*

"Me."

He drew back hard, aiming to hit the creature square between the eyes, instead landing the punch on its left shoulder, causing it to drop the girl onto the floor, allowing her to get away. She screamed loudly, and the other three children got out of bed and ran out while she hid underneath her bed, leaving Xander alone with it.

The creature righted its posture, staring down at Xander with big, blank eyes, its mouth open in a joker-like sadistic smile.

"You... *are* afraid," it drawled, in a voice that reminded Xander of a cartoon snake with a throat infection.

"Of ewe?" Xander smirked, almost falling over all on his own, his eyes glazing over as sweat began to bead and dribble down across his face, tasting salty when it reached his lips in large quantities. "I was. But now... Why would eye bee scared of ewe?"

The demon backhanded Xander across the chin fast, sending him flying across the room. He landed on one of the children's beds, breaking the springs in the mattress before rolling off onto the floor and hitting his head.

"I see," he grumbled to himself, even as the creature walked toward him, the slithering sound coming from everywhere. He tried to get up and face the thing again, but was instead forced back onto his knees by the burning in his stomach. He clutched his sides and threw up, splattering warm bile all over the floor.

"Guh," he gasped, breathing deep, wiping the puke and snot away from the lower half of his face.

"Brilliant," he said sardonically, cursing himself. "Five minutes into the fight and I've managed to heave all over myself. This is fifth grade all over again."

The creature grabbed him by the scruff of his shirt and flung him across the room. He smashed into the far wall, removing paint and plaster with the impact. It sprinkled down upon him as he lay dead-to-the-world on the floor, drool coming out of the left side of his mouth, blood out of the right.

"You fear life," the creature stated, suddenly next to Xander again, lifting him up by his collar.

Xander fumbled around a nearby desk, trying to grab at something that he could use for a weapon, finding nothing. He gasped for air, and the bits that he did get were further stifled by his stuffed nose and sinuses. The world waved about before him, shaking and convulsing with each hit he took as the creature held him up with one arm and slapped his head back and forth with the other, laughing mechanically as it did so.

"You fear living," it reiterated, slapping Xander again.

"You prey on the sick, the people that can't defend themselves," Xander spat, fighting for the breath and strength to form each word. "That tells me something too: you're afraid of losing. You're afraid to fight fair. Oh, scary. A monster only fit to hunt scared, sick children. I cower. I may be scared of a lot of things..." he said, glaring at where the demons eyes would be. "But you're not one of them."

He reached out fast, grabbing at its tender facial muscles and digging his nails in, ripping off its face, expecting to find a mass of bone. Instead there was nothing, just the same abyss that made up its eyes. The creature screamed, clutching at the void that Xander had created.

Its hand disappeared into its face.

Then its arm.

Slowly, its entire body was sucked into its own face, imploding upon itself as the hissing, slithering sound became deafening, and its scream seemed to pierce the very walls of reality. Xander watched in horror and shock, as the creature finally blipped out of existence.

Mike burst in through the door, sending it slamming against the wall.

"Xander!" He screamed, seeing his friend standing there, looking dazed and confused. He looked around the room helplessly, panic washing over him as Cathy came in behind him. "Xander, I can't see it! Tell em where it is so I can help!"

Xander smiled, raising an arm to point and laugh at his friend, when in fact he was pointing just a little to the left. The effort made the blood rush to his head, and his eyes rolled back as he fell to the floor, hitting his head off the footboard of the bed as he did.

Mike and Cathy both looked at him, their eyebrows raised.

CHAPTER FOURTEEN: ONE WEEK LATER

Xander lay in his bed, smiling, as the fan his Mother had brought up from downstairs for him turned toward him again, blowing his hair back. He laughed to himself, taking another gaping handful of salt-and-vinegar chips and shoving as many of them in his mouth as would fit, then tried hard to chew, still grinning like an idiot.

"Hey!" Cathy groaned in a cute, flu voice, her lower lip protruding. "Stop hogging all the chips."

"My chips," Xander said territorially, hugging them closer and sniffing back mucus. "Not your chips. My chips."

"It speaks," Mike said, then sneezed, wiped his nose with a well-used tissue, then turned back to them. "First time in twenty minutes."

"Hey!" Xander said, pointing at the computer he had hooked up to play movies for the three of them. "I've been watching the - -" he paused, looking at the blank screen.

"You stared at the credits rolling for ten minutes, the blank screen for five, and then you became very interested in the fan until a moment ago," Cathy informed him. "Looking after you is like watching one of those Discovery Channel specials on autism, I swear."

"Quiet."

She rolled her eyes and sniffed back a helping of phlegm. "I think the anthrax would have done it, you know. You could have kept it confined to the non-contagious illnesses."

"I couldn't take chances," he shrugged, an act that caused his shoulders to ache violently.

"Did you ever get those files cracked after?" Mike asked, motioning toward the thumb drive that rested atop Xander's keyboard.

"Ayuh."

"And?"

"And Dennis Marx was a douche-bag... just not a child-killing douche-bag."

"Then what was - -"

"Was trying to come up with a cure for a couple of different diseases. Found this weird kind of kola plant while he was in Niger that he was convinced had medicinal properties... tried testing it on a bunch of locals without their consent, got him drummed out of Doctors Without Borders... but he never *killed* anyone. Far as I can tell, not even his treatments harmed anyone. May have not made them better, but didn't harm."

"But, why would that thing have been so interested in his patients?"

"Like I said: guy was a douche-bag. Had no bedside manner. To me and you, that's just annoying... To a sick kid, it's terrifying."

Mike sighed, laying his back down against the pillow.

Cathy frowned, then held out her hand to Xander.

"Give chips," she ordered.

"Not your chips," he repeated. "*My* chips."

"Give her the frigging chips," Mandy moaned from her seat at Xander's desk, wearing a flannel nightie that was just a little too small for her. "The only thing worse than having to be sick is having to listen to you two bitch while being sick."

Xander groaned, then tossed the bag of chips onto Cathy's lap. She gave a handful to Mike immediately, who thanked her with a kiss.

Mandy looked at the two of them, resting her chin on her wrist and smiling. "Those two'll never stop, will they?" She remarked to Xander, as both Mike and Cathy watched each other's movements longingly.

"No, they won't," he replied groggily.

"What?" Mike asked, smiling.

"You two. You two will never stop loving each other. Even when you guys went through that rough spot, there was still so much love there. It was like, you couldn't be that mad without passion, and you can't have that kind of passion without love... y'know?"

Mike smiled, leaning in and kissing his lover.

"Yeah, I do," Cathy grinned, kissing him back. "So, what brought that out all of a sudden?"

"Ah," he said, grabbing the remote as if to disregard it. "Just thinkin' about what Mandy said."

There was silence between the three of them then, as they all avoided eye contact with each other.

"She always did know what was going on," Mike said finally, his eyes welling up although he was smiling. He grasped Cathy's hand, as tightly as he dared. "I'm really going to miss that about her. She was a special girl, wasn't she?"

"Yeah," Cathy agreed, tenderly putting pressure on his hand, stroking it with her thumb.

"A whole week of the three of you sitting there sick, and finally someone gets it out of him," Mandy tisked, flicking through the remaining movies. "Hey, how about the Ninja Turtles movie? I haven't seen that since I was a kid."

"Ninja Turtles?" Xander responded, cocking his eyebrow at her.

"All right," Mike chimed in agreement.

Cathy nodded, then got up to change the disk.

CHAPTER FIFTEEN: CH-CH-CH-CHANGES

She picked through the garbage tin that the wind had blown over a few minutes before, fumbling about it for any food that had not spoiled yet. During her years on the streets she had become adept at taking advantage of the wastefulness of humans, a trait to which they seemed to ascribe in endless amounts.

With her keen vision she found a small scrap of ham still moist with sauce sticking out from underneath a battered can of preserved beans. She reached out slowly and carefully, always mindful of her surroundings, then finally hooked it and pulled it out from beneath the can. It fell to the ground in front of her. She brought it to her mouth immediately, clutching it between her teeth and feeling the rich, flavorful texture against her tongue.

The porch light came on.

She turned and ran into the woods without so much as looking where she was going, so fast that Ms. Engleman did not even see the blur of motion she created as she zipped away. She still clutched the chunk of meat between her teeth, so tightly that she was afraid she would bite through it and send the excess falling into the grass below her.

When the light was obscured by a large oak tree she stopped, still able to hear Ms. Engleman shuffling about on her front step but knowing well that she was safe. She laid the meat down on the ground and, holding it down with her paws, began to tear away at it with her sharp teeth.

Her name had been Tawny once, and she was a tabby cat. At least she had been, before her owners had moved and not taken her with them. Now, she was just a stray. She closed her eyes and started to purr happily as the sugary taste of marinated pork bathed her taste buds and found its way down her throat.

The oak next to her made a long, croaking sound as it settled. It sounded like a frog at rest on a lily pad.

She stopped eating, her ears going flat against her head as she glared out into the open wood. There was nothing around her, just the black silhouettes of trees painted on the blue curtain of the night.

Tentatively, she turned back toward her feast.

Suddenly she found herself hoisted into the air, the skin on her neck and face pulling tight and making it nearly impossible to move. She hissed, flailing and spinning and trying to make contact at her assailant with her claws.

Her eyes went wide as she felt something penetrate her gullet, going in fast and coming out the other side. Her growl slowly faded until there was nothing, and she went limp.

"Stop it..." she giggled, gently moving his hands away from her hips, but making no effort to stop him as he put them there again. She laughed as he groped at her loose clothing, pulling it and then stopping, biting his lip with temptation.

"Why should I?" He cooed, looking around and seeing nothing but the back porch of her house between the trees just beyond her yard. "Nobody can see us..."

Trina Kennessy smiled as John brushed his hand along the side of her face, the tips of his fingers gingerly tickling the short hairs on the back of her neck as he did, sending cold shivers up and down her spine. "Cathy walks back this way sometimes. What if she..."

"She won't," John whispered in a hushed voice, grabbing her by the waist to bring her up close enough to give him a kiss. He was much taller than her, and quite a bit older as well. She melted into the kiss, barely noticing as his hands inched their way up the inside of her shirt and began to fondle her breasts. She bit her lip, stark white on top of lush red. She ran her hands through his gelled blonde hair, the pointed tips pricking at her as she did. She started to pull away just a little, but he kissed her deeper, bringing her back into the moment.

Her hair was a dark black much like her sister's, and was pulled back in a pony tail until she reached up and let go, allowing it to fall to the moss covered ground next to the tree roots below. She finally realized that he was touching her, and she smiled, reaching around to the back of her shirt. She fumbled for just a second then took her bra out through her left sleeve.

He smiled hungrily, his thumbs touching her nipples underneath the shirt; he stared at the moving cloth as though he had x-ray vision. After a moment he wouldn't have needed it, as she lifted up the front of her shirt to give him a clear view of what he was doing to her. She was thin and white in the overhanging moonlight, the shadows cast by the leaves of nearby maple trees dancing over her body and making it come to life as she quivered beneath his touch.

He bent down, scooping up her tiny body and bringing it to him, his lips sucking at her breasts out of pure, uninhibited sexual starvation, making him convulse and burn for more.

"Hmm..." she giggled, laughing as she pulled the shirt back down, wrestling away from his grasp. Her hands moved quickly as he lost his grip on her, touching him ever so briefly in the place he longed for her to linger. She skipped away from him a step or two, bringing that hand up to her open, circular mouth, her tongue dancing along her own fingers, as she playfully lifted her shirt and put it back down, letting her navel appear and disappear from view.

John smiled at her, taking a step toward her.

She quickly took a step back, waving a finger in front of her, as if to say "oh-no-you-don't."

Smiling through clenched teeth, she began to play with the button of her jeans. With aching slowness she rode the top of her jeans down with her thumbs, exposing her slender midriff and the white freckled swells of her hips. He swallowed hard and took a step toward her, but she moved a step back to match, holding out a scolding finger to him and smiling.

"Catch me if you can," she laughed, turning and skipping over a log, running further into the forest.

He grinned and started after her, his mind a gaggle of things that she might let him do once he caught hold of that tiny, thin form of hers. She zigged and zagged through tree branches that scraped against the meat of her arms, but kept going, laughing and giggling all the way as evergreen needles fell into her hair. He gained on her quickly, catching her just as she was about to fall onto a log, causing them both to fall to the cold, wet ground, him on top of her.

"Oh!" He cried, feeling his own head to make sure it wasn't bleeding. "Are you okay?"

"Yeah," she said, her frown slowly returning to a smile.

His hands touched something, and her over-biting tooth again pressed against her ruby lips.

"How about now?"

"Yeah," she gasped between breaths, nodding her head quickly. "Oh, yeah." She tilted her head upward and closed her eyes as his lips started to trail down her neck, his spare hand shoving her blouse up again, revealing her small, tea-cup-sized breasts. She moaned, opened her eyes halfway, and then screamed.

Lying not four feet away from them was the mangled body of a German shepherd, its fur and organs spread out over a two foot radius, blood soaking the snow all around it, steam still rising from the open wounds.

ʎʎ

Mike sat in his room and stared up at the ceiling, clenching a red stress ball in his right hand every few seconds then feeling it expand as air reentered the tiny holes on either side. He glanced at it every once and a while, its nature perplexing him, as it went from being almost flat to spherical within a matter of seconds, and then back again at his command.

"Are you having fun?" Cathy asked. She was rotating around in Mike's swirly chair, closing her eyes and then opening them again to see how each affected how fast she got dizzy.

He turned to her, watching as her spinning slowly came to a stop, until she finally put her foot down to halt it, the chair facing him, and crossed her legs.

"Actually, yes," he answered truthfully, after only a moment's hesitation to mull over whether or not this was another of her infamous trick questions that would no doubt leave him gasping for metaphorical air.

She rolled her eyes, then threw her back onto the chair, sending different parts of her hair bobbing in all directions at once, making it frizzy. She looked all around at the posters on the wall, of Curt Kobain, Megadeath and one movie poster from *The Care Bears Movie*, hidden slightly by his closet door.

"Is that Tender-Heart?" She asked, pointing at it from her relaxed pose.

He paused, sighed once, and then hung his head. "No, it's Brave-Heart Lion. That's the movie where they meet the Care Bear cousins."

"Right," she nodded, smirking as she recalled the exact plot of the movie. "Much more masculine, really. You have in no way weakened your stature as a grown heterosexual male. Not at all."

He frowned, turning to watch for shapes to appear out of his ceiling tile again, placing pressure on his ball.

"You know that only works with stucco ceilings... right?" She asked, cocking an eyebrow in his direction.

He stopped mid-squeeze, clicking his tongue against the roof of his mouth.

"Yes," he said finally. He coughed. "Have you been talking to Xander to-day?"

"Eh," she passed, shrugging off the notion. "He was feeling well enough to get around outside the house today, so I'm pretty sure that he's going down to the hospital to check on Julie. I don't think she's doing a whole lot better."

Mike sighed, remembering the way she had looked with bloodstained sheets wrapped around her body, trying to find a position that wouldn't send pain coursing through her. "Does he want tag-alongs? We could pick up some more candy for her, I think she should be able to eat it now."

Cathy shook her head. "No, I got the impression from Xander that, after what happened the last time, this was going to be a solo outing. I think he really wants to spend some time patching things up between them."

"Do you think he can?"

Cathy smirked. "We managed, so I guess anything's possible."

He smiled at her, getting up in one quick motion and walking over to her, a sparkle of mischief in his eyes. He placed both of his hands on either armrest of the chair, boxing her in, in essence, then leaned in and kissed her, softly and passionately, on the lips. She tilted her head up to meet his as his tongue darted in and out of her mouth like smooth lightning. Slowly, without even realizing it, she felt her own legs uncross and move apart, spreading out before him. He paused, looking down at her lap, and his hand began to quiver. He turned his gaze back toward her, coughed again, and inched back a pace, then back again, coming in quickly to kiss her, his hands meeting with her hips and clutching them tightly.

RIIIIIING

"Aw," Mike sighed, clenching a fist playfully and softly tapping it against the arm of the chair.

"Have you... um, ever considered getting that disconnected?" Cathy asked, exhaling as though she hadn't done so in several minutes, her face red and hot.

"I was just thinking that," he drawled as he picked up the phone and brought it to his ear. "Hello?" an odd look came over his face, and then he shrugged and passed the phone to Cathy. "It's for you."

Cathy made a face, taking the phone from him. "Yeah?" she said in an almost agitated tone of voice, bringing a finger to her mouth to bite. "What?"

ʎ⟨ʎ

Jesse Larkin heaved a sigh as he stepped out of his car and into the parking lot. He always hated this time of the year, when everything was cold and wet, and the snow always came, then melted, only to come again a day or so later. He wished every time that it would simply stay for the season or leave so that spring would start, but it never did.

Soon he'd be out for winter break though, and that was always something to look forward to. But then again, after that there was midterms. And then, of course, there was the fact that soon his mother was bound to decide that it wasn't safe for him to be driving on the roads any more, just as she had last year, just weeks after he had gotten his license.

He pushed back a mound of his curly blonde hair as he locked up the car,

68

revealing a gash near his left temple. He winced and cursed a little as his finger accidentally brushed up against it, making him grit his teeth in pain.

TUNK!

He swirled, turning to see what the noise had been, seeing nothing but the empty parking lot. He frowned to himself, then turned back and walked toward the mall. It had been closed for hours, but he still had some business to take care of out back.

There was a sound, like someone running across pavement, dragging their feet.

He turned again, this time looking all around him, examining every shadow.

"Is someone there?" He called out, his New England accent thick. "Is anyone there?"

ʎ‹›ʎ

Xander stumbled on the stairs of the hospital, catching himself before his face became a smear on the concrete steps, but not before his kneecap struck them. He grunted as he felt the pain surge up from his leg, not quite bleeding but bruised enough for blood to come to the surface anyway, making it feel moist even though it was not. He cursed on the slick walkway, then continued into the hospital, waving at a familiar nurse as he did, mentally making a note to take the wheelchair entrance for the rest of the winter. The nurse waved back to him but avoided eye contact, continuing to sort through the mounds of paperwork in front of her.

He passed by the green plastic chairs of the waiting area, its denizens each looking up at him with a mixture of envy and anger as he strolled past, bypassing the call from the receptionist and going straight through the big, white doors into the main part of the hospital.

He grinned as he passed by a wall full of pages from children's colouring books, each a different picture coloured by a different child patient. Most where incoherent scribbles by children that had spent way too much time in the waiting room bored out of their minds, but some of them were genuinely good. He saw one very good rendition of a doctor giving a boy a lollipop done by Charles, a kid from Xander's neighborhood. Panning the wall a little more, he saw one by Chanelle McDonald, one without any blood, or anything else out of the ordinary on it anywhere. Just a girl playing with her cat, putting a red bow around its neck.

There was also a sketch there by Mandy.

"You like that one, huh?" Mandy asked, coming up behind him, her arms folded as she turned her head sideways and stuck out her tongue, sizing up the colouring of a boy and girl riding their bicycles down a country road from a different angle.

"A little prosaic for me, thanks," Xander said dryly, his eyes still darting over the wall, looking to see if there were any more by people he knew, like Kerri or Trina. "I prefer the work by the children five and under, usually the girls, but not

69

exclusively. They just seem so much more creative. It's like modern art, except, done well."

"Life does mimic art," she said knowingly, nodding slowly.

He raised an eyebrow, turning toward her. "What's that supposed to mean?"

"I dunno," she shrugged, spinning around one full rotation before turning left and walking down the hall, Xander following her after another quick glance at the wall. "I heard it in a movie once, thought it sounded cool."

"Ah," he smiled, chuckling a little. "Very emulative of you."

"'Prosaic,' 'emulative'? What's up, did your Mom give you a word of the day calendar for your birthday or something?"

"Actually, yes. This month is descriptive words in sentences. What do you think?"

"I think you sound like a character from *Frasier*."

"Crap," he sighed, moving his mouth around as if he could place it somewhere different on his face, until it was finally a smile. "So, when were you in the hospital here?"

"Back when Mom was dating a real dick named Strickland. Guy took a hot clothes iron to the side of my face."

"Ouch."

"Yea. That's how I got that scar."

"Huh."

There was a silence between them then, and Mandy stopped walking, turning instead toward the door to their left. It was Julie's room door.

Several moments passed, in which they both stood, facing the door but not looking at it.

"You gonna go in, or are we admiring the paint on the door now?" Mandy asked, smiling from ear to ear as she leaned in front of Xander's blank face.

"I don't know if I can," he whispered, his lower lip shaky.

"Sure you can! You just turn the knob, push, and -"

"Not what I meant," he sighed, slumping his shoulders in frustration. "Can you come in with me?"

"Absolutely not," she replied, with no hint of her usual humor.

"What?"

"This is not one of those things I can play audience for," she said, then turned and walked toward the cafeteria. "I'll be around after if you need me, kay?"

"You always are," he smiled, watching her go until she was around the corner.

Taking a deep breath, he turned the knob and entered the room.

A nurse looked up at him, a brief look of shock on her face as she finished snapping in a fresh bag of clear liquid into the top of Julie's IV.

"Oh," she said, simply, blushing slightly as she was taken off guard. "I'm sorry, I wasn't expecting her to have any more visitors today."

"More?" Xander poised, raising an eyebrow.

"Yes, that nice boy from town Tommy Irons was in to see her earlier, but she wasn't awake. She still isn't now, but you can sit with her if you're very quiet."

Xander nodded, then stepped into the room, sighing as he saw the almost worried expression on Julie's face as she slept. She looked as though she were very uncomfortable.

"Do I... know you?" The nurse asked as she passed by him, turning her head and giving him a slight smile. "I've seen you around here, haven't I? I'm Nurse Reilly."

"Hmm," Xander hummed, moving forward without paying so much as a seconds attention to the woman before she shrugged and walked out. He moved to her bedside, sniffling back a sinus full of mucus, then reached out his hand and touched hers, holding it tightly. He gazed at her beautiful face, so white and flushed out, willing the colour to return to it quickly, and just for him.

But it didn't, and it wouldn't.

"Come on, Jules," he coaxed, shaking her hand a little, sighing. "I don't know why I'm here," he admitted finally. "You've made it pretty clear that you don't want to be my girlfriend anymore. I'm pretty sure that if you actually did wake up with me next to you like this you'd slap me and call security or something to that effect... I just need to know that you're going to be okay. I rounded up all the Tees, I... I'm doing everything I can to try and make things better and it's just not..."

He looked at her longingly, then sat down at the chair next to her, buried his face in her sheets, and began to weep.

CHAPTER SIXTEEN: CRASHING

Trina sat before them both as they stood over her, both of their arms crossed.

Mike and Cathy both glared down at her little sister, anger and astonishment in their eyes as she tried to evaluate what she should say next.

"I'm... really sorry?" She said, flashing her brightest, toothiest smile as she fixed the shoulder of her top from coming down her arm.

"Oh, you have no idea," Mike fumed, his nostrils flaring.

"John Stein?" Cathy asked for the third time, raising an eyebrow in disbelief, trying to stop herself from laughing.

"Yeah?" Trina responded, almost defensively.

"Didn't we used to call him Hubble?" She asked, turning to Mike.

"Yeah," Mike smiled coyly, nodding. "He had lenses so big they looked like the Hubble Space Telescope."

"Right. Guy was like Piggy from *Lord of the Flies* all through High School, from what I recall."

Trina rolled her eyes, fumbling with her fingers on her knee, looking around the kitchen for anything that would captivate her attention so that she wouldn't have to face their icy stares again.

"Hey," Mike said, calling the girl's attention back to him. "Are we boring you? Because if we are, I'm sure your folks could come home and find a way to keep you entertained."

"Oh no, Mike, please... you wouldn't..." she pleaded, whining.

"But I would," Cathy corrected, stepping forward and leaning in at the same time, trying to be as menacing as she could be. "I thought you'd learned from my mistakes, and then you go running off with an older guy in the woods and take your clothes off? What were you thinking?"

"She wasn't," Mike snickered. "It's a Kennessy family trait."

"Shut up," Cathy spat, forcing back laughter as she shot him a look, then turned back to her sister. "If you ever do anything like this again, Trean... you won't have to worry about Mom and Dad, because they'll have to put you back together to deal with you after I'm done."

Trina swallowed hard, never once breaking eye contact with her sister.

"Because I love you, and I would rather destroy you than watch you do it to yourself," Cathy added, snorting air through her nose for effect. She turned to Mike, cocking her head toward the door. "Go check out that dog she's so worried about."

Mike nodded, getting up and walking out their back doors, heading off into the woods.

Cathy turned to her sister. Slowly, a smile crept over her lips, until it spread from ear to ear. "He is quite a dish, isn't he?"

Trina smiled.

Mike walked out into the woods, following the footprints in the slush that Trina and John had made. Smiling and shaking his head, he thought of the very similar thing that had almost happened between him and Cathy back at the house.

I'm not ready for that again, he thought, pushing past a tree branch. *I mean, I love her and I want to be with her, in every way... but after everything that happened last time, I just wonder if it's worth the risk to hurt her, or to hurt the two of us that way again. And if it's not worth the risk... why are we even together?*

He bent down and picked up Trina's bra off the ground, rolling his eyes and shoving it into his jacket pocket and trying to imagine what would be the most embarrassing way to give it back to her.

The footprints veered left and traveled over a log, so he hopped over it. Glancing around, he saw it. All of it. The dog, strewn out as though it were being sliced open for a meal, parts of it taken out, examined, and then tossed aside, as if uninteresting. There was blood everywhere, along with a stench that was unmatched to any dead thing he had ever been close to in his life, like blood and feces and wet dog all rolled into one. He balked, turning away quickly.

Then he stopped, glancing back at the beast, his eyes growing wide.

"Aw, no," he whispered, turning and running back toward the house as fast as he could, the bra dropping out of his pocket again as he went.

CHAPTER SEVENTEEN: WAKEUP

Xander stirred, waking up laid back in the chair next to Julie's bed. She was still asleep, and at some point it had gotten dark out. He looked around quickly, then checked his skin for the familiar feeling of dried blood. Finding none, he breathed a deep sigh of relief, then relaxed back in the chair again.

Julie was still in the same position she had been when he had cried himself to sleep, laid back with her hands outstretched, her face as white as a ghost with the clear expression of pain on it.

He gazed at her, sighed, then slammed his hands against the armrests of the chair and got up. He marched toward the door, cursing under his breath as he went. When his hand touched the knob he stopped, his eyes softening, and he turned and took a step back toward her.

Leaning over her bed, he gave her the smallest, softest kiss possible on her lips, never once closing his eyes. He turned back, opened the door, and exited the room.

Sweat poured off him as the room seemed to sway this way and that, like the deck of a boat during rough seas. He thought he might throw up, so he leaned against the wall to wait for the feeling to pass.

"Jeez, you look like crap," Mandy smiled, chomping down on a Butterfinger bar as she walked toward him. She peeled the wrapper down a little more and took a large bite that sent flakes of clustered peanut brittle sprinkling to the floor around her.

"Don't hold back..." he smirked, his voice gruff and sickly. "...Tell me how you really feel."

"Don't worry, I always do." She smiled perkily, grabbing his arm and throwing it over her shoulder to help him walk. "The Womb's healing factor still hasn't helped much, huh?"

He shot her a glare. He hated it when she brought up that she knew about the Womb, especially in public, wishing that it hadn't flowed off him when he saved her from the Tees a few weeks ago.

"No, it hasn't," he answered, when it became clear that she wasn't about to accept his glare as a viable response. "Mike had this theory the other day that the Womb may not have the antibodies to properly deal with what's in me."

"So...like, in that case, you just, like, swallowed toxic bacteria, and you'll handle it just like I would?"

"I doubt that's actually the case," he smiled, hearing the concern in her voice. "Before we met, on one of my first times out as the Womb, I got into an explosion out on the highway. It was bad stuff. The Womb wouldn't even turn on for almost two weeks."

"Weird," she drawled, shoving her candy bar into his face. "Want a bite?"

He stared at it for a long moment, then at her. "No," he said finally, starting to walk on his own again. "No, I don't. Why are you still here, anyway?"

"Waiting for you," she said in a cheery, matter-of-fact voice, popping up next to him and putting her arm around his.

He paused a moment at that, looking at her in a different light.

The both of them stopped for a moment, turning into the children's ward.

Xander opened the door, and a few of the children looked up to see who was coming in, but not many. His gaze fell over the room, until finally coming upon the empty bed of Chanelle McDonald.

His brow furrowed.

"What?" Mandy asked, her gaze following his. "Oh, right. That girl you helped. She's gone. She got sent home while you were out playing sick."

"Wasn't playing," he corrected.

"I know, but it sounds funny."

"Really doesn't."

She pouted, finished off her candy bar and then tossed the wrapper into a nearby trashcan. "What's the big deal? She's fine."

"I know. I just wanted to see her."

Mandy gave him a slack-jawed look for a moment, and then promptly closed her mouth, looking away at an assortment of "Get Well Soon" cards along a pegboard.

"Oh," she said, trying not to look too disappointed.

He turned, grinning at her. "But now I'm glad she's not here, because now I get to spend more time with you."

She smiled, her features becoming soft, then she turned back toward the door and started walking away, hiding her face from him.

"Actually, I've got to go," Mandy said, wiping something from her eye. "I, um, I promised Aunt Sam that I'd call her and tell her how Julie's doing, y'know?"

"Yeah," Xander groaned as he watched her leave the room. "Sure."

He turned back toward Chanelle's bed, reaching under it and pulling out her colouring book. A bemused expression came over him as he flicked through it page by page, watching the artwork as it steadily progressed into happier, healthier things, until the last page, which was torn out. He assumed that had been the page that he had seen posted on the wall outside.

"What are you doing?" Came a voice from the doorway.

The voice brought Xander out of the hypnotic state he'd placed himself in, and he quietly pushed the book back under the bed, turning to smile at Mike. "Nothing much. What are you doing here?"

Mike gave him a look, both tired and saddened and angry.

"What?" Xander asked again, rising to his feet. "What is it?"

CHAPTER EIGHTEEN: GHOSTS OF THE PRESENT

"And you're sure?" Xander asked again, as he, Mike and Cathy marched down the street as fast as they could without seeming suspicious to the passerby. A few hours earlier and they would have gotten looks from behind every window, but people in this part of town shied away from looking out their windows at night. Too often, they saw something they wished they hadn't.

Again, Mike shot him a glare.

Cathy frowned, unable to hide the intense worry on her face, eyes sparkling with newly shed tears. "A poor dog, and now a murder? What else could it be, Xander?"

"Any number of things," Xander contested, his shoulders slumping in defeat.

They still hadn't said it yet. Neither of them wanted to, neither of them would dare. It was as if they were in some cheesy horror movie where simply saying the creature's name would draw it out.

"It's Zakron," Mike blurted finally, the name slicing deep into each of them like a knife. "It fits his profile. Animal deaths, and now Jesse Larkin? I saw him in the hospital before I came down and got you, man. He was ripped to shreds. There is no way anything but that monster did this."

Cathy didn't say anything, just kept her head down and stared at the sidewalk below her feet.

"The Anti-Womb," Xander grumbled, running his nails through his hair. The veins in his eyes had become varicose from his sickness and the sudden rise in blood pressure since hearing the name. "Last time I saw that thing, it was getting carted away by Circe."

"But you beat Circe," Mike said. "So this is how they're getting their revenge?"

"We should call Megan," Cathy said in a neutral tone of voice, eyes still glued to the pavement. "Last time it went after Adam. She could up the security around his room."

Xander pointed at her, affirming her suggestion. "Right," he agreed, turning to Mike. "And we need to get busy. We need to know how to fight this thing or we are screwed. The Womb's out of commission, and Zakron is always ready to party."

Mike nodded, then looked up, as if a light were going off in his head.

"O'Toole," he said, slapping Xander on the arm, as if to scold them both for not thinking of it sooner. "He released Zakron the last time. He must have files on him in his old office. All we gotta do is break in there and they're ours."

Xander smiled slyly. "Good idea."

"I was overdue."

"Guys..." Cathy said, stopping dead in her tracks, her body ridged and stiff.

"What is it?" Mike asked, his voice going from stone hard to completely soft as he touched her face, stroking it gently. "What's wrong?"

Xander looked around, his nostrils flaring as he sucked back snot and spit it out, trying to clear his sinuses. He turned, seeing the top of the mall peeking over the roofs of houses one street over. "Mike," he asked, looking at the long drag marks going down the sidewalk. "Didn't you say that the murder was around here somewhere?"

Cathy pointed to a bush, then collapsed into Mike's arms. "It's going to happen again," she whispered, stroking his chest. "We were thinking about it and now it's going to happen again, all of it."

"No, baby..." Mike said, eyes growing wide as he saw what she saw by the bush. "...Xander?"

"Yeah?" Xander asked, nose twitching as he turned back toward them. He followed both their gazes to the base of the bush, where the body of a small tabby cat lay skinned.

"There's a joke there, but it's just too easy." Xander sighed, his nostrils flaring again.

"Do you smell something?" Mike asked, taking a step toward him.

"I thought your senses were dulled back?" Cathy questioned, moving with her boyfriend, not wanting to let go of his arms.

"They are," he assured them, looking toward the house that the bush belonged to, "But I'd never miss that smell, not once you know it."

"What's that?"

"Fear," he said, curling his lips with disgust as they all looked at the name on the mailbox.

It read: McDonald.

Xander stepped back a little, retracting the hand he had extended toward the child's activity book. "Okay. That's... that's okay," he said soothingly, crumpling his forehead. He glanced down at the girl's arms, seeing them bruised and swollen, her legs larger than normal as well. He sighed, then got up to walk away.

"So, what do we do?" Mike asked, rubbing Cathy's shoulders as she finally stopped crying.

"Just what we planned to," Xander growled, clenching his teeth so hard that they ground together.

Xander pulled his hand back out of the broken window of Dr. Warren O'Toole's office, grimacing as the glass cut into his flesh. He motioned to Mike, who rolled his eyes before reaching through the smashed glass and unlocked the door, opening it.

On the floor, the letters of the good Doctor's name were scattered about and rearranged. It made Mike smile, just a little.

"You break, I enter. We make an excellent team," he said, looking around the dark of the office.

Xander stared at the open wounds on his hand as the blood drained down them. Slowly, the wounds stopped bleeding and began to close, at a tenth of their usual rate, making it much longer and more excruciating, like the glass was being ripped through each cell individually.

Mike moved over to a filing cabinet, then opened it and started flicking through the papers. A queer look came over him as he lifted one file out and opened it.

"What is that?" Xander asked, sniffing and grunting as his hand finally pushed out the last few slivers of glass.

"It's Mandy Peterson's file," Mike said absent-mindedly, not taking his eyes off the page.

Xander shook his head. "Do you really think Warren would be stupid enough to keep his Circe folders here, in an unlocked cabinet? They're probably in his loft."

"We'll have to make a point of retrieving them," Mike resolved, snapping the file shut and putting it back in the cabinet, flicking through some more until he found what they were looking for. "Here we go. Chanelle McDonald."

Xander leaned over his shoulder, reading the file along with him. "Says here she came to school every few weeks with fresh bruises, the last time so bad that the school remanded her to the hospital."

"Look at this," Mike said, pointing to an entry near the top of the page. "Chanelle and her family only moved here three months ago. Before that they were living in Indigo, Utah. There was a fire at the house, with Chanelle trapped inside. Firefighters found bars on her windows and her door locked from the outside. Before that, the McDonalds lived in Oregon, where neighbors and a family member were found murdered. The deaths were never solved."

Xander glared at the file photo of Chanelle, one of her eyes black, ruining her beautiful face.

"We need to see that body," he said decisively, turning toward the door as Mike put the file back.

ʌ⟨ʌ

Chanelle McDonald lifted her mug of hot chocolate to her lips and took an enjoyable sip, several tiny melted marshmallows squiggling down her throat as she did. She smacked her lips together dramatically, like the child on the commercials for grape juice, and exclaimed: "Ah!"

At the end of the table, her father looked up and glared at her. He squinted hard, and then slowly turned his attention back toward his paper, scanning through the business section.

Chanelle's gaze lowered, a frown spreading across her lips as she brought the cup of hot chocolate back up to them and guzzled down the last of it.

"Okay," her father said, putting down the paper and stepping toward her. "You've had your treat, now it's time for bed."

"No!" Chanelle cried defiantly, a touch a fear in her voice as she jerked away from him.

He reached out and grabbed her arm so fast that she barely saw it coming, as though he'd been sitting in one frame of her mind's reel and then on her the next. Standing, he dragged her through the hallway and opened the door to her bedroom, forcing her inside and then finally letting her go. There were red lines on her arm from where his hand had been.

She spun and clacked her teeth at him as though she could bite him from across the room, her cheeks flushed with red. "No!" She screamed again, as though he hadn't already forced her inside.

He slammed the door even as she was protesting and turned the padlock on it with his thumb. It slid into place with a firm *cl-clack* before he slid his hand down further and found a second padlock, sliding it into place as well. *Cl-clack*. Finally his hand fell upon the key that rested in the doorknob and turned it all the way around. When he heard the mechanism inside click, he put the key in his pocket and walked back down the hallway. Returning to the table he picked up his paper again. The Mets had won.

ʌ⋁ʌ

"Get out of the way," one doctor screamed, waving for both of them to move. Julie jumped up right away, but Mike stayed there, still as a marble statue, looking down at the woman he loved as blood poured from his body, but he paid it no mind. It was of no consequence to him.

He was pushed out of the way and backed up a few steps silently, as two men laid a stretcher out between him and his love. They hoisted her up onto it, and immediately the clean, white sheet turned to dark red. Blood seeped out from between her legs, and she did not move. Never once did she move. He reached out and touched her hand, and it was chilled, her lips blue.

Soft
Lime
Tender
Moist
Wet
stop.

"She's so cold," he said in a hollow voice, as he watched them wheel her away into the back of an ambulance. Julie slowly walked up behind him, reaching out and grasping his hand, then wrapping both arms around him, bawling into his shirt. He turned to her, surprised that she was there, having not noticed her before. He stroked the back of her head, his stare falling past her at the rubble at their feet. "Should we get her a blanket?"

Cathy awoke with a start, her head numb after so much time pressed up against the library desk. She groaned as the blood rushed to her head, wondering how long she had been asleep for. Groggily, she turned her head (with one eye partially closed) to the clock on the wall, and realized that she had missed gym. Stopping to think about her schedule for a minute, she realized that she had Family Education with Miss Waller again now. Thinking back on her performance at their last class, she decided against attending.

Soft
Lime

78

Tender
Moist
Wet

She blinked twice, and the thought vacated her head again. She sighed, slumped her head on one hand, reached to the nearest book, and opened it. She winced, trying to force the thought not to come back.

What if it happens again? What if I get pregnant again? I can't put Mike through that. I just can't. Oh gawd... what are we doing...

She sighed again, pulling the book closer to her, getting out of her own light, and trying to immerse herself into the literature.

CHAPTER NINETEEN: VIVISECTION

Harry Ford took a deep bite of his chicken sub, the honey mustard on it dripping down from the bottom in huge yellow dollops that splattered against the wax paper in his lap. He stifled a laugh as the cartoon duck on the screen in front of him slammed into a wall, then peeled himself off as though he had no more substance than a Post-It Note .

Lance snarled at him, shaking his head. "I don't know how you can watch that."

Harry wiped his mouth in his sleeve. "I get one, one lunch break. I'll spend it how I please."

"The screen is so small."

"It's a phone."

"But... still."

Harry rolled his eyes and then went back to his meal.

Lance continued to poke at his fruit cup idly, curling his lip at the chunk of red sponge that was in it. He wasn't sure what it had been in life, but now it had just absorbed the tastes of everything that had been around it, coming out as a mix of cherry and banana. He wondered if it had actually been a sponge.

Around the corner, Mike took a deep breath, then continued counting down.

"Ninety-eight, ninety-seven, ninety-six..."

He wasn't counting down to anything per se, it was just something he'd discovered helped calm him. The numbers helped bring some order and focus to the chaos around him.

He wondered, briefly, if he would grow up to be an accountant.

He then wondered if he would live to grow up at all. That thought stayed with him, even as he raised the cheap Bic lighter he'd lifted from Xander up to the sprinkler head above him and struck the flint. Fire shot out, moving smoothly over the metal surface.

Nothing happened.

He stood there and stared at it for a long moment, until the top of the lighter got so hot that he thought it would burn his hand.

"Dammit!" He yelled, then punched the wall next to him. It made a loud, heavy thud.

Harry looked up from his sandwich. "Did you hear that?"

Mike's face went white. He turned around quickly and made his way for the stairwell.

"Sounded like something dropped..." Lance answered, even as he got up and started walking down the hall.

Harry followed, and they both rounded the corner just in time to see the stairwell door close. "Hey!" He yelled, and the both of them bolted for the door, trying the handle and finding that it was locked. "Hey! Let us in!" They banged on the door fiercely.

Around the opposite side of the stairwell, Mike came around the corner. Tiptoeing, he made his way to the morgue entrance and ducked inside.

"Are we there yet?" Mandy whined, rolling her eyes as she walked alongside Xander, her pigtails bobbing up and down on either side of her head like little pom-poms.

"Yes!" Xander hissed at her, pointing to the house they were standing in front of. "Yes, this time, we are actually here. Not like the first five hundred and fifty times you asked."

Mandy gave him a look, taking one last suck of her popsicle before tossing it into the bushes next to the house. "I really don't think it was that many times. You're greatly exaggerating your math here, boy-o."

"Boy-o?" He repeated, raising an eyebrow at her.

"I always call you boy-o."

"Never once in your life have you called me boy-o. I mean, ever. Ev! Er!"

"Oh," Mandy clicked her tongue, eyes darting to one side, away from him. "Maybe that's just from one of the conversations I had with you in my head and didn't out loud."

"You have conversations with me... in your head."

"Uh-huh."

"Yeah, and I'm the weird one."

"No, you're the boy-o. Say it with an Irish accent. It's fun."

He stopped, turning to glare at her.

"Words fail me," he groaned, starting up the path to the house of Lindsey McDonald. "What are you doing here anyway? I'm going after a child-beater. Probably not the safest mission for you to accompany me on. Besides, everyone knows Mike's my sidekick."

"I think you're his sidekick."

"I'm the one with powers, so he's my sidekick."

"I think it takes more than--"

"I'm the one with powers, so he's my sidekick."

"Touched a nerve, have I?"

"My last one," he growled, knocking on the white, metal door, then ringing the door bell. "Seriously, Mandy, you shouldn't be here. You could get hurt, and if anything happened to you..." his voice got quiet suddenly, as he looked away from her. "...Your cousin would never forgive me."

The door opened suddenly, and Lindsey McDonald loomed a good two feet over him, glaring down.

"What do you want?" He said in a gruff voice. A blind man could have told that he was from Utah with that accent. He wasn't necessarily strong looking, just very tall and broad. He was unshaven and his eyes and nose were red, either from excess alcohol or not enough sleep. Or both. He looked like the type of person that could snap at any given moment, in Xander's experience.

And I should know, we can smell our own.

"Um..." Xander stammered, eyes widening. "Me and my friend here were just going to talk to you about, um, about Jesse Larkin. If that's alright." He turned to motion to Mandy, discovering that she had taken his advice and left. Oh yeah, that makes me look real good, he sighed, then turned back to the man.

"What about Chanelle's sitter?" Lindsey asked, leaning in and raising an eyebrow.

"He's... dead?" Xander said slowly, sizing the man up and down.

Sweat immediately began to pour down the man's brow, as he stood back from the door to let Xander inside.

⋔

Cathy sat back with the large brown bound book in front of her, resting comfortably on her legs. She flipped through it aimlessly, not looking for anything in particular but becoming more and more interested the more she discovered.

There were dozens of articles on the Salem witch trials and myths about ogres and werewolves from the eighteenth century. She stopped at a section on Dracula's connection to Vlad the Impaler, winced at an etching of a silhouetted man impaled on a spike, then turned the page.

The Boogey Man that Xander had fought looking back at her, grotesque smile and all.

She jerked back a bit, a shudder traveling down her spine so powerful that she almost dropped the book. She turned the page to get away from it, then stopped.

Sitting up straight, she flipped back to the text on the Ok' La' Zarr.

Her eyes grew wide. She got up from her desk and ran for the door as fast as she could.

⋔

The metal shelf opened with a clang. Mike put his hand on the cloth covering Jesse Larkin's body.

He shivered. The cold, sterile environment of the coroner's office bit at his skin. Steeling himself for something he knew would be unseemly, he pulled back the cloth to reveal Larkin's entire form. Holding his breath, he forced him-

81

self to look at the punctuated remains of Larkin's stomach. It was covered in nearly identical, sharp little holes. They looked like mouths.

He let out the breath he'd been holding and brought one gloved hand up, pulling at the skin on Jesse's stomach to open the wound. He started to count again.

The wounds were slanted downward, their tracts leading toward the more extensive wounds around his pelvis.

He stopped counting, even in his head.

A curious look came over him, and he bent down to one of the stab wounds just above Larkin's penis. There were chunks of denim fibers caught in it from where he'd been stabbed through his jeans.

The wounds were the same as before, the tracts slanted downward.

His brow furrowed. He turned around and walked toward the far wall where a model of a skeleton stood erect. Imagining that the dummy was Jesse, he stood next to it, clutching his tweezers as one would a knife or dagger.

Holding the "handle" firmly he stabbed Jesse in the lower gut. Looking down at where the tweezers entered the model, he saw that they slanted upwards, toward the head. He tried several more times from different angles, but the result was the same, the knife, and wound tract, would have to be pointing upwards.

A haggard look slowly came over Mike's face, his muscles relaxing, as he knelt down onto both knees, swinging the "knife" over his head to strike, coming into contact with Jesse Larkin's abdomen, the tweezers pointing down, toward his crotch.

He stopped, thinking about what he had just discovered. *Concealment? Maybe he was knelt in a bush when he struck, or...* he stopped, his eyes growing wide as he scrambled to his feet and ran for the door as fast as his legs would carry him.

CHAPTER TWENTY: JERUSALEM

"God, I'm so sorry..." Lindsey gasped, sitting down at his kitchen table again. He held his head in his hands as tears started to dribble down his cheeks, dotting onto the newspaper below, still spread out to the sports section from the night before.

Well, this is a new one on me. Xander frowned, watching as the man broke down from the simple confrontation of hearing his victim's name.

"There was blood," he said, looking at Xander and then turning away. "Oh, my gawd, there was so much blood."

"Jesse's blood," Xander said, completing the thought as Lindsey seemed incapable of getting a full one out. "That is what you're saying... right?"

"I tried forever to get it out. It just wouldn't come clean, it wouldn't... couldn't..."

"Yeah..." Xander sighed. "It never comes out easy."

82

"I swear..." he moaned, his body racked with sobs. "I swear I didn't mean to, I was just trying to protect my family..."

"How the hell were -" Xander started, growing more and more confused by the second.

The phone rang, startling them both.

Xander turned to Lindsey, who just continued to sit there and weep.

"Yeah, sure, I'll get it then," he said under his breath, walking to the far wall and picking up the receiver. "Hello?"

"Xander!?" Cathy screamed frantically into the other end, followed by a sigh of relief.

"Cathy?" He spat, whispering now, turning his back to Lindsey. "What are you doing calling here -"

"You have to get out of there!" Cathy screamed into the other end, panic taking over her voice again. "You have to leave, now!"

"Cathy, what are you talking about?"

"The Ok' La' Zarr... it's a body jumper!"

"What?"

There was pain then, a blinding white pain that took over his entire field of vision. It was accompanied by a hollow ringing sound and continued to gong like a bell even after the blow had been struck.

Xander hit the floor hard, his face beating off the edge of the wall, sending blood and mucus in all directions. He rolled over as his sinuses clogged, his vision getting hazy, just in time to see Chanelle raise her father's baseball bat again...

Another loud smack echoed through the house, and for a moment Xander thought he'd been hit again. The world spun around in front of him, but Chanelle still stood there. Her eyes were alight with rage and she was wearing a grin so wide it showed off all of her round, tiny teeth right to the gums. The bat hadn't come down though, and she turned and hissed at something he couldn't see.

He tried to turn and his whole world shifted to the right.

There was another loud crash as the wood around the McDonald's deadbolt finally splintered and Mike fell into the house, stumbling once and catching himself. His eyes locked to Xander's only briefly when he saw Chanelle, her arms raised as she held the bat taller than her into the air.

"Okay, kid," he coaxed, holding out his hand and stepping toward the child cautiously. "Why don't you just give me the bat, and then we'll get you some double-fudge-mint-chip ice cream or something, huh? You in the mood for a sugar..."

There was a groan to his side, and Mike turned to see Lindsey McDonald laying on the floor beside the couch. There were two other pairs of feet poking out from behind it as well. One was clearly a child's. The other wore heels.

"...rush," he finished, turning back to her.

She grinned at him, and then swung the bat. It slammed it into Mike's side with more force than she should have been capable of and sent him stumbling across the room and into the far wall. Two pictures and a vase fell off a nearby shelf down onto him as he landed on the hardwood floor, feeling something in his tailbone bend to the point of breaking then go back again.

"Ah!" He hissed through his teeth, closing his eyes tight as pain ripped through his body from several points and all converged on his skull as if on a race.

Xander's eyes opened suddenly, his face blank of all expression. Something deep inside of him twitched once, and then again.

Groggily, Mike opened his eyes. Chanelle was standing over him, her bat gripped tight between both hands. Her hair was wild and out of control, sticking out in all directions. Her cheeks had become crystalline, bloodshot and shiny, like dried flakes of desert dotting her face. Her eyes were no longer there... instead there were dual black holes, gaping maws that seemed to stretch on for eternity. He gasped, even as she drew back the bat again and brought it down across his face, sending him sprawling into the couch, a quick spurt of blood splashing onto the dark fabric.

The veins in Xander's eyes became prominent, making them red and bulging for a moment. That thing deep in him twitched and his eyes went quickly from red to a thick black. He rose quickly to his feet as the gash on the side of his face healed, sewing itself back up until there was nothing there but smooth skin.

He grabbed Chanelle by the back of the throat, turned her around, and slammed her against the wall just as she was about to strike Mike for a third time.

"Boo."

He tightened his grip on the possessed child's neck as the rest of the family started to stir and Mike ran to their aid, blood streaming down an impact wound on his own head as well. His ear was bleeding heavily.

Xander let his claws out of two of his fingers, puncturing the girl's neck just a little as he squeezed. She tried to scream, but found that she could not get enough air. Suddenly, her demonic eyes began to glow.

Xander's own blackened eyes widened, even as he continued to tighten his grip.

Something shoved Xander back as the room filled with light.

Chanelle dropped to the ground, coughing violently, holding her throat as tiny droplets of blood started to flow down it.

The light faded quickly and the Ok' La' Zarr stood there, looking dazed, its muscle tone slightly more green than it had been before. It looked less graceful, and its erection was gone as well. It screamed a high-pitched wail that made Xander cover his ears, his enhanced senses returning quickly.

"Discani!" It spat angrily. It took off toward the door and ripped it off its hinges as it passed.

Xander stammered to his feet and bolted over to Mike.

"It's corporeal," he said, helping the mother to her feet. "We can end this now."

"You go!" Mike nodded, taking the son onto his shoulder. "I'll take care of things here!"

Xander got up and ran toward the door as fast as he could, the Womb blood already coursing through his veins, waiting for the release, the pressure in his body building and building. As soon as he was out of earshot of the house, he bellowed "Black Womb lives," the reverberations of which came back at him almost immediately, attracting the attention of several dogs within a block of him.

"What was that thing?" Chanelle's mother exclaimed as she rose to her feet, aided by Mike. "What the hell is going on here?"

"They know, Mary," Lindsey barked, sighing as he hoisted his son onto one arm. He walked over to where their daughter still knelt, coughing. He grimaced as she looked up at him, her eyes pale and innocent. "They know what she's done."

"Wait," Mike said as he sat down on the couch, smearing his own blood onto his jeans accidentally. "It wasn't her. That... thing you saw, it was like... a parasite. It was inside her, acting through her."

Lindsey furrowed his brow, as his daughter smiled up at him, leaping up into his arms. Fresh tears spilled down his cheeks, as his smile spread from ear to ear, the way it hadn't since all this began.

Mike smiled, laying back against a cushion and clutching his side. He watched as the father held his daughter as tightly as he dared, squeezing her as though he had not seen her in years.

The Ok' La' Zarr ran through the woods, shoving past trees and shrubs as it went, sweat beading on its skinless brow. It glanced behind its shoulder, breathing hard as it struggled to see if it was still back there, following him. Trying to see if it was still coming to get him. Fear washed over the fear demon's face, a look that didn't quite fit it, though the poetic nature of it would have been noticed by anyone who had been around to see it for what it was.

Its teeth ached with the cold winter air that flew around it in all directions, stinging its large, unprotected canines, like the feeling one gets when they drink cold juice. Its suit was torn and ripped by the foliage all around it. Deep inside its lanky chest its heart thumped loudly, sending blood coursing through its veins faster and faster until it thought that its head might explode.

It had never seen anything like that... thing... before. Never in its long life had it ever been touched by something so black, so dark. Never.

He looked over his shoulder again, then turned back to the front, slamming face first into the Black Womb and falling backward to the ground, scuffing its pants on the muddy, half-frozen ground.

"Take me not back there you can!" The creature hissed angrily, letting a glob of spit hanging from his mouth finally fall to his chest.

The Womb stepped toward it, not speaking. Not taking its large, red eyes off it.

"Not you can!" It bellowed again. It dove at the Womb with incredible speed, its hands spread wide and its long talons all seeming to point at him at once.

The Womb brought its hands up to defend itself as the creature plunged forward into it, then vanished into vapor.

A ripple of gooseflesh traveled over the Womb's black flesh, covering him in that same pins-and-needles feeling one got when a limb lay pinned for some time.

Xander turned around, fists still raised, trying to see where it had gone.

He grunted, feeling something drip onto his foot. When he looked there was a growing puddle of thick black soup growing between his feet and the Womb-flesh melted off of him. Fresh, human blood started to come out from his nose. He brought his hand up to catch it then held it up, confused at how much there was. It coated his fingers and palm in thick crimson, as though he were wearing some satin glove.

"What the hell?" he coughed gruffly. Pain erupted from his head like a massive migraine and his hands jolted up to clutch either side of it. It felt like his brain was ripping itself it two. "Oh... fuck."

It was dark.

Darker than it had ever seen, ever known in all its years. There was nothing for its senses to find there but the slow, methodic dripping of its own blood as it leaked from its veins. The demon took several slow steps to the right, gazing all around him with those eyes of nothing as it did.

Chills ran up and down its partially exposed spine as it explored its environment, unsure of what to make of it. It growled deep within its throat. Somewhere in the dark it thought it heard a child's whimper.

The Inner Child.

It smiled grotesquely, stepping forward and licking its lips with a long, sick tongue. It stepped toward the voice, looking from side to side for it, ready to pounce at a moment's notice. Drool salivated from his gums as it anticipated what it would be like, the first bites of the flesh and the final beats of the heart.

"Come outs..." it hissed, smiling as warm as a thing with a face like that could. "You have nothing to fear..."

Suddenly, two aqua eyes opened in the maw that surrounded it, glowing brightly as if from nothing.

The creature balked in shock as the Womb stepped out of the shadows toward it, opening up a full row of teeth.

"Make me go back you won't!" It screamed, lunging at the Womb.

It was batted away carelessly as the Womb opened up its mouth, bellowing at the very top of its lungs: "Black Womb lives!"

The Womb grabbed the demon by the head and snapped its spine with one skillful slice of its massive claws, paralyzing it.

Tears streamed down the demon's face as it tried to hold out its hands to block the Womb from coming toward it, but found itself unable to. All it could do was watch as the creature slowly slunk toward it, blue-green eyes large and unblinking.

"Didn't expect this, did you?" Xander snarled, blood gushing out his nose, ears and mouth as the last of the Womb seeped off his naked body and into the snow. "Trying to take me over you'll have to step in line."

It screamed as the true Womb leapt upon it, its massive jaw unhinging and growing to envelope the Ok' La' Zarr's entire body, swallowing one section at a time like an anaconda.

"The human, that's the part you like," Xander laughed, even as he began to even cry blood. "The Womb... that's a different story now, ain't it?"

It screamed, only its head remaining visible as it bawled for life, its eyes watching as the Womb's mouth came over them, bringing new pitch to the blackness all around it... and then, slowly, it began to laugh.

"What's so funny?" Xander asked himself, lying down in the snow now, unable to move. "You won't be taking little girls away where you're going, y'know."

"I never has to go back..." it laughed, even as the Womb took it into itself. "I never has to go back there again. No control. No help. Trapped we was, trapped. Trapped by the prey."

Xander's eyes lit up as the creature finally stopped laughing, light fading from Xander's eyes as it died, finally.

Chanelle laid the book down on the bed for him to see.

Xander's eyes went wide. His hand trembled as he picked up the book.

What had originally been a boy in a hospital bed with one leg in a cast and a doctor coming in through the nearby door had been turned into the same boy with dark red smears dripping from his eyes, mouth and ears. The doctor had been coloured in black, making him look shadowy and evil.

He grinned as he passed by a wall full of pages from children's colouring books, each a different picture coloured by a different child patient. Most where incoherent scribbles by children who had spent way too much time in the waiting room bored out of their minds, but some of them were the genuinely good. He saw one very good rendition of a doctor giving a boy a lollipop done by Charles, a kid from Xander's neighborhood. Panning the wall a little more, he saw one by Chanelle McDonald, one without any blood, or anything else out of the ordinary on it anywhere. Just a girl playing with her cat, putting a red bow around its neck.

Mike's eyes grew wide as he saw what Cathy saw by the bush. "...Xander?"

"Yeah?" Xander asked, nose twitching as he turned back toward them. He followed both their gazes to the base of the bush, where the body of a small tabby cat lay skinned.

Just a girl playing with her cat, red blood around its neck.

"Oh..." Xander said softly, staring up at the sky as he laid back against the snow, his muscles refusing to move. "... my god."

Lindsey McDonald took the last screw out of the lock on his daughter's door, smiling as he chucked it to Mike. "Done," he said, unable to contain his enthusiasm.

"Done," Mike smiled in return, tossing the lock in the bathroom garbage. "So you were locking her in to stop her from hurting things?"

"Broke my heart every time," he sighed, the smile still on his face, his eyes bright and glimmering.

"That's great," Mike chuckled. "That is so much better than the way I thought all this would turn out, you have no idea."

"And you're sure your friend can handle that thing?" He asked, a touch of concern in his voice.

"Yeah, no problem," Mike smiled, handing him the screwdriver, which he placed on a shelf near the bathroom door. "He can handle himself."

Lindsey nodded, still unsure of what to make of everything that had happened. "I just can't believe it... all the bad things that have happened over the last few years, all because of that creature somehow?"

Mike smiled, nodded... and then the smile slowly faded from his lips.

"Years?" He repeated, as the two of them turned the corner into the living room again. He grabbed Lindsey by the shoulder and started to turn him around. "Did you say years?"

Both men stopped quickly, eyes wide as they saw Lindsey's wife and son sprawled out on the floor again. Blood was hemorrhaging out of Mary's back. They were both covered in a viscous fluid that Mike recognized automatically.

He turned back down the hall just in time to see the bat swipe across his face again, connecting with his nose. He hit the ground hard, his eyes glazing over as he felt something splash over his legs. The smell got worse as his eyes started to close, just in time to see Chanelle McDonald put down the can of gasoline.

She smiled down at Mike, holding up a book of matches. "The boy said that if my family dies... I get a new one."

CHAPTER TWENTY-ONE: BURN

CH!
TCH!
CH!

Chanelle sighed, pouting out her lower lip as she tried to light match after match, throwing the useless sticks to the floor.

CH!

Cathy came into the house slowly, walking around the corner and into the living room, refusing to so much as blink to take her eyes off the child.

"Hi, Chanelle," she said, sweat pouring off her brow from the run she'd had trying to get to the house in time.

CH!

Chanelle struck another match, the last of the powder wearing off before it even got to spark. Indignant, she threw the useless stick of cardboard to the ground.

"Hi," Chanelle said warmly, taking a moment to smile up at Cathy before she ripped off another match and tried to ignite it.

TCH!

Cathy winced every time the sound occurred, staring at the matchbook and watching for that one spark that would send the situation up into flames.

"What are you doing?" Cathy asked, in the nicest tone of voice she could muster, brushing a strand of hair back behind her ear. She smiled even as she looked down at Mike, his lower half drenched in gasoline.

CH!

"I'm starting a fire," the girl said simply. "Then I can have a new family."

Cathy nodded. "Okay..." she said, taking a quick glance around the room and spotting the bat a few feet to one side. "Why do you think you need a new family, Chanelle, sweetie?"

"Oh, I know I do," she said, not so much as throwing a glance at Cathy. "I have to get a new one so they can make me happy, so I can do whatever I want."

TCHC!

"You know, you don't have to set a fire just to get a new family..." she coaxed, slowly stepping forward, moving just a little to the right with each step she took, toward the bat.

"Oh, I know," the child assured her, smiling. "Fire's just fun."

CH-isssss!

The flame lit up on the edge of one of the matches, and Cathy's eyes went wide, the spark caught in both her pupils. "Chanelle, no!" She screamed.

Chanelle looked at her finally, the child's smile gone.

"Don't tell me what to do!" She screamed, tossing the match down onto her mother's gasoline-soaked dress.

Flames erupted all around, sucking all of the air of the room and filling it with smoke.

"No!" Cathy screamed, raising her hands to block against the flames. They spread quickly, the fire moving from point to point along the spots in the carpet where fuel had dripped, like a bright orange stone skipping across the water and making ripples as it went.

The baby boy began to scream, the shrill wail heard even above the roar of the fire. The fire sounded like a dragon and the flames that kissed the undersides of Cathy's arms were its molten teeth.

Her eyes began to water from the smoke and the heat. She had to force herself to open them, her every instinct telling her not to. She squinted past the hole that her arms made in front of her and saw Mike, lying unconscious on the floor not far from where Chanelle's mother lay.

89

His arm was on fire.

Her eyes went wide, the smoke and the humidity stinging at them.

She dove forward into the flames, past the orange wall that stretched up to stain the ceiling a deep charcoal black already. It felt as though she were inside an oven. The heat that had hit her like a wave a moment ago was now all around her, pressing in on her from all sides and making her feel as though she might implode. Her lungs ached for air but every breath brought more pain, the smoke searing her flesh on the way down like millions of tiny axes. She coughed, gasped for air and got more smoke, then coughed again.

Her hands found Mike's chest and she forced herself to stop coughing. The wall of fire was dissected by her abdomen and seemed to have quelled the fire directly beneath it, a long doorway having opened in the flames all the way to the ceiling. She discovered now that the orange wasn't so much a wall but a large and ever-expanding box, within which was just more flames.

Her hair catching and filling the room with the disgusting and unmistakable stench of burnt hair, she grabbed him by his shoulder and the neck of his shirt and pulled with everything she had in one mighty tug, bringing him over to the other side of the fire.

She gasped for air from the exertion and immediately regretted it, her lungs rebelling wildly against the smoke and screaming in pain. Her vision blurred and large red dots decorated all sides of it. A migraine came out of nowhere, the first in her life, so blindingly painful that she clenched her teeth hard enough to crack a molar. Forcing herself not to faint, she kicked Mike in the ribs as hard as she could and sent him tumbling toward the front door, where he slammed against the jam and stayed there at an obtuse and painful angle. His mouth was open, his eyes were not.

His shirt was still on fire.

Pursing her dried and cracked lips, she turned back to the flame. Chanelle was still standing beyond it, her back to the wall. She looked at Cathy expectantly, the fire dancing in her glossy, moist eyes.

Closing her eyes, Cathy dove forward into the flames once again. She felt the tips of it against the skin of her chin. Her hand connected with hot fabric and she pulled back, throwing herself away from the fire with such force that she knocked her head against the doorframe and pushed Mike out of the house and onto the walkway.

The baby was clutched tightly to her chest.

"No!" Chanelle cried from the house, coughing as her little lungs filled with smoke. "You can't! I don't want you to!"

Cathy grabbed sand and dirt from the walkway and threw it against Mike's shoulder, burying not only that side of his face and torso but the fire as well. The ground she'd piled there smoked and smoldered like a volcano about to erupt.

"I don't want you to!"

The baby cried, finally able to again now that its lungs were filling with the night air.

Cathy turned back toward the house as flames engulfed the door she had just come through, making it impossible for her to get back in.

Firefighters arrived on the scene twenty minutes later, when the house and the three people remaining inside were nothing but piles of charred ruin.

EPILOGUE

"So... it was the kid all along?" Mandy asked, as she and Xander walked down the darkened sidewalk a few days later. The streetlight cast long shadows on each of them.

Xander nodded, taking a puff of his cigarette and then throwing it aside.

"That's so awful..." she trailed off, looking down at the sidewalk. "Give me a straight bad guy any day. This stuff, when you don't, like, know what's right and what's not... it's just too much. You know?"

"Yeah," Xander sighed, turning to smile at her briefly. "I do."

She smiled at him coyly, one eyebrow raised suspiciously. "So, where are you taking this innocent teenage girl on this cold winter's night that you can't tell me, anyway?"

"You're not innocent, by any stretch," Xander said, without humor, even though he meant for there to be.

She frowned, knowing full well what that tone in his voice meant. "Hey... there was nothing that you could have done. You did your part... more than. Like always." She drew her hand in close to his cheek, tilting his head up to look at her. "I love you, boy-o."

Xander smiled as best he could, his eyes welling up. "I love you, too."

He turned off the main road then, heading up the path toward the cemetery.

"Hey, what're we going up here for?" Mandy asked, looking around cautiously, sweat beginning to dot on her brow even though she was shivering.

Xander did not answer, just continued to walk up the trail, with her no less than three paces behind him at all times.

"Xander, I don't like it up here," she whined, shivering again. "I'm cold, can we go please?"

Again, he said nothing. Tears started to draw forth from his eyes and he batted them free, trudging his way silently up the steep slope.

"Xander please, I don't want to -"

And then there was silence. Xander stood staring down at the grave before him. Engraved on the stone was the most beautiful name he thought he might ever hear : Amanda Peterson.

"Goodbye," he said softly, bowing his head.

Several long moments passed, and then someone else stepped up next to him again, gazing down at the grave with him.

"Hello, Alex," she said simply, her eyes pinned to the letters and date engraved into the stone.

"Hello, Julie," he sighed, touching her hand briefly. "When did they let you out?"

"Few hours ago," she said, her voice and lower lip quivering, her face still a little flush. "I came here as soon as I could."

Xander nodded. Neither of them looked at the other.

"She was so brave," Xander said, his eyes getting red and puffy. "Oh, gawd, Julie, you should have seen it. She looked soooo pretty, she did, and her eyes were sparkling right up until the spark went out, I swear... nobody has ever seen anything so beautiful as her eyes right before it happened. It was like all the wonder that was meant for the rest of her life got crammed into that one second, and I was there to see it."

Julie nodded, tears dribbling from her chin as though it were a faucet. "It's good that someone was there with her," she said simply. "I just wish I knew why all this had to happen."

He opened his mouth and let it lay slack for a moment, then he pulled a knife from his jacket and brought it to his wrist behind his back.

"There's something I have to tell you," he whispered softly.

"Don't," she spat, taking him by surprise. "I mean... just don't." She looked down, sniffing back hard. "I'm going back to Coral Cove tomorrow, Xander."

"What?" He exclaimed, putting the knife away quickly.

"I can't do it anymore. And my Aunt needs me now, me and Mom. I asked her and we're both going now, so that she won't have to be alone anymore. It's for her, I just..." Again, she sucked back tears, turning to face him for the first time since she'd joined him. "I just can't keep competing with dead women."

He stepped back a pace, shocked.

"It's not Sara... it's not that you still love her, in ways you can't love me. That's not it, Xander. It's what you really love more than anything. You love *death*, Xander Drew... and as long as you do, death will keep following you, wherever you go, and I can't be a part of that anymore."

His lower lip quivered, so she reached out and kissed it, lightly. "I love you, Alexander Drew," she said, wiping tears from her face as she walked away from him, heading back down the hill into town.

In his room, Mike held Cathy close to him as they lay on his bed, looking up at the posters on his wall. He stroked her hair and just held her, as she snuggled up closer to him, fitting perfectly against his body.

"About... what we were talking about the other day..." he said slowly, kissing her on top of her head.

"Yeah?" She smiled, looking up at him longingly.

He sighed. "Everything's just so different. Everything's changing all at once again, and I don't know when it's going to stop. I just... I just want us, right now, to be the one place that I can go and know what to expect for once. I want us to change, to go to that next level..."

"...But not yet," she smiled, leaning up and kissing him, softly, on the lips.

"I feel the same way."

He smiled, cuddling her close to him again, just staring up at the walls.

"In the darkness it followed them, just enough light for them to see. It chased them through the brush and the woods, the tree limbs scraping past them, tearing at their limbs, cutting deep, deep, everything cut deep. The wind whistled through the branches as they ran past, singing the songs of their deaths, and it was beautiful.

"It was not an evil thing that pursued them, for its need to kill went far deeper than what we mere mortals define as right and wrong. It was simply a need to be, an urge to sate the growing hunger for flesh. It did not hate them, nor they it, because they knew that it was its instinct to give chase, as much as it was theirs to run.

"The ground beneath its feet stuck to it, keeping it moist and warm; a loud sucking sound accompanying every powerful stride as it broke the twigs that sliced at its prey, its eyes never batting for fear of being prodded. It thought only of the hunt, of the taste of victory.

"The moon overhead and the ground beneath, it chased as they were chased. It ran as they did run. And as it caught them, their flesh biding mercy to its claw, they became one under a common need, a common goal, and came to know and understand each other in the hour of their passing.

"The need to go on.

"In the shadows it caught up with them, and they did not turn away, for they found that they could not bear to fight it any longer, and more than that, did not want to.

"They came to it willingly, tired from the hunt, and felt its tingle wash over their bodies as its breath hit them, and they were surprised at how good it felt. How freeing it was.

"They let the monster take them whole in its passion, biting their lips as they disobeyed all that their parents had instilled in them as children.

"All for that one moment of pure, unrelenting ecstasy.

"Their bodies throbbed and convulsed with pleasure as its tongue draped over them, and from their vantage point, naked and writhing in the shadows, it could see the world of the light out of the corner of their eyes, but the world could not see them, as the darkness sank snugly inside of them.

"And even as it filled them, clouding their thoughts and their actions, their hands going places they were told never to let them go, they could not help but remind themselves how wrong it was.

"That they were bad.

"Suddenly, it began to hurt. Then more and more, until the pleasure was gone, leaving only agony and death that wrenched at their hearts, the darkness enjoying it more and more with every swell of pain that surged through them, barring its massive teeth.

"And when they died it ate them, from the bottom up.

"And all they could think was how bad they were.

93

"And how much they deserved it.

"And how they could not wait to do it again.

"And how it had all been worth it.

"It came at them from inside the mirror, arms reaching out with tiny mouths at the end of each and every fingertip, devouring them like tiny cannibals, so hungry that they would eat even of their own flesh.

"And when they screamed it was neither piercing nor did it render any help as blood started to pour from their gaping, open wounds, for it was a silent scream, turned inward on themselves. As the scream pierced their very souls, they stopped feeling the thousands of razor sharp teeth, and eventually all they were was the tone of the scream.

"After time, the teeth were always there. The teeth had become a part of them, hard and sharp, covering their exterior so that no one ought see them, and no one would dare touch them for fear that they, too, would be devoured.

"And without the warmth of another the teeth sank deeper and the scream grew louder. It grew until they could no longer even hear it, becoming white noise, and they became deaf to all else.

"So great was their hunger for human contact that they turned on themselves, and became the teeth, both devouring until there was nothing left.

"With nothing left to feed on, the teeth on the tips of the fingers turned to their eyes, gouging them out.

"They heard nothing.

"They saw nothing.

"They felt nothing.

"They were nothing.

"And the teeth on the tips of the fingers went back into the mirror,

"To wait until tomorrow.

"They did not run, for they did not wish to. Instead they stayed there, bathed in light as the darkness swirled around them, taking each breath long and deep, just in case it was their last.

"The beast circled them, clacking its nails against the ground, making them twitch as the suspense rose to a nearly tactile level of unbearableness.

"It was maddening.

"At first, they did nothing. Then, all at once, they turned about and lashed out, pounding their fists into the creature, sending it scampering away, laughing at their attempts.

"That they would try to harm that which they simply did not understand, such being the plight of all mortals.

"But the blow missed, of course, and the arm traveled around the curvature of the earth, picking up speed as it went, until finally, they hit themselves.

"And the blow that would start to harm others

"Would cause their suicide.

"They looked deep inside themselves,

"And they realized that the darkness had been inside of them the entire time,

"Following them like a shadow."

94

Xander stood on the edge of his bed.

The knife dropped to the floor, tiny droplets of blood spraying off it onto the wall as black ooze took over his body, slithering its way from his veins out into oxygenated air. His eyes turned coal black... then stark red...

... then finally, a sea-green aqua.

He growled, opening his mouth wide.

BOOK NINE

GANG WAR

PROLOGUE

Tommy Irons held the knife firmly in his right hand with the blade pressed tight against his left wrist.

The knife belonged to his father. It was a simple hunting knife, its rubber handle wrapped in black grip tape. The faded six-inch blade came up sharp on both sides, without any serrated edges or designs in the metal to make it appear fancy or frightening.

Against his tender, loose flesh, it looked much more impressive than when it rested casually on his father's worktable.

His hair was spiked high, as it usually was, belaying its long length. His heart-shaped face, usually seen with a smile (or at least a grin), was now sewn up in a frown of deep resentment. He wore a stained and tattered white tee shirt under an open blue one. The shirt was denim, like his jeans. He'd fallen in love with that style three years ago after staying up late and watching old teen movies from the nineties and had gone shopping the next weekend. He owned at least a dozen identical pairs.

He sat on the edge of his bed, arms leaned against knees and feet thrown over the side. There were pictures scattered all around of the most recent person to leave him with nothing: Julie Peterson.

His walls were covered in images as well. Pictures that he had taken, pictures that had been taken of him and of his life.

That had always been an annual ritual of Tommy's. Every year, he'd change all of the pictures on his wall to those he'd taken the year before. His father had always called him Shutterbug for it, back when he'd given Tommy's actions any thought.

This year, however, had been different.

This year everyone had started to abandon him, from the beginning of the school semester starting with Jamie Dawkins and continuing through to Julie Peterson. The weeks could almost be marked by a personal loss on his part, either through death or choice or circumstance.

Every time one of them left him, he would turn their picture around. He would never take it down completely, merely flip it so that it faced the wall, sticking a pin in its corners and trying his best to forget the faces contained within them.

Now they were all facing front again. They glared at him again. Judged him again. The eyes that had once seemed warm and inviting now scowled and belittled him.

Jamie, forever frozen, held his cue stick as he awaited Mike to finish his turn. Half cut off by the table, his face was also lost but this time in the shadows of his red Cougars baseball cap. In the darkness, his eyes sparkled from the flash, looking sinister as they stared out at Tommy no matter where he sat in the room.

There were sunspots in Sara's picture, but they worked so well that they enhanced the image. Tommy had zoomed in on her face as she was sipping from the straw of what he thought might have been a Cherry Coke, although the can wasn't visible in the photo. He had framed the shot around her flawless face, accented with wisps of her blonde hair puffing out in stringy wet spikes from each of her black hair bands. Her eyes were wide, showing almost all of her pupils. The girl just didn't seem to believe in blinking, as he used to tell her after examining a roll of film in his darkroom. Now those eyes gawked at him, as if daring him into a staring contest he had no hope of winning even if she wasn't merely an image on glossy photo paper. It was so condescending, the way her eyes seemed to give him the once over, then push any thought of him aside, choosing death over him.

Then there was Derek.

There was no imagination needed to vilify that photo. Staring directly into the lens, arms crossed, eyes squinted and one eyebrow cocked -- he looked ready to leap from the photo and cut Tommy's head off, which he no doubt would have done if given half the chance. Then there was that grin. The sly smile prickling at the sides of his face, the one that he'd always worn. He wore it every day at school, while everyone around him talked about the murders, wondering who would be next and who could do such a thing. He smiled and joked and made light of it every single day... knowing all along that it was him. That he could have stopped and put their fears to rest at any time, but didn't. It was all to impress his father, who spent more time at his job than with his own son. The smile, those eyes... they made you feel like you were being stalked. Like it was only a matter of time, even through the camera's lens.

Then there was Julian Grendel, one of his best friends growing up, sitting back against the couch in his rumpus room, arms stretched out around Cathy and Liz as the both of them leaned in and pretended to give him a kiss on either cheek. His smile was broad. His big blue eyes clearly visible, their color brought out by the sea-green tee shirt he was wearing. He was mocking Tommy, holding out his hands around all that he had and Tommy did not. He was laughing at him, egging him on and yelling at him to do it -- to slice the flesh and let it bleed all over him.

Then there was Randy Owchar, hanging out at The Factory with Justin Langley and Sven Douglas. Never aware that Tommy was taking their picture, they were just loitering by the counter. One of them (Sven, maybe) was holding a Pepsi. As it turned out, all three of them had been Tees, a gang of idealistic thugs that thought way too much of town pride and formed by Randy's mentally disturbed father. Randy had betrayed and hurt them all in many ways, but none more than Tommy.

In the photo each Tee, but especially Randy, was turned away from him. If anything, it was more natural that -- like always -- they didn't give him a second thought. From his place on the bed, Tommy glared up at Randy's face, turned away and sneering at the former friend.

In the background of Randy's picture was Roxanne, the waitress at The Factory. She, at least, was looking directly at the camera. A small grin stretched across her gorgeous face, which was framed by the few scattered wisps of her curly red hair, otherwise drawn up in a bow. She was bringing Randy a Coke, for which he was already reaching into his pocket for change. She, at least, had always been kind to him. She was also one of the women killed by Derek Smith, who explained to a reporter that his reason was to throw the authorities off his trail by killing people outside his circle. Ever since she died, The Factory had not been the same. Joan, the owner, hadn't had any spirit since that day. None of it was fun anymore, instead just a grim reminder of what it had once been, when they had at least been able to cling to the illusion that everything was normal and that they were all friends, despite their differences.

Tommy turned and closed his eyes tightly, batting away a few droplets of tears as he turned to the next picture. His grip relaxed around the knife, then tightened again. He sighed, opened his eyes, and looked straight at the photo of Frederick Windser, who most people just called Sud. The picture was a bust of him, his bald head gleaming under the flourescent lights of the school. He had a fist connecting with the palm of his hand in front of him, wrinkling his dark green sweater at the elbows, distorting the triangles that adorned its chest. He had a vivid, fake grimace on his face as he posed, but the truth of the matter was in his eyes. His eyes sparkled with the mischievousness and playfulness of his true spirit as he posed for his friend's picture. In those eyes were all of the many years of friendship that he had given to Tommy... and the question of why Tommy had betrayed him. It stung more than any photo yet. The night before Sud's death, Tommy had been with his killer. Randy murdered him simply because of his hometown – dead because of a few measly miles -- and the artificial importance of the tags 'Tee' and 'Omega.'

And then there was Mandy.

Amanda Peterson, the light that shone on all their lives, bringing hope to all it touched. She had come to them in their darkest hour, when it seemed like there was no good left in this world, and gave them a glimpse of something better. Her flame burned strong, even as darkness threatened, and maintained her cheerfulness, zest for life and ability to forgive those who had wronged her.

This was part of the reason that Tommy had loved her so much.

In the end it had taken a beating, both physical and spiritual, to finally break her body... but not her spirit. Raped, beaten, tortured, mocked, spat upon... the hope was still in her face, even long after she was dead.

Now, from its perch on his wall, that glow bathed down on him from her pictures on his wall... a mockery of what it had been, for no picture could ever do it justice.

The first was of Cathy, Julie, and Mandy at the Factory. It was one of those spur-of-the-moment pictures that he had taken only because he had his camera on him at the time and they had not noticed that he was standing there until it was too late.

Those were the ones that he liked best. Not the ones where everyone stood in a line like they were getting their driver's licence photo, looking stone-loaded out of their minds with red eyes and pasty expressions or had fake smiles plastered over an otherwise dreary expression.

No, he preferred the pictures that were natural. When he could look and remember what people were like, not when they were all dressed up, but everyday normal, in case he ever forgot.

The three of them were sitting on one of the park benches that The Factory owners had bought from the city and fixed up, with an old fashioned street lamp hanging overhead. Where they'd gotten that piece of nostalgia, he'd never know. Never ask, either.

In the picture, Cathy was sipping on her bottle of Cherry Coke via a straw, her head turned slightly. The angle made her hair drape down over a good portion of her face, dividing it into angular lines. She was wearing a tank top with red and black vertical stripes. One of the shoulder straps had fallen over her shoulder, turning the picture from something simple into something sensual.

Julie had actually managed to see him right before he pressed the shutter. She'd been looking past him, at Xander. There was a quirky smirk on her face. When developing the photos and finding he had captured it, Tommy got so happy that he pinned it up while it was still wet, permanently staining the bedspread beneath it with photochemical dots.

And Mandy. She was doing something with her hair. She had both hands up, fixing her pigtails, inadvertently presenting her breasts through the sweater that she almost always wore, or at least some variation of it. There was nothing sexual about the pose, though. It was like looking at a portrait, a painting of a beautiful woman. If done right, there was nothing sexual about the nudity, just beauty. That was the way this was. It was simply her being her, as no other person could, with mouth open to say something to Julie, who was completely oblivious to Mandy's presence.

Tommy had loved that picture for that exact reason. The fact that there she was, being perfect, and nobody was paying attention to her.

Nobody else could see her glow.

Sighing, he turned from the wall to the bed and floor surrounding him.

There were thirty or more photos sprawled out on the floor. Some upside down, some overlapping the others, and none of them in any particular order. There were close shots, wide shots, medium shots, group shots, portrait shots, and the one semi-nude she'd let him do that time they got drunk in Grendel's cabin with Sara. All the shots, no matter their composition, had one thing in common:

They were all of Julie Peterson.

In some she was looking at him, others she was interacting with others. But in all of them, she had cute freckles across the bridge of her nose. She had effervescent green eyes that formed the basis by which every other color in the photos were judged. She had perfectly white teeth, just a little crooked in the front and always in a smile. She had a heart shaped face. She had brown hair with natural light streaks.

In all the photos, she was who she was: never posed and never fake.

One in particular had Julie sitting with Mandy on a bench just outside of school. He told Mandy under false pretenses that he was taking the picture solely of her, so she was posed perfectly, pretending to be a kind of funny-sexy. Julie had been turned toward the smoking section, saying something to Xander when he had called out her name, just before pressing the shutter release button. What resulted was the most natural shot of her possible, from the back wearing a slinky tank top, her head turned over her shoulder to look at him.

He also lingered at the semi-nude shot, in which her shirt was off, revealing a black bra underneath. Nobody in attendance had remembered him taking that picture, including Tommy himself. When he discovered it he had told no one, not even Sud.

Turning away from the pictures, he let a single tear dribble down his cheek as he pressed the knife in; slowly increasing pressure, hissing air as he drew blood, which gradually streamed down his arm.

Pursing his lips, he continued to push, driving deeper into the tender flesh. The pain was overwhelming, shooting in violent bursts between wrist and brain, then everywhere in-between.

Biting his lower lip as the pain got even worse, he held his breath, trying to summon the strength to push down just a little deeper...

His lungs fought back and Tommy heaved a great sigh. He relaxed his grip on the blade and let it fall to the bed. He stood. Cursing softly to himself, he looked around the room at all of the faces staring back at him again.

Sud
Mandy
Julie
Xander
Sud
Randy
Mandy
Cathy
Xander
Sara
Julie

"Argh!" he screamed, eyes bloodshot from pain and rage. He picked up the knife again and sliced it across the wall. Several pictures tore in half, some just below the neckline. Bellowing again, he sliced at the picture of Sud again and again, ripping it up with each strike until it was barely recognizable. He then turned the blade on Sara, and Jamie, and Derek, and Grendel, and Roxanne, and Mandy, and Julie. He tore them all to shreds, sending tiny pieces of photo-paper confetti fluttering in all directions as he waved his arms about wildly with the blade.

He sliced a photo of Xander directly in two vertically, splitting him into halves. He turned to the part of the wall that mainly portrayed Cathy and Mike, grabbing at them with hungry fingers and ripping through the glossy finish on the paper as though it were nothing.

Finally he stopped and looked at what he had done. Sweat poured down his brow and blood down his arm. His breath came in heavy, great gasps.

One photo remained on the wall, hanging from a single tack.

It was the shot of Randy, Sven and Justin, all hanging out at The Factory, awaiting their drinks. Slowly, he reached out with the tip of the blade, gently slicing away Sven and Justin and sending their pieces falling to the floor.

Stepping back and turning away for just a moment, he spun back around quickly and threw the knife as hard as he could at the picture. The knife burrowed a whole two inches into the wall, splitting Randy directly between the eyes.

Tommy stood there, breathing deeply as he squinted at the knife and waited for it to stop vibrating.

CHAPTER ONE: SHOCK

She threw the vase as hard as she could, without aiming it at anything in particular, just heaving it with as much force behind it as she could muster.

It burst against the wall just to the side of Lee Piercey. He had to duck just to avoid the shards of pottery and soil coming back at him.

"Jaylen!" he cried, his face livid with anger as he stood up again, brushing the dirt off of his shoulder. "What the hell is the matter with you?"

"Me?!" she screamed, pointing her finger at herself to bring the point home. "Excuse me, you son of a bitch. I found the goddamn letters!"

Lee's face went white.

She reached into the kitchen drawer behind her, pulled out a bound wad of envelopes and heaved them at him. They connected with his forehead, knocking him back a pace. The elastic band binding them snapped, sending letters fluttering about everywhere, spinning to the ground all around him like fake plastic flakes in a snowglobe.

Lee fumed as he watched them fall around him. He turned back to face his wife, finger extended, and a fiery red color now very apparent on his face.

"Well, maybe if you were doing your fucking job, I wouldn't have to go sneaking around like a goddamn child!"

"Me?" she laughed, pointing at her own chest. "I couldn't get it up if I *wanted* to, you impotent fuck! What the fuck does this one got that I don't? Testicles?"

"You shut the hell up," he barked, taking several menacing steps toward her, his jaw set.

"Get out!" she screamed, stepping back against the wall, fear flashing in her eyes.

He realized what she thought he was going to do, shaking his head spitefully. "You'd like that, wouldn't you?" he drawled.

"Leave," she repeated, standing up straight again.

Smiling and calming down, he nodded and turned back toward the hallway.

Lee entered the bedroom, slamming the door behind him. He knelt down and reached under the bed quickly, pulling out a leather suitcase and opening it. It was already full of clothes, razors, and a few other toiletries. He looked it over quickly, then zipped it up, slung it over his shoulder and headed back out the door.

He walked to the front door of the house, slipping off his loafers as he went. When he reached the porch, he pulled on his shoes and grabbed the keys to his car off the rack. He looked down at them, smiling. Slowly, he removed the house key and the mail key off of them. He held them in the palm of his hand, feeling their weight.

"Jaylen!" he called out to the kitchen, a smug look on his face.

There was no response.

He frowned, turning toward the room and tilting his head to try and see in. "Jaylen?"

Again, no answer.

Sighing, Lee walked across the carpet, tracking mud over it as he did. He turned to look at it, worried at first, then smiled. "Jaylen, I'm leaving the fucking keys on the kitchen table!" he yelled out, wondering where she had gone on such short notice.

He turned the corner to enter the kitchen and saw her, lying on the floor with a long red line drawn across her gut. Blood leaked out of her mouth and her glassy eyes looked into the distance.

"Jesus!" he screamed, dropping his keys and the suitcase to the floor.

He felt a sharp pain in his back and fell to the ground. He hissed, then looked at the rapidly pooling blood on the floor next to his face until his eyes finally closed and he drifted off to sleep.

Xander Drew stared forward, entranced, at the row of lockers spread out before him. They were painted in the school's colors, an alternating pattern of red and orange.

His brown hair looked almost black, only accented by his attire: a tight-fitting black tee-shirt, leather jacket, and dark blue jeans. Even his eyes, usually a dark blue, looked exceptionally black.

His brow furrowed, scrunching his bushy eyebrows as he stared at the sight before him, letting out a sorrowful sigh.

One of the lockers, an orange one, was left hanging open.

There were squares on the inside that were not as faded as the rest of the painted metal, where photographs and a schedule had once been taped down. On the front of the locker were paper swatches in the shapes of flowers where stickers had been ripped off in a hurry, along with the unmistakable sight of eraser-burn where something had been scrawled in pencil and hastily eradicated.

Slowly, he brought a hand up to the fragmented bits of paper stuck and traced one finger along the edges of the once shining flower, feeling its coarse edges against his skin. Again, he let out a long breath of air, which was almost visible as it reacted with the metal in the cool school hallway.

His hand relaxed and clapped against his side as it fell limply. His eyes continued to trace out every detail of the door, trying to remember what each shape and line had once been.

Quietly, respectfully, a figure came up beside him. Then another, on the opposing side.

Cathy Kennessy held her schoolbooks tightly against her chest, hiding the majority of her red tank top under both them and the black wool sweater that was draped around her shoulders and arms. Her raven hair fell down flat on either side of her face, hiding it in effect, except for one eye, her nose, and part of her lip. Blowing at a strand to get it out of her way, she quickly pushed both lengths back behind her ears, revealing a pale round face that nobody would ever want hidden. Her feet shuffled beneath her loose-fitting blue jeans and heels as she followed his gaze to its target.

Opposite her, Mike Harris frowned and folded his taut arms as he saw the sight in front of him, shaking his head and making his blonde hair shimmy out of place. His shirt read 'SE MAG D NIM' across it, which his mother had had specially made for him a few years ago. It read 'MIND GAMES' when switched around, something he had once found mildly amusing. He watched Xander for a minute, waiting for his friend to address him. When he did not, he shot his girlfriend a look.

She crunched her brow at him, moving her head from side to side ever so slightly. Sighing in defeat, he turned toward the locker as well, looking at the faded decals and removed decor.

Finally Xander moved again, opening the door the rest of the way until it clicked against the locker next to it. Inside, almost hidden by the shadows, was a small white square of paper. Hand trembling, he reached in and carefully picked it up by the edges. He turned it over, even though he already knew what it was.

It was a picture of him, taken two months ago at one of those four-photos-for-a-dollar booths. He had a goofy smile on his face but it was the only one that Julie had of him.

"She's really gone," he said simply, the despair in his voice palpable as he gently slid the photo into his pocket, resuming his glare into the empty void of her shadowed locker.

"Yeah," Cathy breathed sympathetically. She placed a hand on his shoulder and began rubbing it gently. "She really is."

He turned toward the floor, looking as though he might start to cry, then sucked it back with one long sniff and changing his look to something between anger, sadness, and resolve. "I really didn't think she'd actually go, y'know?" he smirked, turning from Cathy to Mike as he fought his eyes from tearing up, acknowledging their presence for the first time.

"None of us did," Mike agreed, looking at the locker now as if using it as an excuse not to make eye contact with Xander. "But I guess she had her mind made up."

Xander nodded. He sucked both his lips in, then plopped them back out. "Good," he said finally, forcing a smile. "Hopefully she'll be happy in Coral Cove, right?"

"Yeah," Cathy chirped.

"That's where Mandy was," he said. He could feel the ridges that the picture made in the fabric of his jeans. "That's where she belongs right now."

They both just nodded, realizing that no matter what they said he would continue talking until he was done.

"It's not like she's needed here," he chuckled forcibly. "It's not like I needed her or anything. We'll be fine without her. Just fine."

There was a long silence, and each of them turned back toward the locker, oblivious to the looks of their fellow students, who formed their own opinions on the trio's actions as they walked past.

Mike let out several long breaths, the last of which he segued into a tune.

Xander turned to look at him. Then Cathy followed suit.

After a moment, he began to mouth words, then say them softly, not quite singing. "... hear them talk about it, on the radio..."

Cathy rolled her eyes and then hid behind her hand, peeking out from between her fingers.

"... did you try to read the writing, on the wall..."

Xander allowed a real, true grin to twitch at the corners of his mouth that grew slowly into a smile.

"... did you hear the voices say, 'I've heard it all before?'"

"It's like deja vu, all over again..." Mike finished, turning his head on an angle and laughing.

"Exactly what made you do that?" Cathy asked, taking down her hand once she was sure that the both of them were done.

Mike shrugged. "The suspense was killing me."

"Yeah. It beat me to it," Xander groaned, placing a palm against the front of the locker door and shutting it tight with a loud clang of metal on metal.

"Hardy har har," Mike said, in his best snot-nosed voice. "You're so funny I forgot to puke on Cathy's heels."

"Heels?" Xander smirked, raising an eyebrow as he turned toward her and noticing how much taller she looked compared to usual. "When did that happen?"

Cathy squinted, as Mike's eyes bugged out and he made a motion as if to duck and cover. "Two months ago," she said icily, squeezing her lips together.

"Eee," Xander squealed softly with a voice suddenly emasculated. He gritted his teeth and turned to the side. "I knew that."

"Of course you did."

"I did."

"I believe you."

"No you don't."

"You're right," she agreed finally, again pushing a strand of her hair back, which promptly fell back to where it had been. "I'm a horrible liar. I admit that now."

Xander smiled, an event that faded as he turned back toward the metal rectangle he hadn't even been aware they were walking away from, even though they were across the hall from it now. "I just don't know what I'm going to do without her."

"Did you tell her?" Mike asked, leaning against the wall with his arms folded, examining the locker to see what magnetic hold it had over his friend.

"Tell her what?" he posed, unsure.

"That you don't know what you're going to do without her?"

Xander's face was expressionless, devoid of all but physical features, as he spoke. "No. I couldn't. If I had, she might have stayed."

Cathy smiled, reaching up and bringing his chin up until she was looking into his eyes. "But, on the other hand, if you'd told her, she might have stayed."

"She made her choice," he said. "I wasn't about to say anything to her to influence it or make her regret it once it was done... it wouldn't be fair."

"Because people in this town *always* play fair, don't they?" Mike drawled.

Cathy shot him a look.

"What?" Mike asked, spreading his arms as if to illustrate his point. "All I'm saying is, how fair is it that Jules had to make this decision without knowing the whole score? It's like playing Texas hold 'em when everyone else is playing straight. She only got to see half her cards before she decided to fold."

Xander pushed his fingers through his hair, making his forehead look twice as big in the process.

"Is it just me... or did that make a little sense?" Cathy asked quizzically, giving her lover a look.

"I always make sense. You guys just don't listen," Mike said smartly.

"None of it matters now," Xander said finally, swiping both hands across the air quickly. "Julie's gone, and I'm here, and why she left or why she didn't stay is irrelevant."

"Maybe she was pregnant," came a voice from behind them, almost so low that they couldn't hear.

Xander's eyes went wide, followed in suit by Mike and Cathy, as all three turned to see Tommy close his locker door and then lean against it. He was facing them, his patented smirk plastered across his face.

Xander took a step forward, his fists clenching without him even realizing it, as he glared at the taller man. His eyes burned with rage. "What... did you say?"

Tommy tried to contain his laughter and failed miserably, the chuckle erupting from his lips like a volcano. "I said someone probably knocked 'er up. Geez, you'd think you'd be in a better mood about it, unless it wasn't yours. First action you'd've gotten that wasn't off a dead chick, right?"

Xander drew back so quickly that the slowly gathering group of students didn't even see his motion, only the result. Tommy spun around quickly, his mouth distorted, blood spitting out onto the locker doors.

He slammed against the floor then immediately started to laugh again. He wiped the blood on his lips away with one sleeve as Xander glared down at him, fists still readied.

Mike came up behind Xander fast, pulling him back and shoving him against the far wall.

Xander tried only once to push away, but a quick look from Cathy ended the struggle.

"Oh, I get it," Tommy nodded, slowly rising to his feet as he tasted a sliver of the blood that was on his thumb. "You're going back to pretending you're not making googly eyes at Cathy, while she pretends not to make googly eyes at you?" he laughed. "Careful Xander, you might end up with another one pregnant... she's good at that."

Cathy turned to face the wall, trying to hide the tears that were welling up in her eyes.

Xander lunged again, something deep inside of him surging, wanting to rip into Tommy. He felt his claws aching within his fingertips, pulling at the skin until they were ready to burst. He let out a low growl deep within his throat, not loud enough for anyone but himself to hear.

Mike stopped him again, placing his palm flat against his friend's chest and shoving. "No," he said, turning from Xander back to Tommy, removing his hand. "He's not worth it."

Unnoticed by all, Cathy stiffened a little, her back straightening to ramrod precision.

Tommy snorted, looking to have too much laughter in him to express in one lifetime. "Oh, I'm so hurt. Whatever shall I fucking do? I'm not worth it. Oh no!"

Mike stepped forward, though not in a threatening way. "Y'know, as much of a jerk as he could be, I'm still glad Sud isn't around to see you acting like this."

Tommy met his gaze and clicked his tongue against the roof of his mouth. That stupid smile of his was still plastered across his face.

"You know what? Me too," he said cheerily, walking away from the three of them before turning left, stopping and deciding to go right instead.

Principal Shnieder watched the scene through the shutters of the glass door to his office as Tommy walked away from Mike and Xander, leaving them to console Cathy. He sighed, letting the plastic strips flip back into place as he held the phone tighter to his ear, laying the base back down on his desk.

"So, you see where I'm coming from," he said warmly. "These kids, they're starting to get out of control again. We can't have that. They need someone they can talk to, before another one decides to go crazy again... yes...yes."

While the person on the other end spoke, he carefully moved the letter opener on the corner of his desk and then adjusted the angle at which his business cards were facing.

"I know..." he said once they were done, nodding even though the person couldn't appreciate the gesture. "... I understand that it isn't the best of conditions for you. No offense, but it isn't for us either. You're my last resort. I need you, Robert. More importantly, these kids need you, and..."

Principal Shnieder stopped in response. Smiling as he went back to his chair, he sat down and put his feet up on the desk before rubbing one hand back through his scalp. "I understand... this will not effect your other responsibilities... we will work around your schedule... tomorrow? Thank you."

He hung up the phone, a sly grin spread across his lips as he leaned back into his chair.

There was a courtesy knock at the door before a pretty brunette popped her head in. "You busy, Mr. Shnieder?" she asked politely. He noticed there was a blonde girl behind her, waiting patiently to see the Principal.

"Not at all, Jennifer," he said, sitting up straight and straightening the papers on his desk.

𝄢𝄢𝄢

Xander leaned against the ripped and torn pool table, lining up a shot at the yellow one ball. He strained his eyes to see it properly and then adjusted his focus to look past it so that he could glare at Tommy.

Tommy sat at the bar, sipping on his cola. He watched as a young waitress passed by him, taking notice of all of her assets, and gave her a quick wink.

Xander tightened his brow and attempted his shot. The one missed its intended mark of the corner pocket completely, instead clacking against the eight and sending them both against the wall. He sighed before getting up again, shooting another sidelong glare at Tommy and shaking his head.

Cathy got up, rubbed some chalk against the top of her stick and then laid the half-used cube of blue powder on the side of the table. She jolted up next to Xander, her hair bobbing against his shoulder. "You missed," she said simply, giving him a curt smile.

He acknowledged her (barely) with a short grunt, wringing his stick with both hands as he imagined walking over to Tommy and using it to beat that smug look off of his lips.

Off to one side, leaning against a corner, Mike smiled at the two of them. He took a bite out of his Skor bar, its crisp almost-too-sweet goodness snapping off in his mouth. He peered at Tommy too, but his gaze was mostly fixated on Cathy. She'd been through a lot the past few months, and he was glad that what Tommy had said had not hurt her any more than that moment. "Keep your chin up, Xander," Mike said, his mouth full of candy. "She always chokes on the third-last ball." As both contestants ignored him, Mike's eyes began to stray around the room. It had been a long time since they had all come here, the three of them, like this. From the looks of things, it had been a long time since anyone had.

There were mock Persian rugs for sale, pinned up against the far wall. Each of them was brightly colored with earth tones, all with completely different patterns but the exact same aroma. Though one he could never quite name, it was in every Asian market or authentic restaurant he had ever visited. Mike loved that smell, it reminded him of his one and only trip to Los Angeles when he'd bought a Japanese dub on Highlander for three dollars at a cart in one such market. It had been two disks for an 190-minute movie, something he had marveled at at the time, but now seemed quite mundane. He had been impelled to choose Highlander from the large pile of DVDs because every other title had been pornos where the preview on the back had been a garbled mix of English and Spanish.

Near the rugs was the arcade section: a special, sunken part of the Factory that constantly radiated swirling lights and different noises and taunts. As a child, it was like a Siren's call. Eventually, the noises faded into the background but every now and then, if one got too close, one would still be pulled in. Most likely to one of the one-on-one fighting games that dominated the area.

Close to that was the bar, kitchen and tables. That was where Mike's senses really kicked into overdrive, making him forget exactly why anyone would not want to come here. Besides the smell of cheap booze and cigarette smoke (a vile combination that wafted not from the patrons but from the kitchen staff), there was the distinct fragrance of burgers frying on a grill. Big, thick, meaty burgers so greasy that you could feel your arteries clog as they slid slowly down your throat. The first time he had ordered one, it had taken him nearly an hour to devour the entire thing. Even then, he had to throw out almost half of it while his friends weren't looking and telling them he had finished the rest in one bite. To this day, this was still considered an impressive feat and was brought up on occasion.

On the wall that was directly in front of him -- the one behind Xander and Cathy as she sank her high ball then moved in for another -- were movie posters lined up with sticky tack, covering the bad plastering like cheap wallpaper. There were about thirty in all, from Timecop and The Breakfast Club all the way up to X-Men, but as far as Mike was concerned there was only one. One that caught his attention the second his eyes fell anywhere near it and any time: the poster for American Beauty.

The one with the blonde girl laying in a bed of roses, looking up at you with that come hither look in her eyes, mouth partially open and hair spread out in a halo around her head. She looked sublimely innocent lying there with dark red rose petals covering her breasts and mid-section, tongue barely visible, as if another petal rest inside her mouth.

As Mike stared deeper and deeper into the poster, he began to wonder if her tongue was like a rose petal. Soft and tender and quick, with such an odd and sweet taste that one would spend the first moments of the kiss trying to pin it down before relinquishing that thought into her body. When the imaginary kiss broke off, it was no longer the girl from the movie laying on the bed, but Cathy.

Cathy lay there, twisting about and moving her legs from side to side, shaking the rose petals that covered her but never moving them entirely. The result was like a quart of alcohol on Mike's system, blurring his vision to anything else. His mouth went dry and he felt his legs buckle.

She brought her finger up to her lip and touched it briefly with her tongue, smiling devilishly. She giggled at him when he quivered, then glanced down at herself, as if only just realizing how titillating she actually was. Grinning just a little, she stood up. All the rose petals fell to the bed, except for a few that stayed in her raven hair. She walked toward him slowly, her supple breasts waiting to be caressed, as were the curves of her soft, smooth body. He could already imagine what she felt like. *Remember* what she felt like. He remembered the hot, the moist... but mostly, he remembered the distinct taste of lime on his lips when he had kissed her...

"Mike," Cathy said again, a little louder this time, bringing him out of his trance. "What were you thinking about?" she grinned, just like she had in his daydream. The similarity startled him at first, making him wonder if her clothes would now fall to the floor and she would walk toward him with that look in her eyes.

He cleared his throat, and took one final look back at the image on the wall. It had gone back to being the young girl from the movie. Still hot, but nowhere near as satisfying as where his mind had taken it. He turned back to Cathy, smiling genuinely. "Nothing, sweety," he said as she pulled him into a kiss, her rose petal darting in and out of his mouth.

Xander watched their lips move for a second, then turned away and scanned the room. There were a few girls sitting closer to the kitchen then they were, each of them about the age that Mandy had been, thirteen or fourteen. Tommy was looking at them, too, and for a moment both men realized that they were thinking the same thing.

Their eyes met from across the room, both steely and cold. There was a silent dare between each, a promise that no matter what happened this would not be over easily. It was like two countries declaring war after years of uneasy peace.

Finally grinning, Tommy got up and walked over to the two girls. They laughed a little at something that he said, then he sat down next to them.

Again Xander felt his hands wringing the neck of his stick, his teeth grinding together. "I really hate that guy," he said under his breath, turning away before he broke the cue in half. "Smug, stupid bastard. I should drag him outside right now and give him what's been coming to him for months. Since Grendel's party. Since that time he kept hitting on Mandy. Since..."

"Since he saved your girlfriend's life and then she got all chummy with him alone in her hospital room," Mike said, breaking off the kiss long enough to breathe the words, then going in for one more peck before the couple turned to face Xander.

"Yes," Xander said, pointing at him in weird agreement. "Exactly. That's..." he shook his head and walked closer to the two of them, his footfalls heavy. "You can't tell me you guys don't see what's happening here?"

Cathy frowned. She reached out and touched Xander's arm, then remembered what Tommy had said about the both of them and let it fall to her side. "He's just... he's going through something too right now. Maybe he's just not handling it as well."

Xander groaned before he leaned over the pool table and fired at the seven ball. It connected, but ricocheted off the eight and sent it into the side pocket. Xander's head sunk down between his arms as Cathy giggled, then held her hand over her mouth to hide it. He sighed, throwing a sidelong glance at her, then fired the rest of the balls into the pockets one by one. When that was done, he reached into his pants pocket and withdrew a plastic cigarette case, from which he grabbed a Camel then pressed it between his lips firmly.

"Must you?" Cathy tisked in disgust, curling her upper lip at the sight of it.

"I really must," he replied, flicking the flint on the Bic lighter until flame spouted out the top of it. He lit the tip of the smoke, then closed his eyes and took a long drag, a smirk spreading over his lips.

"Maybe Tommy isn't the only one handling this the wrong way," Mike sighed, watching his friend inhale.

"Give it a rest, already," Xander barked back, smoke puffing out of his nose and mouth.

Cathy recognized the way he exhaled. There was a different way for every emotion he was feeling, she discovered. The quick, short burst of smoke from both his nostrils and his mouth meant that he was hurting, typically. "Look, Xander, Julie's leaving was hard on all of us."

"You hated her," he returned, almost laughing.

"I did," she nodded, in the exact same, sympathetic tone of voice. "I really, really did. But you didn't. You..."

"Don't even say it, Cathy," Xander ordered, pointing two fingers at her, his smoke lodged between them. "Don't even think it."

"You loved her," she said, making his arm drop.

His other hand rose, massaging the bridge of his nose and covering his eyes.

Mike looked away, realizing that he probably wouldn't be a part of this conversation.

She stepped toward him and tried to get his hand away from his face so that she could look at him, but he refused. Frowning, she tried again. This time he relented and immediately threw both arms around her, placing his head on her shoulder (a feat much easier now that she wore heels).

Mike turned away from the two as Cathy cooed soothingly, feeling his chest start to heave as he tried to force it not to. He looked over at Tommy, who was chatting away with the two young girls. At that moment, he looked up and glared at Cathy and Xander, smiling briefly at Mike.

From behind Tommy, the door to the kitchen opened and Joan stepped out with a tray full of nachos and laid them down onto the bar.

Joan was a big woman, and she reminded most of the Factory's patrons of Roseanne Barr with her witty, sarcastic nature. Up until a few months ago she would have come out of that kitchen with a wide smile on her face, laughing at something one of the kids had done or stopping to tell a quick joke. But since Roxanne's death there were dark circles around her eyes all the time. There were no more jokes or laughs, only the grim reality that things weren't as they were supposed to be.

Maybe things wouldn't have been quite so bad if business hadn't taken such a horrible turn after all of the murders. It didn't matter that Derek Smith was behind bars, and would remain there for what he had done. The streets weren't considered safe anymore, and neither was The Factory.

Mike watched her cross the room, keeping his eyes anywhere except for Xander and Cathy, trying to give his friend as much space as possible. The last thing he needed right now was to feel crowded or boxed in by the two of them coming in at him.

Xander's cigarette hung loosely on his bottom lip. The smoke drew up into his eyes and made them sting harshly. He put up with the discomfort as the smoke served a more devious purpose: it kept Cathy from getting too close, despite her manoeuvres and attempts to get him to look her in the eye.

His eyes began to well up and he blamed it on the smoke. Xander removed the cigarette for a moment and rubbed the tears away, yet still managed to keep Cathy mostly out of his field of view.

"I loved Sara," he said finally, barring his lip to keep in from shaking. "Julie was just... more convenient."

"This may shock you Xander, but it is possible to love more than one person at a time," she soothed, finally catching one of his hands between both of hers. She rubbed it with both her thumbs. "Like the way I love you and Mike."

"I didn't love her," he spat as he finally turned to look at her. Anger and pain drenched his voice and his nostrils flared. "I didn't. Maybe I thought I did, but I was wrong. You, I love. Sara. Mandy was lovable. Julie was difficult. She was unattainable. She was something I could chase but never have... basically something to occupy my time that went just a little bit too far. So, in other words... she was convenient."

"Just about anything's more convenient then a dead bitch," Tommy said as he sauntered over.

The three of them turned, their gazes following the looks and stares that the words had left in their wake, until they found the person who'd spoken them.

Everyone was silent for a moment. It seemed like even the deep fryers in the back had been hushed by the words, too shocked to form a coherent sentence. When it came time for someone to finally break the silence, it was Mike that found the words first.

"What did you just say?"

Tommy smirked as he leaned back on his chair and popped two chocolate chunks into his mouth. His voice was soothing yet venomous, like a combination of charmer and snake. "Well, Michael, I overheard Alexander and Catherine talking about the former's recent romantic woes, terrible bit of luck that it was. I distinctly heard Xander state repeatedly that Julie was more convenient. That lends to the thought that, to be more convenient, she had to be more convenient than someone else. Since the only other candidate is Sara... that makes a lot of sense. I mean, Julie puts up less fight getting her into bed then a dead girl, after all."

Again there was a silence. He had somehow managed to make his original statement even ghastlier.

Xander took a step forward. His smoke dropped from his lips and landed against his shoe, sending little sparks in all directions before it rolled away. His eyes were transfixed and wide. Another step forward, less slow and mechanical this time, brought a great scowl to his eyes. By the third step, he was almost flying through the air at Tommy. Cathy held him back, though she wasn't trying too hard.

"I am going to kill you," he said under his breath, pulling just slightly on Cathy's grip.

"Why not?" Tommy shrugged merrily as he popped more sweets into his mouth, chewing on them even as he spoke and making great smacking noises with every syllable. "Maybe me and Sara could do the undead bedroom squiggly. Then I'll have been in *both* of your girls."

Cathy let go of her grip on Xander.

He took a moment to register his freedom from her grasp, and only half of one afterward to act upon it. He lunged from where he stood, his feet barely touching the ground as he crossed the twenty feet of dead air between he and Tommy in a heartbeat. He grabbed the mocker by the scruff of his shirt and pinned him against the wall, wrinkling and tearing the posters that adorned it.

"I will rip you in two," he said, so low it was barely audible, using every ounce of restraint he had in him not to completely let loose.

"Why? I'm only telling you the truth," Tommy grinned. He wiped some saliva from his chin and then patted it onto Xander's cheek. "Why do you think she wanted to talk with me at the hospital? She wanted to thank me for putting it to her so good. She even slipped me a twenty for it."

Nobody else in the room moved as Tommy watched Xander's face be at war with itself, looking like every emotion he was feeling was fighting for dominance. And while everyone else in the room could know what Xander must have been going through right now, nobody else could *understand*.

Nobody else was the Black Womb.

Xander felt pain pulse from the tip of each of the fingers in his left hand, the one that held Tommy to the wall. The one that was irritatingly close to the foolhardy youth's neck. It was pain that could have easily been ceased, simply by giving in to the urge that had been building for years now. The urge to end Tommy Irons.

The urge to pop his claws.

Four-inch retractable claws positioned at the end of each finger, each one made of the same dense bone that was inside his lean, muscular body. His lanky form and loose clothing hid a being of formidable physique, capable of world-class athleticism. Blood filled his mouth as a second row of teeth emerged behind his normal ones: this set razor-sharp and able to regenerate. Shark's teeth. His eyes, although they appeared normal, saw more than anyone else in the room. They saw through shadows and the tricks of light. His hearing was strong enough to perceive Tommy's heartbeats, and to know how calm and relaxed the arrogant prick was about this entire situation. Most phenomenal though was the organ which lay deep within his right side. It had the ability to act as any other organ and heal Xander's body past the point of what was previously thought possible. It could even cover his body in a thick, black liquid armor, transforming him into the thing that stalked the nights and punished evil men.

As Tommy squirmed in his hands, the thought of transforming right then and there and gutting him like a fish became almost too appealing to pass up.

Tommy smiled, waiting to see what Xander would do.

Xander drew back, then felt a firm hand on his shoulder. He turned slightly, just enough to see Mike standing behind him, a somber look on his face. Xander panned around the room a little, seeing Joan, Cathy, and a few other Factory patrons watching and waiting on the outcome.

"Come on, Xander," Mike said, squeezing a little. "Tommy's a jerk. I'd like to hand his face to him, too. But he's not worth this."

Cathy tensed.

Mike kept his hand on Xander, and after a moment Xander began to feel the full weight of it. It felt heavy. "He's not that bad."

Xander sighed, turning back to Tommy, who was still smirking wickedly.

"Yes he is," Xander said after a moment, raising Tommy about two inches higher, much to everyone's surprise -- especially Tommy's.

"Am I the only person who still sees it?" he asked rhetorically. "It's like everyone got used to having him around or something. 'Hah Ha, Tommy did this.' 'Oh my gawd, I can't believe Tommy said that,' and everyone thinks it's all in fun. Fun?" he sighed, almost laughing. "Well, what everyone seems to forget is that this guy is going to grow up and become a *man*. A man that grew up getting away with what all of you let him get away with. Grow up actually being encouraged by most to act this way. And he's going to be one of those truly awful human beings that will do something to one of *your* children and then you'll all get on the evening news like ignorant idiots and say 'Oh, he was always such a nice boy. We exchanged cards every Christmas. I never saw this coming.'"

Xander relaxed his grip on Tommy, who was no longer smiling, and slowly lowered him to the ground. "Well, when it happens, don't forget to mention the guy that warned you of it years before, and you were all too stupid to listen."

Tommy twisted away from Xander's grasp, then chuckled a little as he fixed his collar. He feigned a smile, then walked back to his table, grabbed up another chocolate chunk and put it in his mouth as Xander pulled out another smoke and lit it.

"You're right," he mumbled under his breath as he chewed. "I'm not a nice guy. And it's about time I reminded everyone of that. Especially you, Xander."

Xander snorted. He turned and nodded to Mike as the both of them walked back toward their table, where both Joan and Cathy stood waiting and looking panicked. Xander slumped into a chair, hunching his shoulders as a bittered look came over him.

Mike regarded his sulking friend and shook his head in dismay. "Was all that really necessary?" he asked in a hushed voice as they joined the girls.

Xander avoided his friend's gaze, keeping his eyes locked in his peripheral vision. From the corner of his eye, he saw Julie leaning against the bar, frowning at him. He turned to see her completely, only to realize that there nobody was there.

Cathy's hand went immediately to Mike's, squeezing it softly.

Joan sighed, all but collapsing into her chair as tears formed in her eyes, only to be wiped away by her sleeve as soon as they came. "It's for reasons just like this..." she half-whispered to herself, drawing the attention of everyone else in the room.

Xander turned to face her now, ignoring whatever it was he thought he saw.

Cathy put a hand on Joan's shoulder, which she immediately shoved aside.

"...this town isn't like it used to be. I just can't anymore," she sobbed. "I didn't want to do this with all of you here, but we're going to be closing. For good."

The entire room was silent now, all eyes on her. Except for Tommy. He was still chewing on his wad of chocolate.

"I'll give it a month, just for you kids... but after that, I'm done. The Factory is done."

There was a stillness in the room. An unexplainable quality as each person looked to the next for clues on how to feel, but nobody really knew. This building, under one name or another, had been a part of their lives since before they could remember. It had been a part of their parents' lives. Many of their parents had actually met and had their first dates in this building. Now, for the first time in generations, it wasn't going to be here.

Cathy again put her hand on Joan's shoulder, and this time it was not rebuked, but welcomed.

Amid the mute motionlessness, one man stirred.

Tommy Irons got up from his table, his horrible grin having been wiped from his face, and fixed the collar on his jacket. He walked to the exit, turned to see if anyone was following him, and scoffed when nobody did. He slammed the door behind him, shaking the entire building.

CHAPTER TWO: ARE

Deep in the dark he swallowed hard, tasting blood from his lower lip. He had spent the last two hours rending it to shreds with his own teeth. The metallic taste filled his mouth and he grinned in grim satisfaction, revealing teeth and gums lined with red.

Drawing back his head, he snorted then spat out a large wad of blood and saliva onto his fingers. Laughing, he brought them toward the concrete wall he sat against and made a line straight down, then a semi-circle on the top on the right side with another, smaller line coming off from that. It was the letter R.

He giggled gleefully to himself, spitting more blood onto his hand.

CHAPTER THREE: DEFINITIONS

"Amalgam."

Xander looked up from the file folder that he cradled in his arms and shot a glance at Mike (who had spoken the word), before turning back and continuing to read.

There was a long silence between the two in the dead of the room, Mike's nose buried deep in a folder all his own, one a kind of tanned green color.

Finally, Xander slapped his folder shut and sighed. "Okay, I'll bite," he said, laying his reading assignment aside. "What is it?"

Mike looked up from the file, as if just now realizing that Xander was there. "Amalgam," he said again, leaning in so that Xander could see his records as well. "He uses that word over and over again. In like, every sentence O'Toole describes you with it."

Xander glanced at his own folder, which they had stolen last week from their deceased Guidance Counselor's office after realizing that he had been involved in a plot against Xander and his friends. "He does it in mine, too. What's your point?"

"What does it mean?"

"Amalgam. Distorted. To distort. To merge. Basically a half-image of what was before. It was also a DC / Marvel crossover in the 1990's before Joe Quesada came in and decided that crossovers were lame, in which Marvel and DC heroes merged to form new heroes, which were amalgams of the originals. Most notable are Dark Claw, made by combining Wolverine and Batman, and Spider-Boy, created from Spider-Man and Superboy. As another fun fact, it is a romance term coming from an ancient Greek word that translates to 'emollient.' This matches its term in chemistry where it is a softening agent, usually with Mercury... Perhaps only with Mercury."

"I knew what the word meant. I meant why does he keep using it. It's like he's obsessive compulsive about it or something."

"I think you're reading a little too much into this. Is it possible he just misplaced his thesaurus? Besides, it's a pretty accurate description of my ties to the Black Womb."

Mike let that bounce around in his head for a moment, frowning. "I guess. It just seems like he was trying to tell us something."

Xander picked up his file again, flipping through it. "Mike, the man hypnotized us -- gawd, I feel stupid saying that -- then tried to mind-fuck us all over the course of several months. Me and Mandy most of all. According to what we've found here, he also performed experiments on us at some point, trying to make sure that I actually was the Womb. He also sicked Genblade, the Tees, Zakron, and Circe on us, and was probably a party to more than that before we even showed up on the scene. We also don't have any clue what *future* plans he might have had in store for us that might be waiting just around the corner. That's why we've got to figure out these files, find out exactly what Circe knows about all of us, and see if we can figure out when and where they'll strike at us next."

"You don't think there's even a slight chance that we beat them and now they'll leave us alone?" Mike chuckled.

Xander shot him a look.

"Right, sorry. I forgot I was living in an episode of Passions there for a second."

Outside his window, Xander thought he saw something move between his house and the Johnson's, but he paid little to no attention to it.

Her eyes stared forward at her husband, without feeling or emotion. This wasn't the first time. Neither of them moved and neither of them spoke: they simply lay there and looked at one another in a still silence.

Blood dried all around them and the foul stench of death rose up in heated wafts, coating the curtains and the walls; it was the kind of stink that future tenants would complain about for years to come. Their eyes were shrouded and cloudy, their lips cold and dry.

If Jaylen had been alive, this might have reminded her of the first few moments after their first time making love. She had been more than a little drunk. He'd tell her years later that he had dropped some ecstacy earlier that night while he was out with his friends. The two had been dating for several weeks, after meeting at one of her college orientations. He'd already graduated, but stayed around campus, still clinging to the last strings of his old life. He'd come over that night just to talk, a fact they both maintained over the years that followed. He had lived all the way across town, and it was late, so they both decided that he would stay the night.

When it was over, they had just looked at one another, their eyes dead and cold, not knowing what to feel or say. They hadn't spoken or moved, or even made the effort to take him out... they had just lain there, staring at one another.

If Lee had been alive, he would have been looking at her breasts. He had always loved her breasts, but now they seemed somehow different. It was one of those subtle ways that dead bodies looked so different from ones that are alive. Her breasts no longer moved and bounced when she breathed the way they would if her lungs were still drawing air. The color had already gone out of them, too. She looked more and more like an extremely well-articulated mannequin, positioned in the worst possible way.

The front door creaked open, and there was the sound of heavy footsteps on the floor, scuffing against the mat as they came in.

"Oh my gawd."

⋏⟨⋋

In his room, still surrounded by ripped shards of the pictures he had taken over the past few years, Tommy sobbed relentlessly, his entire body shaking. He scooped up the pictures and was tossing them into a burnt up coffee tin, stuffing as many of them down inside at a time as he could. Images of his family and his friends, of lovers and hopefuls, of enemies and idiots, all crammed together in the small pot until there was nothing left but a bare, lifeless room.

Fumbling in his pockets he found a pack of matches, and struck one dramatically. It illuminated his face in the dark room, casting eerie shadows over his features and the walls. After gazing into the flame for a moment, he dropped the match into the tin before it could burn his fingers, and watched as the images began to melt and contort as the fire found each one.

He watched as the fire found an image of Randy and his father, smouldering its way up their bodies until only their heads were left. Eventually those were burned and distorted too.

He wiped the last of his tears away, smiling wickedly.

⋏⟨⋋

The Factory was empty now, nothing but cobwebs and dust to keep Joan company as the radio blared some junk in the background that she thought was by Billy Talent, so she tried her very best to ignore it, using it only to drown out the sound of the silence.

She swept her broom against the tiled floors, wondering with each stroke why she was even bothering. It was over. She stared around the room at the posters and memorabilia she'd put up over the years. Pictures of her and Roxanne back when they'd bought the place together, both smiling wide, sitting in one of the corner booths, holding up their glasses of champagne to the camera. For the life of her, she could not remember exactly who had taken that picture, but it was right on the tip of her tongue.

Forcing herself to turn away, she continued to sweep the dirt from her patrons' shoes into a large pile in the center of the room, letting out a heaving sigh that shook her entire body.

It wasn't supposed to be like this. She wasn't sure how or why anymore, but she knew that it was supposed to be different, somehow. The world used to be something brighter, sunnier, and now it was just a dank room filled with dirt and musk.

As she walked by a table she picked up a bottle of cola and tossed it toward a garbage can about ten feet away. It made the odd sound of hollow plastic as it ricocheted off the rim of the can, bouncing to the floor before rolling under a nearby table.

She cursed to herself, then rested her broom up against a chair and walked over to the table.

There was a sound behind her and she turned quickly, expecting to see some teen settling into one of the video game machines that adorned the walls.

There was nothing but the stereo, still blaring out mindless drivel, finally getting toward the end of that insipid song. Scanning the room just once, paying close attention to the shadows and the crevices, she turned back toward the table.

Her bones ached in objection as she bent down on her hands and knees to collect the wayward bottle. As it lingered just out of her reach, she briefly considered adding a recycling bin to the Factory, before reality closed in, squeezing ever tighter on her psyche.

The song finally ended, and she closed her eyes in thanks, wondering why she never listened to anything but this station. After a brief moment with a stuttering DJ who tripped over nearly every word, a new song came on. Its jazzy beginning immediately identified it as Livin' La Vida Loca. She suddenly found herself wishing for Billy Talent again.

"She's into superstition, black cats and voodoo dolls. I've got a premonition, that girl's gonna make me fall..."

She heard that sound again behind her, but couldn't quite put her finger on it. There was also a damp, musty odor in the air that would have driven her into obsessive-compulsive cleaning on any night but tonight. She turned away from the bottle again in an attempt to identify the sound.

A sharp pain erupted in the back of her neck, followed by a warm trickling sensation around it on both sides, down around to her chest. The smell became as overwhelming as the heat of her attacker's breath. She turned as she fell back to the floor, staring wide-eyed as she struggled for breath that would not come, the air lost in the obvious hole in her neck.

In that instant before death, as her murderer's hands wrapped around her shirt and pulled her close, she remembered exactly who had taken the picture...

CHAPTER FOUR: BETWEEN

Xander stared at his hands as he sat between Mike and Cathy against Julie's old locker. He was trying to command the Black Womb, to force its vaunted stealth and bodily control and bend it to his own will, but was failing miserably. It seemed to matter how hard he tried, he could not stop his hands from shaking.

"How did it happen?" Cathy asked finally, her own hands buried in her armpits to try and stop them from being so cold, as she rocked back and forth ever so slightly.

There was an almost tactile silence between Mike and Xander then, as each urged the other to speak first. In times like these, they'd discovered that the wrong words could be the death of you.

"We're not sure," Xander said finally, letting his head fall back against the locker, followed by a reverberating echo from within it. "All we know is that she was killed. That it was... savage... even by the standards we've set over the past few months. That the first blow killed her, and that whoever did it just kept hitting her long after she'd died."

"This wasn't just a murder," Mike nodded, staring at the opposite wall. "This was somebody's idea of a party."

"Maybe," Xander added quickly, raising a finger. "We're not sure of anything yet. From what I've been hearing around town, Joan wasn't the first, which probably means she won't be the last. They haven't released the name of the first victim yet, but they have given Joan's. There has to be a reason for that. We find that reason, and we'll find out why Joan was killed. And by who."

There was a pause as Cathy absorbed all of the information. She opened her mouth as if to speak, stopped, then leaned forward and looked at the both of them. "And what good will that do?"

"What?" Mike whispered, squinting at her.

"What good will come of that?" she reiterated, her eyes a mix of pain and fear. "Are we stopping what's happening? Are we making people die less? Every time we do this, someone else decides that they want to be a serial killer. Julie left because she didn't want a part in this life anymore... maybe we should start thinking of doing the same thing. Just getting out of the way and trying not to get killed."

"Cat..." Mike soothed, placing a hand on her elbow.

"No," Xander interrupted, shaking his head at his friend. "No, she's not wrong. You guys should steer clear of this one. Of every one. I've been saying that since the first time we went out. This is my fight. My vow. You two should never have been --"

"You, too," Cathy stated bluntly, grabbing his chin and turning him toward her. "This isn't where you should be either. We've got to stop this. We can't just keep leaping into harm's way like this."

"We have to protect --" Mike interjected, only to be again cut off.

"*I* have to protect these people," Xander said, stopping him. "I started this... horror, and I have to be the one to finish it. Otherwise everyone'll end up dead like Julie!"

The three of them fell silent again. Mike and Cathy stared at Xander as his chest heaved up and down furiously.

"Mandy," he corrected, his voice softer now. "You'll end up like poor Man-dy."

All three looked down at the floor in front of them, letting out a sigh in near unison.

As people continued to walk past the trio, ignoring them, the friends sat and considered what had just been said.

"Hello, my son," came a calm, gentle voice from somewhere in from of them.

They looked up to see Reverend Robert Gallagher smiling down at them, regarding them with a curt but kind nod, his hands clasped in front of him.

"Father?" Xander said, speaking first, scrambling to his feet.

"Hello, Mr. Drew," said the man as he extended his hand, which Xander accepted. The younger man's skin grew goose-bumps at the older's soft touch, and he thought he felt the Womb deep inside of him twitch, just once, ever so slightly. "It's been a long time since I've seen you in my confessional."

Mike regarded Xander with a quizzical glance as both he and Cathy rose to their feet as well, smiling politely at the Reverend.

"Yes..." Xander agreed, finding himself feeling more than a little sheepish. "I am sorry. I always mean to, but can very rarely find the time."

"I still see you up in the graveyard every couple of days. It would do you well to come in some time and talk. And just so you know... we are still open on Sundays."

Xander almost laughed at that, then turned his head toward his friends. "This is Mike Harris and Cathy Kennessy," he said quickly, realizing that he had failed to introduce them.

"A pleasure," Mike said under his breath, shaking his hand just as Xander had.

"The same," Gallagher smiled, then turned to Cathy. "And you I know. I was there at your confirmation... if I do recall."

Cathy almost blushed, then leaned in to give the man a quick hug. "What brings you here?" she asked once they'd parted.

"Actually..." he smiled, although his gaze shifted from them for the first time since the beginning of the conversation.

"You did," came a decidedly less comforting, whiny voice from down the hall. Principal Shnieder walked toward them in his typical marching stance, the lights gleaming off his nearly bald scalp.

Mike raised an eyebrow. "How's that now?"

Shnieder smiled wide, also shaking the Reverend's hand. "Thank you for coming," he said, before turning back to the students. "All of you, actually. He's come by to lend this school a hand in her time of need, and we all thank him very much for it."

The three of them exchanged the same look, then turned back again.

"How's that?" Mike repeated, making it clear that Shnieder had in no way answered the question.

"I'm going to be the new Guidance Counselor," Gallagher smiled, again clasping his hands before him.

Xander's nostrils flared at the thought of it, his eyes darting toward Mike, who he could tell had the exact same feeling. "Well," he said, plastering on a fake smile. "That's just super."

CHAPTER FIVE: AWOL

"Stab wound number three, victim one," he sighed, leaning in close, bending and twisting the overhanging light to get a better look at the wound in question. Lance Berkshire used tweezers to scrape congealed blood into a clear plastic bag and sealed it tight.

He had been a forensic pathologist at Coral Beach Precinct Morgue for almost ten years, and in the last three months, the sheer number of dead bodies he had seen easily tripled. Behind him, his associate Harry Ford performed a similar action on one of the wounds sustained to victim number two: a middle-aged male named Lee Piercey. The victims had been husband and wife.

"What have you got?" Harry asked as he went over the body systematically with a large magnifying glass, using the system that had taken him years to hone and perfect. "Anything probative?"

Lance squinted. "This wound... all of them, they're... very odd."

Harry looked up. With the number of cuts and stabs the pair suffered; he was surprised to hear Lance say that anything was odd. "What's so weird about them?"

"Well..." he sighed again, placing a hand against her cold body to help him get a closer look, "Most wounds move in some kind of order, depending on the direction of the blade and the position of the killer: right to left, and more importantly, deep to shallow. The depth of the slice isn't consistent."

"And hers is?" Harry asked, removing something from Lee's body, putting it into another plastic bag, then labeling it carefully with a felt tipped marker.

"No. Far from it, actually," he almost laughed and then stopped himself self-consciously. "It starts shallow, then goes deeper... then becomes shallow again. Like a letter V. If I didn't know better, I'd say it was a straight stab, but it doesn't match any of the other weapon marks we've seen on either victim."

"You saying there was another weapon, used for just one blow... or maybe she was forced against something in the house, a corner or something? Gimmie a hand, will you?"

"No, I don't think," Lance said, getting up and moving over to Lee's side with Harry. "I think the killer made it that way purposely, like he was playing... you know? There's no bruising around the wound and it's pale, it was postmortem... I really think the killer was just playing doctor."

"Creepy," Harry agreed, putting two hands under Lee. Lance did the same. "Three!" Harry said at once. They'd done this so many times no explanation or further count was needed. They rolled Lee over onto his back to continue their autopsy. The back was caked in blood and bile, shaped into the pattern of the floor due to the amount of time he had spent on it.

Lance's eyes went wide, and Harry stepped back a pace as they both saw it, clear as day, imprinted on Lee's upper right shoulder.

"I think I know why they haven't released the names of these two yet," Harry said.

Tattooed on Lee's shoulder was a bright red letter T.

"They don't want to alarm the family."

"Omega," Cathy said simply, taking the buckle out of her hair as she did and placing it on Xander's night table. Her hair immediately fell in front of her eyes, as it always did when not restrained, and she quickly brushed it back behind her ear with one smooth motion of her fingertips.

The radio played 'Have a Nice Day' by Bon Jovi just low enough so that they could hear it, keeping the awkward silences to a minimum.

Xander looked up from his file folder, which contained a detailed account of the Anti-Womb and the events surrounding it, and stared at her. She looked so cute, her legs crossed Indian-style, a folder in her lap, looking down at it as she took a bite of her Crunch bar. "You and your bo... somebody's gotta start talking to you about speaking in full sentences."

"No..." Cathy huffed, getting up and moving over next to Xander on the bed. "This is it. He's talking about the Tees and the Omegas... and the Snakes, whatever they are."

"Rival gang here in town. Only a few members. Nothing like the Tees. They pretty much just steal from grocery stores. Bumped into one or two here and there. Nothing to write home about."

"Ah," Cathy nodded, continuing. "Anyway, this is it. This is where he talks about the deal he made with Randy... I think."

"You think?"

"His handwriting's all lopsided here... and every second word is misspelled, misused, or misplaced."

Xander took the file from her for a second, bringing it to he nose and taking in the scent of it. "He was drunk. It stinks of Rye and Coke. And a little Vodka."

"Ugh," Cathy grimaced, taking the folder back. "Anyone ever tell you that that enhanced senses junk can be majorly creepy sometimes?"

Xander turned toward her, inhaling deeply, his nostrils flaring. He calmly turned back to his own file. "Mike got to third base with you last night on the couch in his basement. There was a scented candle. Vanilla."

Cathy's mouth dropped, and she slapped him once. "Isn't it some kind of super-hero rule that you can't use your powers like that?"

"You don't need super-human senses to see somebody's tongue hanging out, or them wearing the same clothes they did the night before," he mumbled calmly.

Cathy grinned. "Any*way*."

"Yes. Something about the Tees?"

She nodded, fixing her hair again, then went back to the file. "It talks a lot about how he approached them; how he told Randy about you."

"Just Randy, right?"

"Uh-huh. Part of the deal. It doesn't say why."

"Doesn't need to. He's a scientist. Needed controlled variables. Too many people knowing messes up all his equations, and then the experiment doesn't work out the way he thought."

"Which it didn't anyway."

"He didn't count on Genblade waking up. None of us did."

"Mmm," she hummed in agreement. "Then it gives us..." she stopped, eyes growing wide.

"What?" Xander said, almost not paying attention, looking over notes on the Anti-Womb by one of its original creators. "What does it say?"

Cathy sat up straight in the bed, her eyes dancing over the page wildly, trying to take in all of the information on it at once. "It's a list of all of the Tees and Omegas."

Xander sat up so quickly that if she'd been looking at him, she still would not have seen him. He looked over her shoulder at the list, which stretched onto the next page.

"How can there be so many?" she said, more to herself than to him.

"You'd be surprised what people are capable of," he growled. "Especially when there are enough others doing the exact same thing. Mob mentality and all that. If you're part of a group, you're not the one doing the damage -- It's the group. No blame, no guilt."

"Justin Langley, Sven Douglas, Ian Char, Duncan Coombs, Quintin Travers, Randy Owchar, Terrance Owchar, Elliot Piercy, Steve Matthews, Dwayne Piercey, Ryan Matthews, George Walker, Jason Moony, Danny Quire, Nicolas Sharp..."

"Wait," Xander stopped, pointing at the last few she read. "I don't recognize those last ones."

"There's a red mark on them... it's on George Walker, too. Kerri's dad. Maybe that's a mark for Tees that are no longer active members, one's that quit?"

"You don't quit the Tees," Xander mumbled, taking the folder away slowly. "They quit you. They tell you when you've had enough." He looked long and hard at the symbol marking each of them. It was a circle with twisted lines coming out of the bottom of it, and looked almost like a squat up stick man. "And I've seen this before somewhere... in the files." He turned the page and saw a list of at least forty more Tees, all with the same red symbol next to them. He scanned down the list quickly, eyes fluttering. "I know a lot of these people... my Mom plays bridge with some of them."

Cathy stopped at one name, pointing to it. "Lee Piercey. Why does that one sound so familiar?"

"Dwayne's cousin," Xander responded. "Family ties, which isn't surprising.

It can't have just been Randy that was a legacy. This type of bigotry is passed down through generations. I always thought that might be the case, but there was never enough for me to act." He clenched his lower lip.

The radio stopped on some mid-90's Bryan Adams song mid-beat, interrupting with the familiar chime that preceded all that station's news broadcasts.

"Following another possibly-related death in the town of Coral Beach, police have released the names of two victims from last night's murders. Jaylen and Lee Piercey were found dead in their own home…"

Xander and Cathy shot looks at one another, staring at Lee's name on the list. "My god…" Xander sighed. "It's starting again, isn't it?"

"I don't know," Cathy frowned. "But somebody sure seems like they want it to."

ʎ⟨ʎ

The sun was almost down when Mike opened the back door to The Factory. He did it in the same careful way he'd watched Agent Tim White do it, so as to not arouse police suspicions. Very slowly and calmly, he shut the door behind him to avoid the click of the old lock.

It did anyway.

The sound reverberated off of the walls back and forth until it seemed to be coming at Mike from all directions.

He turned around slowly, looking at the place where he'd spent so many nights, just hanging out or playing pool or hitting on girls. It all looked the same: the posters, the games, the tables… everything. That surprised him more than anything had in a long while. He had expected it to be different, to be tainted or stained with the act that had occurred here, but it wasn't. Each one of the games still hummed away, playing their sound clips and voice-overs, inviting people to come and play them.

He sighed and adjusted his jacket, which had been bunching in the back the whole way over, then walked toward the bar. As he got closer, he could see the outline of white tape that the police had left to mark where Joan's body had been, not that it was needed. The large, human shaped void in the pool of blood was a sufficient reference point.

Careful not to step in anything, he knelt down next the where she must have lain for her last few moments, looking at the redness that surrounded it. He followed one trail that went up and to the right, noting where it splashed on the stools, then onto the bar itself, the Beatles poster on the wall, and finally created a splash or two on the ceiling. He followed the trail back down, his eyes scanning every last droplet.

His brow scrunching as he began picturing the murder, Mike leaned over the body the way the killer must have. He cupped an imaginary knife and began slashing at the air just above the chalk line. Craning his neck, he watched the direction his arm went in after every slice, trying to calculate where castoff from the weapon would go. It completely bypassed the bar, and would have ended up across Van Morrison's face.

127

Adjusting the angle at which he struck to a backhanded slash, he watched where the blood went now. Across the bar, onto the Beatles poster, and depositing one or two drips on the ceiling. He allowed himself a smile.

Glancing to the left, he saw two more distinct blood trails, and tossed his pretend blade from one hand to the other before repeating the same series of motions. Again it worked, sending the castoff in the exact direction the blood actually went.

He stood again, unclenching his hand in the process, and stepped away to follow the third trail. It didn't go far, and it didn't go up. Instead it stayed on the floor, away from the walls, not like the others, until it reached the corner. Then, it turned. There was a single drip on the other side of the corner. Turning to look at where he'd walked from, Mike imagined himself walking again, holding the knife... blood dripping from it onto the floor, shaking the last bit off as he turned the corner. He looked up the wall, seeing the tiniest smear on the ledge of a still open window.

Again, he smiled a little. Just a little.

"Oh man! You did great!" came a whiny voice from behind him, and he turned quickly, fists clenched and ready.

He was standing face to face with a Marvel vs. Capcom arcade game, which was displaying a list of top scores, scrolling across the screen in blue flashing letters. He walked over to it slowly, the light from the screen bathing his face in blues and reds. The violence on the screen reflected in his eyes and took him back to a time not so long ago, when he wouldn't have had to do things like this.

ʎ∨ʎ

-clack, crack!-

He pressed the pinky of his right hand against the palm of his left, cracking the bone and feeling the slight rush as pressure released from the joints. He grinned slightly as he sat on the edge of his bunk, moving from one finger to the next, cracking his knuckles, and looking forward at the bars of his cell.

The cell bar's shadows made lines across his tanned, cracked face as he glared silently into the hallway outside. The smooth, clean walls taunted him, as he yearned to simply open the door and step out into freedom.

A stiff breeze came through, bringing with it the familiar stench of urine that one never got entirely accustomed to, making all the hairs on both his massive arms stand on end. He sniffed back a glob of mucus, spitting it as far into the hall as he could, then wiped his mouth with the sleeve of his orange jumpsuit. It was ripped and torn in places from too many fights in the prison yard, so many that they now only allowed him access to it at certain times when there weren't as many inmates. When it was just him and the crazies -- the ones they didn't mind seeing ripped limb from limb. Hell, the guards set up an online shop where they sold security footage.

One such tear was right over his heart. Some punk kid from the next cell over had given it to him with a homemade shiv fashioned from an old toothbrush.

From the smell of the little bastard, it had been all he'd ever used the toothbrush for. Though the fabric was ripped, one could still see most of the letters of his name, but not all: Char.

Terrence Owchar.

But that wasn't what they called him, and it wasn't what that kid had yelled right before he lunged at him.

He had called him Roulette.

⋀⋁⋀

Xander poured steaming hot water onto some oats, brown sugar, and apple slices, watching as the steam rose up from the concoction slowly, turning it into mush. He flared his nostrils and breathed deep, taking in as much of the aroma as he could.

"That smells so good," Cathy said from her spot against the window at the kitchen table, practically salivating as she spoke.

"Your favorite," he smirked, adding a little canned milk, followed by the slightest squirt from a re-sealable bag of sweetened condensed milk that his mom didn't think he knew about. Taking a spoon out of a nearby cupboard, he stirred it quickly, until most of it looked the same; its various ingredients spaced evenly throughout the blue bowl that had long ago been deemed Cathy's bowl when at this house. He placed it down in front of her, and she quickly ran her fingers through her matted black hair, forcing it behind her shoulders to avoid making a mess while she ate.

"Thanks," she replied honestly, as she picked up the spoon and dug in, trying harder than one would expect for a bonus apple slice. "Been a while since we've done this."

Xander smirked and set down a glass of cold milk on the place-mat as he sat on the chair opposite her. "Too long," he agreed, then raised his glass to her in a pretend 'cheers' before downing its entire contents.

She frowned at him. "That's not all you're having, is it?"

He nodding, laying down the glass. "Don't need to eat, remember? Only reason I'm even having this is my throat feels dry."

She smirked.

"What?"

"Do you realize I slept on top of you last night?" she asked, taking another spoonful of oatmeal, this time getting one of her much-sought apple slices.

"Yeah..." he trailed, blushing a little. "How about we leave that part out when Mike asks where you were last night?"

"Not that, silly. You didn't... you know... go out."

Xander smiled and started watching his fingers dance along the edge of his glass, trying to avoid eye contact with her. "You noticed that too, huh?"

"How long has it been, since the last time you went out at night without trying to?" she asked as she leaned forward excitedly, her hair falling off her shoulders again.

"At least a week and a half, but I think its been more. A lot more. I just only

129

really started noticing enough to pay attention a week and a half ago. I also don't notice it... I dunno, twitching?... for no apparent reason anymore. It's like..."

"Like you're getting control."

Xander smirked, again looking down at the table.

"Why didn't you tell me?"

"Didn't wanna jinx it. Plus, I don't get to see you as much anymore. You've got Mike, and I've been spending a lot more time with..." he trailed off, his voice growing dim as the smile slowly faded from his lips. "You've got Mike, so we haven't been seeing each other as much anymore."

She sighed, reaching out a hand to touch his. "It's her loss, you know. Any girl would be lucky to have you."

He finally met her gaze head on, as her thumb rubbed the tender flesh between his thumb and forefinger, sending shivers up and down his spine.

Inside him, the Womb flinched, making him adjust his position uncomfortably.

"Any girl would," she repeated, bending her head down to reestablish their line of sight.

"Sara used to say that, too," he said glumly. He took a long pause, then got up and brought his glass to the sink to rinse out. "Is it some kind of girl code, or something 'I think you'd make a lot of girls happy, but not me and not anyone I know?'" He sighed.

"That's not it at all," Cathy pleaded as she dug her spoon back into her breakfast.

"Isn't it?" he almost snapped, but stopped himself and pursed his lips. "It seems like everyone wants me to be with someone, that everyone thinks I'd make this amazing boyfriend, but no girl will actually give me the chance to be it. And you know why? Because we both know that I make one crappy fucking boyfriend, Julie."

She looked like she was about to say something, then stopped and tilted her head to one side.

"...Cathy," he amended, leaning against the counter as if it were all that were holding him up. "We both know it."

"Oh, is that so?" she smirked, almost laughing.

"What's so funny? Ha hah, Xander's in pain?"

"No, it's..." she motioned down at her cereal bowl with her spoon. "We're not even together, and look at this. You spent all night snuggled up with me in your arms and never once even tried something that could in any way be considered a move, you get up and make me my favorite breakfast, you talk to me about what's on your mind... Xander, you're right, you wouldn't make a good boyfriend. You'd make an amazing boyfriend. And if you think I wouldn't take full advantage of that if anything happened between me and Mike..." she let that sentence fall off, not needing or wanting to finish it. "It's just that things keep getting in the way. You have to choose not to let them."

Xander nodded, smirking at her. But his eyes looked distant, lost in some horrible thought.

"What is it?"

"Something Julie said. When she left," Xander sighed, rubbing the bridge of his nose. "She said that it wasn't Sara... that it wasn't that I still love her, in ways that I couldn't love Julie. That it was what I really love more than anything. Said that I love death and as long as I do, death will keep following me, wherever I go, and that she couldn't be a part of that anymore."

Cathy let those words hang in the air for a moment, picking her time to speak carefully. The right words said at the wrong time right now could mean the difference between closing up the walls he had around his heart again, something that could take months to undo. "Do you think any part of that's true?"

He looked up at her, and she expected to see tears in his eyes, but there were none. "I think it's all true. I think she's right... and more than that, I think you were right."

She grinned mischievously to herself. "I'm always right," she said coyly. "But, be more specific, which part?"

"Back at the school, before Gallagher interrupted us. I think you were right. After this one... I'm finished. I've got control now. I've avenged Sara's memory a hundred times over... I'm done. This is the end of the Black Womb."

Her eyes went wide, her smile spreading from ear to ear. "Are you serious?"

"More than I ever have been. If I'm going to make it work with Julie, or the next girl that comes along, I've got to stop seeking death out. If I need to, I'll be able to stop it... but I'm through looking. This is it."

She smiled wider than she'd ever thought possible, then helped herself to another mouthful of oatmeal.

The knob of the front door squeaked, and boots stamped on the mat in the porch.

Cathy threw a look at Xander, who gave the same one back in return. His parents weren't supposed to be back for hours.

Mike walked past the entrance to the kitchen, heading toward the stairs to Xander's room.

"Hey!" Cathy called after him, making him turn and notice the both of them at the table, "What's up?"

"What do you mean, 'what's up?'" he asked, breathless, looking as though he had just run the entire distance from his house to Xander's, which he probably had. "What are you guys doing just sitting here? Don't either of you turn on a tv or radio? Ever?"

Xander's brow furrowed, and he stood just a little straighter, a little taller. Cathy had seen this happen before, a change more dramatic than the one between Xander and the Womb. The walls were back up again, and now it was all business. "What's going on?"

Mike huffed, still trying to catch his breath. "This just became bigger than we thought it would."

CHAPTER SIX: GANG WAR

Xander stood back from the cell, with Mike not far behind him. A few feet further down the narrow corridor police tape sectioned it off from the other cells, wrapped around on of the bars and held in place firmly with sticky tack. He could see it all, but for some reason still felt the need to step closer. With every step he grew more and more repulsed, disgusted... and oddly peaceful. There was a sense of closure in the bleak concrete walls.

Though police procedure was often lax to the point of ridiculousness in Coral Beach, when the tape was up Xander had learned to mind it. He'd never really noticed any fault with the justice system in his corner of Maine before a few months ago. But then, he'd never been exposed to any real issues before then either. He had been blissfully ignorant, it the same fashion that he now described the officers themselves. He'd noticed it first just after the Engen Corporation kidnapped him. While the surviving kidnapper had been (and was still) behind bars, the building itself had never been thoroughly investigated, to the point that several items left behind continued to cause havoc even weeks later. Things had gotten so bad that, after helping out one too many times (catching Darren Phillips, assisting in the search for Kerri Walker, and successfully finding Charles Frank, to name a few) there was now an open door policy between Xander, Mike, and the Coral Beach Police Department. Of all the times he'd felt the urge to comment on the issue, this was not one of them.

Blood ran down the drain in the center of Roulette's cell, making a tiny dripping sound that only Xander could hear. The stench was unimaginably potent, coming at him from all sides. He swallowed back a glob of bile as he nodded curtly to Warden Tim Greyson. He stretched his fingers until they cracked, then took the last step forward until his midsection pushed against the police tape.

The floor of the cell was drenched in blood. Against the bunk on the adjacent wall was a void in the almost-black redness, distorted slightly by the absorbing effect the mattress had. There hadn't been an outline done yet, but the body had been removed.

"Couldn't have happened to someone more deserving," Mike said coldly, stepping in behind Xander, crumpling his nose and bringing a hand to his face briefly. "Lord, how can you stand that smell?"

"Barely notice it," Xander sighed. He reached into his jacket pocket and produced a thinly rolled cigarette, placed it between his lips quietly, lit it, then took a long drag. "I can still smell it on Cathy from the... from a few months ago. It's everywhere for me now."

They both stepped along the edge of the tape, until they could see further into the cell and the bunk came fully into view. In the center on the void where Roulette's body had been there was an oval-shaped yellow mark, mostly faded.

"Guy went and pissed himself," came the Warden's voice as he walked by, glancing in at the two. "Made one hell of a mess in his trousers, too. Just be glad we removed the damn thing. An hour ago, you couldn't step in there without a mask on."

Xander nodded without turning toward the man, then crouched down until he could see under the tape that blocked their path. Mike raised an eyebrow, about to ask him what he was doing, then thought better of it. Instead he examined the blood spatter that ran up the walls from the direction of the body. The droplets were pointed upward, meaning the killer was hunched over Roulette when he'd been slashing away at him. He imagining the blade again, like he'd done back at The Factory. "He did it back-handed again," he mumbled to himself.

"Did what backhanded?" Xander asked, flicking the remains of his cigarette out the cell window.

"The cuts the killer made, they were all backhanded. Like at the Factory."

There was a noise somewhere to the left, and both men froze. After a few seconds of silence, the two resumed. "How do you know what kind of strokes the killer made at the Factory?"

Mike paused a moment, pretending to examine a particularly large blood drop to avoid his friend's gaze. "Police report. I've still got some friends here in the department from when me and White took down Phillips."

There was a noise again, almost like the creek of springs, and Xander swallowed hard; his mouth went dry for no reason at all. "Ah," he said, pretending he hadn't heard anything. "So, we're pretty sure this was the same guy, right?"

"Mm-hm," Mike hummed, glancing at the grated window to see if there were similar smear marks on it, like when Joan was killed. "I don't know about the police, but there's no doubt in my mind that we're dealing with one guy."

"He didn't move," Xander said finally, standing up.

"What?"

"He didn't get up from his bunk. Guy as big as Roulette, didn't even try to defend himself. Killer had to open the lock, open the door, come across the cell, stab him (repeatedly)... and he didn't move. Didn't even fall or slump over after he was dead. Just stayed there."

"Maybe he didn't think he had something to be afraid of," Mike offered. "Maybe he knew the guy, or it didn't seem threatening. You getting any scents?"

Xander closed his eyes and tilted back his head, breathing in deep through both his nose and his mouth. "Too much blood, can't get anything decent. It's all covered in his scent. There is something though, but I can't put my finger on it...."

"But it's familiar," Mike finished for him, seeing where it was going.

"Very. Whoever it is, I've met him before. I just don't know from where," Xander agreed, twitching his nose to try and get the foul smell out. "Come on, we've learned all we will here."

Mike nodded, turning toward the cell door.

133

The two of them rounded the corner back out into the halls, then stopped.

The cell next to Roulette's was dark and shadowed. The light that hung from its ceiling had been broken and the barred window covered shut somehow. Both men looked into it. Not a sound came from it, but there was somehow a loudness in the silence. It screamed.

There was a shuffle in the darkness, and something that could almost be called a giggle.

Deep inside of Xander, the true Womb surged violently, so hard that he thought he might throw up or just plain keel over right there on the floor.

"Come on," Mike said, unable to take his eyes away from the cell while they stood next to it. "Cathy's waiting out in the lobby."

ㅅㅅ

"Well, that was useless," Mike grumbled, as the trio walked by the playground on their way back to Xander's house, trying not to look in at the children playing in the snow and slush. "Did you learn anything from the officer out front?"

"No," Cathy drawled, looking a little disappointed in herself. "The security cameras didn't catch anything, but the view of Roulette's cell is distorted in all the tapes anyway. Don't know why they wouldn't have better surveillance over the cell of a gang-lord who just happened to be a rapist and murderer."

"Simple," Xander said harshly, finally speaking up. "So that when somebody finally got up the balls to kill him, they'd have an excuse not to catch the guy."

Cathy looked shocked at the response, then remembered how many policemen had been killed by Tees over the years, and realized the idea made sense. "So, what about you guys? Are we any closer to finding out who this creepola is and getting it over with?"

Xander smirked at her briefly. The use of the word 'creepola' reminded him that not everything in this world was dark and black.

"We think it's someone we've encountered before," Mike piped up, tapping his nose twice and then motioning in Xander's direction.

"And it's becoming pretty clear that they have some kind of grudge going on against the Tees. So, let's start there."

"Well, there's the three of us, and Julie," Cathy frowned, only half meaning the words coming out of her mouth.

"Tommy's got a pretty big mad-on for all those gang-types," Mike added, tightening his fists.

"Mm," Xander thought. "There's also the Circe. They seem like the type who like to tie up loose ends, and they definitely have the means to pull off something like this, even if you don't count Zakron into the equation."

Cathy's eye twitched at the mention of Zakron, but she said nothing on the subject. "Then there's that Sebastian jerk. We never did hear from him again, and we don't really know what he was all about."

"We've also got a list of former Tees and Omegas about a mile long back at

134

the house. Any one of them could have a reason to pull a stunt like this."

Mike frowned, looking thoughtful. "I dunno. I feel like we're getting further away from it here. Sure, all these people have reasons to go after the Tees... but who would want Joan dead?"

Joan sighed, all but collapsing into her chair as tears formed in her eyes, only to be wiped away by her sleeve as soon as they came. "It's for reasons just like this..." she half-whispered to herself, drawing the attention of everyone else in the room.

Xander turned to face her now, ignoring whatever it was he thought he saw.

Cathy put a hand on Joan's shoulder, which she immediately shoved aside.

"...this town isn't like it used to be. I just can't anymore," she sobbed. "I didn't want to do this with all of you here, but we're going to be closing. For good."

The entire room was silent now, all eyes on her. Except for Tommy. He was still chawing on his wad of chocolate.

"I'll give it a month, just for you kids... but after that, I'm done. The Factory is done."

There was a stillness in the room. An unexplainable quality as each person looked to the next for clues on how to feel, but nobody really knew. This building, under one name or another, had been a part of their lives since before they could remember. It had been a part of their parents' lives. Many of their parents had actually met and had their first dates in this building. Now, for the first time in generations, it wasn't going to be here.

Cathy again put her hand on Joan's shoulder, and this time it was not rebuked, but welcomed.

Amid the mute motionlessness, one man stirred.

Tommy Irons got up from his table, his horrible grin having been wiped from his face, and fixed the collar on his jacket. He walked to the exit, turned to see if anyone was following him, and scoffed when nobody did. He slammed the door behind him, shaking the entire building.

"Tommy," Xander said, growling deep inside his throat. "It was Tommy."

Cathy nodded, shocked at the fact that she wasn't shocked. That it sounded true; sounded right. "Tommy," she said aloud, and it felt correct.

"I dunno," Mike said, stopping in his tracks. "I mean, no doubt the guy has been a jerk lately, but murder? That's a bit of a jump."

Xander met his friend's gaze with something resembling frustration, though much more intense.

"A bit of a jump?" he barked. "It wasn't even four months ago that this guy beat you over the head with a piece of two-by-four to help his friend rape Cathy. That he was chummy with not one but all of the Tees, whether he knew what they were or not, plus his best friend was an Omega. He had that crush on Mandy he couldn't let go of, then the Tees killed her... who else could it be?"

Mike put his hands into the air, relenting. "All I'm saying is that maybe we should wait a little while before going after the fucker with guns blazing. We don't want to make any mistakes here, right?"

Xander squinted. "And while we're waiting, more people are going to end up dead. Maybe you. Maybe Cathy, depending on how pissed off the little dick is at everybody. No..." he trailed off, shooting a glance at Cathy. "... we end this now."

Cathy paused, then nodded in agreement. "Not without me. Not this time."

Xander nodded curtly. "I think it's time we showed Mr. Irons what a Black Womb is capable of."

Mike huffed. "Fine, I just... there's some stuff I want to check on first, okay? Can this wait until later tonight?"

Xander threw a glance and Cathy, who simply shrugged her shoulders. "We'll go to my place and wait until ten. After that, we're going after him, and we're not stopping until we get the truth out."

Mike nodded, gave Cathy a kiss, then went off the other direction -- toward The Factory.

Warden Greyson peered out between the blinds of his office window, glancing quickly from side to side.

"Any sign, sir?" came the voice of a much younger officer, who still had a bit of an acne problem across the forehead, and tried to hide it unsuccessfully with long bangs.

"No," Greyson replied, turning from the window and letting the plastic snap shut, killing the lone streak of light in the otherwise dark room. "But you never can tell with those kids. That Harris especially. Shows real promise. Hope he decides to join the force some day, if he keeps his nose clean and manages to keep himself alive."

The younger cop -- with a badge that read Lanus-- nodded, looked down and remembered the thick file folder in his hands, then placed it on the Warden's desk.

"Do they know anything?"

Greyson took a long sip of his coffee, soaking his greying moustache as he did so. "Only what they hear on the news, maybe a little more. They have their suspicions, but right or wrong, they don't know the scope of it yet."

Lanus stood quietly for a moment, mumbling a little, choosing his words carefully. "With all due respect sir, why aren't we telling them everything? The media, I mean?"

Over the brim of the Warden's cup, Lanus saw the older man's eyebrows raise.

"Son," Greyson started, putting his cup down. "A dead gang-lord is bad enough before you take into account that it happened while he was under our protection. *Thirty-eight* missing Tees with enough blood at each scene to tell us they were killed, yet no body in sight? Now that's pushing it. I'm just glad Harris bought my story about moving Owchar's body -- they didn't need to know the killer managed to drag it away without us or the cameras seeing it."

"Sir... what are we dealing with here?"

"It's a gang war, son," Greyson sighed, picking up his coffee again. "'Sit next to the river long enough, and the bodies of your enemies will float by.'"

"What was that, sir?"

"Nothing, son."

Mike opened the front door to The Factory again, not taking the time to look around now. He ignored the blood spatter on the walls and the chalk outline where Joan's body had been, moving instead to the pool table where he and Xander had been playing just the other day. Frowning down at it for a second, he hopped up and sat against the ripped green fabric. Steadying himself, he took a long pan of the room now, making note of every little thing.

What's different? he thought to himself, trying to force his brain to work. *You were here just the other day, idiot. The killer must have been, too. Now what's different?* His eyes darted all around, trying hard not to let them focus on any one thing in particular, but on the room as a whole. To see it as one large object and then find the flaw in its composition.

The air felt wrong here, just as it had back in Roulette's cell. Something was out of place, something was different.

"You can't do this, bitch!" Tommy Irons screamed as he drew back the dagger and lashed out in a backhanded slice that ripped open her breasts. She fell to the floor in an awful slump, her head smacking off one of the bar stools. Her eyes were wide with terror.

Mike, frowning, turned and looked at the row of posters behind him. It wasn't back there; everything looked fine. No, something in front of him called out, crying to be seen. Begging for it.

"Beg for it," Sebastian sneered coldly, the gem on his forehead sparkling in the low flourescent lighting, his eyes alive with a glee that his face did not portray. He raised up his sword again, twirling it and slicing through her flesh with each spin, sending long, repetitive tendrils of blood all over the walls.

"I don't even know you!" Joan screamed, holding up an arm in a vain attempt at self defense. "I don't know what you're talking about!"

"The stone! The stone is here, it has to be! Just tell me where the stone is and you can live, witch!"

"No..." Mike sighed, standing up and walking slowly toward the wall, as if narrowing in on what was wrong with the room. He knew it was close now, but still couldn't see it, and the closer he got to the far wall, the more wrong it seemed. Not something added, but something missing.

"Zaaa- Kraonnnn!" Zakron bellowed, thrusting his massive head up into the air; spraying blood from his lips in all directions as its black, oozing face contorted with rows of teeth moving about in its mouth as if they had a will all their own.

Joan screamed as the life drained out of her, watching as the puddle of blood next to her head grew larger and larger, trying to look at anything except the dark beast lingering above her, bobbling from side to side like an animal toying with its prey.

"Zak," it grunted, the breath that jutted out from its nostrils visible in the coldness of the bar area. "Ron." It ripped forward with its massive claws, tendrils whipping around to hold her, to stop her from shaking as its massive tongue draped its way all over

137

her body.

Mike was almost nose-to-nose with the wall now, looking around him. There was a long space with nothing but pictures... one was missing. It had been a picture of Roxanne and Joan on the day they had bought the Factory. Right where it had been, there was one tiny blood smear... far away from any of the others.

"You took it, didn't you?" he asked aloud. "You took it when the blood was still wet on your hands. Why did you want this? What could it have meant to you?"

He touched the bare wall briefly, noticing that it was a slightly less faded brown then the rest from being covered by the picture.

The picture.

Officer Lanus walked past Roulette's cell, gazing in again at all of the blood. He felt bile rise up from his gut as he tried to find one square foot that did not have at least some on it, and found that he could not. And from what some of the other beat cops were saying, this hadn't even been the worst. They said that when the killer had hit some guy named Quire's house, they first hadn't thought there was any blood... until they'd realized that the walls were *painted* with it, a smooth coat smeared over the entire interior of the bedroom.

He got wobbly for a second and gripped the iron bars of the cell for support. His stomach did a back-flip, complete with an accompanying -- and very attractive -- plopping sound. He gasped, sighing just a little as he closed his eyes, took a deep breath, and then opened them again.

Setting his jaw and straightening his shirt, he composed himself and turned to the right to continue his run of the grounds.

"Boo."

A large hand jutted out from the adjacent cell, grabbing Lanus by the collar and pulling him against the bars, slamming his jaw against the cold metal. He screamed, even as a second hand jabbed a light bulb into his eye then twisted, sending dark blood rushing down his face and gathering in his open mouth until he thought he was going to choke on it. The hand released the now-shattered glass, wedged in the young officer's face, reached putrid-tasting fingers into his mouth and then pressed his thumb against his Adam's apple, trying to make a fist while clenching the lower half of the man's face.

The attacker yanked forward with one hard tug, pulling the man's head against the bars. There was a sick, wet snap as the two collided, then he pushed back and pulled again. One side of Lanus' jaw shattered.

Trying hard to scream but finding it very difficult, Lanus' good eye searched the darkness of the cell for any trace of his assailant and found nothing. All of a sudden, he heard a groan, followed by a squeak. He was silent, then, gazing into the darkness for any sign of motion.

There was a flash of something that looked like it might be metal. He felt the sting as sweat billowed from his forehead into his open eye socket.

Something came toward him out of the darkness, swinging at him. It crashed into the left side of his head, jarring it and snapping his neck, his entire body going limp, slumping against the cell.

From within the darkness, there was a small chuckle.

The hands reached forward again, this time patting down Lanus's midsection until they found what they were after. They returned from his body with his weapon, a .357 caliber Glock. The hand fell into the darkness again and came back empty, lingering on Lanus for only an instant before returning with his keys.

Carefully, he found the right one and placed it in the lock to his cell. He turned until he heard it snap open, then slid the cell door to one side, stepping out into the light.

Derek Smith inhaled deeply, pushing his long auburn hair back behind his head. The smile on his face undeniable. His beady little eyes were alive with excitement beneath thick, bushy eyebrows. As he turned his muscular body toward the exit, his finger was already putting first pressure on the trigger finger of the gun.

At the end of the hall, another cop darted around the corner responding to the violence on his co-worker. He was followed by two more, all reaching for their holsters and shouting something at Derek that he was just too happy to listen to.

"Look," he smirked, raising his weapon. "More people want to play."

CHAPTER SEVEN: KILLERS

Xander and Cathy sat in his parents' car, parked across the street from the Tommy's house. The radio was playing something by Three Doors Down, but God only knew what: all their songs sounded alike anyway.

"Can't believe they let you take the car," she said, frowning. "Is this like the time in fourth grade, when Mike 'gave' you his heat-seeking Optimus Prime doll, but you really stole it?"

"First of all, it was not a doll, it was an *action figure*, okay?" he started, pointing at her to enunciate the statement. "Secondly... no." He smiled, gripped his hands around the steering wheel. "No, Dad wasn't going to let me. Then I made up a reason and Mom threw me the keys, gave me fifty bucks and shooed me out the door as fast as she could."

Cathy raised an eyebrow. "What did you tell her?"

"That I was taking a girl out. Which wasn't technically a lie, I suppose, but she's been so 'get back on the horse' about the Julie thing that she didn't even want to know the details. As long as it was a female capable of one day giving her a grandchild, she was happy."

Cathy smirked, tilting her head down to avoid him seeing her blush.

"What?" he chuckled, craning his head toward her. "What is it?"

"Nothing..." she responded musically, almost laughing. "It's just... ah... me and you, and kids, in the same sentence. Can you imagine how weird that would be?" She snorted a little, taking a sip of her drink through her straw and looking out the windshield at the street lights up ahead.

He stared at her for a long moment, the glean of the lights stuck in her hair, making it shimmer, her face palely lit. "Yeah."

He gripped the steering wheel, turning his head away to face forward, letting the radio fill the silence between them.

"It's just you and me, and all of the people with nothing to do... nothing to lose and there's you and me, and all of the people and I don't know why, I can't take my eyes off of you..."

He took a deep breath, then looked down at the glowing green lights of the dashboard clock.

"Nine fifty," he stated bluntly. "Mike's got ten minutes to get here and tell us he's got something, or I'm going in there and kicking some serious ass."

Cathy frowned, staring at the clock herself, then letting her eyes dance over the street, wishing for Mike to come running around the corner.

Xander noticed. "Do you not want to be here? I've got time to swing you home."

Cathy shook her head. "I want to be here. If this is your last time out, I want to be here for it. It's just... the idea of it being Tommy. Someone I called my friend, someone we fought beside."

"Seems a little too familiar, huh?"

"Yeah," she heaved glumly. "I just can't wait for this to be over finally. To get back to some kind of a normal life. I miss worrying about, 'Hey, that guy looks cute. If I wasn't with Mike I'd kiss him. Oh, my gawd, how can I think that? What's the harm in one kiss? Nobody has to know.' Instead, it's, 'Hey, that guy's a serial killer. He's trying to kill my best friend. Oh, wait, everyone I know dies or leaves or becomes a serial killer. Oh, wait, my best friend's the serial killer...' Y'know?"

A smile perked over the corner of Xander's lips. "Who did you think was cute?" he asked, as a slow song by the Backstreet Boys started playing.

Cathy blushed a little and turned away.

His hand danced along the edge of her shoulder, subconsciously playing with the strands of hair that dangled there; hairs that always went off in their own direction despite her best intentions to keep it tame, yet always looking so amazing.

She looked back up at him, her eyes shinny and bright, her lips gleaming against the dashboard display.

At once they leaned into one another, neither of them separately starting it, but instead each finishing the other's motion. Their lips met open-mouthed: her lips soft and supple, his moist and intensely strong. She reached up with both her hands, holding each side of his face and pulling him closer, even as his own hands slid up her arms, reaching her shoulders and gripping them, dancing between them and the nape of her neck and then back again. He broke off from her lips and kissed her lower cheek, then down to her neck as she pulled him closer

140

toward her, on top of her.

-Bing!-

They both stopped, frozen by the sound that came from the radio, as if it had been the timer on their motion. He leaned back a moment, away from her neck, and looked at her.

"That was 'Incomplete' by the Backstreet Boys here on WCBR1. This is Tara Samp-son and we've got lots more of today's hits and yesterday's classics here for you tonight, but now, here's the news at ten..."

He looked at her, almost laughing. She looked back up at him, her hand still rested on the back of his head. She wasn't laughing.

"This probably isn't a constructive course of action," he chuckled, moving off of her. He felt her hand tighten, and stopped.

"Yes it is," she whispered, pulling him back toward her. Their lips met again as she wrapped one leg around him, pulling his entire frame into her.

"Following an incident at the Coral Beach Penitentiary that resulted in an uncon-firmed number of deaths, the murderer known as Derek Smith is at large. Residents in the greater area are urged to stay in their homes."

Xander shot up in his seat, followed by Cathy, the both of them forgetting everything that had just happened a moment ago and sat staring at the radio.

"We will bring you more details as the situation develops. For now..."

Xander stared the radio, paused for only a moment, then turned the key and felt the engine roar to life.

"What are you doing?" Cathy snapped, grabbing him by the arm.

"Bringing you home," he responded dryly, not even bothering to look at her as he turned around to see if it was clear to pull out.

"Yeah, I'll be safe there," she said, rolling her eyes. "I'm sure Derek doesn't remember where I live. Me, the girl that shot him and put him in jail. I bet he can't even remember my name."

"You're abusing sarcasm at this point," he said in an even tone, and with-out looking at her. "We're getting you home and I'm getting the cops to come over and watch your place. It won't be a hard sell for them. Then I'm going out and I'm finding Derek, and then I'm going to feed him his intestines. And..." he stopped, turning his head to the left and staring at Tommy's front door. "And by that time Tommy could have killed again."

She frowned, nodding at him and running a finger through the hair above his ear.

His face contorted with frustration as a million thoughts bounded through his head, and he looked as though he were about to cry. "I know, baby," she soothed, stroking the side of his face, "Believe me, I know..."

"Genblade or Randy?" he whispered to himself, staring at the odometer.

"What?"

"I've had to face this kind of choice before.

"Womb!" Hale shouted as Genblade drove the blade forward. It sliced clean through him, spewing blood out through the treads of the sword.

Genblade withdrew and let Hale fall to the ground, still alive. Blood was coming out of the gaping hole in the man's chest. It was so dark and bubbled out so furiously that it looked like oil escaping from a sprung vein, soaking through his clothes and into his skin. He was bleeding to death, and quickly.

"Isn't this interesting?" Genblade sneered, watching the life pump out of Hale's veins. He danced around Hale in a small circle, then leaned down to grin right in his face. "After all this time it's you that's going to fall, not me. Not like you always said. And I'm not even going to give you a decent death, you see that? You're going to die bleeding and mewing like a stuck cat and I'm going to watch. It's over now, do you get that? The Circe is done, do you hear me? Are we clear?"

"Crystal."

Genblade turned just in time to see Xander's claws coming toward his face.

They connected, all four of them ripping a different line through Genblade's skin, like tiny ditches dug for blood to flow through.

"Argh!" Genblade screamed, his head flying forward into his palm as his face burned. "Can't I ever be rid of you?"

"When Mandy died, I had a choice. I could have left and been there in time to stop Randy and save Mandy, but I didn't. I chose to stay and fight Genblade. To rip him open and put him in a hospital bed for the rest of his life. But if I'd left... sure, Hale would have died, but that'd be it. Worst case scenario is that Genblade would have come looking for me again afterward and I would have beaten him then. I made the wrong choice and now..."

"Shh," she cooed, bring his head to her shoulder and stroking it softly. "It's okay. It's ooookay."

"I can't make this choice. I can't... I can't do this again. I can't feel responsible..."

"Then let me," she said calmly.

His head rose, and he looked at her, forcing back tears. "What?"

"Let me make this one. Let me decide what we should do, and you just listen. Right or wrong, black or white, I'll take the heat if we fuck this one up. You don't feel any guilt about it either way, okay?"

Xander looked thoughtful for a minute, sniffing back tears, then nodded.

She smiled a little. "It's ten-oh-six. We're late for our appointment with Mr. Irons."

He smiled at her, then turned off the car and opened the door.

Mike stared at the televison screen for a long moment, watching the images dance across them. There was no sound on the black-and-white footage, and yet he could hear each shot that Derek took and feel them sink swiftly into his gut. His lower lip trembled, but he stopped it quickly, raising a hand to his mouth and coughing. He was unable to blink or even to move as he watched Derek leave the building, playfully blowing on the tip of the gun he'd stolen, like a cowboy in some 60's spaghetti western, long hair billowing backward as he opened the front door.

"That's enough," he said after a moment, tearing his eyes away from the screen long enough to look up at Warden Greyson. The footage was now just an empty hallway, with the body of one police officer half hidden from the corner camera's view.

Greyson nodded solemnly, pressing stop on the DVR and ejecting the disk, letting it dangle between his fingers for a second. "Fuck," he said under his breath. "As if this town didn't have enough to worry about."

Mike didn't answer, still staring at the screen even though it was now covered in snow.

The Warden sat down, tossing the tape onto his desk atop a mound of files and folders. "Derek Smith," he said in a hushed voice. "Of all people, it had to be Derek Smith."

"Mm."

"I'm sorry we even have to bring you in on this. Known acquaintances always get the third degree when anything like this happens. And you and Derek --"

"We have a history," Mike finished for him, still staring at the blank screen. " I know."

"I don't think we have any more questions. Sorry to bother you."

"I was coming in anyway. Wanted to take a second look at Owchar's cell. Something just doesn't seem right about any of this. It's right on the tip of my tongue..."

"Like a goddamn piece of food stuck in your teeth. You know it's there, and you can pick at it all you want, but that fucker ain't coming out until he's good and ready."

"Yeah," Mike sighed, still keeping one eye on the screen as if expecting it to do something else. In his mind, it was playing his memories of Derek. When they'd played together as kids, when Mike had taught him how to win at arcade fighters, when the both of them had worked together to stop Dr. Phillips... when he'd held a knife on Cathy and tried to kill her. When he'd stabbed Xander. When he killed a good percentage of the school and almost got away with it.

Greyson stopped talking and just watched Mike as he mulled things over in his head, letting the thoughts bounce around over and over again.

"I'm gonna wanna see his cell," Mike said finally, reaching out and turning off the screen.

"It hasn't been cleared or swept yet..."

"I'm gonna wanna see his cell," Mike repeated in the exact same tone of voice and manner.

Greyson nodded, reaching for the keys that hung at his side and slowly rising to his feet, moving down toward the containment block.

The pair stepped into the cool, white hall, and Mike was convinced he could see his breath rising up from his nose every time he exhaled. The walls were covered in bloodied hand-prints. He recognized them immediately as Derek's. He had the massive palms of a bear, with tiny, thin fingers. Once the two men turned another corner to get to Derek's and Roulette's cells, Mike stopped dead in his tracks. His mouth dropped open as he turned to face it full frontal, putting his hands on his hips.

Written across the wall, about three feet high and stark against the white primer, was a message written in blood. It said: THE REASON.

"You still wanna see the cell?" Greyson asked, raising an eyebrow.

"I think this'll be good," Mike drawled, mentally shooting the cop a look, but unable to tear himself away from the image to actually do it.

"What do you suppose it means? The *reason*? What's the little bastard talking about?"

"Dunno," Mike shrugged, letting all the air out of his lungs. "But you can damn well bet we're going to find out."

CHAPTER EIGHT: THE REASON

Mike burst out of the police station and bolted in the direction of Tommy's house, cutting across the playground. He was running so fast that his feet hurt already; so badly that he thought they might fall off.

-Squeak!- came a noise from his right, and he turned quickly, his fists clenched and ready to strike.

There was nothing there, just a tire swing swaying back and forth in the winter's breeze. He stayed there, watching it for a second. Back and forth, back and forth.

The Reason? he thought, so loudly that it made his head hurt. *What in God's name is...*

Back and forth, back and forth.

"Maybe I'm not being... direct enough for you."

Back and forth, back and forth, like the gears churning in his mind, the piece of food in his teeth shaking loose and slipping down his throat like poison.

Back and forth, back and forth.

Slowly everything fell into place and Mike's eyes went wide. He turned swiftly on his heels, changing direction, then took off down the street.

I just pray I'm not too late.

Tommy sat in his room, surrounded by broken and torn pictures that he'd taken over the years, watching as half-faces stared back up at him. Their eyes still borrowed into him and their smiles still taunted him, no matter how many times he cut them down.

He let out a long breath and closed his eyes, letting his head slump down a little. The blade he held in his hand shone in the low light of his bedroom, and he felt the cool of the metal between his fingertips. The edges were still stained with dried blood, tiny dots of it congealed around the very tip. It made it look more menacing somehow, transforming it from merely an object into a weapon.

His spiked hair was matted and sticking off around the ears from days of leaving the gel in it, sleeping with it in, and letting the rain get at it. His face was tense and serious. The mouth that was typically drawn upwards in a sly, almost devious grin that had earned him a reputation with the females of the school was now hung low, looking to be almost set in stone there.

"Has it got to you yet?" came a voice from the doorway, familiar, and twisted by anger.

Tommy's eyes shot open and grew twice as wide once he turned toward the speaker. Xander, with hatred burning in his eyes, was half hunched over with his fists clenched so tight that his knuckles were turning white. Cathy was behind him, hanging back but looking ready to move forward at a moment's pause.

Tommy did not respond to the question. He just glared, squinting his eyes a little.

Xander stared back, moving his thumb over his forefinger and cracking it.

"What do you want?" Tommy asked finally, turning away from the pair to face the pile of photos again.

Xander almost laughed. "What do you think, you little runt?"

"Xander-- " Cathy started, but was cut off when Xander raised a hand for silence.

"I'm going to rip you limb from limb," he finished, looking around at the walls, so bare now.

Tommy snorted. "You're not John Wayne, Drew," he said coldly, still not turning to face them.

Xander could see the knife now. He could smell the blood on it from the second he'd entered the house two floors down. "Let's step outside," he said simply.

"Xander--" Cathy repeated, more urgently this time, touching his shoulder.

He shrugged her away, and she realized that, just like in the car, she wasn't talking to Xander anymore. He'd transformed again, into the dark person that always brought a taste of fear to her.

"Leave me alone," Tommy said in a flat, low voice, his head hanging down to look at the blade now, again moving it in the light and watching its gleam.

Xander pushed off his heels, moving forward in one fluid motion, like water flowing through the air. Before either party could blink, he had grabbed Tommy by the back of the shoulders and spun him around, slamming him into the wall and pinning him there.

"I will *not* leave you to kill anymore!" he bellowed, gritting his teeth, the Womb rose a little from the outburst but he choked it back, wanting more than anything to do this himself.

"Xander!" Cathy yelled, grabbing his shoulder and digging her nails in, pulling her friend's one arm off of Tommy.

Xander turned to Cathy and snapped, "What?" His face, reddened with anger and hatred, burned even when he looked at her.

She said nothing, just looked past him at Tommy.

A quizzical look came over Xander's face and some (but not all) of the wrath drained out of it. He squinted at her a moment, looking for an answer, then turned back around to see that Tommy was crying.

His eyes were swollen and puffy and his cheeks were wet with hot tears that showed no sign of stopping any time soon. Xander raised an eyebrow, then let his hand slip and fall away from Tommy, who now sobbed uncontrollably. His whole body was shaking and his hands were over his face in a desperate attempt to try and hide it from the world...

... that's when Xander noticed the scars and scabs that lined his wrists and lower arms.

He stepped back from the sobbing youth, backing up a pace or two until he stood on par with Cathy, the both of them looking at Tommy in shock.

"Go ahead..." Tommy sobbed, his whole body shaking. "Just do it. I'm sick of this. Sick. They all die or leave or hurt... now you are too, I can't... I'm so sorry. I'm sorry about the things I said, I just..." he was overcome by sobs then, burying his head into drawn up knees, holding himself in the fetal position.

"You didn't kill Owchar..." Xander whispered, more to himself than to Tommy.

Tommy looked up, his whole face soaked now. "He's dead?" he said quietly, his eyes darting around in their sockets, confused.

"You didn't hear?" Cathy said in a soothing voice, finally speaking up.

He snorted back mucus, then shook his head.

Xander let out a breath, then placed a hand on Tommy's shoulder. "It'll be okay, you know," he said sympathetically, glancing at the thin cuts and knowing what the boy was feeling. The frustration of the pain, the added frustration of failing to release it. The thought that he couldn't even kill himself right. He'd felt it all many times in the past few months. Realized how many times after Sara died that he had been mean to Cathy, had taken it out on her... how he had been even worse than Tommy at times, many times, and still was even now. He sighed at his own stupidity while rubbing the boy's shoulder.

"It won't," Tommy sighed, shaking his head as more tears came down.

"Yeah it will. Believe me, man. I've been there."

Tommy looked up, meeting Xander's gaze for the first time since the whole thing started. "You?" he said, shock and awe in his voice.

For the first time, Xander noticed something in Tommy he never had - a twinge of jealousy, and envy. Not much, but enough. He smiled a little and hugged Tommy briefly, patting him on the back. "Yeah," he said softly, as Cathy moved in and joined in the embrace. "...me."

ʎⱯʎ

Xander slammed the door to the car, pressing his head against the steering wheel in frustration. The horn beeped for a second from the impact, and he stared at its red imitation-leather center for a long moment, focusing in on every crack and indentation.

Cathy opened the passenger side door and slid in alongside him, leaning her head back on the rest and heaving hard. She turned to him, the light from the dash illuminating her pale face. "Do you think he's going to be okay?"

146

"He's talking to his Mother. That's all we can do."

She looked as though she were about to speak again, then nodded.

He chuckled softly to himself, a smirk growing over his lips.

Cathy turned on the headrest, looking at him with an odd expression on her face. "What's so funny?"

He sat up straight and turned toward her, running his fingers through his hair and then scratching the back of his head. "Given the choice between two murderers... I go after a suicidal, emotionally unstable teenage boy," he snorted, then laughed again, clenching his hand into a fist and slamming it against the dashboard, cracking it slightly with an audible -snap!-.

"You couldn't have known," she pleaded, touching his arm gently.

"Oh, yes I could have. I *wanted* it to be Tommy, and we both know it. I needed it to be him," he said, thumping his chest right over his heart once.

"Why?"

He paused as the gears turned inside his head. His eyes had a far off, distant look as things started to fall into place. "Because the alternative was too much for me to handle."

Xander reached into the back seat and grabbed his mother's cell phone, the one thing she insisted he bring with him if he took the car. Flipping it open, he dialed the number he'd come the have burned into his frontal lobe over the past few months, then pressed talk and brought it to his ear. Cathy just watched his mouth silently chanting the word 'please' over and over again.

"The cellular customer you have dialed is outside the service area, or has the phone turned off..."

"Ah!" he grunted angrily, snapping it shut again. "She never has her phone off."

Cathy nodded slowly, getting that same far-off gaze that he'd had a second ago. "Julie."

Xander just frowned at her as he dialed another number, nodding once curtly. "Julie." This time the phone rang.

After what seemed like an eternity, someone picked up. There was a moment's pause and then a hacking cough that made Xander yank the receiver away from his ear. "He 'lo?" came the tired-sounding voice on the other line, her voice slurred and sloppy.

"Miss Peterson?" Xander asked, pressing a finger against his free ear to hear better as static clogged the connection. "Dee? Is Julie at home?"

"Julie?" Dee responded, waking up a little, sniffing. "Haven't seen her all week. Came by and dropped off her bag, left again."

Xander sighed and closed the phone, not wanting to continue the conversation further. "Julie hasn't been staying there," he said to Cathy, tossing the cell back on the seat and turning the key in the ignition. "Hasn't been there in days."

Cathy sighed, rubbing one temple at the spot that Xander had once classified as the 'Peterson Syndrome' headache. "So we're looking at Julie?"

"'Death will keep following you, wherever you go, and I can't be a part of that anymore,'" he quoted as he pulled out onto the street, the entire car jolting

147

with the sudden burst of acceleration as he sped down the street. "She wants death out of her life... no better way than to kill the killers."

"Where are we going?" Cathy almost screamed, gripping the handle on the car door and tightening her safety belt.

"Coral Cove," he growled, gripping the wheel. "There are some things you can only talk about with an ex."

⚤

The room was mostly blackened by shadows, so much so that one could barely see the walls to get a grip on its size. In reality, it was massive. An abandoned poultry farm from Coral Beach's more industrious days. Sometimes you could still smell the hen droppings, if one tried hard enough.

There was one light hanging from a beam in the very center of the room, its metal shade ensuring that it shone on no more than a small circle.

Under the light, four men stood in a square, each looking more solemn than the next.

Ian Char's devilish grin was gone now. His face was panicked and sweaty, with two perpendicular scars down the right side of his face, a remnant of his last duel with the Black Womb. He was wearing tight jeans and a muscle shirt, not overly appropriate for that particular time of year, made obvious by the chill-induced goosebumps covering his arms.

Duncan Combs was silent and had a face like a statue. He just watched the rest of them, his icy stare moving from one to the next.

George McGyver stood tall; his posture perfect. His broad chest made him look strong for a man pushing sixty and his greying hair was combed neatly at all times. He might have been intimidating, if not for worried look his eyes gave as they darted back and forth in the darkness, as if petrified of its black.

Finally there was Quinton Travers. A fat, older man who was one of the people who'd been in the gang the longest. He had a laugh like a rabid hyena when he used it, but that time wasn't now. Now, he was deadly serious as he regarded the other three, stepping forward.

"Roulette is dead," he said simply, and they all hung their heads for a moment.

George reached up and touched his right shoulder, where his Tee tattoo had been placed years ago by Owchar, feeling the pull of sadness at his heart.

Travers paused, letting the words sink in. "So are at least thirty of our number, maybe more. It's not always easy to contact non-active members... not anymore. But we're trying. The police are trying to keep it quiet, but this is nothing short of an attack on our way of life. With Roulette gone, I'm taking control of our group. At least until we destroy whatever's doing this."

Ian's head shot up and he pushed the words through clenched teeth. "The Womb?"

Travers frowned. "I don't think so. He could have killed each of us so many times now and didn't... why all of a sudden, like this? It isn't his style. He likes to play the hero."

148

"Could be the Snakes," Duncan added, staring at a spot on the floor, his voice low. "With all that's been happening, they might think it's a good time for a power struggle. A lot of ex-Snakes are cops."

Travers nodded. "Maybe," he conceded. "But I think we're dealing with the Omegas. I think they're finally stepping up to the plate after that whole business a few months ago, right before the Womb started dogging us."

"What are we gonna do?" Ian asked, smirking a little.

Travers reached into the seat of his pants and produced a handgun. He cocked it once, letting the slide snap into place.

"We go to war."

⋏⋎⋏

Mike burst in through the front door of the Smith home, wood splintering around the deadbolt as he did so and flying out in all directions. The door swung hard, hitting the adjacent wall with a thud that echoed off of the walls of the house, reverberating back at him from every direction. Small fragments of wood sprinkled the floor in a semi-circle from the door, bouncing off of the carpet like confetti. He quickly looked around, hot sweat making his hair stick to his brow as he frankly searched for what he sought.

The door had opened directly into the living room, where a solitary sofa and ratted coffee table were all that kept it from being completely vacant. There was a pile of dirty magazines against a space heater near the sofa as well, and he could smell the distinct aroma of dust inside those heaters. Straight ahead was the entrance into the kitchen, where only a chair and part of the table were visible. To his right were the stairs, going both up and down, with extensions of the wall covering most of them, making it impossible to see the next floor without being on them.

"Mr. Smith?" Mike called out, blinking twice to adjust to the low light in the room. The muscles in his neck tightened as he clenched his fists and became stiff. He took an uncertain step forward out of the doorway, checking behind him only briefly to make sure there was nobody there. His eyes darted around the room feverishly, looking for anything that might be used as a weapon, or any spot where someone might be lying in wait. "Mr. Smith, are you home?"

There was no response.

Swallowing back hard, he took another step forward, then another, heading toward the kitchen. He had no desire to go upstairs or down to floors where no exit was readily available until he was absolutely sure he had to.

He stepped into the kitchen and felt the tile giving just a little beneath the weight of his boot. He realized he was tracking in snow and water, and briefly considered taking off his shoes, then thought better of it.

Unlike the front room, everything here was white and clean. The dishes were carefully put away, chairs neatly positioned at equal points around the table. On the table was a jar of pickles, a ketchup bottle, a loaf of bread, a two liter of Pepsi, carrots, and a head of lettuce.

Mike squinted at the arrangement, trying to determine what could possi-

149

bly be made from the accumulated items. He took a step toward it, old floor boards creaking beneath him. His toe hit something under the table, propped up against the leg of one of the chairs, and knocked it over with a clang that made him jump.

Taking a deep breath, he knelt down to pick up the item. It was a metal grate, cut into even squares over and over again, and white except for a few twinges of rust where it had obviously sat for a long period of time

Standing again to examine it in the light, he recognized it as a shelf from a fridge.

Looking up and actually bringing the fridge into focus, he realized what could be made from the items assorted on the table: Room.

Letting out a sigh, he laid the grate onto the table and walked toward the refrigerator. He put a hand on the cold handle, pausing briefly, hoping he wouldn't find what he thought he would. Summoning his reserve courage, Mike opened the door wide.

His face turned white. Staring back at him with wide, open eyes was Don Smith. The eyes were fogged now, taking on a glassy, china-doll eeriness. His mouth was agape, several teeth conspicuously absent as blood dripped from it onto his naked body. Flesh had been torn away from his chest, ripped open like a suit, revealing the muscle and tendons beneath, stiff from the cold and exposure, but still moist with blood. His fingerless hands hung limply at his sides, caked in blood. His legs and arms were covered with cuts and bruises, many of them without visible surface trails of blood… they had been done after Don's heart stopped beating. His genitals were missing, replaced instead with a gaping maw… a crater that looked like it might have been created by a shotgun at close range. The man's face stared out at Mike, frozen in a scream that told all of his last horrible moments of life.

"Hey," came a voice from behind Mike, and he spun around in shock.

Derek Smith stood in the doorway of the kitchen, blocking the only exit from the room. His face and hair were spattered in blood, as was the knife that he held loosely by his side.

"I was saving that."

CHAPTER NINE: STRANGE

Reverend Gallagher sat in his office. The door was open, swaying back and forth slightly in the wind. The old hinges bayed mournfully each time their rusty joints were forced to move. The room itself was small and cluttered, filled with books and notes, and a bookcase full of diaries that he'd kept for years -- carrying them with him from one town to the next. The first Bible he'd ever gotten (a red-leather New Testament, given to him by his Godmother when he was confirmed) sat mounted like a trophy atop the case, its edges worn and the spine creased. On the walls were pictures of his mother and father, one oil painting of

Jesus that had been in this office longer than he had, and many drawings and finger paintings given to him by the children in the Sunday-school classes over the years. There was also a simple wooden cross, splinters forming at the edges of it, held up by a nail is its apex.

The Reverend stared up from the growing pile of paperwork to gaze upon the cross, and the shadow it cast almost to the baseboards. He took a deep breath, shoulders rising, and then let out a heavy sigh.

The last file was of a mentally challenged girl named August Styles who had seen a steady decline in focus and willingness to cooperate of late. He closed the case file in front of him and then put it on a small pile on the floor. He frowned at the pile, only a few folders high yet he'd been at this for hours. He turned to the stack before him, at least three times that height, and he hadn't even taken all of the files from his office at the school. Even though Principal Shnieder had told him that he was free to use the office on school premises for as late as he needed, he was more comfortable here. This place felt like home.

Gallagher reached over to the next file folder atop the pile, a young man named Chesley Norman. He stopped, his fingers resting against the smooth, yellow surface of the folder. His thumb perused down through the rest of them, bending their edges up so that he could see the names of his students slowly flick by: Calla McFadden, Darrel Page, Karen Bennet, Cathy Kennessy, Alexander Drew.

He stopped, staring at that file for a moment.

He recalled once, months ago, when Alexander had come to him seeking solace after the death of one of his friends. Many of his friends, really, but one in particular. That had been at the beginning of all this madness, when the first wave of murders had happened, and he had thought that his flock would take forever to recover from the wounds. In truth, it hadn't taken that long, because more and more just kept coming, over and over again. And now, once again, they were in the same place.

He wondered how young Mr. Drew was handling it this time.

He let the pile go, picking up the file on Chesley Norman and opening it. She was a straight-A student, interest in technology...

He reached for his coffee mug (which read 'On the Eighth day, God created coffee... and it was good') and brought it to his lips, frowning when he found it to be empty. Sighing once again, he got up and walked over to his instant percolator, sliding the cup into its place and flipping the switch on its side. The light on the top of the ingenious device came on, and the water inside started to boil.

He turned as he waited for it to be finished, holding Norman's file before him, flicking down through the family history. The door squealed again, and he looked up at it. Just outside, he could see his confessional, looming ominously.

His brow furrowed as he looked at it, focusing hard. Something was wrong, and he couldn't put his finger on exactly what. Something was different, something small... but it tickled at the back of his brain nonetheless.

As he continued to stare at it, his focus changed suddenly, concentrating instead on the window beyond the confession box. His eyes became wide and his face pale as Chesley Norman's file dropped to the floor. "Lord Almighty!" he cried, backing up a pace and bumping into the shelf, jittering the coffee mug and causing it to fall from its perch, sending steaming hot coffee everywhere before shattering against the floor.

As the pieces of the mug danced and bounced about, one chunk stared upward, casting a shadow as long as the cross had a moment ago.

It said: God

CHAPTER TEN: CASUALTIES

"Derek..." Mike said softly, holding out his hand carefully, palm out, trying to appear calm, not wanting to get the killer excited. His eyes kept darting, almost uncontrollably, from Smith's small, beady eyes, to the knife that he gripped tightly between narrow fingers -- gripped so hard that he veins were popping out of his arms. "...How bout we put that down and talk?"

Derek smirked with the same cocky grin that had won him affection of the female variety right up through school. It smacked of confidence and self-assurance. His eyes squinted at Mike, the way they did at almost everything, seeming permanently narrowed. He licked his lips quickly, then spoke. "Or, I could keep this, and we could talk," he reasoned, his voice harsh yet full of lividity, as if he found the situation darkly humourous.

"Okay!" Mike spat out, just a little too quickly. "Okay, let's just talk then, man. We always used to talk..."

"Yes..." he laughed and took a casual step forward. Mike fought the urge not to take a step back and keep the distance between them. "...let's talk. 'Cause out of all the little fish swimming around this town, I think you were always the smartest one. Even smarter than me, most of the time."

"Thanks," he accepted, voice wavering.

"No problem," he chuckled, spinning the red-tainted blade between his fingertips. His square jaw moved from side to side, popping the bone within one of the joints to relieve some pressure. Mike's eyes wandered over him now, noting the blood covering his hands and arms... his clothes were clean, not even a spot on the white shirt that used to fit him perfectly, but was now stretched over large chest muscles. He'd been working out. And he must have changed his clothes after what he'd done to Don.

"You knew to come here. To you it was obvious. 'Go to his home.' Everyone else is out searching the woods, even after I gave them a clue..."

"The reason."

"Like that, did you?" Derek laughed, throwing back his head and opening his mouth wide, revealing blood-stained teeth. "I did that for you. I figured you'd want to be the one to play this hand of the game."

"The reason you killed to begin with, to help your father get ahead. To try and give him a story he could write about, win the Pulitzer prize and become famous, so that he might be able to spend some more time with you, instead of at work."

"Oo, good guess, but there is *another* reason..." he trailed and tossed the knife from hand to hand before it tight again. "And I kinda liked the song. You know, 'The Reason'? I think it kinda applies to this situation."

Mike was silent, his jaw set.

"Oh, you know the one... the one where the guy apologizes for all those things he did, says he's not a perfect person... and then just has one last thing he needs to do. Before he goes... Come on, Mikey, you know the words."

"Yeah," Mike nodded, forcing a smile.

"Tisk, man," Derek chided, bringing up his free hand and waving a finger back and forth scoldingly. "You're not speaking your mind here, buddy. Haven't we known each other long enough that you can tell ol' Derek how you feel?"

If I try to be nice, he'll know I'm lying and he'll snap anyway... Mike thought, mulling his words over in his mind. "I think you're ill, Derek. I think you need to get help, and I don't think they were giving it to you in jail. I think they were content to just lock you up and throw away the key, and that's not right."

Derek paused then tilted his head to one side to regard his friend. "That's the truth, isn't it?" he asked rhetorically. "Wow. Just when I think I know you... you throw me for a king-sized loop."

"Didn't see the point in lying to someone who's smart enough to know what I was thinking anyway," he said, again forcing his mouth into a lop-sided smile and hoping that Derek was ignoring the fear sweat that was pouring off of him now.

"Good boy," Derek mused. "I was going to kill you when I heard you down here... but you may just be fun enough to keep around after all. Nothing like that trigger-happy bitch of yours."

Mike clenched his teeth, resisting the urge to cry out in response, to play right into Derek's hands. "Pfft. We're not even together anymore. She went south and dug Xander after she and he attacked you months ago. You can take her, but lemme tell ya, that's one ride that isn't worth the price of admission."

Derek paused, and then smiled a little wider. "Nice try. Didn't you just finish telling me that I knew a lie when I heard it?"

Mike swallowed hard.

"Just for that, I think I'll pay that price of admission before I go. She always had a thing for me anyway. Besides, you've got bigger things to worry about."

Mike's brow furrowed, his entire body clenching. "Like what?"

"Like what's really out there. Like who killed Owchar and the others. The Scooby Gang is about to head into the big leagues, Mikey."

"You... know?" Mike said, and even as he did, the realization was spreading over himself as well.

"Me and Julie always were such good friends... had so much in common... maybe I'll pay her a visit..." Derek mumbled, almost nonchalantly, as he brought the knife up to bear. "... Right after I'm done with you."

Derek leaped forward, crossing the distance between the two of them in two mighty strides. In flight, he tightened his grip on the blade, his thumb riding its edge. His eyes seemed alive, sparkling and glistening, mouth open wide and salivating as he thrust the knife forward.

Mike's eyes went wide, and he brought up both his hands to block the blow. He yowled as the sharp metal edge dug against the back of his arm near the elbow.

"Well, that was dumb," Derek laughed as he drew the blade back again.

Mike lashed out and slammed the base of his arm against Derek's side, knocking the wind out of him. The killer stumbled as air forced itself from between parched, cracked lips. Not wasting the moment, Mike football-tackled his opponent, sending the both of them sprawling against the kitchen floor. He drew back and struck quickly, slamming a fist against Derek's face, hearing the gratifying crack of a cheekbone as he did. Holding the man-monster's arm down with one hand, he pried the knife from his fingers with the other.

Derek shot his left knee up quickly, connecting with Mike's groin.

"Oh!" Mike bellowed, but did not let go of the knife and instead tightened his grip. He got up quickly so as to recover while Derek scrambled to his feet. Mike felt something sticky covering the rubber handle of the blade, and realized that it was blood. Don's blood. His mouth distorted from sickness and he watched as Derek steadied himself against the kitchen table, smirking as he wiped blood from his mouth as even more came out. Feeling the rage of the last few minutes build up inside him, he brought the blade up high then bellowed and lunged at Derek.

Derek moved to one side quickly and managed to intercept his foe's downswinging arm. He forced it to continue the motion, lodging the blade into Mike's own leg.

Mike fell to the floor in agony as the blood rushed, pumping out with each beat of his speeding heart and sick from the overload of adrenaline.

"Heeeha," Derek laughed and slowly wrapped his fingers around the knife's handle, then yanked it out violently. He kneeled on the floor and grabbed Mike by the collar, forcing him to eye-level. For a moment, he just stared and smiled at his friend.

"I'm going to miss our talks." Derek plunged the blade deep into Mike's side. The bloodied teen's eyes bulged as he fell forward, only to be shoved back. His head knocked first against the table and then the floor. Derek withdrew the blade, paused and watched Mike tremble, then pushed it in again. He smirked with delight as the torso's tender flesh parted way to make room for the metal, again and again.

The third time he left the blade and rose slowly to his feet, never taking his eyes off of the body of Michael Harris and the blood that slowly expanding into an uneven puddle around him. After a moment, he turned and grabbed his black plastic jacket off of the couch as he headed toward the door.

"And Cain slew Abel..."

154

Warden Greyson turned his flashlight around, watching as the light bouncing eerily off of the snow-covered trees back at him. Although the night was cold, he couldn't help feeling hot underneath his uniform. He did his best to ignore the scent dogs barking all around him, each held back by a fellow officer searching for Smith, trying to pick up some sign of the murderer.

He breathed hard, each exhale sending a puff of crisp air from his lips. He watched it travel upward, then dissipate in the moonlight like smoke.

One of his men ran past him, the disappeared quickly into the foliage as if he had never been there. Although Greyson could hear him only scant meters ahead, the officer had vanished from sight.

He let out a sigh, even as he heard another come up behind him slowly. "It's hopeless. This place is like a maze, Davis," he said, his voice full of defeat.

Behind him, Davis heaved a heavy breath as well. "Smith stayed hidden for weeks, right under Tim White's nose. He's had months to think about this. We won't find him, sir."

"We have to keep looking. While there's snow on the ground, he can't keep his trail hidden," he said with confidence, turning the beam of his light to the right. Although buried under a snowy layer, he thought he noticed a patch that seemed disrupted and misplaced. He raised an eyebrow and called out to Davis, who'd moved on to the left. "Has one of the men been this way?"

Davis turned, counted the different flashlights and did some quick math in his head. "No, sir. Nobody's been down there."

Greyson turned, readied both gun and flashlight, then inched closer to the brush beyond the displaced snow.

"Now, I've got you."

He stepped forward slowly, circling around a large tree, keeping his light fixed on the spot just beyond the brush...

... until it came into view.

"...my God..."

CHAPTER ELEVEN: WAR GAMES

Xander gripped the steering wheel, feeling its texture give way beneath his warm touch. Cathy gripped her armrest as trees sped by at a blur. The only thing in steady focus was the full moon off in the distance, so far away it seemed to follow them across the highway.

"Will you slow down?" she squealed as the car fishtailed slightly on the slippery, slush-covered roads before righting itself. They passed a sign that indicated Coral Cove was some distance ahead, but zipped by it too quickly for her to see how far. "Do you want us to die before we ever even get there?"

"Please," he scoffed, his face twitching upward into a scowl.

"Fine, right. You've got a healing factor, I get it. That won't save me from cracking my head open against the pavement!" she huffed angrily, digging her nails into the upholstery as her eyes began to sting. She struggled to find something to focus on; to take her attention away from the high speeds while her stomach did back-flips inside her gut. As they went over a small hill, the vehicle became weightless for an instant and Cathy began to feel light-headed.

"How much further?" she managed to spit out, closing her eyes as the feeling subsided.

"One-point-nine-eight miles," he said matter-of-factly, cutting the wheel hard to get around a sharp turn, thrusting Cathy about in her seat.

She made a low, frustrated noise, but he did not tear his eyes from the road to see the expression on her face. He knew it too well by this time anyway. She closed her eyes and took a deep breath, steadying herself in the passenger's seat. When she reached some level of relaxation, she opened them again. "What are we going to do when we get there, anyway?" she asked, trying to find steadiness in her voice. "If she hasn't been with Dee, she could be anywhere, Xander. Coral Cove is a small town, but it's big if you have to go door to door."

He didn't say a word. Didn't even move except for his hands sliding over the wheel, navigating the meandering highway.

"That's assuming she's even in a house; that she's even in Coral Cove... she could be back home right now, if she's the killer."

Again, nothing.

She ran all of her fingers through her hair, stretching the skin of her scalp so much that her eyes widened against her will, then dug her nails in and ruffled her own hair just so that she could fix it again. She glanced briefly at her reflection in the side-view mirror. "Are you going to say anything, or am I just talking to myself? A few minutes ago, you couldn't decide which plan to follow through on, and now you've got none. Meanwhile, Mike's still back in Coral Beach, and he has no idea what's happening. This isn't smart, Xander--"

"It's Julie," he stated finally, turning to glance at her briefly. The moment that their eyes locked seemed frozen in time. It wasn't even a second, but it lasted so much longer. She watched the pain, anger and frustration swirl about in his pupils, like all the colors of pain mixing together, to form a look on the verge of tears.

"I know," she said softly. "But we still have to know how to find her."

"I can find her," he responded, as the first few houses started to whiz by. He let his left hand slide from the wheel onto the automated controls at his side, lowering his window and letting the cold winter air billow in. "All I have to do is get close to her."

Cathy's skin covered itself in gooseflesh, and a shiver crept its way up from the base of her spine into her shoulders, head and back down each arm.

Xander looked over at her involuntary movement and frowned softly. He took one hand off the wheel and placed it on her knee, squeezing it lovingly. She resisted the urge to bite her bottom lip as she placed her hand over his.

"I'm glad you're here," he said honestly, as he refocused on the road ahead. "I'm glad it's you. If it was anyone else, I'd be worse. And even though it's Julie... in some strange way, it feels right. It feels like if this is the end, it has to be the end of she and I as well... so that I can really move on."

Cathy nodded slightly, gazing upon his face from the side. At that moment, she felt in tune with his thoughts. She knew each word before it came and could almost mouth along with his lips.

"Me too," she whispered. "I'm glad, now, that we can finally--"

She was cut off as she car screeched to a sudden halt, slamming the both of them forward against their seatbelts. The car spun to one side until it faced the woods on the side of the road evenly, displacing everything in the back seat. "Ah!" she hissed, as the seatbelt loosened itself once they'd stopped, revealing just how much it had dug into their skin.

Xander quickly removed his own before opening the door to the car and stepping out onto the road, heedless of oncoming traffic; just standing there on the pavement and snow with his arms stretched downward.

Cathy took off her own belt, letting it snap back against the wall of the car as the winch tightened. After waiting a moment for a car to pass by them, she stepped out and slammed the door behind her. She turned to face him, the car between them and yelled, "Have you gone ultimate bat-shit crazy?" Slamming a hand against the hood for effect, "You could have just killed us both, you fuck-ing madman!"

His back turned to her; he curled all but the index finger of his right hand back into his palm, silently mumming her before taking a deep breath through the nose.

"What in God's name are you doing, anyway?" she asked, her voice calmer, but still audibly frustrated. As she spoke, she twisted her shoulder about to see if it was even still in its socket.

"I've got her scent, I just need to lock onto it," he said simply, taking another sniff.

She raised an eyebrow. "You can do that? From, like, anywhere?"

"Not with everyone," he said, eyes still closed. "But I know her scent. Know the aromas her body produces that she's not even aware of. I've spent the last week trying to get them off of me, showering day in and day out, smoking men-thol, wearing cologne, hair spray... it's clinging to me. So it's not difficult for me to pick it up now."

"Huh," she said, tilting her head back a little. "Can you do that with me?"

His eyes opened wide and he spun around, much of the stiffness leaving him as he once again entered the car and put on his seatbelt. "Got her."

Realizing that he wasn't going to wait, Cathy scrambled in as well. Her feet were barely off the ground when he slammed his foot down on the pedal and the wheels screamed to life.

Julie Peterson brushed back a strand of her auburn hair, smiling devilishly as she braced herself against the kitchen counter. There was a mischievousness in her eyes as she opened the cutlery drawer, her long fingers dancing over the array of knives within. They settled finally on a long, slender blade with a black handle, clean and glistening in the light of the ceiling's fixtureless bulb that swayed slightly in the wafting breeze.

She smiled, biting her lower lip as she felt it between her fingertips, the soft rubber giving way a little from the heat of moist palms. Her freckled cheeks curled up as her grin grew wider still. She gripped the blade, turning toward the living room, where someone lay motionless against the couch, his head tilted back in an odd, obtuse manner, moaning.

She laughed a little, taking a step forward.

-SLAM!-

The front door to the house burst open, slamming again when it hit the adjacent closet door.

"Or, we could do it that way," Cathy sighed from a few steps behind Xander as he stepped in menacingly, both fists clenched at his sides.

"This ends," he said simply, his voice a deep, guttural sound. His voice box continued to reverberate even after the words were gone, emanating a low growl.

"Alex!" Julie yelped, jumping back a pace and nearly dropping the blade but instead clenched it tighter.

"You could have knocked. And there is a doorbell, you know," Cathy chided, folding her arms across her chest as she took her place at Xander's side.

"Hello, Julie," she said coldly, finally regarding the girl, looking her up and down. She was wearing a light blue terrycloth robe tied off at the waist, and there were purple pajama bottoms sticking out from beneath them. The edges and sleeves of the robe were worn and there was a conspicuous red stain traveling up one of the arms.

"What are you two doing here?" Julie yelled, her eyes going from shocked to angered. Her brow lines moved down and crunched in the middle, like two fault lines coming together to make a mountain. She tilted and glared specifically at Xander. "What are you doing here?"

"Don't play dumb," he spat accusingly, taking one menacing step into the house and pointing at her. "You don't need to, if you thought you were going to get away with this... you haven't been home all week. You went there and dropped off your bags and left again."

"You've been keeping tabs on me?" Julie screamed, tossing the knife down on the table so hard that it skidded and fell off the other side. "What the hell is the matter with you? Give up the hero bit for a stalker role much?"

Xander narrowed his eyes and slightly shook his head. "Don't play the innocent role with me. I know you too well, Julie."

Her eyes darted to one side and she looked downward. Cathy noticed it too, taking a step forward to remain at Xander's side, but keeping silent.

"What's in the living room that you don't want me to see, huh Jules?" he poised, almost laughing at his ex's indignance.

"That would be me," came a deep voice, followed by its shirtless speaker. He stepped out from around the corner before leaning against it casually. He wasn't overly toned, but he was shaped as though he might be one day. He was older than all of them and there was even the slight indication of greying hair scattered throughout the beard that covered his square, chiseled jaw quite evenly. His hair was short, black and curly, and more than a little bit messed up in the front. He glared at Xander with large brown eyes, that although angered, regarded the boy with an air of humor. "This is your ex, I take it?" he asked Julie, without once looking at her.

Julie looked at the floor, then back up again, blushing a little. "Go wait in the living room, Jason," she said, turning back toward Xander. "I can handle this."

Cathy licked her lips, took a step back behind Xander and pretended that she had never been there to begin with.

Xander clicked his tongue against the roof of his mouth and blinked twice, but kept the line of sight between the two of them.

Julie's face was becoming even more red now, not with embarrassment, but with rage. "How dare you?" she grunted, her cheeks shaking.

He didn't say anything. He didn't move.

"What in God's name is the matter with you, Alex? God, why can't you just leave me the fuck *alone*?"

Xander's mouth twitched, and each of her words felt like it strapped another weight to his heart. "You've been here these last few days, haven't you?" he said quietly, feeling terribly ashamed, the feet which had been so well planted a moment ago now scuffing aimlessly along the floor. He took in a breath of air that confirmed what she was about to say even before she did. Her scent was everywhere, against everything... along with the stench of weed and beer and cigarettes. All three were also on her breath.

"Not that it's any of your business, but yes."

Xander's hand loosened, and Cathy stepped out from behind him, taking it, trying to give him some level of support. "Julie, listen..." she started.

"Don't," Julie spat, her eyes narrowing at her intruders' intertwined hands. "Where's Mike, anyway? Shouldn't he be here too?"

The both of them looked downward.

"Gotcha," she laughed. "I don't think either of you are in a position to call me any names right about now." She turned, honing in on Cathy. "At least when I was with him, I could keep him under my thumb."

The words hit them both straight in the gut, and her hand slipped away from his.

Xander looked up, seeing the cake on the table behind Julie for the first time now. "Julie, I'm--"

"Just get out," she snapped, waving him away in a final act of dismissal. She turned her back to him and leaning against the table.

He frowned, then turned toward the door. He lightly grabbed hold of the knob as Cathy walked ahead of past and out of the house.

"Xander?" Julie called as he was closing the door.

He didn't turn. He didn't need to to hear her robe falling to the floor as the couch springs expanded.

"He likes it when I surprise him in his room wearing next to nothing."

He did not make a single sound. He merely closed the door and walked back to the car where Cathy was waiting.

CHAPTER TWELVE: NEW RELIGION

Again Xander and Cathy passed a sign welcoming them to a town, but this time it was Coral Beach, and it was done at a much slower speed.

They had driven in silence ever since they'd left Jason's house with not even a stray look shared between them. Xander was driving casually with one hand now, his fingers loose, guiding the wheel with his palm. The momentum had gone from his thoughts, which now drifted in and out of one circumstance to another.

Cathy opened her mouth to speak, for at least the third time, then closed it again. She simply turned toward the window and looked down to watch the rocks and dirt fly past.

"Well, that was a waste of time," he said. The words were empty and hollow, and far too honest.

"We ruled her out," Cathy said matter-of-factly, her voice barely a whisper.

"Mm," Xander groaned. "We've ruled out all our suspects, Cat. The only person we know for certain did anything remotely close to wrong has had hours to hide, to run... or to kill half the population of the town, if he really set his mind to it."

"No road blocks," Cathy said pointedly, as they got closer and closer to town. "They either don't think Derek's going anywhere or they're very sure he's left."

Xander nodded, accepting that piece of information. He was silent again for a moment before speaking again. "She calls me Alex."

Cathy frowned, sighing. "I know. It bugs you, doesn't it?"

There was a pause, as he mulled the question visibly. "It did, once," he said honestly, pressing lightly on the accelerator.

"Listen," she said. No longer plagued by images of her head splattering against the road, now that Xander was going at something resembling a normal speed, Cathy was able to keep her eyes on him. "About what Julie said... about us..."

"Would you turn on the radio, please?" he interrupted, as if she'd never spoken, but politely all the same. When she did not respond, he looked at her and smiled. "There must be a good song or two on."

She smiled, laughing a little. "On this station, I wouldn't bet on it. The DJ's taste in music is like a pop star's taste in husbands."

He raised an eyebrow, not quite understanding that particular pop-culture reference, and making a mental note to ask Mike about it later.

She turned on the dial, and it came on midway through a word, making it hard to tell exactly which song it was. There was an acoustic guitar strumming along almost aimlessly, and every couple of beats there was a single piano note. It was clear that the song was ending, even the words were few and far between, and yet it lingered on. For the briefest of instants, Cathy closed her eyes and let the notes enter her and grow into something tangible within her mind. sparkling down over her like rainwater.

She opened her eyes and looked out as the last wisps of forest gave way to familiar houses and buildings that greeted her with memories.

It was years ago now, too many for her to be exactly sure when. Before she and Mike had become an item, before high school, she was almost certain. There was a waterfall somewhere just outside the boundaries of the city, not too far from where she now sat. She had walked all of the way there, the sun blazing down on her bare back, burning it for days. There had been a towel wrapped carelessly around her neck. She had been wearing an extremely loose t-shirt of her father's, one far too big for her, over a one-piece swimming suit and flip-flops.

She remembered the way the trees felt as she brushed past them one by one, their branches caressing her sweet skin, sharply at time, but always taking care not to harm her. The leaves were bright green by this time, and their smell made the city seem far and away. She hopped over a rock covered in moss and mushrooms, then stepped carefully down a steep slope made more difficult by her choice of footwear.

On the radio, another piano note rang out, softly traveling along the air.

She had then come to a slippery ledge, overgrown with plant life that seemingly defied gravity as it grew down the slope. Some large fruit hung over the gorge by the thinnest of threads, but making no effort or strain of it. She leaned over it, letting a few small stones tumble downward, clacking off of the large, flat rocks below. There was the pool, just like Dawn had said. It was a great, circular deposit of water fed by a waterfall that started even higher than the ledge where she now knelt. It was so deep that in its middle it looked black.

She scurried down the side of the cliff, no longer noticing the awkwardness of the flip-flops, her heart pounding in her chest with excitement now.

When she got to the bottom, she stopped, taking a moment to observe the calm flatness of the water. Except where the falls hit it, of course. But even that created barely any ripples. It was like a painting and the artist had carelessly forgotten to add waves.

Slowly, she let the towel fall to the rocky shore, kicking off the sandals and letting her feet into the water without even testing it first. A chill ran up her, but she quickly got used to it; it even felt warm once she was chest-deep. She felt the ground in front of her would give way, and extended her right foot to test the ledge's depth. The water there was black, and she could feel no sign of bottom, just the swirling moss and weeds and one or two sticklebacks brushing past her, curious as to what the girl was doing here.

Closing her eyes and taking a deep breath, she leapt into the deep water, feeling it caress every part of her body as she moved down, down, down until pressure started to build in her lungs and ears. When the ache meant she could go no further, even though she had yet to touch the bottom, she opened her eyes. There was no light to see, but there were snippets of motion all around her, surrounding her... and she became a part of it, silent and forever, all knowing.

She started kicking her chubby legs, moving back up toward the surface with her hair swirling about her with every motion. When she broke the surface again, she was beneath the waterfall, its cool onslaught pressing down upon her. She found a gap in its flow quickly and took in air from it, then moved to let some of the water travel down her throat and over her hair, washing the dirt and muck out of it and back into the river.

The piano sounded one last time, ending the song.

"That was Forever and One-Eighth of a Day by my personal favorite, Nine Stops Ten. You should find this album. I myself own three of them. I'm Tara Sampson for WCBR1 radio, and this is your hourly news..."

Xander watched the road, squinting at something up ahead. Meanwhile, Cathy came out of her trance and turned toward the radio, waiting to hear any news of what had happened while they were in Coral Cove. She wondered briefly why her thoughts had brought her back to that place, one of the most peaceful memories she had.

"Tragedy has struck Coral Beach yet again. A search party for escaped convict Derek Smith located the bodies of 30 recently-reported missing persons."

"Thirty?!" Cathy exclaimed as her eyes went wide, turning to Xander for some direction on what to feel.

He did not even break his concentration from the road ahead, turning the wheel slightly to follow it.

"Police say that Smith is not a suspect in the latest murders, explaining the disappearances were reported days before his escape. Although names were not made available, sources tell us the victims were fellow convicts or linked to area crimes. Police urge residents to be on alert as the manhunt continues."

"Tees," Xander said simply, his face not changing expression for even an instant.

"We have to go, Xander!" Cathy bolted frantically, suddenly unable to sit still in her seat as a million thoughts bounced back and forth inside her head. "Mike could be out there somewhere, not to mention Derek! We can't just wait for this to..."

"Cathy," Xander interrupted calmly, not looking at her.

"The killer's done all of this, what if Mike found him? What if Mike found Derek? What if Derek and the killer met one another, what if they were working together all the time, plotting this whole thing so that Derek could escape..."

"Cathy," he repeated, cocking his head forward this time as he slowed the car down.

"What if they're planning something huge with the Circe or Engen or something like that, and we're all too busy to notice before it's too late."

"Cathy," he said, looking at her finally as the car eased to a stop. Red and blue rays of light flashed rhythmically all around them. "Look."

She took in her surroundings for the first time since she'd turned on the radio. There were police cars everywhere, parked so close together that even if the two of them had wanted to keep going, they would have had to find some other route to take.

The building they were piled around was so tall and massive that Xander and Cathy had to get out of the car just to see right to the top of its steeple, or even its large wooden doors.

It was the Apostle Church, est. 1952.

"Lord," Cathy said in a hushed voice, bringing her hand up to her face. "What's happened here?"

Xander did not answer, unless the grinding sound his teeth were making could be considered a response. He started walking toward the door, watching nothing but their heavy iron knockers as they seemed to get closer and closer to him. Cathy circled the car and followed him, hurrying to catch up and even then to simply keep pace with her suddenly driven friend.

He heard a sob to his left, and turned to see Reverend Gallagher holding onto the door of an ambulance for dear life, as though it were the only branch keeping him from being sucked down into a mighty whirlpool. Tears flowed freely down the old man's cheeks as fast as he could dab them away with a handkerchief. His moans were deep and mournful, and he did not even bother to look up and see the two teens watching over him.

Xander stepped inside cautiously, looking from one side of the old church to the other. Reverend Gallagher had walked up to an aged table set up near the back room and poured up two cups of coffee, motioning for Xander to sit down. Drew smirked at the old man. "Isn't this traditionally done at a confession booth?" he joked.

Gallagher's bushy grey eyebrows lifted. "You have sins to confess?" he asked, almost shocked.

Xander smirked, "I'm not what you'd call a religious man."

"That's not what I asked."

Xander sat down, taking up his coffee cup in one hand and chancing a sip on the hot liquid. It burned his tongue, and he felt the Womb veer up to repair the damage instantly. His eyes darted around the church nervously, always coming back to the visage of the son of God upon the cross, hanging dead center in the archway. He could still feel the spikes in his wrists from his own crucifixion, and felt a new empathy for the man on that tilted x. He looked at the kind old Reverend, who was smiling back at him expectantly, patiently waiting for the young man to speak.

"I can see I'll have to start," Gallagher laughed. "Shouldn't you be in school?"

Xander smiled, but it was fake. The smile that you give to older people when they ask questions such as those. "Schools got too many memories. Those old walls talk, y'know?"

"Indeed." He motioned all around him. "As do these walls. Often, late at night, I can hear the echos of a thousand spirits," he paused, staring Xander in the eye. "Recently, the voices of the dead have gotten louder."

Xander looked down toward his feet. "Yes, they have." There was a pause then while they both sipped on their coffees. "I'm having... problems... telling my friends about the events of these past weeks." he admitted.

Gallagher nodded. "I take it you lost someone close to you."

"Yeah. You don't get much closer then... her."

He nodded again. "Find guidance in the Lord, my son. He will help you."

Xander took a sip of his java. "I feel like the Lord had abandoned me, Father. I feel like I'm alone."

"Have faith, my son," the man said, touching him on the hand. "The Lord exists in all things. You may not find him here, but rather in a person. A loved one."

Xander took a last sip of his coffee, then put it down onto the table. He got up and began to walk toward the door. "Thank you, Father," he said, distantly.

Xander clenched his hands into fists, walking past Gallagher toward the mighty door of the church. He stopped then, because nobody had stopped him yet.

"What's wrong?" Cathy asked, coming up from behind him, looking over her shoulder at Gallagher again, who still had not noticed them. "Xander, talk to me. What's happened here?"

He didn't speak, merely turned and saw where many of the policemen were. They were out back, at the graveyard.

He turned and walked, slower this time, Cathy easily keeping pace with him. She heard him swallow back a large gulp of fluid, and there was something to his gaze that told her that he had at least some idea of what they were going to find here. At least, more than she did.

Halfway up the hill, Xander turned and acknowledged something simply, closing his eyes and nodding respectfully, but did not pause or break his stride.

Cathy looked where he had. It was a grave, one with no headstone. She furrowed her brow, and then realized that, in the darkness, there were shards of where a headstone had been sticking up from the ground. Behind that were the shattered remains of it, turned mostly to dust and pebbles. She became confused, looking around for a moment to get her bearings, then realized whose grave it was.

It had belonged to Frederick Windsor, whom most people had called Sud. He'd been shot by the Tees while at school.

Her hand immediately came to her mouth as she gasped, tears welling up in her eyes. She turned away from the horrible sight, running to catch up with Xander, who was almost at the top of the hill.

"Xander!" she called, the salt water reaching her cheeks now, and then the snow and grass below.

He stopped, his face hanging downward.

She thought he was stopping to wait for her, but when she reached him, she realized he was again paying his respects. They were standing next to another shattered headstone, this one covered in flowers and cards and letters. This one she recognized instantly. She had not long ago written one of those letters, and some of the roses had been bought by she, Mike and Xander together, trying to give the grave some light in the bleak weather.

It was Amanda Peterson.

Xander continued without a word as Cathy fell to her knees, digging her hands into the snow and making them cold and blue. She reached out and grabbed a rose in the palm of her hand, squeezing until juice ran forth from it from between her fingers. Rose oil mixed with her tears and fell to the snow, staining it the same dark red as blood.

After a moment of fighting the heaving gasps that attacked her body now, she turned to Xander, wondering why she could not feel his comforting, warm touch on her somewhere.

When her eyes found him, she realized why.

"No..."

He stood at the top of the hill, which was covered completely in snow, many sets of tracks going to and from it, including his own. He was looking downward, his hands shaking and then becoming fists, clenching tighter and tighter until she saw tiny drops of blood slither down his palms and drip from his knuckles. All at once, he fell to his knees without warning, his upper body still perfectly straight and rigid, staring down at what lay before him.

Even though he had his back to her, she knew that he was crying.

He was standing at the grave of Sara Johnson.

Her lower lip quivering, Cathy rose to her feet and followed his footprints up, keeping her eyes glued to the snow. They caught a shard of granite as she got closer to him, followed by a mound of displaced dirt, frozen and crystalline. She swallowed hard as she came up behind him, seeing the headstone smashed into at least two dozen separate chunks, but that was not where he was looking.

And then she knew, just as he had from the start. And just like him, she could not believe it until she saw it for herself.

Xander bent over quickly, pressing his face into the snow, as the shake that had started in his fists now enveloped his entire body. When he moved, all at once she saw what she knew had been there all along.

Sara looked up at her with eyeless sockets, removed from the ground from the waist up, a light layer of snow covering her body. Her skeleton showed through in places, but much of the skin of her face had remained, blue and pale and clinging to the bone with nothing but the fact that nothing had displaced it yet. The shoulder-length blonde hair that had once bounced and shook magically with her every movement was now longer, and it had taken on the appearance of dead hay, stiff and brittle. Her clothes were stained brown from the decay of her body and time spent in the ground, but it was still the white blouse and black satin dress that she had been put to rest in. Her mouth was closed, and for a moment, she almost looked as though she might wake up.

Xander reached out, carefully caressing her cheek with one finger, the flesh moving against his touch and never going back once it left, having long ago lost all its elasticity. "I'm sorry..." he mumbled between tears, almost inaudibly. Even Cathy hadn't really heard him, so much as she knew in her heart what he had said.

He let his hand trail down to her shoulder, grabbing it. As his head began to shake, not from side to side but rather vibrating in general along with the rest of his body, he pulled her carefully close to him, finally bringing her head to rest against his lap, stroking her hair, a great deal of which came out under the pressure.

"Xander..." Cathy said, soothingly, reaching out to touch him on the shoulder.

He thrust his head back, mouth open wide, and let out a long, deep bellow that echoed off the hills that were still miles away, clutching his dead lover close to his heart before collapsing onto it again.

Cathy returned her hand to her side, just watching her friend as he cried, knowing full well that that was all she could do right now.

"... Harris..."

She turned, seeing an officer standing a few meters down from them, smoking a cigarette and holding a cell phone to his ear. She squinted at him, as if focusing her eyes upon him would make her hear him better.

He turned in her direction suddenly, then dropped the smoke to the ground.

She took a step toward the Officer, again, knowing exactly what was about to happen, yet having to experience it to be sure.

When she got close enough that he could see who she was he turned away again, stepping to one side of his squad car.

She turned to one of the other officers. "Do you have a phone I could use?"

He eyed her suspiciously. His jaws seemed too large for the rest of his head.

"Please?"

He frowned, then took a small flip cell phone from his back pocket and handed it to her. She paused a moment, trying to remember Mike's number.

"Put it down."

"Excuse me?"

"You heard me, Xander Drew, put it down." Sara Johnson's voice echoed her own words. Her voice was like springtime. "Are you going to? Or are you going to make me repeat myself again?"

Xander looked at her with surprise and puzzlement, and not for the first, or the last, time. "And again I say, excuse me?"

"You have been at those damn Chemistry books for ten hours straight. You need to relax, and something tells me that I'm just the person to help you." Her back was arched, making her even more sexy then Xander could've ever thought possible. She wore cut-off jeans, with a sleeveless tube top, a modified fish-net stocking providing a sleeve for one arm, which held a smouldering smoke in it. The summer sun beat against the back of her head, creating a halo effect around her hair. She looked like an angel.

"But Sara, I still have to go over the Bronsted-Lowry acid and base tables, and ... "

She smacked the books to the ground. "Give it up! Come outside. Have fun. For me?" When she said "For me," she gave him little puppy dog eyes. He loved that. He loved her. More than life.

"Let me get my coat," he sighed.

"Yah!" she chimed, walking in with him and waiting in the hall. She looked at him for a second. "I love you, Xander," she said suddenly, cheerfully.

He looked up from tying his sneakers and into her eyes. She was serious. "I love you, too."

Xander lay on the ground, broken and beaten by Julian Grendel, who was Sara's current boyfriend. Blood seeped from his upper lip, making the bottom of his face warm and wet.

"When are you going to stop doing this?" she had asked him, using his shirt to wipe a bit of the blood away.

He looked up at her, smiling. "I guess when I start winning fights."

"Not that," she giggled, wiping more blood from his forehead. "This. Chasing after every boy I go out with like some... jealous father."

"Oh," Xander said, looking downward. "I guess when you start going out with reasonable guys."

"What do you mean?"

"Gee, I wonder. Grendel, Derek, Sud, Tommy, Jamie, Travis, Cecil... the list goes on. Guys that are... okay, but they don't deserve you. You deserve someone special. Someone who'll treat you right and make you feel good and... and not look at you like you're an object. You're better then you think you are, y'know. You deserve better than you think you do."

She smiled, then leaned in and kissed him on the cheek. "That was the nicest thing anyone ever said to me. Make me a promise."

"Anything."

"Don't ever give up."

"Huh?"

"Don't ever stop protecting me. And when I finally do find that guy you were talking about, protect someone else. This world needs a protector, Xander."

"I promise."

"Don't ever give up"

"So, you going to Julian Grendel's party on Friday?" Saraasked him, paying little attention to his response or even if he gave one.

"Uh, I'm not sure. I was thinking about hitting the Factory with Mike," Xander replied, half concentrating on her and half watching out for Grendel himself.

"Oh, come on, Xander," she whined. She said his name like it was some kind of a joke.

"All right, I'll come. But you have to promise me you'll make sure Mike and Cathy don't ditch me like the last time," he reasoned, heaving a massive sigh as he gave in.

"They didn't ditch you."

He gave her a droll, tired look.

"They didn't!" she laughed, slapping his arm playfully.

He frowned, then rolled his eyes and nodded.

"Oh, come on. Don't sulk. You know I'm right. They love you."

"They do," he agreed finally. "They really do. They love me and they're there for me and they are the best of friends - except in public. In public, it's like we never met."

"Drama Queen."

"Oh, I'm not saying they try it or anything... it's just the way things are. I get it." He forced a smile, making eye contact with her. "I don't even think they realize they do it."

She gave him a little smile, the right corner of her lip curling just enough to make her irresistible as she fixed her black tube top, even though it hadn't really needed it.

"I promise," she said, after she had spent enough time fiddling with her attire to make him twitch. "They'll be good little boys and girls, as long as you are."

He snorted, rolled his eyes, and closed his locker door with a clang.

"So, what's new today?" he asked, shooting her a smile. "Anything scandalous going on?"

"Well," she started, smirking to herself proudly. "I heard from Julie Peterson today that the reason Derek has been so on edge lately is because Theresa had to take the test."

"Yeah," Xander nodded. "That Family Living test was bad news. I think I must have only gotten an eighty-five or something..."

She turned and gave him a little slap on the arm. "Not that test, you halfwit. A pregnancy test."

Xander's eyes went wide for a moment as he held open the front door for her, which she barely acknowledged. "Oh."

"Yeah."

"Why would Derek be messed up over that?" he asked naively.

She shot him a look.

"Ah. Forget I asked."

"Done."

"Wasn't she supposed to be with Jamie?"

"They broke up."

"Why? I mean, besides the 'she may be pregnant from another man' thing?"

"That's just a rumor. The real reason was because he cheated on her," she smirked to herself coyly.

"With who?" he moaned, feeling a relantionship headache coming on.

"Me," she said proudly, and he realized that this would become a migraine before it was over.

Xander finished walking home with Sara, like always. They lived next door to one another, and had since either of them could remember. Since they were children. Every day he'd remember little things like where he'd fallen out of the tree trying to sneak up to her room when they were six, when she had been sick and wanted to play. Or on his lush, green lawn where she had found out how he felt when they were twelve.

He had had a huge crush on her that summer and had been sitting on the sidewalk between their houses, burning their initials into a piece of wood. She had started toward him on roller blades and he had dropped the wood and ran into his house. She'd picked it up and looked at it, then thrown it into the trees on her way down the road, never actually speaking of it. He could still remember the scent of the wood as it burned every time he thought of it. It was the way love smelled.

At that age, most children were confident of their own immortality. That they could do anything, and go anywhere. But it was then that he realized how different he was from his friend. She was a princess in their school. Other kids wondered why she lowered herself to talking to him. He was . . . abnormal. Subnormal. Less than human. Those who actually took notice of him could barely stand him. But when he was around her, none of it mattered. On that ten minute walk from home to school and back again, the world could fall down around his ears and crush him every day, and he wouldn't care. He would ask for more.

She walked up her driveway and through the off-white door into her house.

He watched it for a second after she was gone as if she were still there, then walked into his own house.

⋏⋏

"Enjoying the party?"

"Most definitely." Xander said enthusiastically.

She smiled at him.

He got lost in it for a moment, just staring at her. Her eyes were glossy, and he could see the brush strokes on her cheeks from where she had applied her makeup before going out.

She smiled at him again, nodding her head and waiting for him to speak.

"Oh!" he said finally, laughing humorlessly. "I had something I wanted to talk to you about."

"Okay," she chirped, still bobbing along to the song in her head. "Anything in particular?"

"Yes," he said. "No. Maybe."

"Glad we cleared that up."

"It's not any one thing. It's... look, we've know each other a long time, and --"

"Hey! You dropped one! You gotta take a shot!" she howled at someone from across the room, pointing at them wildly with her drink hand. She was still laughing when she turned back to him. "Sorry."

"That's okay."

"What were you saying?"

"Yes. What I was saying. What I was saying was -"

"This is the end of this year's flute hanger!" someone called from the next room.

Sara laughed, so hard that she almost fell over onto Xander.

"Hey, listen, you wanna go talk?" he asked, smiling as she helped herself back to her feet. "This place is a little loud."

"Yeah, sure."

He motioned toward the curtains he'd been playing with. When he pulled on the drawstring next to them, they opened and revealed a sliding glass door that lead out onto the balcony.

"Sly," she said, tossing him a playful wink. "If I didn't know better, I'd have thought you planned this."

Xander laughed.

The two of them walked out onto Grendel's balcony. The cool night air whipped at them, her light blonde hair blowing gracefully backward, exposing her neck and chest. He found himself looking at her unintentionally.

"Dear God you're beautiful," he said finally, with the honesty of a person who had been waiting forever to say it.

She smiled at him, with those beautiful lips that she had painted a sparkling platinum for the occasion. "Excuse me?"

"I said you're beautiful," he repeated, turning to look her square in the eye.

"Yeah." she laughed. "I got that. But why?"

"Because," he said, taking her hand. "You are."

He leaned in to kiss her. She looked up at him, moving in slightly herself, her lip quivering in an anticipation she hadn't even realized she had had until now. Her eyes fluttered back and forth between his lips to his eyes and his did the same, making eye contact every so often. He could smell her perfume and it overwhelmed him. He could feel the softness of her body, so close to his and yet still not touching. Slowly, they moved closer together. Closer...

"Xander," came a voice from inside.

"What?" Xander turned, angrily.

"We need you for something in here." It was Dave Marston, a jock friend of Jamie's. "It's this weird thing with Gren's computer. Some kinda net nanny keeping us off. You wanna...."

"Yeah. Just... gimmie a minute."

"All right."

Xander looked at Sara for a long moment, smiling. "Hold that thought."

If you're innocent, you're hurt, or you're scared... I'll be there.

"Xander, we have to go!" Cathy cried, more tears than she'd ever thought possible.

He had laid Sara back down now, and in fact was standing again, looking down at her upturned head. He did not respond to her, just stood where he was, seeming to be off in a daze.

"Xander, Mike's been hurt! The cops found him at Derek's and took him to the hospital! They're not sure if he's going to make it!"

"...gonna get them..."

"Yes! Agreed! We'll get Derek for this, and we'll get the murderer, and if someone different did this to Sara we'll get them too, and if we have time left over maybe we'll round up the Tees..." her entire face was red and puffy, and looked almost deformed with grief. "But right now, Mike needs me and I need to go to him and I need you to help me, Xander!" she wailed, curling her hands against her chest in some version of the fetal position.

"...Julie..."

Tears still coming, she furrowed her brow in absolute frustration, her mind unable to handle what he was saying at the moment. "What?"

"I'll kill them all," he said, his voice so low that it had moved past a growl and become almost like the harsh voice of the Black Womb.

"No..." she whispered, backing away from him a pace. "Please, no..."

Blood started to gush from the wounds his fingers had made in his palms now, and she realized that he had popped his talons *after* he'd made his hands into fists. The redness seeped down onto Sara's rotting corpse, then turning slowly darker and darker until it was black.

"Tommy, Travers, Roulette, Derek, Julie, Raine, Black Heart, Zakron, Genblade..." he thrust his hands into the air, even as the Darkness flowed over them, meeting at the center of his torso and splashing outward, doubling the speed at which they covered his body. "They'll all pay! They will! I'll make them! You hear me? I made a vow on this woman's grave once before... that if you were innocent, you were hurt or you were scared... I'll be there! Well tonight, I make a new one!" he screamed, his entire body covered now as he screamed in rage and hate at the city below him.

"No..." Cathy sobbed, stepping back steadily now.

"Unless you're innocent, I'll be there! I'll make you hurt, make you scared! You're all guilty, and I'll have this town shake with fear!

"Black Womb lives!"

He cried, as the ooze covered his head, quickly forming three red slits, opening to form his eyes and mouth. He turned, his muscular form looking Cathy up and down, then with one great leap was at the bottom of the hill, and seconds later in the forest surrounding the graveyard.

"God, no..."

CHAPTER THIRTEEN

Mike lay on the stiff, metal bed of the operating table as a doctor finished sewing the last of his wounds shut.

"We've got some seepage over here," called a nurse.

The anaesthesiologist rushed to Mike's side as the monitor beside him began to beep and flash wildly.

Cathy buried her head in her hands as the cab sped ever closer to the hospital. It was easily going as fast now as Xander had been going down the highway earlier, but she did not notice this time.

She was all out of fear.

The Black Womb landed against a thick tree, burrowing its claws in deep as it slanted its red eyes, surveying the homes just beyond the brush and the people that walked the streets near them.

Reilly changed Mike's IV bag quickly, tossing the empty one aside. "His heart rate's fading..." she cautioned, keeping one eye on the monitor as she worked, her face a stone as more liquid ran into his veins.

"...I can't stop the bleeding..."

The Womb slammed Tommy against the wall of his bedroom, making him scream in terror and pain, unable to look away from the creature's glowing red pupils.

"Tell me!" it demanded, turning and tossing the boy against the far wall.

"I don't know!" Tommy cried, cradling his newly dislocated shoulder.

Mike's face twitched, looking pained as the doctor finished suturing a long gash near his leg. The numbers on the monitors still changed constantly, rising and then falling again before repeating the process. As he watched in horror, blood started to seep out into the table from a wound he'd thought was closed.

He pushed his way past Reilly and the anaesthesiologist, a panicked look coming over his face as he tried to deal with the new bleed. "I need some help here!"

Cathy threw a wad of bills at the cab driver, not even stopping to see if she'd paid enough or too much as she leapt from the cab. She took off running toward the revolving doors of the hospital emergency entrance. Her eyes were bloodshot.

The Womb smashed through Derek's window, startling a police officer that was hunched over and pressing a cotton swab to a puddle of blood in the kitchen.

"What the fuck?!" he yelped, falling backward onto his ass and then fumbling for his gun.

The Womb lunged feet first at the cop, driving both its heels into his jaw. The officer went flying against the cupboards before he cracked his head and was knocked out cold.

The monster raised its nose high in the air even as it moved to the open fridge, sinking its claws deep into the back of Don Smith's cold shoulder and pulling him out. The body tumbled to the floor and the Womb peered inside for any clue. It sucked back air and closed his eyes. When they opened, the light glistened off their cherry surfaces, and it realized that the scent of Derek Smith had not been here in hours.

It bellowed.

Cathy pressed a hand against the glass door of the OR, watching as more and more people rushed in to help. Reilly left, urged once into the garbage can just outside the room, then continued down the hall.

Cathy turned and buried herself into Mike's father's shoulder.

The surgeon heaved a sigh of relief as he closed the last of the wounds. Mike, still intubated, was wheeled out of the operating room into the recovery area.

Black Womb jumped from the shadows of a bush, pressing his hands against the shoulders of a twenty-something man, forcing him onto the pavement.

"Where!?!" it bellowed, smelling the whiskey on the man's breath.

Cathy sat next to Mike, her hand touching his, listening to the steady beat of his heart monitor. She was afraid to do anymore. Afraid she might somehow hurt him. She wanted to get closer, to let his hospital gown soak up her tears, but instead they fell to the floor in a rapidly expanding puddle.

The Womb turned over Megan Greene's desk, sending her backward onto the floor. She raised a hand to defend herself, her eyes sparkling with horror between her shaking fingertips.

Mike's eyes opened slowly, and he turned toward Cathy, smiling a little.

She laughed, the tears of sadness ending, replaced immediately by a different sort. "Hey," she said simply, her voice squeaky and uneven.

"Hey..." he tried to reply, then gagged, noticing the tube in his throat for the first time. He looked as though he was about the throw up, and the monitor next to his bed began to scream again.

Cathy got up and backed away from the bed, cupping her mouth with her hands as two nurses rushed back into the room.

A panicked, fearful look came over his face and he clutched at the tube and tried to pull it out, feeling as it slid along the inside of his throat, scratching and biting at it and his muscles tried to contract to stop it.

"No!" one of the nurses shouted, but he pulled away.

Cathy screamed.

The Tees turned as one, the smile fading from Travers' face as he swirled his gun around to point it at the doorway, which hung open awkwardly.

There was nothing there.

"What..." George mumbled, even as his question was answered in the form of a guttural hiss.

"Honey, you've got to lie down!" Cathy pled, placing her hands firmly against Mike's chest.

"No, Cathy! You don't understand! I know who the killer is! We have to stop him!"

All four men turned toward the center of the room, where the Black Womb sat crouched, its elbows resting against its knees. Swirls of aqua had appeared in the redness of its eyes and grown like whirlpools until there was nothing left but the blue-green tint.

"It's the Black Womb."

-Bang!- Ban-Bang!-

Quinton shot wildly, bursts of light predating each blast for a fraction of a second, illuminating the rest of the room like lightning. The Womb flipped aside, landing back against its toes and then using the momentum to spring forward.

"Black Womb lives!" it bellowed mid-air as Quinton fired twice more. The three others pulled their own pistols out from their jackets and Ian double-checked to make sure that his was loaded.

The creature ignored the shots, swiping out with its massive claws when it got close enough to Travers, not batting the gun away but instead stabbing its index claw right through the man's palm then pulling backward in one mighty stroke. The gun went in one direction, off into the darkness... the man's middle finger and a great deal of blood went in the other direction, spattering some of the red liquid against Duncan's face.

Quinton fell to the floor, clutching his disfigured hand as blood spewed uncontrollably from it, some even going into his mouth as he cursed wildly.

All three of the others opened fire at once, six bullets finding their way into the Womb's chest and gut within seconds. It stumbled backward from the sheer force and its healing factor kicked into high gear. George watched in horror as the bullets squeezed their way out of the holes they'd created, rattling against the floor in the order they'd entered.

He changed his aim, firing up slightly.

The Womb's left eye seemed to explode in a splash of aqua and the creature screamed, bringing both its clawed hands up to it's face and only causing more damage.

"Yes!" Duncan cried, pumping his arm in the air while using the sleeve of the other to wipe Quinton's blood from his face.

"Keep firing, you idiots!" Travers belched out between gasps of pain.

The Womb looked up from his hands, its monstrous face expressionless, its eye back as though it had never been gone.

It swiped its claws down low, its arm seeming to extend as it did, like swinging an elastic with a weight on the end. They dug into George's ankle, shattering the bone and flipping him onto his back. With one massive leap it was on the man, who was now screaming almost in perfect tune with Travers. The demon dug its claws into the gang-lord's chest ripping downward. George brought the gun up point blank to the Womb's face, putting quick first pressure on the trigger.

The Womb opened its mouth as wide as it could, revealing duel rows of long, yellowed, jagged teeth. It shot its head forward, biting down on George's wrist even as the rapist's shot blew out the back of the Womb's skull.

The Womb, still holding George's hand and gun in its mouth, twisted its legs in a way no human and few animals could, propping them against George's chest and shoving backward into a back-flip that took him halfway across the room, taking George's hand with it.

The creature landed right next to Ian, spitting the now useless appendage out and slashing quickly under the man's arm and simply tossing his against a wall twenty feet away before he could even fire a shot.

It turned its focus to Duncan, whose gun was shaking and empty.

Growling darkly, it leaped.

Cathy opened the door to the barn.

She gasped, closing her eyes.

Xander knelt naked in the center of the large storage room, the air thick with blood and gunpowder. All around him was a huge puddle of discarded black ooze, and his body was covered in a thin layer of congealed blood from head to toe, weighing his hair down tight against his scalp.

The only light was directly upon him like a spotlight, making it hard to see anything else until her eyes adjusted.

When they did, she saw the parts.

There was a hand in the corner.

A head with a large, animalistic bite mark taken out of it lay not far from where they stood, a look of terror frozen onto its face, a horrifying tribute to Quinton Travers's last few moments of life.

Propped up against the wall closest to Xander was a naked body, fat and covered with hair, shards of his clothing scattered all around him, so weighted with blood they did not blow in the draft created by the open door. Cathy recognized it as George McGyver. He was missing a leg and both his arms... and his genitals.

Somewhere in the room, someone still breathed heavily, quick, small breaths. For a second, Cathy dared to hope that someone had survived... and then the breathing stopped, and there was the sound of something hitting the floor. She winced.

Xander turned toward her, tears rolling freely down his cheeks. He opened his mouth to speak but found that he could not. It hung there, open, waiting for words, the layer of blood stretching over it, which he made no effort to remove.

Slowly, Cathy stepped toward him.

She stood next to Xander and looked down at him. His eyes were still partially black.

All at once he moved forward, wrapping his arms around her legs and hugging his face into her mid-section, covering her lower half in blood.

And he wailed.

. . .

Xander sat on the corner of his bed, facing the wall but not quite looking in its direction. He gripped tightly onto his pillow and curled around it in the fetal position. He rocked mindlessly, back and forth, back and forth...

He'd hardly said a word since they brought him home from the warehouse. Cathy had helped him into shower, but she didn't think he had even been aware of it. He would periodically stop crying, sometimes for a full twenty minutes, then something would flip a switch inside his brain and he would start again. There were always more tears, and as Mike watched him start again, shoving his head into the pillow, he thought maybe the Womb regenerated, replenished his tear ducts, giving him more moisture to seep out.

He briefly thought of that as a good thing, then turned back to the tiny print of the file folder he cradled in his hand.

Cathy sat next to Xander, her index finger gently caressing the back of his hand in a fluid, repetitive motion, but achieving no response. It was as if she were touching fresh mortar, cold and wet. She turned from Xander's blank stare to the bandages revealed by Mike's open shirt, unable to find a sight that would allow her mind to rest.

Xander didn't seem to be breathing.

His eyes shot at her for a split second, then returned to their forward gaze at the screen saver bouncing around his screen, displaying the time, counting away the seconds.

Mike flipped back a page, scanning through the document that seemed to randomly change font and size, sometimes escaping into O'Toole's scrawled version of handwriting. "Got it," he said finally, but without satisfaction.

Cathy looked up, leaning forward just a little, but not taking her hand from Xander's. "Yeah?"

"What does it say?" Xander said haggardly, though his lips barely moved. The sound startled them both, as if they'd forgotten he was capable of it.

176

"It's that word again... amalgam. The one he kept repeating over and over. He finally decided to explain what he meant by it."

"And?" Cathy persuaded, coaxing her boyfriend to continue.

Mike scanned through the rest of the document, flipping over to read the first few lines of the next page, his eyes moving back and forth quickly. "Says he'd drugged you. He calls it an 'association-response chemical molecular adhesive.' Something the boys at Engen or Circe cooked up more than likely, though it doesn't say for sure. He used it on you during the hypnosis sessions... all of us for a while, until he started to narrow down exactly which one of us he was looking for."

"What did it do?" Cathy asked, hushed; she felt shocked and violated.

"Whatever he wanted it to. He'd introduce it before each session, then use the session to program that specific dosage. He really laid it on Xander though... keeps using the word 'amalgam'... and 'merge'... doesn't say how he administered it, though."

"So, how do we do this?" Xander asked, trying desperately not to make it sound like a groan.

O'Toole smiled at the young man's compliance, although it had to be forced out of him. He reached into the breast pocket of his faded blue shirt and pulled out a gold pocket watch. "I'll be placing you into a hypnotic state, Mr. Drew. While in that-- "

"With that?" Xander said, raising an eyebrow and pointing at the pocket watch, engraved, 'To Warren, for many years of loyal service.'

"Excuse me?" O'Toole stuttered, trying to find his words after being interrupted.

"You're seriously going to try and hypnotize me... with a pocket watch?" he laughed skeptically.

Warren smiled, dangling the golden circle confidently. "Why, yes, actually."

The younger man clicked his tongue against the roof of his mouth a couple of times, letting saliva slosh in and out of the gap in his two front teeth. "Can I see it first?"

O'Toole smiled wide, handing him the trinket.

Xander held it in the palm of his hand, watching as the lamp light from the Counselor's desk gleamed off of its gold plated surface. He bit his lip as he saw his own reflection in it, and could almost picture himself transforming. Could almost feel the beast inside of him breaking down barriers, clawing at the doors of Drew's consciousness, waiting, wanting. Wanting the blood. As he stared at the watch, O'Toole's heartbeat seemed to get louder and louder until it was all that Xander could hear; like a soft drink machine with 'drink me' scrawled across it.

"I'd like to have that back now." O'Toole coughed, reaching out and grabbing the clock by its chain. "Is there anything else before we begin?"

O'Toole cleaned his thick, round glasses, placing them back on his face. He grabbed

his pocket watch from its perch, pinned to his lapel, and let it drop, dangling from its chain.

Warren picked up the watch by its chain, handing it to Xander, who watched it (as if already in a trance) for a moment as it spun in one direction, then another.

He cleaned the watch, making it gleam, then carefully placed it back in his breast pocket, careful not to smudge it again by touching it with his bare hand.

Xander held the watch, spinning it slightly between his thumb and forefinger.

"It was on the watch," Xander sighed, raising his head from the pillow, his eyes looking tired and old. "He never, ever touched it with his bare hand. And I always asked to see it before I went under, to touch it... he always pretended to resist. That lying..."

"That was probably one of the predominant suggestions he implanted," Mike nodded slowly, recalling his own experience with the watch, even though he himself had never actually gone under. "A desire to hold it whenever you saw it."

"What else did he get us to do?" Cathy almost whispered, shifting uncomfortably on the bed covers, imagining what such a drug could have gotten her to do without her even knowing about it.

Mike saw his lover's discomfort and quickly found her section of the passage. "Umm... not much for you, actually. He was getting you to repress bad memories, but there was also some kind of associative trigger on them. He was locking things away on you... the effect should have worn off by now though, without steady doses."

Cathy thought of the piano, how that song had triggered her memory of the waterfall, and that she had had no idea why. She recalled O'Toole playing the piano in the music room one day, and a similar memory having come to her. She remembered how relaxed she'd become in the car with Xander, practically throwing herself at him, when the piano solo had started. "They were to relax me," she whispered. "To calm me down. But why?"

"Doesn't say," Mike sighed. "I guess we'll never know, now."

"What else was there?" Xander asked, still just staring forward at the time ticking by.

"Oh, gee..." Mike huffed, running a hand through his hair and wincing as the motion stretched some of his stitches. "He did it to some of the teachers... he'd offer them coffee every day and use that damn handkerchief of his to smear it onto their mugs. Getting them to stay quiet about his techniques and what he was doing with our files, probably."

"Especially Shnieder," Cathy finished.

Mike nodded. "There were other students, too, making sure they repressed memories... like the time the Black Womb attacked Tommy in his bedroom during the whole Tee/Omega thing. He didn't forget it, just never talked about it. Did the same thing to Mandy, made her not talk about what the Tees did to her." He paused, again turning the page, his eyes growing wide.

"What?" Xander said, finally looking over.

"He also programmed certain responses to situations, made her not fight back against the Tees the second time. He made her eat less, made her hormone levels fluctuate, sometimes on an hourly basis... he'd make her period stop suddenly for a month, to make her think she might have been pregnant..."

"She never..." Cathy stammered, he mouth dropping. "...She would have come to me."

"Yeah," Mike agreed, raising a finger. "But he also did that 'think, don't tell' thing to her, too. Made sure she wouldn't say a word."

"What'd he do to me?" Xander asked, turning toward the wall now.

Mike swallowed. "Made you forget about your first few encounters with the Anti-Womb... probably because he was there, although it doesn't say that outright. Made your bloodlust grow whenever the name Genblade was mentioned, in case you ever needed to defend Circe against him. Made you repress the memories of Sara, Sud... even Julie, unless certain key words activated them... those are all worn off by now, probably months ago."

Xander nodded. "What else?"

His friend sighed, closing the folder. "When you went under the hypnosis, he brought out the Womb. Awoke it in its own trance-like state, triggered memories of killing and maiming inside of it, sated its hunger for blood, all the while merging both of your personas... or at least trying to, seems he didn't get too far with that part."

"Trying to get me in control. Into something they could use," he finished, eyes growing wide.

"So..." Cathy drawled, her mind snapping onto what the boys already had. "You were never getting control, just borrowing it?" she asked, horrified.

Neither responded, just sat there in silence and avoiding eye-contact.

Finally, Cathy looked at Xander, and he at her. Each knew what the other was thinking. That it couldn't end now. Not yet. That all they'd managed to do was go three steps forward... and ten steps back.

"What now?" she said softly, no longer trying to hold back her tears as she pulled her hand away from Xander's.

Neither of them had an answer. They sat in silence.

After a few minutes, Mike's shoulders heaved upward, then relaxed again in a heavy sigh. He spoke three small words that said everything of the situation: "Black Womb lives."

BOOK TEN

CHAINS

PROLOGUE

It always starts off small.

They say that even an ant can start an avalanche, and now I know it to be true, even if I don't quite grasp how yet.

It all started about ten years ago, with an event that's more common in today's society than most people realize: with the abuse and neglect of a small child, only five or six years old at the time. That child's name was Derek Smith.

He wasn't beaten or accosted or molested like some of the suffering children in this world, but the abuse was no less real and its effect no less grand. His father and mother worked, one a journalist and one a grade school teacher. As a result, little Derek never got the attention he deserved and needed to develop as a child. He was raised by the media around him as opposed to those that loved and cared for him. Surrounded by third-person-shooter video games and movies that glorified acts of terrorism, he grew up callas and unable to distinguish between right and wrong, or recognize the effect of his actions upon others or to empathize with the harm he caused them, feeling only whatever the event brought to him at the time, which quickly away like a autumn leaf on a spring breeze.

As the time with his parents became less and less, he reached a breaking point when his mother passed away at the age of eight. Now his workaholic father was his sole support system, and proved lacking. So with his father working harder and harder at getting that Pulitzer prize to prove himself worthy to his only son, Derek worked to make sure that his father would get it: and began murdering the people of Coral Beach, Maine in an attempt to get his father that award-winning story so that they could spend more time together.

It was in that act that... that...

...

..

.

Cathy Kennessy stopped typing and watched the curser blink at the end of the line. She frowned as it winked at her from where she had left it after the end of the word that.

It was early morning, roughly five am, and the first bare hints of sunlight were beginning to perk their way above the trees that stood beyond her bedroom window. The air in her room was cool enough to make her breath show when she exhaled, and she had snuggled her feet into fluffy red slippers to protect them.

She shifted her focus from the blinking curser to the clock in the lower right hand corner of the screen and then back again, let out a huff of frustration, then brought one red-painted fingernail over the backspace button, as if threatening her writer's block to come undone.

"What are you doing over there?" Mike Harris chuckled from his place snuggled into the sea of pillows that covered her bed. He pressed pause on his DS for a moment and laid it atop his chest, then squinted his eyes to see what she was typing across the room. "'Surrounded by third-person-shooter video games and movies that glorified acts of terrorism'... hun, what are you writing? 'Derek Smith : The Unauthorized Biography'?"

Cathy smiled, turning around on her chair to face him, giving him a smug look. "Something like that."

Mike snorted, then turned his game back on and started to play, the three-note melodies of the game humming away once again. The game was nearly enveloped by his massive hands, which occupied her line of sight and prompted several inappropriate thoughts. His forearms and shoulders were no less large or broad. He had always been strong, something that she had always guessed was a trait amongst his birth parents, but in the last few months he had been pushing himself to be bigger and better than everyone else. Especially since winter set in, he had been spending a great deal of time at the school gym after hours training himself, and now he was positively rippling.

He paused his game again and looked past it to Cathy, her eyes still lingering somewhere in the vicinity of his tricep muscles. He raised an eyebrow to her and pretended to be annoyed at her ogling of him. "Can I help you?" he asked impatiently.

Cathy's gaze jolted up toward his face, as if only now realizing that she had been staring. She laughed, and then a wry smile began to curl its way up the edges of her lips. She stood up slowly and made her way over toward him. "I'd rather help myself," she said in a hushed, deep voice. She leaned over him and opened her mouth and brought it down until it was just above his, letting it linger there for a moment as her hair fell onto either side of his face. His breath quickened the longer she waited before actually making contact, and when she finally did the smooth wet sensation of her lips drove shocks through his entire system, her tongue leaving her mouth and entering his just once, briefly, before she broke off the embrace. His eyes still closed and mouth still open as she backed off ever so slightly, watching the as the effects of her kiss lasted even after she had stopped. Putting both her hands on the bed for support, she got off of him and then moved back to her chair.

"Um..." he said when his brain became a little less foggy and his ability to speak returned. "Was that your fantasy, or mine?"

She smirked, giggling at him. "Let's go with both."

"You're a cruel girlfriend," he reminded her as he sat up against the wall and let his feet dangle off the edge of the bed. He fixed his suddenly too-tight jeans to be more comfortable.

"I try." She flashed him a goofy smile that always made him laugh, then turning back toward her laptop and starting to backspace over what she had just written.

Mike watched her as the words erased one by one, except for the first two paragraphs, leaving it at :

It always starts off small.

They say that even an ant can start an avalanche, and now I know it to be true, even if I don't quite grasp how yet...

"I'll ask again," he sighed, switching off the game and laying it on his lap. "What are you doing?"

Cathy turned and gave him a look of dismay. "How many lives have you saved in the past few months?"

His head bobbed back a second, shocked by the suddenness of the unexpected question. "I don't know-- a dozen, maybe? I don't really keep track."

"And what about Xander, how many has he saved? Or taken, for that matter? That's if you don't count the whole thing with Alpha, when he pretty much saved the world, so, like, seven billion lives right there."

"What are you getting at?"

She laughed, in such a way that let him know she thought that question was absurd. "He - saved - the - world - once!" she said, pronouncing every word slowly to hammer home the point. "I know all those video games and comic books and science fiction novels and all that make that seem like no big deal-- but it is, Mike. I mean I don't think anybody has actually ever done that before. Or since."

Mike's brow tightened toward the center, as he started to understand. "I guess it is a big deal. But that still doesn't explain what you're doing."

She frowned and touched a hand against the soft skin between her neck and her left shoulder, tracing a finger around the intricate network of scars that were only now covering themselves over with a fine layer of flesh.

"Ah," Mike smiled, nodding. "It's about that," he said, motioning to the wound.

"No, it's not -- it's --" her eyes cast downward, then back up to meet him. "When the Womb attacked me, my whole life flashed before my eyes. I know how cheesy and fake that sounds, but -"

"No," he interrupted, his voice as soothing as he could make it. "It's not at all."

She smiled. "Anyway, that was the first time he ever attacked me... alone, you know? And on my way to the hospital, even though I wasn't hurt that bad, all I could think was that it could have been worse. It could have killed me, right there. I starting thinking that I'd never get to see Trina grow up, or tell my parents how much I loved them, or get to move in with you, or tell Xander that I forgive him. All the people we've seen die since September, you would think that I would have learned not to leave so many things undone."

"You wanna move in together?" he smiled stupidly.

She gave him a look, then continued. "I know there's nothing I can do about that. I know that if I die, you'll find some way to explain all this -- madness -- to my parents so that they understand. But what if we all die, Mike?"

He sat up now, leaning close enough to take her hand and run his thumb rhythmically against the back of it. "What?" he asked patiently.

She tisked, unsure of how exactly to get her point across. "What if you, me, and Xander all died? At once?"

"That's -- not going to happen, sweetie."

"Oh, really?" she laughed, taking the statement as an insult to her intelligence. "We almost did when the Tee's attacked the school. And when Zakron came after us. That thing could have easily killed all three of us. That's not even considering that two of the greatest serial killers in the country have a serious hate for all three of us, and one of them is out there somewhere right now!"

"Shh --" he calmed, stroking her hand until she lowered her voice, mindful of her little sister in the next room.

She got off the chair and knelt on the floor, snuggling in close to him. She draped her arms around him and rested her head on his stomach. It was less soft since he'd started working out regularly, and she found she missed the comfort of a little fat. "What if we all died and nobody knew? Nobody knew why or for what... or what we'd done and the lives we'd saved? What if nobody realized how close the world came to ending once?"

"I get it," he smiled warmly, touching the side of her head. "I do. I get it now."

She smiled. "Thank you. So, I decided I'm going to write a book. A novel, really. Kind of like those dramatic reenactments from Unsolved Mysteries."

"Yes, because our lives need the added drama."

"Shut up," she teased, giving him a little slap before kissing him quickly, then moving back to her chair. "I mean I know most of what happened, either first hand or from being told, but there's some stuff I'm going to have to make up. Like, there's no way of knowing what Hale might have said to O'Toole behind closed doors, so I'll make it up. But I'll make it sound real -- y' know?"

"I gotcha," Mike nodded, then thought for a moment. "I like the line in that case. The whole 'ant and the avalanche' thing. It suits it, I guess."

"But--" she coaxed, wanting more feedback than that.

"I think it's wrong to start the story with Derek. It's not supposed to be about him. And the way you were writing it, you would have written yourself to an end in like, four more pages."

She frowned, looking back at the horrid blinking curser. "Actually, I already had," she admitted. "But isn't that where it all starts, with Derek? He's the one who killed all those people."

"Yeah, but that's one of the reasons it shouldn't be about him."

"Well, I'd make it about Xander, but that 'd be too hard. There's so little we know about where he actually came from or how he was made yet, it'd just confuse whoever read it."

Mike motioned in agreement. "Why not write it from your point of view? That 'd be simplest."

Her brow furrowed as she considered that for a moment, then looked back at the screen with confidence. "Yeah... I could do that. Tell the whole story from my side of things. It's going to end up that way whether I try to or not, seeing as I'm the writer."

"Exactly. And that way, you can put in how you feel about stuff. You can put the font in italics and do like a voice-over monolog or something, like: 'Star Date 0.8765.765.9, I was making out with Mike, when --'"

She shot him a look. "No Star Trek now please. I'm not in the mood."

"I thought you liked Star Trek?"

She rolled her eyes at him, dangling her fingers over the keyboard again.

He took this as a sign that she was starting again and picked up his game.

After a pause to collect her thoughts, her fingers once again began to flutter over the keys.

... It always starts off small.

They say that even an ant can start an avalanche, and now I know it to be true, even if I don't quite grasp how yet.

The Factory. The Factory was a local arcade where we all went to hang out when there was nothing better to do, which was just about all the time. It existed in this limbo where nothing happened and everything happened. Couples became couples there, and often became singles there as well. There was money and there was change at a time when it seemed like everything was changing. It was a giant living room outside our parent's homes, always loud and exciting and neon.

Jamie Dawkins leaned over one of the many pool tables which adorned the club, raising an eyebrow as he tried to figure out his shot. His leather sports jacket crumpled and scrunched noisily every time he moved, impeding his ability to shoot. Many times he had pushed up the sleeves, but they always fell back down almost immediately. But he dared not take it off. His brother had worn that jacket when he was captain of the Coral Beach Cougars, and his father before that. Now that he was finally the captain it barely ever left his back. Some even said he showered with it on...

She stopped, her shoulders falling.

Mike glanced up, taking a quick scan of the screen. "That sounds good."

"It's crap," she corrected flatly. "It's going to come into my point of view in a second. I couldn't think of where to start it, so I figured right before Jamie died would be as good a spot as any. And I'd have to spend a little bit of that time introducing Jamie and everyone else, so I thought maybe I'd do it from my point of view, watching the two of you play pool at the Factory that night -- but it's stupid."

He winced, remembering the pain he'd felt when he heard of Jamie's death as though it had just happened. "That's great, baby," he said, swallowing back hard.

She turned to look at him with regret, then quickly pressed save on the word document and closed out of the program, then walked over to him. "It still tears at you, doesn't it?" she asked, though it wasn't really a question.

Mike's eyes grew distant for a moment as he stared off at nothing, then turned back to her as she sat down beside him. "No, it doesn't," he admitted, raising up his arm so she would be able to snuggle in against his chest. "And I think that bothers me more than anything. There's been so much since then, that it seems..."

"Small?" she finished for him, reaching one hand up inside his shirt to keep it warm, then running her nail around the groves of his familiar frame.

He nodded, but did not respond.

She opened her mouth to continue, then stopped. There really wasn't anything to say. As horrible as it sounded, it was true and she knew it. The death of Jamie Dawkins did seem small now.

They sat in silence for several minutes until the glowing red letters of her clock read five thirty. She turned to Mike, whose eyes were closed but she knew was not asleep, and poked him twice in the leg. "Come on," she coaxed, then waited for him to move.

CHAPTER ONE: DISCOVERY

It watched her from the corner of its eye, her every movement reflecting off its opaque, aqua-marine retinas. She was holding a tiny plastic statuette of a bird sporting a green Mohawk. After examining it carefully for a moment she placed it back atop her dresser along with several others, including a duck that was smashing an electric guitar in grand Who-style and a long-tailed mouse playing the maracas.

She turned toward the window and looked almost directly at it, not quite right into its eyes but close enough. She lingered, and it thought that perhaps it might have been spotted. It let go of a frustrated grunt into the cool fall air, which became visible in the chill and traveled up past the leaves of the tree on which it stood perched. She stared out the window, then turned back toward her bed. She moved the pillow and pulled back the covers. She should have been in bed hours ago.

She had light blonde hair with white highlights, which had made her head shine like a halo. She was beautiful and graceful, sweet and innocent. Somewhere deep within the creature's mind it remembered someone else that had fit that description, although it couldn't quite remember who just now.

There were stuffed animals all over a shelf near the ceiling, the bright colors of each drawing its gaze. It focused in on a red one in particular, turned an odd purple in its always-blue distorted vision. There was a hole in the wall that had been hastily patched, about the size of a quarter, and an old stereo that looked as though it might have been handed down from an older sibling. It rested atop a bookcase, the lower shelves of which were decorated with Baby Sitter's Clubs, Harry Potters, and Chronicles of Narnia. The creature regarded them with some degree of fascination, then turned back toward the girl.

She was wearing a floppy nightgown now with a faded printing of a teddy bear on the front of it.

The creature jumped off of its branch, its black, scaly form glistening in the starlight for a moment before landing on the roof over her window with a soft thud, digging its talons into the tiling and tar.

The noise, no matter how slight, made the girl jump. She looked around her room, then out the window into the trees, trying to find the source of the sound. There was none to be seen.

She picked up her copy of Harry Potter and the Prisoner of Azkaban *and lay on her bed for thirty minutes reading it before she had assured herself that there was nothing in her room that was going to jump out and hurt her. She laid the book on her night stand and turned off her lamp, shrouding the room in darkness. She rolled over and closed her eyes and went to sleep.*

The creature's eyes opened, their blue-green glow illuminating the room surrounding them. The eyes were all that were visible of it now, here in the blackness, if the girl had been awake to see.

It reached out quickly quietly as it crept ever closer, bringing a claw ever so lightly up -- up -- raising it to just the right height. With one lightning fast motion, it brought its arm down, digging it deep into the girl's chest. Her eyes snapped open and she opened her mouth to scream. The creature's hand was already there, holding the noise in as it ripped upward agonizingly slow, spilling blood onto clean sheets --

Cathy awoke with a start, hot sweat flying off her forehead. Her breathing was labored, drowning out even the roaring winter wind outside, which shook the whole upper floor of the house down to the very last nail. Her full lips gasped for air as her nightmare slowly eased its way out of her mind, the bane of consciousness forcing it away.

She pushed her covers away, her warm body sticking to them where flesh was exposed until only her flannel pajamas covered her. Her chest heaved and her hands shook as she struggled both to remember and to forget what her mind had just been experiencing.

She looked out her window and realized that it was dawn. The sun was almost invisible through the clouds that constantly threatened to snow. There was a defused glow over the trees and buildings outside, bathing everything in light, making every wind-swept snow drift visible.

It almost looked peaceful.

She put her feet down on the cold carpet that lined her spacious room. She stood there wriggling her toes for a moment, an exercise she was convinced forced her feet to get used to whatever temperature they were in (and that Mike was convinced was just plain crazy). Satisfied that she was as warm as she was going to get until her father got up and turned up the thermostat, she walked over to her closet and opened it, her back turned to the rest of the room.

She stopped, her eyes growing wide.

She heard a sound behind her, a long, scraping slice like the sound of metal against metal. She closed her eyes in a silent prayer, then turned around slowly.

The room was empty. She knew it was for a fact, now. A few months ago she'd arranged the furniture into the corners and asked her parents for a new bed, one that you could not fit a person under, but went straight to the floor. She's told them that she liked the idea of having all that space to do her exercises in, but in reality it was for reasons just like this, so that she could be quickly assured there was nobody in her room that shouldn't be.

Allowing her dark eyes one last sweep of the room, she turned back to the closet and ruffled through the shirts she had there, settling after a moment on a black tank top that said dumpster across the front of it in glitter. She threw it hanger-and-all against the bed, then tapped her finger against her lip for a moment while deciding on her jeans.

Gripping each door of the closet in a hand she closed it again (it so rarely got left open these days) and headed toward her vanity.

There was a tickle in the back of her mind, a memory to do something that had almost reached the point of habit, but not yet. She opened her jewelry box and took out a small silver packet with twenty-eight pills in it, each in their own tiny blister-pack bubble of air. She snapped one small pink pill out and pressed it between her lips. She swallowed it without water and the ritual was done, the twinkle in the back of her brain quelled for another day.

She removed her top, and her shoulder cried out in pain when she did. She craned her head awkwardly to look at the scar on her left shoulder, administered by one of the Tees months ago and never having healed quite right. She tisked, then reached for the shirt she had picked out and slid it down over her head.

She stopped again when it was almost completely down over her, swearing that she heard something.

-Nok - Kock-

She turned toward her bedroom door even though she knew that wasn't where the sound was coming from. She glanced briefly at the glowing red numbers on her alarm clock. It was not yet six in the morning. Mike shouldn't be picking her up for school for at least another two hours.

-Knock!-

That one was louder, and she decided that she had better go down and see who it was before one of her parents woke up and did it, because if it was Mike at this hour it would be the last time he would be allowed to knock on the door until long after Christmas.

She moved down the stairs with the speed and grace of a pedal on a breeze, her long black hair continuing in that direction as the rest of her turned toward the front door, released the latch and turned the knob, then opened it just a little.

"Shouldn't open the door... without asking who it is first," Xander Drew said, leaning his entire body against the doorframe. He was covered in blood and snow. "Never know who might be there."

Her eyes grew wide and she opened the door the rest of the way. Xander fell and crashed onto the hardwood floor, slamming his teeth against it as he did so.

CHAPTER TWO: SEARCH

Mike wriggled his toes inside of his size eleven shoes, hoping that it would somehow force his feet to adjust to the cold -- or at least ward off frostbite as he walked knee-deep through a snow drift that seemed to go on for miles in every direction, pulling his parka tight to protect against the freezing wind.

He stopped a moment and looked at the ground around him for footprints or any sign that somebody had been there before him. He turned off his flashlight, realizing that he no longer needed it.

Strands of his hair had become frozen together, making them now just stems of yellow icicles coming out of his scalp. He shivered against a biting wind and wished to high heaven that he could get the Friends theme out of his head. It had been stuck there for several hours.

He saw a police officer about ten feet away, just coming into his peripheral vision. The tall man had a pot belly and still held his flashlight out in front of him, apparently not yet having realized its uselessness in the dawning hours. He held a smoldering cup of coffee in hand and brought it to blue lips at regular intervals.

Good, Mike thought to himself. *One of the officer's wives must have put on another pot.*

At the thought of it, he could almost feel the warm liquid traveling down his throat, thick and sweet with far too much sugar and just the slightest hint of cream. If he was lucky they'd still have some real cream, which had made the entire experience nothing short of perfect. The fat from it made the warm from the coffee last hours instead of minutes.

Licking his lips, he forced his eyes away from the coffee and back to the wilderness ahead, a frown making his cracked, freckled cheek-bones smart. He stumbled once against the mounting snow, then pressed forward.

It's been twenty days, he reminded himself, feeling his foot dig into the virgin powder. Realizing that it was now morning, he corrected himself. *It's been twenty-one days. Twenty-one days since Derek escaped, and since then nobody has gotten a look at him.*

There had been sightings. Many, to say the least. It seemed that for the last twenty-one days, every time a shadow moved in the night or a sound was heard echoing from the winter darkness, it had been Derek Smith back to finish the job he'd started months ago and kill them all one by one. But as for somebody actually seeing him... that had yet to happen. And in a town where there was more than one thing out there to make noises in the night, one could hardly pin ones hopes on them.

What there had been, however, where signs of his presence.

The night after he broke out there had been a break-in at The Factory. His fingerprints had been found all over several of the video game terminals. One even had a spot of his blood on it, though god only knew how he had come to shed it.

The night after there had been two occurrences. One had taken place in the city morgue. One of the coroners had come in to close up for the night and had found the body of Derek's father strewn across the operating table. The body had been ripped apart, much like many of Smith's victims months ago -- and his hand was missing.

That same night, an old man answered his doorbell only find a flaming brown paper bag left on his porch. It was a childish prank that Derek, Mike and Tommy had often played when they were young, filling a bag full of a dog's excrement and putting it on a doorstep. When the man would try to stomp out the fire, he would get it all over his shoes and legs.

Only this time, when the man had attempted to put out the blaze the afore-mentioned hand had been inside, causing the elderly man to go into cardiac arrest. He died short hours later as doctors attempted to revive him.

Somewhere deep inside him, Mike knew that Derek had gleaned a sick sense of self-satisfaction from that incident in particular.

Having come a few feet over the snow bank he took another look around, squinting against the wisps of air that made his eyes water and want to close. Again, there was nothing. No sign of life whatsoever, except the occasional squirrel. He sighed, the air forming a cloud as it came out of his mouth, hanging for a moment before rising up and eventually disappearing. It was what Mike feared the most. That, like his breath, Derek was just hanging around for a moment or two after being released -- and that then he would disappear, and the only thing left of him would be a town that would always be gripped in fear.

He heard the snow crunch just over his right shoulder. He turned and clenched his gloved fists in one quick motion, but his grip automatically relaxed when he saw Officer Banner holding out a paper cup filled with coffee toward him, the cup balanced precariously in his thick mitten.

Mike nodded in thanks as he took it carefully, not wanting to spill a drop of the precious liquid.

"You looked like you could use it," Banner said, watching as he took a cautious first sip. "You've been at this all night. There's bagels waiting at the parking lot when you get back. If you wait a bit, the wives are talking about putting on some ham and sausages -- maybe even a boiled egg or two. You should head back and get some."

Mike nodded. "I will. Believe me, I will. I just want to get this quadrant mapped off first. We need to know where he is." He took a much longer gulp of the java.

"Slow down, son. You'll burn your mouth off like that."

He was right of course, and Mike could already feel the numbness of liquid burn all over his mouth. But more importantly, he could feel it in his gut and chest. Still, he slacked off.

"You're the only one out here besides the wives not wearing a badge, son.

Why're you doing this to yourself?"

"How much ground have we covered since you gave me my last cup?" Mike asked, not responding to the question.

"At least two miles. We'll know better in a few minutes, when all the squad leaders radio in their reports."

Mike shook his head and bent down to look over the snow at eye-level, looking for any inconsistency in the sea of white. "He wouldn't come out this far," he grumbled to himself.

"I don't know," Banner grinned, tipping back his parka with his thumb to look up at the rising sun. "I've seen them come out further than this. When we were huntin' down the Snakes, they were stretched out over miles keeping in contact somehow -- the furthest one was twenty clicks into the north wilderness, almost to Canada. We felt lucky that we'd nailed him before he made it, too."

"I didn't say he couldn't," Mike corrected, handing the now empty cup to the officer. "I said that he *wouldn't*. I don't think Derek would come this far out -- away from people. It means he has to go farther to play his little pranks -- plus he likes to be near the aftermath. Likes to watch the masses talk and scream and be paranoid. It's his favorite part."

Banner eyed Mike for a moment as he rose to his feet and brushed the snow off of his pant leg before it set in and made him more moist than he already was. "You knew him, didn't you?"

Mike nodded, but did not look back. "He was one of my best friends."

There was a long silence then as Mike stared into the wilderness with his fists tight, daring Derek to jump out at him. To attack and get it over with. To end the wait. The silence was interrupted by a snow bird singing its morning praise and scraping its talons against the bark of a nearby tree. Mike sighed, then turned with the officer back the way they'd come. He winced in pain and brought a hand to his right side to stop it at the source.

Banner regarded him with a look of even greater concern then, but decided not to voice it, as the both of them imagined the taste of ham, sausages -- and maybe boiled eggs, too.

But inside, Mike was looking around, taking in every square inch of land as they walked back, studying for any place that Derek could be hiding -- any place he could start looking when it came time again.

Cathy lay Xander's head upon the inflatable back rest that had adorned the downstairs bathtub since her sister Trina was an infant. He fought it for only a moment, then relaxed his neck against the foamy material as she loomed over him, the ends of her black hair tickling his face and chest. He opened his eyes for the first time since he had collapsed in her hallway. It caught her attention and she returned the gaze with soulful brown eyes. He was trying very hard to look alert, but both pupils were lazy and one eye was open further than the other, then they switched, like scales that could not reach balance.

"Are you hurt?" she asked curtly, trying to disguise the pain she felt at seeing him like this. She avoided continued eye contact by removing his socks. She had managed to coax his pants and shirt off of him while he was throwing up in the toilet, but had had to explain to him several times not to remove his underpants. She still wasn't sure he understood why.

"N... No. No," Xander replied, his thick brown hair weighed down flat against his head with congealed blood, making it look blackish red. "'Mjus all fucked up."

She glanced back at the bathroom door to make sure it was locked tight, then grabbed a towel from a nearby shelf and rolled it into itself, forcing him to lift his back and then using it to raise it slightly. "Why is that?" she asked, her confusion making the stress and concern show through a little. She pushed some of the hair out of his eyes, making no attempt to hide her disgust as long tendrils of bodily fluids stuck to her fingers. "I thought that after you -- after Black Womb -- went out, you were supposed to get all (what's the word?), *rejuvenated* or something?"

He nodded, which visibly took a great deal of energy. "It usually comes out when I sleep, so I feel all rested. Last night it forced itself out. I tried not to go to sleep, but it came anyway. So I didn't sleep, my mind didn't go to sleep. It just -- it took over."

She nodded, tending to a few parts of him that seemed to be extremely strained... his wrists, neck, and the femoral artery in his leg she'd come to learn was very tender after a transformation. She didn't even think he realized that yet. She reached out and turned on the faucet, pouring hot water into the tub. If it had just been him she would have made it boiling, but as she pulled up her sleeves she added a hint of cold for her own benefit, grabbing the softest cloth she could find as she pulled the lever for the shower head to turn on.

"Did you kill anyone?" she asked, fighting to keep her voice even as the carefully dabbed the blood off of his hands, watching as it was discarded and floated along the top of the water all the way down the drain.

He closed his eyes, and after a moment, a single tear escaped one, turning red upon contact with his still spattered cheek.

She was wearing a floppy night-gown with teddy bears printed on it.

He nodded.

"Was it anyone we know?" she sighed, he voice wavering now.

"No," he replied after a moment, his voice solemn. "I think -- I think it was a child."

She dropped the washcloth without realizing it, her mouth pulling inward and making her chin wrinkle. She forced herself to pick the cloth back up and continue. "Oh."

"I think it was looking for Derek, but it found her first. I remember it like it was a dream -- it was remembering the way Derek killed Sara, then it was remembering the way Sara looked when she died -- then, the way Sara looked when she lived, as a child... and then it saw a child that looked like that..."

He looked down at the water, the level of which was rising steadily as the blood poured off him, revealing the pink skin underneath. It crossed his mind to just slide down and let the water envelop him. To open his mouth and breathe deep of it and let it fill his lungs until there was no life left in him. "I want this to end, Cathy," he said, his head snapping in her direction. He made full, open eye-contact with her.

Her tears came easily now, as the comfort of her bed upstairs seemed so far away. "I know," she choked, reaching out her arms in an embrace that he gladly accepted, bringing her body close to his, getting soaked as the boiling water poured down -- but could not wash away their sins.

Nothing could.

CHAPTER THREE: CUP

August Styles took a brown paper bag out of her locker, then opened it and pushed her face down in it to see what her mother had packed for her today. It was a turkey sandwich (not real turkey, the kind that came from a can and got mixed with mayonnaise), a can of off-brand cola and a Jell-O pudding cup, complete with small plastic spoon.

She smiled a little as one of the more obnoxious boys in the school walked past her and purposely bumping into her. Her body slumped against the sharp metal door for a second, then she righted herself. She ignored the boy and turned down the top of the bag, placed it carefully into her sack, then closed the locker door.

The locker had no lock, which some said defeated the purpose, but she could never remember the combination anyway and she could always see it from her classroom. Besides, the only thing she kept in there were two pictures, her lunch, and her gym clothes. She looked at the door for a second, almost absent-mindedly, then turned toward class. They were learning more about trees today, and she had always loved in when they talked about things that grow.

August was fifteen, had blonde hair, and blue eyes. She was short, and quite chubby to match, but was usually wearing a rather large smile, one that was infectious to anyone else that saw it. She was happiest when she was at school, but she also liked doing things afterwards too, with her mom and her friends. Her clothes rarely matched, but she found she rarely noticed and absolutely never cared. She was friends with all the teachers, and most of the students.

She also had Down syndrome.

That was the technical name for what made August a little different from most of the other people at Coral Beach High School. Her mother told her that nobody was exactly the same, and that she just had the special honor of her difference having a special name.

Now she walked to her classroom and sat down at her desk near the back. Mrs. Foxx, their teacher for everything except gym, was at the front of the class going through the attendance sheet of who had been on the bus but was not in class. She had short brown hair and thick glasses that curled upwards at the ends into points with little sparkles on them. She was usually smiling once class started, but not right now. Right now all her wrinkles seemed like they were trying to stretch down and escape from her face, like they did every day when she was doing attendance.

There were three other people in the room. There should have been four. One was missing.

There was Tim, he was her best friend. He was really smart, and he had shaggy brown hair and glasses that reminded August of the bottoms of Coke bottles.

There was Robyn. She was younger than them. She was only twelve. She was really pretty, August thought, and she liked to draw things while she was in class.

Cory was here today, he was big and always had a smile and was laughing and trying to make jokes, even though Mrs. Foxx once told him that his jokes "Were not in good humor." He had glasses too, and a buzz-cut hairdo. People called him Buzz sometimes and it frustrated him horribly.

The only person missing was David, but he was missing a lot.

The classroom itself was full of colors. There were plenty of things on the wall, a few height charts, Robyn's drawings, and hand-prints each that of them had made on their first day of class. August's hand-print was purple. She had always liked purple. There were different spheres hanging from the ceiling, each one a different color. They were the different planets in the solar system. There were four computers lining the far wall, one for each of them. Tim's had a program on it where you could type something in and a purple monkey would say it, which August had always thought was funny. Partly because it was purple.

August opened her science book and turned to the part about trees. There was a picture of an evergreen there, and she thought for a second about how pretty it looked, taking up the entire height of the page.

All at once her stomach started to hurt. It felt like it had done a flip inside her. Her face crunched in pain and she bent over in her desk.

"August?" Mrs. Foxx asked from the top of the class, holding her dry-marker and getting ready to write something on the board. "August are you okay? Do you need to go to the bathroom?"

August nodded. Her face was already very pale.

Mrs. Foxx nodded.

August got up and made her way through the brightly colored door. The other three students watched her go.

A worried look came over Tim, stretching out his thin, long face.

Reverend Robert Gallagher moved quickly to one side as August bumped past him, nearly falling over as his entire weight shifted from one foot to the other. He steadied himself quickly, then turned to frown at the child as she bolted down the hallway. He considered calling out to her and telling her to slow down, but decided not to bother, instead turning and continuing his walk toward his office.

He wore a dark blazer with suede patches on the arms, the kind of suit which looked like it should be worn with a tacky tie... but no tie was there, only a paper-white collar. Carrying his briefcase by his side, he appeared quite the oddity to anyone who did not understand his specific place at Coral Beach High School. He was aware of the contradiction, to the point that he had decided to poke a bit of fun at it, putting an Ichthys on the side of his briefcase.

Gallagher had been brought on board as the newest Guidance Counselor to help console the youth at Coral Beach High through the everyday trials of adolescence as well as the often remarkable situations that presented themselves in this particular facility. He recalled Principal Shnieder saying those exact words to him, just as he passed a section of hallway where the molding and paint were slightly discolored. It had been replaced after an eight foot tall black animal had broken through it and attacked several students.

All the same, Gallagher had taken the position with a degree of pleasure. He had been trying for years to get young people into his church to console them and help them, only to find that young people were not interested in faith.

"When you can't get the world to come to you, you go to the world," he chuckled softly to himself as he turned the last corner before his office door, situated very close to both the bathroom and Shnieder's office -- one of which he regarded as a dumpsite of dung, the other where it was created.

He lifted his right arm high, revealing the watch he had been given on his tenth anniversary with the church. He let out a guttural sound as he realized that he was going to be late again. He rubbed his tired, bloodshot eyes and made sure once again that his balding head of hair was not wild and crazy. He quickened his pace, so much so that he barely noticed Xander Drew sitting against the wall outside his home-room, waiting for classes to begin.

He afforded Xander a quick nod, which was not returned. The gesture (or lack thereof) didn't seem to be an act made out of unkindness. The boy simply seemed to be off in his own little fantasy world -- and not a particularly happy one at that.

Adding it to an ever-growing list of mental notes, Gallagher finished the last few strides to his office, his name freshly painted on the glass front.

The child in him couldn't help but wonder what new challenges the day might bring him.

ʎ⟨ʎ

Cathy stared at the open window of Chem room 103, examining the snow-covered trees and buildings that surrounded the school with a concentration she'd never had before, wary of the things that could be hiding behind them.

When she turned back to Miles' lecture she realized that she must have drowned out more than she thought as she picked up half-way into a sentence on a topic she did not remember him starting.

"... a chemical element that has the symbol Tc and the atomic number 43," he explained, marking the letters 'tc' and the number '43' in bright pink on the dry board. "The chemical properties of this silvery grey, radioactive, crystalline transition metal are intermediate between rhenium and manganese. Its short-lived isotope 99mTc is used in nuclear medicine for a wide variety of diagnostic tests. 99Tc is used as a gamma-ray free source - -"

"Gamma rays?" Tommy interjected, as though he had only heard those two words.

"Yes, Thomas. Gamma Rays. A form of electromagnetic radiation or light emissions of a certain frequency produced from sub atomic particle interaction, such as radioactive decay and electron positron annihilation; most are generated from nuclear reactions occurring within the interstellar medium of space. However, as I was about to say, technetium is a gamma-ray *free* source of beta particles, which can be used to treat medical conditions such as eye and bone cancer."

Tommy was thoughtful. "So, if this is a gamma-free source of this, then there must be a way to get it that had gamma rays, right?"

"Yes. It's still used in some countries."

"For medicine?"

"Yes," he smiled, delighted that he'd caught the boys attention. He had been trying to for several months now.

"Wouldn't that turn people into the Hulk?"

The smile left his face. "No, Thomas, it would not."

"Sure it would," Tommy urged. "That's how the song goes, isn't it? Dr. Banner, belted by gamma rays, turned into the Hulk, Ain't he unglamou rays!"

"Banner didn't turn into the Hulk *because* of the gamma rays," corrected a scrawny kid with thick glasses and bad acne near the front of the class. "The transformation of the gamma rays latched onto a long-dormant personality inside his brain caused by his multiple personality disorder."

Tommy pondered this a moment. "Ok, so what if someone with multiple personality disorder was hit by gamma rays --"

"That's not what gamma rays are used for," Miles spat. "Now if you want to consider this discussion, I suggest you drop this course and join 'flights of fancy 101'."

Tommy stared blankly at him a moment, then leaned over toward the person next to him and whispered, "Why wasn't that on my course sheet this semester?"

Miles' head fell, and he let go a long sigh, rubbing the bridge of his nose.

Cathy turned back toward her desk, opened her exercise book to a fresh page, and began to write.

Tommy Irons watched the pool game from the other side of the Factory, taking a sip of his Diet Coke and playing with the tips of his gelled hair, which always seemed to be just a little too long to be spiking up, but he did it anyway.

She couldn't remember if Tommy had actually been at the Factory on the night Jamie was killed, and the more she thought of it the more it made her head hurt. She remembered seeing him there that day because Mike had punched him in the arm a few hours before. Had he left right after that? She wasn't sure.

After a few moments of going back and forth on the subject she decided that it didn't matter all too much and to just leave it alone, continuing the paragraph from where she had left off.

He wore a big grin across his face, and together with his pointed chin it always made his face appear to be the shape of a heart. He was tall and lanky with long legs that ended comically at his big feet that looked like a clowns on him. Next to him, Fred Windsor (who everyone called Sud) slurped his own Diet Coke.

Sud was short and bulky and still caught in those awkward years when some parts of the body seem to be growing faster than others, his arms hanging further down than they should have. This was exaggerated by the baggy sweaters and jeans he seemed to wear perpetually. His head was always shaved, except for a five o'clock shadow around the ears, and made his brow seem all the more pronounced, punctuated by a deep scowl and beady eyes.

Apart they were both likely targets of a snicker or two, but together they were outright hilarious, one tall and skinny and the other short and big. They looked like they had just stepped out of an episode of Fat Albert. Both men were almost always misunderstood by their friends and peers. It was easy to misinterpret Tommy's crude comments and Sud's constant mimicry his friends as signs of stupidity and inauspiciousness, but in fact they were just trying their best to do what every kid at Coral Beach High was trying to do : fit in. And most days it seemed like they would do anything to do it.

That's why he picked them.

"Hey, guys," smiled Derek Smith, as he walked over to the three of them.

If she had been uncertain as to whether or not Tommy and Sud had been there, she flat out *knew* that Derek had not been there. Nobody could be sure, but it had been accepted that he had been in his house, while all this was going on. That he'd watched as Jamie had been attacked by Genblade and Spider -- and that in the opposite direction, the Black Womb had been watching as well, both young killers learning *how* to kill by watching two of the best. But she wanted to get Derek in as soon as possible, and she'd wanted someone to come over and start talking to Tommy and Sud. At first she was going to use Grendel, but had decided against putting him in, at least for now. She wasn't going to say he was never there, but she saw no harm in lying by omission when it came to the man that had hurt her so much.

She tapped her pencil against her pad and her mind began to drift. She felt horrible that at the same time that her friend's life was at an all-time low, her relationship with Mike seemed to be hitting an all-time high again finally.

She stopped tapping her pencil as she remembered how far she and her lover had fallen the last time they had gotten so close, and suddenly became very, very afraid; her pupils dilating and her lungs growing short of breath.

Even though she was trying to make a conscious effort not to think it, her brain screamed at her: *What else could go wrong?*

Xander let his head fall back and thud against the painted brick of the school corridor.

"Ow," he said emotionlessly. He was sure he could feel the impact reverberating through his skull, as if it were an echo in an empty room. *Your mind is an empty room*, he snickered to himself sarcastically.

The bell to end home room shattered the quiet of the corridors. It was only then that he realized just how 'turned up' his enhanced senses had become in the silence, the sudden noise making him cup his ears so tight they formed suction.

Classmates poured out of their classrooms, heading off to the first classes of the day like sheep moving from field to field, each one moving past him without paying him any notice. He watched their legs and feet pass by one by one, recognizing a few of them by what they wore and guessing the rest. They passed him as though he was a statue, until eventually one pair of legs stopped squarely in front of him.

He didn't need to look up to see who it was.

He was so tall that Xander couldn't see his waist. His ripped blue jeans were baggy and rolled up at the cuffs. They were soaking wet from the knees down and led into new brown boots, the kind that you had to lace up every time. Xander had always hated footwear like that. If he could have gotten away with wearing loafers or velcro-laced shoes every day and not had Cathy kill him, he would have.

"Mike," Xander regarded, still not looking up at him.

Mike sighed, then knelt down until he was just a little above eye-level with Xander. "How's it going?"

Even though Xander had not altered his gaze, Mike had placed himself in a position where he would have to shift his vision to break eye contact. In doing so his entire body became uncomfortable, as if the illusion that he was in fact a part of the wall had been destroyed. "Been better," he answered, his voice low as he found a new point just beyond Mike's head to stare at.

Mike nodded slowly. He glanced at the clock on the wall and decided that he had a little time before his Biology teacher got irreparably mad at him, then sat down next to his friend. His legs cracked with relief as the hours of pressure he had built into them was relieved. "I hear you there," he sighed, letting his own head fall back against the brick. "Ow."

Xander took deep breath through his nose, then exhaled. A confused look passed over his face, his brow furrowing in deep thought. He turned slightly toward Mike, taking in another, shorter breath. "Have you been in the woods?"

Mike nodded. "Out helping the cops look for Derek."

"How's that going?"

The look on Mike's face said all that was necessary.

"That good, huh?" Xander groaned, turning back toward his staring spot on the opposite wall.

"Every day we don't catch him, the area he could be hiding in expands just a little more. We're just lucky that the public transportation departments are working with us, not selling any bus tickets to people who match Derek's description, or we'd already have the entire country as a search zone."

"And you're sure he's on foot?"

Mike raised a hand, counting each point off on a finger as he made them. "No public transport, no stolen vehicles, nobody stupid enough to pick up a hitchhiker matching his description. Unless he's learned to sprout wings and fly, Derek Smith is still somewhere in the Coral Beach Coral Cove area."

Xander nodded. The silence between them became palpable then. It was tradition among good friends. One told what one did last night, the other told theirs. So when it was obvious that it was Xander's turn to speak, the silence became a very tangible thing.

"I bumped into Cathy coming in," Mike said finally, breaking the quiet. "She told me what happened."

Tears welled up in Xander's eyes, but he pushed them back. "Have the police heard anything yet?"

"Not when I left, no," he replied, resting a hand on Xander's shoulder. "They'll probably blame it of Derek. It fits his usual M.O."

"That's a great comfort," Xander said sarcastically, unable to fight the tears now as they dribbled down and pitted against his dark green shirt. "That I won't be blamed for killing a young girl -- again. Really, a weight has been lifted off my shoulders."

Mike's entire upper frame seemed to fall into the lower. "We know now that it's possible for you to get control. All we need to do now is - "

"Control?" Xander yelled, whipping his arm out from behind him. He let the force of the motion carry through to his fingertips, thrusting a three-inch long serrated talon from each one of them, an action accompanied by a quick sucking sound and a dribble of blood from the digits. "Is this what you call control?" He brought the razor-sharp shards of bone up to his cheeks and dragging them down, making four ridged slices.

"Jesus!" Mike screamed, grabbing Xander's arms and pulling them back. As he watched in horror, the flesh on Xander's face seemed to take on a life of its own, bending and shuffling until the cuts became scars, and then the scars gave way to the pale flesh he had started with, marked only by a few thin trails of blood.

Xander slumped back into his relaxed pose. "I don't even have control over whether or not I bleed," he said, his voice filled with despair and hopelessness.

Mike watched intently as the claws slowly reverted back into Xander's fingers, refusing to relinquish his grip on his friend until they did. "Then we'll have to find something new. Something to reign it in. We'll get there, man. We will."

Xander turned and was about to say something very unsavory in response to Mike's well intentioned words when he stopped, his gaze shifting past him. "Cathy," he said, his voice immediately warmer.

She smiled down at him, big and bright, with ruby lips and pure white teeth as she approached the pair. She regarded Xander first, then bent down and kissed her boyfriend, lightly, on the lips.

Xander closed his eyes and gave his head a little shake, his still-enhanced sense of sound picking up the wet smacks of their lips pressing together, something that was disturbing enough to him without his powers amplifying the experience.

"How are you?" she asked Mike. "Did you eat anything today?"

Mike nodded, allowing himself a smile. In truth, even in the horrible situations their lives had managed to become wrapped up in, he couldn't keep it off his face whenever she was around. "Yeah. Some of the wives made a big breakfast for everyone."

"Sounds good. Keep it up," he grinned. She turned to Xander, her expression more serious and concerned, the smile smaller and pasted on now. "And you?" she asked him, her eyes sparkling with the pain she felt for him.

He wiped the sleeve of his jacket across his face, drying the blood and tears. "I'm fine," he lied through his teeth. He wondered if a lie was still a lie if all parties involved knew the difference.

She nodded, agreeing with the truth behind the statement if not the statement itself. She reached out and hugged him tightly, kissing him briefly on the cheek. When their bodies parted she tweaked the kiss away with her thumb, giving him another grin.

The three of them sat in silence then, each trying to think of something to say.

"Oh," Cathy said, reaching into her book-bag and pulling out several pages of paper, all folded together neatly, and handed it to Mike. "Here. I was reading this article the other day on dietary supplements, and how some of them can actually reduce the risk of heart disease. They were saying that..."

Xander turned his head until it faced almost perfectly forward and stared at his spot on the wall again.

"... eems pretty cool. I saw something on CNN like that, said with just a little gene..."

Slowly their conversation started to drone away from him, their voices sounding more and more like they were underwater, until finally it was just a hushed mumble, like the teachers on the old Peanuts cartoons.

"... thought about us, because if we were, you know, ever going to..."

Xander got up suddenly and without a word. He pushed himself off from the wall and walked down the hall the way Cathy had come, shoving his hands deep into his pockets.

Mike and Cathy turned to watch him go, waiting until he was long out of sight to say anything.

Mike turned to her, a puzzled look on his face. "What was that all about?"

She frowned, moving in close to him, putting her back against the wall. "We're losing him," she said softly, no longer feeling the need to hide the pain she felt. She never felt the need to hide anything from him.

He wrapped his arm around her instinctively, pulling her close into a lover's squeeze. "I know. I can't figure a way to pull him back either -- and with everything that's going on, I don't have time to think of one."

"We have to help him Mike. He needs it. More than that... I don't want to think about what'll happen to us if we can't keep him from going over the edge."

Mike raised his eyebrows. It was the first time he's heard her vocalize any sort of worry that Xander might hurt her, although he'd suspected that she'd thought it before. Not knowing what to say, he turned his head and kissed her on the top of hers.

Huffing, she bent her head back and knocked it against the brick wall. "Ow."

CHAPTER FOUR: FAITH

Calla McFadden stood alone in the smoker's section just off the south wing, brushing ash-stained snow from side to side with the long heel of her leather winter boot. She did this over and over again until there was a semi-circle of clean flat snow big enough for her to sit in, and then did, pulling the tail of her coat down. Her face had a healthy roundness to it, along with the rest of her. Her eyes seemed too big and sparkly for her head, her mouth a little too small and cutesy, both outlined by generously sprinkled freckles. Her hair (naturally a light brown) was mostly jet black and straight now, with one curled lock that hung in the left corner of her face dyed hot pink.

Samara Reynolds was standing next to her with her arms crossed defiantly in front of her chest. She wore a padded vest in lieu of a jacket, her hair done up in a bun with long stands spider-webbing out the back of it. A few similar strands hung down in front of a slender face, giving her a spiteful look. She watched as Calla reached into her pocket and withdrew a small plastic bag that she opened and started picking through. "What do you think you're doing?"

Calla looked up quizzically, as if completely unaware that she was doing anything out of the ordinary. She smiled politely and tilted her head to one side in a way that Samara had come to recognize meant that she was about to say something either very patronizing or very condescending. Or, in this case, both. "I'm rolling, sweetie. What are you doing?"

"I know that," Samara huffed, crouching down to be on the same level with Calla but not actually sitting, her eyes darting back and forth for any sign that they might be seen. "Why are you doing it here?"

Calla looked down at the clumpy green substance in the baggie, then back up at her friend, an annoyed and comically exasperated expression on her face. "Because when I do it at home, my parents get mad."

"I think they'll get mad when you do it here too, Cal."

She shot the shorter girl a look. "All the crap that goes on at this school, do you really think they're gonna get on my case about possession?"

Samara nodded slightly, conceding to the point as she lay her back against the wall and relaxed a little.

Calla pinched the marijuana and sprinkled it onto a thin piece of paper she'd taken out of her jeans pocket, dipping her hand back into the bag twice to get more before deciding it was enough. She turned to Samara expectantly, who reluctantly produced a single flattened cigarette from her vest. Calla rolled its tip back and forth between her fingers, sending tobacco raining down onto her concoction until the paper appeared full enough, then licked along the inside edge until it was damp and rolled it together, the glue holding properly as she twisted both ends so that nothing would come out. "There, see?" she smiled at her friend, holding up the joint between her thumb and forefinger triumphantly. "That's how it's done."

Samara rolled her eyes and plucked the bone from between Calla's fingers, then placed it into the top pouch on her vest.

"Hey, I was gonna smoke that," she fake-whined, pouting out her tiny lower lip a little.

"Come on, Cal. We've got Geometry. What's with you, anyway? You've smoked *maybe* three times in your life. Suddenly, what, you're a pothead now?"

Calla scoffed, bracing herself against the bricks as she got up. "Just trying to enjoy life, that's all," she murmured, brushing the snow off of her jeans until there was hardly any there anymore. "Speaking of which, we gotta find us a couple of guys. It's been a while since we've really partied, y' know?"

"Excuse me, I have a guy."

"That's not what I'd call Travis."

"Shut up!" Samara laughed, slapping Calla's arm. "Come on, we gotta get to class."

"Fuck that. Gimmie back the smoke," she demanded, though in a pleasant tone of voice, putting her palm out and motioning with her finger for the joint's return. "I'm gonna stay out here myself a while, if you're going in."

Samara tisked, tapping one foot against the ground as she pulled out the rolled up square of paper and placed it in Calla's open palm.

"Thank you very much," Calla beamed, her cheeks shining in the morning light when she did so.

"Whatever. I'm going to class. You need some serious help, girl," Samara said, smiling briefly before walking off to class.

ʎ⟨⟩ʎ

Xander stalked the hallways of the school, his hands deep inside his pants pockets. He reached the front lobby looking out into the cold outside. He took a quick glance around the corridor for Shnieder. There were bullet holes in the walls. He stared at them and they stared back, like the gun that had put them there had given the concrete eyes. Walls had always been said to have ears that could hear and mouths that could talk, but now they had two holes for eyes that could see everything. Soon Coral Beach High would just sprout legs and walk away from him, he thought, transfixed in the dead gaze or the stone.

He pulled a cigarette pack and a lighter from either pocket and started toward the front door.

Outside the wind blew fiercely, making his coat dance and flap at his side.

He barely noticed it, instead fighting against the breeze to light his smoke and using the small porch of the school for what little cover it provided. Finally the cherry lit and he took a long drag, feeling his tension melt away as his throat burned.

The healing factor made every puff feel like his first, his esophagus healing between breaths.

After a moment he stepped off the balcony and down the concrete stairs, fearful that the Shnieder was still about.

"Hello my son," came Gallagher's warm, instantly recognizable voice. He smiled up at Xander from just around the corner, leaning against the school in his winter coat.

Xander turned, surprised. "Father? What are you doing out here?"

"Not killing myself with those blasted sticks like you are, I'm happy to say."

Xander immediately threw the smoke to the ground behind him, pretending as though he had no idea what the holy man was talking about.

"Last night I was so pleased when I'd made my way through all the student case-files... and when I walked into my office this morning there was a whole new pile, marked M through Z'." He smirked. "I decided I needed some air, no matter how bitter it might be this morning."

"M-Z... so, you've read mine, then?" Xander poised, failing to hide his interest in the subject.

"Yes," Gallagher smiled, looking down at an odd shape he was unconsciously making in the snow with his feet. "In fact I was hoping to get you into my office if I got some time today... but now I guess that isn't necessary."

Xander raised an eyebrow, cautiously strolled over to the older man, then leaned against the school next to him. "What about?"

Gallagher opened his mouth to speak, then stopped. After a moment of continued silence, he chuckled to himself. "You know, in my line of work I get to listen a lot, and then I give my opinion and best advice, if it's warranted and appropriate... it never occurred to me how hard it was to start a conversation."

Xander grinned a little at this, and his face felt weird in the expression, his suspicion of the good Reverend melting away at his clumsiness. "Just say it, Father."

"I'm worried about you, boy," he said, needing to get the words out as quickly as possible lest he trip over them again. "Tell me... are you feeling all right?"

Xander bit his lip, and now it was his turn to look down at his feet. "I don't know how to answer that, Father."

"A few months ago in my chamber, you told me you felt as though God had forgotten you... do you still feel that way, Alexander?"

The use of his full name made Xander flinch. He'd been named for a saint by the nuns that had overseen his adoption, and since then he'd never been comfortable with it being said by members of the clergy. It felt too formal, somehow. "No..." he said, meaning for it to be both the beginning and the ending of the sentence, then he continued. "... No, lately I feel as though God has been paying far too much attention to me."

Gallagher raised an eyebrow, then caught the child's meaning and nodded. "The Good Lord does test us all, my son... though I would agree, he seems to test some more than others. And there has been so much death..."

"They're the lucky ones," Xander interrupted, saying the words before his mind could filter them out.

"Excuse me?"

"All the people that I've buried -- I've noticed something about them. Most of them didn't deserve it. They were innocent. They were purity."

"Nobody deserves to die, my son."

Xander shot him a look. "I think you and I both know the difference of that, Father."

Gallagher said nothing in response, which Xander took as an agreement.

"What I've come to think is that death is God's reward for good people. He takes them out of this earth, so that they don't have to live in it anymore. I look around and I see all these people living here, so afraid of dying... but I'm not, Father. I'm afraid of living forever. Of watching all the good things in my life lift up to the heavens... because I know that if I'm right, I'll never get it. I'll never be released from this world."

Gallagher looked at him astonishment for a moment, then smiled.

"Something funny?"

"No," he grinned. "But I was going to ask how old you were, not to demean your sentiment."

Xander smirked, then let it fade. "Sometimes I do feel old."

Gallagher nodded, then patted him on the back. His body was angled as though were about to leave. "My son, understand that when I say this, it is not as a faculty member nor as a priest. I wish to give you my best advice... as a man. Is that all right?"

Xander looked up, hopeful and a might curious.

"Find relief in the Lord, my son. No matter what you believe... I have never seen it steer anyone wrong."

Gallagher turned and walked up the concrete steps, clouds of breath spiraling over his head every time he exhaled on his way back into the school.

Xander stood there in the snow for a moment, his brow furrowed as he bounced the idea in his head over and over again. His head rose slowly as a flash of inspiration sparked in his head so bright that his eyes lit up. A smart, sinister grin played over his lips as he laughed at his idea, then jumped out of the snow onto the pavement and headed back up the stairs into the warm.

CHAPTER FIVE: WITH

August Styles sat in the bathroom floor with tears streaming down her young face. There was cold water touching her hand on the floor, but she made no attempt to move it as she leaned against the dingy toilet, comfortable for the first time in what seemed like days.

Her chest quivered a little as her breath slowed from the breakneck pace they had been going, each one throbbing in her throat, strained from countless urges and heaves.

There was an odd taste in her mouth, like the tang of a penny, and her sinuses were assaulted with the scents of human waste and pine cleaner, stuffing her nose and making her eyes water even more.

Her stomach wretched again and she thought she might throw up for the tenth time, but instead it slowly calmed itself, like water brought to a boil then allowed to cool.

There was a clacking together of heels and tile floor moving steadily in her direction, and she turned away from the open stall door, hiding her face and trying not to get noticed.

The girl walked by at first, but then the sound of the heels stopped and the tall brunette stepped back a pace, looking in at August sitting on the floor. August recognized her instantly as Jennifer Bradley, a girl from her grade that wasn't particularly nice to her.

Jennifer glared at August for a moment, curled her lip, then grabbed the handle to the stall and closed it, leaving August alone once again. The sound of her heels moved away once again.

August's gut turned and she buried her head in the toilet and threw up again.

CHAPTER SIX: CHAINS

"This is a stupid idea." Cathy frowned, squinting through the gaps in the dried plywood and watching the sun set for the evening. Her arms were crossed across of her chest and her hair fell in two straight lines on either side of her down-turned face. Her bottom lip stuck out as a visual act of her dismay. "I just want to state that for the record."

"It's not a stupid idea," Xander heaved, wincing just a little as he watched Mike clamp the first large, metal cuff onto his right arm. It pinched his skin a little, and the jolt it caused wasn't altogether unpleasant. Thick, sturdy chains traveled from the half-inch-thick bonds to three huge copper circles that were screwed into the wall and then out the other side where a second cuff hung, waiting to be attached as well. "It's a smart idea. Waiting around for the bodies to pile up, that, was a stupid idea."

Cathy's frown only increased, her lip sticking out even more.

"As long as we're putting it on the record," Mike said, careful of his tone when dealing with an obviously already frustrated girlfriend. "I think Xander's right. We've tried everything else to keep the Womb in check, and right now we do not have the time to devote to watching over it all night. This seems like the best option."

"Thank you," Xander smiled, giving Cathy an over-the-top nod to flaunt his victory.

"Whatever," Mike shrugged, picking up the left restraint. He pulled it to its fullest length, making Xander's arm jerk back to the point that it might have bent backward. It made Cathy flinch. In her mind, she could hear her friend's joints straining.

Mike clamped the second restraint shut with a loud clack that echoed off of the halls surrounding them, then gave them a firm tug on each side to make sure they would hold before stepping back a pace. He gave it all a once over, then nodded.

Xander's arms were stretched out as if he were on a crucifix.

Mike brought a hand up to his mouth as he surveyed the situation, a thoughtful look coming over him as he looked down at the base of the apparatus. "You sure we don't need the feet as well?"

Xander looked down, shuffling his legs in every direction, trying his best to get free to test the restraints. "I really don't think so," he said, still trying to get free. "It shouldn't be a problem. And, call me a whiner, but I don't want any uncomfortableness that isn't necessary to getting the job done."

"Cool," Mike nodded, holding up a key ring with two pairs of keys on it, one for each cuff and a duplicate. He took off one set and handed it to Cathy. "Come morning, if I can't make it over here to let him out I'll call you on your cell."

She nodded, unable to look at either of them. Her expression had gone from frustrated to angry as she snatched away the key.

"Make sure you leave it on..."

"*Okay,*" she stressed, giving him the hint to drop it, which he did. Finally, after huffing twice, she turned to Xander. "Did I hear you say that this was Gallagher's idea?"

Xander nodded.

She raised an eyebrow at him. "One Guidance Councilor's a serial rapist, another worked for a evil genetics company that manipulated events for months to try and recruit you, then the third tells you to chain yourself up in an old church... and you listen?"

Xander smiled. He looked around the abandoned Catholic church, which the residents of Coral Beach had used until the back end burned down in the sixties. That part had been boarded off, but when the repair crew discovered that the entire place was rank with asbestos, they'd decided to just close it up and build a new one (which Gallagher now presided over). The rings that held his bonds to the wall had once held a large two-hundred pound cross there. It had hovered just slightly off the ground before some teenagers had stolen it and tied a freshman to it, setting him naked in the middle of the baseball field several years back.

All of the pews were empty and most were falling apart, just like the rest of the place. Many of the stained glass windows had been beaten in with rocks, but the confessional was still mostly intact, something that Xander found disturbing for some reason. "He didn't exactly put it like that," he said finally.

"How did he put it then?" she demanded.

"He told me to find relief with the lord."

Cathy's eyes widened slightly. Mike snickered. He'd seen that expression on her before.

"And *that's* what you took from that?" she said, taking a step closer and rapping him on the head with her knuckles.

"Ow. Stop it," he grimaced, trying in vain to bend his head away from her attack.

"What are you, dysfunctional? That is the most fucked up logic I have ever heard in my entire life! What is *wrong* with you?"

"Are you done?" he asked, as she finally stopped hitting him.

She sighed, shaking her head and making her hair dance in all directions. "Yes. Yes, I'm done. I just wanted it noted that this is -"

"A bad idea. Right, got it," Xander interrupted.

"Do you want us to stay until you transform?" Mike asked, putting his key in his pocket as he grabbed up his parka, already prepared to go out in search of Derek again. He winced a bit when he did, his side still sore.

"No," Xander said, forcing cheerfulness. "I don't think I would with you here anyway. I'd never go to sleep, and that would defeat the purpose."

Mike nodded, then took Cathy by the shoulders and led her out. Neither looked back, even as they snuck back out the front doors, closing them as they left with a loud slam.

Xander stared at the spot where they had disappeared, trying to get as comfortable as he could... and waited.

ᚠᚢᚠ

Gallagher ran his fingers through his silver hair, ruining the comb over that he'd labored on in the faculty washroom just thirty minutes before. He stared at the pile of files in front of him, which seemed as though it was only growing.

When he'd been a child, his grandmother had told him stories about the Devil. She'd said that you could never rest when fighting the Devil, because it would never rest. Didn't have too. The Devil would just keep coming until it got the upper hand. Right now, he felt that the Devil was being represented primarily by file folders.

"No wonder the last three went crazy," he mumbled to himself, finishing off another spot of coffee.

A few minutes ago he'd finished a file on a particularly troubled young man named David Walton. A solitary boy, he was prone to jolts of enthusiasm and loud behavior, and was constantly striving for the attention of others, often causing him problems with the faculty and the rest of the student body.

Before that, there had been Evan Lucas, a young man with questionable social skills who seemed to be taking a darker spin on his adolescent misgivings around females. Both O'Toole and Shnieder had separately marked him on their observation list.

Prior to that had been Nick Carry, a student who had always been the victim of ridicule, something to do with his appearance. That child hadn't even been seen in several months, with some reports stating that he'd gone to another school, but there was no record of the transfer ever happening.

He heard a sound up ahead of him, finally pulling his tired eyes away from the mountain of files that seemed to be growing out of his desk.

Leaning against the doorway to his office was a pudgy blonde girl with a long face. It was dirty and covered with that certain sparkle that could only be left by tears. She sniffed and turned her head downward as soon as he made eye contact with her.

He smiled, although there was pain and pity in it that he tried to hide, rising from his uncomfortable chair. "Can I help you?" he asked, motioning for her to come in if she wanted too.

She took a step forward, and now he could see the tiny white speckles of vomit that dotted the corners of her mouth.

"Are you all right?"

August looked up, her eyes welling up with tears once again. Her hands were both planted firmly around her stomach.

"It's my baby..." she sobbed, her voice whined, as she collapsed onto the floor.

Gallagher stood in shock for a moment before moving forward to help the girl up.

There was a tree in the courtyard of Coral Beach High, pressed against the far wall directly in front of the rear exit. It was a massive elm that had been planted decades ago as a sapling when the town had still been a mining town, and had grown ever since even in times of poverty. There were names carved in it going all the way up, carved there when the trunk was young and close to the ground and carrying them to the sky as it went. Some said there were three generations of sweet-hearts, all on the one tree.

The leaves were green and full of rich veins despite the snow, turned up toward the sun that shone from overhead and nourished it. It sparkled and glowed, its halo stretching out in all directions until the entire courtyard was bathed in its heavenly glow.

CHAPTER SEVEN: PAST AGAIN

Xander took a deep breath, held it for a long moment, then exhaled and opened his eyes once again. Before him all he could see was blackness, without the slightest trace of light to give him any sense of direction or depth, and he blinked once or twice just to make sure his eyes weren't still closed.

The air around him stank like nicotine and old books, assaulting his senses over and over again with its stale odor. His face twitched with every scent of it, yet welcomed it, as it was the only thing letting him know that the void before him was real. There was a sickening taste in the back of his throat that carried the coppery tang of blood, but tinged with something else. It was sweeter than it should have been; with a bitter twist. It was like vomit when the only thing in your stomach had been sugar-water. He cleared his throat, trying to make the taste go away. It only made it stronger, and the sound he'd made echoed off the walls he could not see, his senses telling him that they were both far away and right in front of his nose, the information muddling his already confused brain. He held his breath for a moment, trying not to make any sound at all, so that the confusion might stop. All at once pressure roared from his central plexus, rocketing into his spine and up his backside, finally exploding out of the back of his brain. He tried hard to scream, but now no sound would come. Had the pain been less, he would have mentally commented on the irony of that.

After a few more moments of trying to scream, and the unbearable frustration of not being able to, he gave up, hanging his head down to stare at the floor that was took dark to make out, letting out a silent grunt of defeat.

Softly, a silky hand caressed his face, then tilted it upwards. As he looked up, the gentle person brought a cold, wet cloth to his head, nursing a gouge he hadn't even been aware was there. At first all he could see was the red cloth being used to treat him, and it looked huge, spreading up and taking a humanoid form. It confused him, and he hadn't realized how skewed his vision was until he had something to focus on. As his sight slowly but surely returned, he realized the reddish glob in front of him was actually the clothing of someone standing very close. The person bent down, revealing long black hair and soulful dark eyes in the shape of almonds. Her lips were thin and coy, the scent of her perfume unmistakable by those that knew it

Eve Spider looked at him, an intense pity in her eyes that he was not used to seeing. He stared in silent shock upon her beautiful demeanor for a long moment, as she finished wiping the blood from his brow and slid her hand down his face gently. "My poor, poor little Black Womb," she said softly.

He tried to respond, but again, nothing came. He choked back the frustration, sunk his head, then brought it back to her again. He opened his mouth in a silent plea, then shut it again, as if trying to illustrate his disability at this moment.

She nodded her head respectfully, bringing one finger to his lips. "I know... I know. Can't talk, can't move, can't see... can't do anything but sit there and wait. And what happens when you try?"

Pain shot through his body, exciting the nerve ending until they couldn't take it anymore, making him feel cold and numb. Then the healing factor kicked in, and started the whole process again.

"What the fuck!" he exclaimed. His eyes grew wide after a moment when he realized that he was somehow able to form words again.

She smiled at him and waved a finger in front of her, like a mother chiding a child. "Language, little man," she giggled, running a hand over his chest before letting it fall away completely.

He grunted once, almost just to prove that he could, then turned up to glare at her. "Why am I here, Spider?"

She smiled, rising to her feet again, stepping away from him so that he could see her. There was a noticeable tear in her otherwise perfect red gown, draped elegantly over her slender form. It was still there from when he'd killed her months ago, and his gaze lingered on it. "First you have to know where you are, then why you're here will become all too clear."

He sucked in his bottom lip, wanting very much to just close his eyes and ignore her rantings until eventually she went away. After a moment, he deciding to take the bait. "Okay... where am I?"

"Where you've been heading your entire life, and every time you try to avoid it you just end up chained, unable to move, unable to speak. Unable to do anything but sit there in pain and try to deny where you are and the reason for it."

He sighed in discontent. "Did you take a class on how to answer direct questions with indirect responses, or is it a natural talent?"

She turned and glared at him for a moment, her ankle-length hair spiraling off in all directions from the inertia of it. Her features slowly softened into a coy smile that on any other woman could have been confused with seduction. "Maybe your question wasn't direct enough," she giggled.

Briefly, he longed for the days when she would just show up out of nowhere and slice him with unnecessarily long blades until he was unconscious. "Tell me where I am, Spider," he said sternly, mustering all of the confidence he had in him. Suddenly, there was a brilliant flash of light! Images began parading past his mind's eye, so fast that he couldn't get a clear bead on what was happening. Sara, being stabbed through the gut by Adam Genblade. Mandy with the life ebbing out of her. Sud shot dead in the halls of the school. Tommy beaten and useless. Warren falling victim to Genblade. Julie with her insides on the out. Cathy, laying in her own blood, dying... and Mike next to her, already dead and beginning to turn blue. Between each image were even more images, people he didn't even recognize. An Asian man who looked to be burning alive. A blonde woman crying as she held a lifeless newborn in her arms. A brunette woman, who just looked at him, her eyes full of pity and hate all at the same time. "Stop it!" he screamed, his body wrenching and convulsing with each new impulse.

"I'm just answering your question for you, my silly Womb," she cooed softly.

Suddenly the chains which bonded him were no longer there and he fell a foot or so to the floor, hearing muscles and bone crack with a wet snap even as he did so. His hands finally free, he brought them up to his head and started pounding at it as hard as he could, trying to make the images stop, succeeding only in feeding a migraine. He popped his claws in desperation, each splitting his skin with an audible -shluck- of ruptured flesh. Insane with pain, he brought the claws up to his temples and was about to start to gouge the images out, when there was a pressure against his wrists that stopped them. For a second he thought he might be in the chains again, but when he opened his eyes Spider was holding both of his wrists.

She raised his hands up high above his head until they touched the floor. At some point during the confusion he must have ended up on his back, the sensation being that he had flipped silently, and without feeling it. It was disorienting, a situation only buoyed by the fact that now he was flat on his back with Spider on top of him, binding his wrists over his head with one strong but delicate hand. "Poor boy," she said. "I often forget how young you are. You're just not as ready as you'll need to be for this, when it comes time."

"Ready... for what?" he said through clenched teeth, adjusting his arms against her grip.

"For hell, of course," she said in a teasing voice, swaying her hips about playfully, either side of her red gown on either side of him.

He paused for a moment, looking at her, and then around him. Even though there was still just the blackness, he now had the undeniable sense that he was being watched. That there was somebody else in the room. Lots of people, as point of fact, though he couldn't begin to think who. "You expect me to believe that this... is hell?"

"It's your hell, little Xander," she soothed, rocking her body back and forth, running her free hand from his face to his chest and then back again. "There are billions of hells... as many hells as there are human souls. This, is yours."

"So why are you in my hell, then?" he grinned, skeptical.

"Because you killed me," she said, bringing a hand to the slash on her side. When it came back it was covered in blood. "You killed me, and now I get to torture you for all of time. Isn't that just lovely? Think of all the people you'll have killing you by the time you get here for good. All those people you just saw, and oh so many more."

"I don't believe that," he spat defiantly, trying to rise against her but failing to.

"It doesn't matter," she said, her eyes full of mournfulness. "Some things are true whether you believe them or not."

"You can't play with me anymore, Spider. You can't fool me. Most of those people you showed me aren't even dead."

Spider smiled, but not out of happiness. For the first time, it seemed forced... as though she were trying to smile for his benefit. "But they will be, Xander dearest... and soon. And inside, you know exactly how it's going to happen... don't you?"

His gaze became distant and he turned to one side, the images returning to him.

Cathy pushed open the door to the battered old church, its heavy wooden frame moaning beneath her effort. She was about to walk in when she heard a loud, metallic sound echoing off of the tiled walls, and stopped. Even though the sun had been up for almost forty-five minutes, she suddenly became aware of how very dark it was in the dank, run-down cathedral. Broken molding and torn curtains hung from the ceiling and walls, making odd shapes out of the few strands of light that seeped in through the knotholes in the wood that boarded up the windows. Dust floated past the rays of sunshine, stirred up by the door, and were now swirling about like little tornados, making it seem like there was movement when there was none.

She took a deep breath and pushed her bangs back with one quick motion, making sure she had the full range of her sight. It was quiet again now... like a tomb. She stepped inside and closed the door behind her, as gently as possible. Suddenly, from behind her, the rattling sound came again, reminding her briefly of the sound of metal on metal, the sound Derek used to use with his blade as a way to psyche out his victims. The memory brought with it a cold chill that rivaled that of the fresh morning air. Her lungs started to ache, and she realized that she had neglected to breathe out, finally letting go of the tuft of air.

Summoning all her courage she stepped forward, crossing the five meters to the entry point of the main hall as soon as possible.

It was more open here, with more sources of light coming in through the gaping holes in the church's structure. Up in the distance she could see him now, chained up as if crucified.

She remembered when he told her the story of how he'd been crucified, months ago. He'd been on the verge of tears, as if facing the memory were making it happen again. She had, of course, been sympathetic... but had never been able to fully understand. Moreover, her young mind was unable to visualize the scene, despite all of the times she'd seen carvings of it in her grandmother's living room. Now that she saw it, the light coming in on his down-turned head and forming a halo, she felt pity well up anew in her gut. It seemed like such a shame, that it had come to this.

She could see the hair on his head, soaked down with the thin layer of congealed blood that accompanied each transformation each time he completely reverted back to the form of Xander Drew. His clothes were soaked down with it too, and despite the horridness of the image, she felt herself free of the thought that he would be naked, which sometimes happened. His right arm twitched and the chains holding him down rattled, amplified as it refracted off of the walls. She sighed in relief, chiding herself for not realizing what the sound was earlier.

"Xander?" she called out, trying to sound chipper. He was in a bad enough mood already, she wagered. Besides the obvious, sleeping in that position couldn't have done wonders to his back.

He grumbled something indiscernible and twitched against his restraints.

"Xander?" she said, a little more cautiously now as she stepped toward him.

"Xander?" Cathy moaned, trying desperately to hold her intestines in as she looked up at him with tears in her hazel eyes. Blood covered his hands, and as they reached out to help her he found himself unable to retract his claws. Instead of taking her hand, he ripped into the tender flesh of her palm, scattering it against the nearby brick wall... and a stone.

It was stone where they had once kissed, years ago. They were behind The Factory, he realized. She recoiled in pain, and when she did she faded from his view and into the darkness that enveloped the entire scene.

Xander screamed, thrusting his head back as he twisted under Spider's grip.

"That's it, baby. Scream," she cackled, holding him as she moved her hips back and forth, her form changing from herself to Cathy then Julie then back again as she twisted about. "You know how to get me there, don't you?"

"Please..." he whispered, his head turned on its side in defeat. "...Please, just stop. Let me be."

"I'm not trying to hurt you, Xander," she cooed with a calm voice that belied her malevolence. "I'm just trying to warn you. The man dressed all in white, and the right switch, and the thing you fear most. Six little angels all in a row, sparks will fly, and not just from the one with the electricity, either."

He turned toward her, brow furrowed. "You make no sense, has anyone ever told you that?"

She paused, halting her movement atop him. "Many people," she said after a moment. "But I was pieced together in a lab. How sane would you be?"

"You're insane."

She smiled at him wickedly, then reached around to something on her back. She leaned down and came in close to kiss him, stopping millimeters from his lips. "That may be true... but remember, this is all in your head... so what does that say about you?"

Their lips embraced, and he found himself enjoying the kiss despite the sadism of it... until she drew her sword from the holster on her back and plunged it deep into his right side. Into the heart of the Womb.

Xander thrust forward toward the sound of Cathy's voice, stretching the chains to their limit and letting out a horrible grunted scream through clenched, razor-sharp teeth.

She yelped loudly and jumped back out of his reach.

He stayed there, pulling against his restraints, his arms held at a ninety degree angle as he thrashed and twisted and tried to get at her. He snarled.

"Oh my god..." she said in a hushed voice, her hand raising up to her mouth as she looked upon him.

The black tar that made up Xander's womb form was gone, laying in a dark puddle at his feet... but the transformation was incomplete. His bone structure was still that of the Black Womb, covered so tightly by Xander's human skin that in places it became translucent and she could see the muscle underneath. His lower jaw was skill disjointed and angular to make room for extra, larger teeth.

His face bumped and contorted into the pronounced brow of the Womb, and Cathy saw for the first time just how much it resembled a Neanderthal man. The eyes themselves were his: small, human and blue... but their sockets were larger and slanted upward in a triangle, the remaining space half-covered by bleeding muscle and bone.

"Wom!" he bellowed, and just the tone of his voice and the anger in it made it clear to Cathy that the word it meant to say was not a nice one. She felt fear rise up inside her like vomit, ready to erupt and overcome her.

"Xander..." she said softly, wanting very much to reach out and touch his face, even starting the motion to do so, and then thinking better of it.

He growled deep within his throat, lowering his bile-covered head but never taking his eyes off of her, burning a hole into her with his gaze. "Wommmmmb...." he repeated. For a moment she could do nothing but stare at him, pulling the black leather of her jacket tight around her as he looked her up and down like a piece of meat. As she composed herself she convinced herself that if the chains had held him all night that they would continue to do so now, and she made a kind of sense out of the situation. It was like when you get woken up from a deep sleep, and you weren't quite awake yet - caught halfway in between.

"Sweetie..." she said as soothingly as possible, trying to hide the fear in her voice. "Sweetie, you have to wake up now, okay? It's time to wake up now."

Spider's visage changed to Cathy for a moment, then back to Spider. It was only now that he truly saw how much they looked alike.

"Mmm..." she hummed, licking his taste off of her lips as they finally parted. She released the sword from his gut. "Love you, baby..." she said mockingly.

"Woomb..." he spoke, and as he did, she could see the jagged teeth retracting somewhere into his complex skeletal structure, revealing the normal, human ones behind it. He was reverting.

"Yes, honey?" she asked, finally daring to get close enough to touch him on the side of the face, gently. He twitched once, but she did not flinch.

"Womb hates you," he said spitefully, like a child tossing an insult at an angry mother. The fact that he actually spoke words let her know that Xander was returning. He continued to glare at her, wanting very much to sink his claws into her, even as his brow sunk back into his scalp.

She frowned, trying not to take the words too seriously, but they sliced at her more potently than his talons ever could. Her lower lip quivered. She sucked it back and put her hand underneath his chin, raising his head up to meet her gaze. "But Cathy *loves* you," she said matter-of-fact-ly, leaning in and kissing him passionately on his distorted lips.

There was a pause when he tried to pull away, but she held his chin tight in her grasp, and he was weak from the transformation. Slowly he relaxed, and their lips began to move as one, with each other rather than against each other. Taking subtle cues from the other on what to do that came as naturally as the instinct to breathe.

Spider began to fade away, as the visions had before. As she did she tried to say something to him, but all he saw was her lips moving. Despite himself, a grin pried its way across his mouth as he left her there, in the darkness.

There was a noticeable pop as his jaw snapped back into its rightful place, allowing him to sink into the kiss. His eyes healed over, and he was Xander Drew again. She released his chin and he did not let go. She brought her hands behind his head, playing with the short hairs there and sending strange sensations rocketing throughout his body.

She ended the kiss and looked at him, finally back to normal. She smiled and tweaked him gently on the nose. "Knew that would get you back," she teased, very proud of herself.

He grinned stupidly at her, unsure if he was trying to shake off the disorientation from the kiss or the transformation. Or both. "Thanks," he said, unable to think of anything else.

"No problem," she said cheerily. "Just don't get any ideas. Mike and I are quite happy."

He chuckled. "Wouldn't have it any other way. I appreciate the gesture though."

She nodded and wiping her mouth. She took the keys to the shackles out of her pocket and moved around behind him, twisting his arm to find the hole. "You know... if I wasn't with Mike... I might leave you in these right about now."

His eyes went wide and his entire body became rigid for a second as he tried to turn and face her. "Excuse me?"

She leaned forward to allow him to see her. "Just kidding," she smirked devilishly, then turned back toward the lock. "You're so easy."

He snorted, then closed his eyes. The memories of Spider were coming back to him, as well as what the Womb had done the night before, trying to get out of the chains. She freed his right hand and he used it to rub the bridge of his nose, the intrusion of all those memories at once giving him a migraine. Suddenly he remembered something else, and his eyes shot open. His limbs went limp, allowing her the freedom she needed to free his left arm. "Cathy?" he said softly, looking downward sheepishly, almost shyly.

"Yes, hun?" she responded, fumbling with the keys.

"I love you, too," he said, almost shamefully.

She stopped, smiling warmly at him although he couldn't see. "I know."

Mike stared forward in disbelief, his blue eyes bugging out of his head. If his mind had not been completely blank at that precise moment, he would have imagined that he looked like a complete idiot.

He was standing knee deep in the snow, his toes numbed far past the point where wiggling them could help with the circulation. He had been stupid enough to have worn jeans, and even though he was wearing insulation underneath he could still feel the cold seeping up his legs. His top half wasn't nearly so uncomfortable, a tan parka one of the wives had given him drawn around him snugly. His hair was again brittle, as he refused to wear a cap - another man had appeared to need it more. There were bags under his eyes from lack of sleep, and his breath stank of stale coffee and even staler donuts.

"You're sure?" he said finally, unable to register what he'd just heard.

"Definitely," Officer Banner replied, tipping back his cap and taking a quick glance at how fast the sun seemed to be rising today. "Matches your description perfectly. But our boy was in prison then, wasn't he?"

Mike grew contemplative, tapping his thumbnail against the dimple of his upper lip, lost in thought. "Mmm," he said in a non-answer. After another moment of deadly silence, he smiled at shorter man. "Nothing. Wasn't anything important, just heard it somewhere and wanted to be sure."

Banner raised an eyebrow, then nodded. He cupped his hands around his coffee mug to try and heat them up.

"Shouldn't do that," Mike said as he peeked over a nearby brush out into the clearing beyond, scanning the area ahead for any sign of life.

Banner shot him a look. "And why not?"

"Getting your hands too close to the heat... makes the pours open up to let it in. Then when you take the heat away they stay open and all the cold comes rushing in. Might heat you up for a few minutes, but it'll make you colder in the long run."

"Hn," he grunted. He did not agree but loosened his grip on the mug all the same.

Mike smiled. His eyes darted around the open areas, until finally he gave a nod to Banner, who nodded back, and the both of them quietly crept onto the next place that appeared safe to scout. Mike glanced at his watch, then up at the sun. *Cathy should have unchained Xander by now,* he thought briefly, his mental image of her serving to warm him up and giving him that odd tingly feeling on one side of his face.

Then he thought of Xander, and what Banner had just told him, and became instantly cold again. *Now what does this crap mean?*

He huffed.

"Tell ya, whole world's gone to hell," Banner grumbled as the two snuck through the dawn into a patch of alders.

"What do you mean?" Mike asked, although he didn't necessarily disagree.

"This Derek piece of shit is walking around free, when they would have given a person just a few years older than him the damn chair."

Mike nodded, sucking in his lower lip.

"That little girl, the one that got killed - - so much death all over the place, and now my wife's niece is giving birth."

Mike stopped in his tracks, squinting quizzically. He considered the statements provided for a moment, then turned to his compatriot. "Forgive me for going Sesame Street here, but, one of these things is not like the other."

"Huh?" he said, then quickly into his intercom, "Sector F-17 clear."

"Derek, death, carnage... new life brought into the world? How does that fit in with the rest?"

Banner sighed. "Well, for one, she's fifteen,"

Mike felt the guttural pang of pain-filled memories, then forced it back. "Hey man, I know what that's like, but she'll be..."

"... she's also got Down syndrome."

Mike's eyes went wide a moment, for the second time in under ten minutes, when he realized who the man was talking about. "Oh."

CHAPTER EIGHT: MOTHERS

Antony Jones stared blankly at the file in front of him, trying desperately to keep his eyes open as he read the pages. He reached for his morning cup of coffee without looking and almost knocked it over, cursed, then spared a glance at the mug just long enough to grip its handle.

Just a few months ago he wouldn't have had to do this himself. Someone would have briefed him on everything he needed to know. A month ago he had asked his superiors for reassignment as soon as possible. His replacement had been found before he had found a new position suitable, so he had taken up with the local office of Grey, Mercer and Suite in the interim.

He was sweating, like a pig. Coffee always did that to him, but it was a trade off for the forty-five minutes of alertness that it bought him. He shook his face after each sip, sloshing it around in his mouth. It was like a Zen ritual for him, and somehow always managed to make him feel awake. He closed his eyes for a moment, willing the blood vessels within them to stop pounding, then went back to the words in front of him.

His office door opened and a familiar strand of dark red hair poked its way in, followed by the rough-hewn yet beautiful face of Megan Greene. She had been the assistant D. A. until she had accepted the Adam Genblade case that rocketed her into stardom, and lead to her becoming a partner in Mayer, Summers and Soul. She'd always dreamed of being a lawyer ever since she was a child. When they'd met, she'd let her ambition cloud her judgment, and they'd started as abhorrent rivals. But they'd both discovered how not take themselves so seriously, and they'd become confidants. Friends. They'd gone against each other in a case involving Adam Genblade. As it happened the killer had been Derek, and the experience had caused the two to become close, in a manner of speaking.

Everything about Megan screamed of power, and yet there was a softness to her nature, the duel signals usually made those around her (men in particular) quite uncomfortable. Which was alright with her. She'd use every edge she could get.

She watched him, unable to keep the smile from her face as he toiled away, completely unaware of her presence. She relished in this rare chance to be a fly on the wall and watch him behave as he would were she not around. After studying him she raised her fist and rapped twice on the thick wooden door. "Paging Tony Jones," she giggled, mimicking the cheesy entrance that had become a ritual of his. "Tony Jones, are you there?"

He jolted his head back and tapped the button on his intercom. "Yes?" he said wearily, the strain in his voice giving away how sleep deprived he was.

She opened the door the rest of the way, and could now see that his clothes were wrinkled and unpressed. "Well, you're with it, huh?" she said.

He turned, sheepishly taking his hand away from the device. "Hey," he said, running a head through his auburn hair as he turned back to the papers, making it stick up in the back.

"Hey," she replied, the spontaneity of her entrance spent. "New case?"

"Mmm," he mumbled, bringing the caffeine to his lips again. "Disgusting case. Family Court stuff, they're the worst. This is not the stuff I took this job for."

She smiled and stepped around to a quaint art-deco sofa he had placed there to make himself look cultured when clients were in. She sat on it in a relaxed position, legs crossed in front of her. "That's the breaks of working in a small district, Tony. Sometimes you've got to sweat the small stuff to keep yourself in the game."

"Still... this is just too much."

"Hard case?" she asked, unsure herself if she were concerned or amused, and settling for being both.

"No, no... it's open and shut. It's just the filing, the dictation... everything about it is done wrong. Some of these things are hand-written, for God's sake. Who's that new girl? Summer's secretary?"

"Jillian Mayer."

"She should be fired," he grumbled, cursing. "How'd she even get a job here? We used to have standards at this office... I dimly recall."

Megan raised an eyebrow and sucked in her lip, not really wanting to say what she knew was the truth to his question. "She was Natasha Mayer's niece."

He looked up from the papers again, recalling the young woman who had put Mayer, Summers and Soul on the map by initially taking the Adam Genblade case... at the killer's request. "Oh," she said, tapping a pencil against his folder. "Well, she'd still better shape up soon."

She snorted. "I remember tales of a certain D.A. who was so nervous his first day in court that he kept referred to a male judge as Ma'am... just couldn't stop, kept spitting it out, the more nervous he got."

"Those allegations have never been substantiated," he said, raising a finger to punctuate his point, while scribbling on a post-it note tacked to the side of one page. "Besides, I sue anyone who states it for slander."

"Except when it was posted in the office newsletter the day you became D.A."

"Then I sued for libel."

She laughed, and it was a good feeling. But when it died off the two were left in silence for a long moment again. She clicked her tongue against the roof of her mouth, trying desperately to think of something to say. "So, what's the case about?"

He sighed. "Some custody bullshit. Mother against daughter for granddaughter / son... it's a mess. I'm trying to make heads or tails of it, and it's just not happening. But this mother really doesn't want her kid to raise the grandkid. Still haven't sorted out why."

"Hope you're not up against anyone too good."

"Naw. They put Stack on it. Was appointed by the state."

She rolled her eyes. "Couldn't get anyone to do it pro-bono, huh? Man, she hasn't got a chance."

"Tell me about it. Going to mop the floor with that drop-out."

She was silent for a moment, just looking at him. "This is Family Court, Tone... maybe that attitude isn't the best going in."

He licked his upper lip, put down his pencil, and folded his fingers together in front of him. He took a long moment to gather his thoughts, then finally made eye-contact with her. "Why do you keep doing this?"

"Sorry?" she retorted.

"Why do you keep coming in here like this? Every single day, always with some pearl of wisdom or sharp comment or cute political limerick... why? I mean, I know we said we were going to stay friends, but we're ex, Megan."

The words took their blow, and she stood up to regain herself. "Thought you said you just wanted some time. For work?"

He sighed, giving her a sympathetic look. "We don't want the same things," he said finally.

She frowned, then nodded. "This is about the kid thing, isn't it?"

"You want children, I don't. To me, that's pretty cut-and-dried."

"Doesn't have to be. We don't have to be.. Ex."

He sighed, turning back to the desk. "I have work to do."

She nodded and headed toward the door, her heels clacking angrily against the floor the only indication of emotion she would allow show through. "Fine. Be that way. But I'll be back tomorrow morning to file for an appeal."

He snickered at that and watched her leave. "Duly noted."

She closed the door softly behind her and headed off to her office to start the work day.

He sighed then buried his face in his moist palms, rubbing his face back to life. He turned back toward the closed door to his office, feeling the sudden urge to go after her. He again reached for his coffee without looking, this time knocking it over and spilling its contents onto his desk.

⚔

Gallagher sat with his elbows on his desk, clenching his hands through his receding grey hair. He had loosened his collar significantly a few minutes ago trying to stop his shortness of breath. It hadn't worked, and since then it seemed to have gotten exponentially worse with each passing second, his adam's apple bobbing up and down as he swallowed nothingness trying to get some saliva going in his parched mouth.

He took a deep breath, then slowly exhaled. He composed himself. It was eleven thirty, almost lunch time. His appointment was almost an hour late. He furrowed his brow, checking his wrist watch just to be sure, then glanced at the door to his office, and finally at the brass cross that hung next to it.

He turned to glare at his intercom, nearly obscured by a pile of papers. He

221

groaned at the idea of using it, letting the pros and cons of such an action rattle back and forth in his head for a few minutes, then reached over a pressed the first red button on the left.

"Tanya?" he said, trying to sound cheerful as he held it down. He waited, but there was no response. Finally a dial tone ensued, along with a series of seven beeps. He raised an eyebrow to the machine quizzically, but continuing to depress his finger. After a few rings there was the unmistakable clicking sound of the line connecting. "Hello, Tanya?" he repeated, slightly less cheerily.

"Hello, you have reached the voice mail of... 'Robert Gallagher'... please input your password, now," came an automated female voice.

He released his finger from the button, heaved a loud sigh, then pressed the next button over. "Tanya?"

There was a squeal of feedback as his voice rang over the school's loudspeakers, and he quickly released the button again, pressing the third and last button immediately. "Tanya?!" he barked, using his free hand to again clench his scalp.

"Yes, Mr. Gallagher?"

"Thank you. Did Miss McFadden give any reason why she would miss our appointment?" he considered correcting her on the fact that it was actually Reverend Gallagher, but decided that it would be pretentious.

There was a rustling of papers, and then several clicks on a keyboard. "Miss McFadden did not show up for class today, Mr. Gallagher, nor did she call in sick. Should I put in a call to her home?"

"No, no," he replied hastily, waving his hand to sweep the idea away, until he realized that she couldn't actually see the motion. "That won't be necessary. When is my next appointment?"

"Well, your eleven thirty has been waiting here next to the office for fifteen minutes."

He fumbled through his own papers, finally coming across the name Jaden Mal, a seventh grade boy here. "Why didn't you send him in?"

"Because you had a ten thirty appointment with Miss McFadden."

"Miss McFadden did not show up for her ten... just send the boy in," he sighed, releasing his finger from the button for what he hoped would be the last time that day (but knew himself it would not), and again made sure that his collar was on correctly.

The door opened and the young man came in. His skin was a kind of tanned brown and his hair dark dark black. Gallagher had become convinced when first meeting the child a few weeks ago that he had been from an inter-racial family, but of course couldn't ask. He was short, and his two front teeth stuck out just a little too far. He wore a green and brown horizontal striped t-shirt with a ketchup stain on the right breast. His jeans were torn and soaked from the knee down from the snow outside. He looked cold. More than that, he looked scared. He always looked scared.

Gallagher immediately felt a swell of pity for the child, walking over to him and smiling warmly, motioning for him to sit. When he did, he placed a comforting hand on the child's knee. "So, what do you want to talk about?"

Xander strained his head to the left as hard as he could, slowly forcing it more and more until he felt the calcium in his joints pop. He breathed a sigh of relief.

"Kinks?" Cathy asked, taking a sip of her Slush Puppy from an orange straw that fit perfectly between her pursed ruby lips.

He shot her a look, almost laughing. "Yeah. I wonder why?"

"Maybe you slept weird," she grinned, jutting the cup toward him in offering, which he shrugged away.

"Never thirsty after a transform."

The right side of her mouth twitched as she processed the statement, unable to have a frame of reference for what he was talking about. "Always thought you would be."

"Naw. Takes me hours to feel anything after. Womb gives me all the vitamins and stuff my body needs... I think."

She nodded, adjusting the way she was sitting on the cafeteria table, her jacket strewn across her lap. He sat on the chair next to her.

"Can't we go outside?" he asked, his hand tapping against the table uncontrollably.

Her hands sunk as she shot him a disappointed glare. "I'm not going out in that cold just because you're having a damn nic fit," she protested, kicking his hand off the desk. The sound had begun to annoy her.

He grunted, clenching both hands.

She sucked more slush into her mouth as a group of kids walked by, churning it about in her mouth until it melted, making her already healthily-chubby cheeks puff out a little with each movement of the half-frozen liquid. After she swallowed it she smirked and turned back to him. "So if the Womb gives you everything you need, then why do you need a smoke?"

He shot her a deadpan look.

"Seriously," she laughed, loving how much this was getting under his skin. It had been a while since she'd had a chance to seriously bug him. "I guess you don't really have to have one... ever, right?"

"Is this going to be the daily : 'you must quit smoking' speech?" he asked, smirking despite himself. "Because you're early. Usually doesn't kick in until we're on our way home from school."

"That's because you smoke half a pack between here and your house, you freak!"

"Do not."

This time it was her turn to shoot him a look.

His eyes went up in their sockets, the way they always did when he was doing mental math. His fingers also counted. When he finished, he simply leaned forward on the table.

"And?" she asked self-assuredly when he did not immediately present his

223

figures.

"Shut up," he scowled, defeated.

"I believe that's another victory for Catherine Kennessy, Woman-Supreme."

He chuckled. "Woman-Supreme?"

"Uh-Huh," she chimed, giving him a goofy, toothy smile.

"Woman-Supreme?" he re-stated, raising one hairy eyebrow.

"It's my code name."

"You have a code-name?"

"You get one, why can't I?"

"I have two personalities. When you can claim that, you can have a second name."

She thought about that. "I don't know... Mike says I'm like a whole different person when I'm on my period, does that count?"

Xander cupped his hands over his ears. "TMI!" he yelped.

"Huh?"

"Too Much Information!"

"Ah," she laughed. She got a coy look about her, waiting for him to remove his hands from his ears. He did, and she said: "You know, with all the congealed blood you had on you last night, I'd think you'd be used too..."

"TMI! TMI!" he yelled, returning his hands to the sides of his head with lightning-fast reflexes.

She laughed as he kept repeating it, never noticing Mike enter the cafeteria and walk over, bags still obvious under his eyes. "Hey, lover," she greeted, above Xander's yelps.

"Hey," he said as cheerily as he could muster, but a confused mind fueled by lack of sleep was apparent even from that one word.

Cathy smiled. She knew her boyfriend well, and was well aware not to ask what was wrong. He wasn't in the mood just yet, so she simply pouted her lips out toward him.

He smiled, taking the hint and leaning down for a good-morning kiss. After a moment he pulled back, smiled, then gave her a perplexed look. "You taste weird. No offense."

"Xander," she said simply, shrugging.

He raised an eyebrow, considered the context for a moment, then shrugged as well. "Oh... okay then."

"Tmi... tmi..."

Mike pointed a thumb at Xander. "Speaking of which, what's up with him?"

"Apparently he got too much information, or something. I don't know."

He turned from her, to Xander, and then back again. "You were talking about period stuff, huh?"

She grinned devilishly.

He punched Xander in the arm, forcing his friend out of the fetal huddle. "Yo."

Xander smirked. "Yo. You're late."

"Slept in. What about you guys, have any trouble with..." he lowered his voice, suddenly aware they were not alone.

Xander frowned.

Cathy rolled her eyes, dismissing Xander's drama before Mike's mind blew it out of proportion. "He had a little trouble getting up on the right side of his consciousness, but he got over it."

"Hmm."

Xander looked up. "Any word about that girl I saw the other night?"

"Yeah," Mike spat, getting into his down-to-business attitude that Cathy despised. "But not here."

Xander stared at Mike blankly for a moment, fumbling nervously with his forest green t-shirt, his thick eyebrows narrowing in response to what he'd just heard. An unlit cigarette dangled uselessly from his lip, threatening to fall with every breath he took.

"You're sure?" he asked after a moment, having to place a palm against the wall of the smoking section to keep himself from falling over.

"That's what I said," Mike nodded, placing a comforting hand on Xander's shoulder. "But it's definitely true. I trust Banner... and even after he told me, I put in a call to the number White gave me... it's legit. That girl you said you killed the other night... she was killed months ago. Back in September, man."

Cathy's brow furrowed, confused. She stood just a few feet back from pair. She had agreed finally that this would be the most secluded spot to talk about their problems of late, but in her own words had: 'refused to breathe in second-hand stinkiness.' Neither of the men had seen that exact expression on her since Jamie Dawkins had died. It was bewilderment at the sentences coming at her. "So... what does that mean, exactly?" she asked finally, extending her hand palm up.

"Well, it puts more players in the game for her death," Mike pointed out, stroking his chin. "I mean, this girl's death happened when Genblade was still active... not to mention Derek. And the Tee's were still around back then, Bram and Raine. Could have been any one of them, really. There's no reason to assume it was - "

"I remember the taste of her blood in my mouth," Xander interrupted, head turned down and eyes shut as he tried to block out the memories that wouldn't stop coming like a slow leak in a huge dam. "I remember that she still had that new baby smell. I remember... everything." He opened his eyes, locking them to Mike's. "This was me."

Cathy had turned away when he had started to speak. She found that if she didn't see him saying the words, she could distance herself from them. "Again..." she said, pausing to find her voice. "What does that mean?"

All three were silent for a moment, the gears in their minds turning.

"Its hidden things from you before," Mike pointed out. "And it showed you them at a later time, when it needed you to know. Genblade said..."

"Genblade?" Xander scoffed.

"Genblade said that the Womb knew that Derek was the killer, and that it hid that fact from you. Maybe it's the same now," he finished, as if his friend hadn't interrupted.

"No," Xander said, shaking his head somberly. "It means that I'm remembering... that someday I might remember everything that it does, all the time."

"Could this be part of learning to control it again?" Cathy chimed, trying hard to find positive options.

"More like it starting to control me," Xander spat, finally lighting the smoke, to which Cathy stepped away another pace.

Mike snapped his fingers. "Warren!"

"Huh?"

"His hypno-therapy crap! What if he was using it to block your memories somehow? Bring them back at key times in order to control the Womb? We could go through his files, and..."

"We've been through the files a million times. O'Toole had to use a bunch of tricks and schemes just to find out who I was. I don't think he had something this major up his sleeve. Especially not without filing it away for Hale and the Circe's say-so... no, I think this is more just to do with," he paused, pressing his hand to his right side, where the womb-organ throbbed in response to his touch, like a kicking fetus. "... This."

There was a silence then as the three absorbed that, trying to find a place to put it in their heads. Xander sighed, sitting down against the bricks and bringing his knees up close to his face.

He just wanted to curl up in a ball and die.

Feeling a swell of pity, Cathy finally walked over and sat next to him, putting her arm around him and giving him a friendly squeeze. "It'll be okay," she said, ruffling his hair. "We'll find a way to beat it. Last night worked out all right... right?"

Xander nodded, but his heart was not in it. "What about the other thing?" he said finally, wanting very much to shift the focus away from himself for the moment, looking in Mike's direction. "You mentioned something else."

"Yeah," Mike stated, frowning. He bent down in front of them, leaning forward to bring his hand into contact with his girlfriend's, to give her support for what he was about to say. "There's a pregnant girl."

Cathy shifted uncomfortably, even with Mike's support.

Xander shot him a dry stare, puffing smoke through his nostrils. "Not exactly our area of expertise. And don't even try to tell me I'm the father."

"She was fifteen," Mike added, clearing his throat.

"Tragic. But still, there's nothing really sinister in..."

"And she had Down syndrome."

Xander's eyebrows shot up.

Cathy's went wide. "I know who you're talking about!" she said, jaw slack. "We used to be in class together in grade three, before they decided to segregate her into the Special Ed room! It's..."

"August Styles," Xander finished, face still locked in the same shocked position.

"Yeah," Mike said. "And, as you can imagine, her Mom isn't very happy."

"I remember that bitch. She was like a Nazi. A Nazi that Hitler would have been afraid of."

"Pulled my hair once," Cathy added absently.

"August?" Xander questioned.

"Her Mom."

"Ah."

"More than that..." Mike sighed. "... her Mom's making her get an abortion."

Xander's look faded slowly from shock, to a dead-serious look the both of them recognized as him trying to hold back anger. "What?"

"She can't do that." Cathy protested.

"Oh, don't be so sure," Mike sighed. "Mentally challenged, underage, and no idea who the father is..."

"Come again?" Xander spat, almost so fast the words jumbled together. "Am I officially the last person in our school to get any?"

Mike shot him a look. "Not funny, man. The doctor's got to do a rape test on her when she went in for a prenatal exam..." he tightened his grip on Cathy's hand. "They did the old rape clock test... but there was scarring on the upper *and* lower parts of her... well, y' know."

"Upper is consensual, lower means rape," Xander recalled.

"Exactly. This isn't as cut and dried as it sounds. Something's up, and her Mom is rushing it into court asap. If we don't do something about this..."

"...we could have another dead child on our hands," Xander finished, looking downward.

"... there won't be any genetic evidence left in August to find the rapist," Mike said, finishing his own sentence.

Cathy frowned. "Won't work," she said after a moment.

"Why?" Mike said, tilting his head to one side.

"Come on, hun. We've dealt with this before. I've..." she sighed, "... if the girl hasn't talked, she's not going to. And can you blame her? She's got the mental functionality of a six year old. She can't possibly process what's happened to her, let alone open up to us about..."

Mike looked at her. A grin started to play over his face, and he shot a glance at Xander. Xander smiled too, turning and looking at Cathy knowingly.

"... fuck," she spat. "I just got the job of talking to her, didn't I?"

Xander gave her a quick squeeze, then got up and doubted his cigarette and dusted the ash off of his shirt.

"Okay, I'll talk to her. If nothing else, I can point her in a direction... there's all kinds of programs through the school board to help pregnant teens. That weasel Shnieder is surprisingly good with it. He even offered me help when I was... you know."

"Really?" Xander asked, surprised by the new information.

"Yeah. Someone told me his Mom got pregnant with him as a teen, so he tries to help and stuff. Anyway, I'll talk to her."

"You find out what you can," Mike said, squeezing her hand warmly. "Xander, you ask around too. See if Tommy and the rest know anything. Find out who she's close to, who would have had the opportunity for something like this... everything you can."

Xander nodded, scratching his chin. "That sounds good... you can do that. I've got a better idea."

Mike stopped. "And what might that be?"

Xander did not answer, merely started walking toward the exit to school grounds.

"Damn him," Mike said under his breath, as he and Cathy started walking back to class.

Gallagher leaned back in his chair with one hand over his mouth as he tried to stop the other from shaking. A cup of coffee sat on the desk before him, completely untouched and cold by now, a few dribble marks going down the front from where he had raised it to take a sip then placed it back down. Next to the coffee was an equally untouched pack of king-size cigarette's, the plastic still on them.

"Didn't realize you smoked," came a familiarly shrill voice from the doorway. Principal Shnieder was leaning there, taking the last few bites of a banana. He was wearing a plaid sweater-vest over a blue shirt and grey dress pants that almost seemed too long for the pint-sized man, the fluorescent light gleaming off his mostly bald head and making his ears (which stuck out as if by magic) glow red.

"I don't," Gallagher grumbled, leaning his elbows onto the desk. "But I think after this week, I might have to start."

Shnieder smirked a little. "A little overwhelming, isn't it?" he said smugly, scratching his beak-like nose as he did. "I tried to warn you, Robert. It's not as easy as it sounds."

"I know. But I never expected..."

"That's when it'll come, friend. When you don't expect it."

Gallagher groaned, already tired of Shnieder's well-meant Holier-than-Thou attitude. "In the confessionals I hear things I cannot repeat, some that I would not want too... but who would do this? To a child that didn't know any better?"

Shnieder looked somber for a moment, as if trying to push it out of his mind. "I can't tell you, Robert. But you have to remember, this is exactly why we brought you on board. I know it's horrible to say, but this type of thing isn't uncommon. It's just who it happened to that is. There have been eleven girls pregnant just this year, and the year is only half over. So many that a few years back I helped set up a program through the school that would help them out financially. I mean, I wish there was more we could do. There just... isn't."

"I understand. I just keep thinking that - "

There was a knock at the door that interrupted him and a student poked her head in to the door. "Principal Shnieder?" she asked, smiling at him politely. "The secretary said you'd be in here. I need some help with the SADD committee snow-day next week?"

"Of course," Shnieder smiled, nodding at the girl. "I'll be right with you."

He turned back to Gallagher, tapping twice on his desk, trying hard to keep his lower lip as stiff as possible. "We'll talk later."

Gallagher lifted his mug, then turned back to his paperwork for the day.

CHAPTER NINE: DELVE

August Styles sat against the wall of the stairwell between the second and third floor of the school, staring out the nearby window and the snow that clung to it. It took funny shapes, some of it falling onto other parts, making even more shapes. One of them looked kind of like a fairy, she thought. Another one reminded her of a hand. And her Mother... she could see her mother very clearly in the foggy glass.

A tear ran down her cheek, and then another... and another, until finally they were plopping against the floor and dribbling off of her nose, making the skin on her face feel blotchy and red. She sniffed it back, and when she did the breath that followed was a wail, one that echoed throughout the entire set of stairs. It was heard by several people, all of whom ignored it.

She hit herself hard in the side of the face and sank down into herself, looking like a lump of humanity created for making tears. She looked bruised somehow, although there was not a mark on her. It was as if she was the bruise, like it was on her soul, or the small fragile heart that was breaking with every thought that passed through her.

Cathy watched her from the doorway to the third floor. As she did, she couldn't help but be reminded of a child. Even though she knew that they were both the same age, the scene brought an almost maternal feeling out in her, rising up from her gut until it overcame her. August's whole body shuddered in a powerful sob, and Cathy had to do her best not to start to cry as well. "Hey," she said finally, composing herself as she stepped forward. She spoke as gently as possible, using the same tone she would have used on an upset child.

August jumped when she heard the voice, then grabbed her lunch bag and began to move. There was a primal fear in her eyes.

"No, it's okay!" Cathy said, forcing a wide smile. "I was just wondering how you were."

August gave her a long, side-on look, as if sizing the girl up to see whether or not she was dangerous. She sat back down and seemed to relax, but still kept her lunch bag clenched tightly to her chest. "My nose is runny," she said honestly, turning to stare down at her feet.

Cathy nodded, smiling. "Yeah... That happens to me sometimes, too. That's why I always carry these," she said, reaching into her purse and withdrawing a bundle of two or three soft, fluffy tissues. "You want one?" she asked, holding them out.

August regarded the offering with some hesitation, but her nose was hurting more and more, so she reached out and grabbed one. She wrapped it around her hand methodically, then used it to blow her nose. "Thank you," she said, almost a whisper. The strain in her voice could be heard now, and it was obvious that this was not the first crying fit that the girl had gone into today.

Despite her better judgment, Cathy could resist it no longer. She reached out and touched the girl on the shoulder, then leaned in and gave her a warm hug. "It'll be okay, sweetie," she said, holding back her own tears as August started up again. They stayed that way for a long moment, and when they released, Cathy gave her a kiss on the cheek, getting the taste of salt-water on her lips as she did.

"I don't know what's going on," August sobbed, wiping her nose again, only this time with her shirt. "I don't know..." the sentence might have continued, but it was lost in a wail.

"I know, honey," Cathy said, trying hard to think of what to say. "But I need to ask you about how it happened now, okay? I can help you fix it, but I need to know how it happened."

"My Mommy says I can't keep my baby..."

A sharp pang was felt deep within her gut, and she fought the urge to show it. "I heard that, too. I know. You and your Mommy need to talk about that, okay? But right now, I need to talk about the Daddy."

August looked at Cathy for directly for the first time, her eyes bloodshot and puffy. "I don't know where my Daddy is."

"No," Cathy said warmly, placing her hand of the girl's knee. "I need to know about your baby's Daddy." There was a long pause, and she wasn't sure how to phrase the next back delicately. "If you're not... sure... I can help you figure it out?"

August looked confused, her eyes darting about inside her head. Her hands started to twist the brown bag, ripping it in places. "I don't know."

"That's okay," Cathy sighed, pushing a strand of her black hair behind her ear. "I can help you figure it out. Just tell me when the last time you slept with a boy was."

Her brow furrowed. "I never slept with a boy."

Cathy stopped herself from outright objecting to the statement when she realized what her words would mean if someone took them literally. "No, sweetie. Um... the last time you made love to a boy?"

"I kiss Tim sometimes. The last time was at the Halloween dance. He says he wants to be my boyfriend but I don't want a boyfriend right now."

Cathy clucked her tongue against the top of her mouth, struggling now. She knew how she would have to phrase it, but didn't want to say it. "No... no, honey. I need to know the last time you had sex."

August leaned herself back, a little repulsed by the vulgar-sounding word. "I've never had sex!" she said, offended.

Cathy let those words bop around in her head, then finally she thought of the correct wording, smiling. She reached out and touched August's stomach gently. "I need to know when you did the thing that made your baby."

August stared at her for a moment, a sad look passing over her, then looked down at her feet.

ʎ꘎ʎ

Mike sat down next to Tommy in Lit class, even as Mr. Reid was talking about an upcoming assignment based on MacBeth in which they would have to break off into pairs. He cringed at the idea, looking around him for people he was close enough to pair with that might have some shred of understanding of Shakespeare and finding none. He silently cursed the entire idea of the assignment, but decided to keep his mouth shut on the subject.

"Hey," Tommy said to him, finally noticing that he was there. He was leaned back in his chair, something every one of his teachers had told him repeatedly not to do, playing with a toothpick in his mouth. Why he was doing that nobody knew, it was just one of those character traits that Tommy seemed to pick up for a week or so and then never speak of again.

"Hey," Mike reciprocated, nodding a greeting.

"You're late," Tommy said, holding out a fist until Mike held out his own and knocked them together.

"Mmm. I've been told that already."

"Something up?" he almost smiled, using his tongue to position the toothpick between his two front teeth. "Anything interesting?"

"Nothing life and death. You?"

Tommy sighed sadly, yet still retained his smile, which Mike now began to think was fake. "I'm still grounded after the drama a few weeks ago, when... well, you heard."

"Yeah. About that..."

"It's cool."

"Good. Grounded, huh? That must suck."

"Pfft," Tommy shrugged, shaking his head. "I wouldn't be going out anyway. I'm actually kind of glad I'm grounded. Mom picks me up here every day after school and drives me home, then drives me to school every day. Not allowed outside. No outside means no chances for Derek fucking Smith to come at me in a dark alley." He shuddered at even the mention of the killer's name.

Mike was startled, but only for a moment. With his attitude and everything that happened lately, it was easy to forget that Tommy had taken quite a beating in the months since school started... most notably from Derek and the Tee Gang. He nodded sympathetically.

"So, I hear you're actually *helping* the cops look for him?" Tommy asked, raising an eyebrow quizzically.

"Yeah," Mike nodded. "Not much, just scoping out the woods to look for signs that someone's been there. Doing my part."

There was a silence, as Tommy looked the other teen up and down. "No offense, dude - you're killer and all - but I think you should take a cue from me and just lock yourself in your room till the fucker's dead or behind bars."

Mr. Reid shot a look in their direction, but said nothing.

"Why's that?" Mike said, lowering his voice. "Give me one good reason."

Tommy reached out quickly and tapped Mike in the side with the back of his palm.

Mike bent over in pain, fighting the urge to yelp.

"There's one," Tommy said smugly, considering his point proven. "Last time you crossed Smith he nearly gutted you. That's not an experience I would want to repeat, I was you."

"You're not me," Mike spat, a trace of bitterness in his voice as he composed himself. "You handle it your way, I'll handle it mine."

Tommy nodded. He took the pick out of his mouth, licked his dry lips, then put it in again. "Fair enough," he said finally, giving an apologetic look.

Tommy never seemed to apologize for anything. Ever.

Mike breathed heavily, willing his side to stop throbbing. "You heard anything around lately?" he asked when he felt he could speak in an even tone again.

"About Derek? Same as everyone, big load of nothing. Nothing since the old man with the hand... which, by the way, ew."

"Yeah," Mike agreed. "Not Derek. Anything else? Anything you might've heard from the guys?"

Tommy narrowed his eyes at him, taking a long breath and fingering the pick. It reminded Mike of the way Xander sometimes twirled his smokes when he was mulling over something. "You're talking about the retarded girl, huh?"

Mike's eyes grew but he decided not to chide Tommy on the use of the crude term. "The Down syndrome girl, August. Yes, her."

"Heard she got knocked up, but everyone knows that. You must too, or you wouldn't be asking."

Mike tilted his head, conceding to the honest, if not sly, response. "Naw, I'm wondering if you've heard any of the guys say anything. You hear a lot. Anyone been bragging in the locker room? Anyone talking about scoring?"

Tommy shook his head. He leaned in close. "No. Even if one of the guys did it, nobody's stupid enough to brag about something like that. They know they'd get in shit, plus no player wants a reputation for that kind of girl. Hurts the chances with the ladies, if you get my drift."

Mike nodded.

"Why you asking, anyway? This isn't anything you usually get up in people's face about. It's not any murder or a rape."

"I wouldn't be too sure," Cathy said, sitting down between the boys in the row behind and laying her purse and jacket across her desk, leaning on them to get in close.

Both Mike and Tommy turned to her, shocked by her sudden arrival.

"What do you mean?" Mike asked, his hand without delay and unconsciously going to hers.

"Yeah," Tommy said, shifting in his seat to face her now. "I've heard some wild stories, but that isn't one of them. You saying someone forced themselves on the girl?"

Cathy shook her head, wiping her face to make sure there were no tears there. She'd spent the last five minutes in the bathroom making sure, but her face still felt dry from them. "I don't think it's that simple," she said, her voice almost devoid of emotion.

"What?" Mike asked, shooting Tommy a perplexed look, who returned it in kind. "What are you talking about? It's either rape or it isn't, right? Is there something I'm missing? Date-rape? Drugs? Was she tricked somehow?"

Cathy nodded, chattering her tongue against her teeth. "I think so, Mike. She doesn't know what sex is."

"What?" Tommy exclaimed.

"She doesn't know *how* her baby was made."

CHAPTER TEN: PREPERATION

Megan took a sip of the martini she had been nursing for the last hour. The olive that bobbed in the fancy, decorated glass bounced against her nose. She was about to put it down again, when she changed her mind and instead downed the three-quarters that was left to the glass then slammed it down on the mahogany desk, sending an echo throughout the room. "Ah," she exclaimed as the liquor burned her mouth, giving it the after-bite which made her love them so much. One of her friends had told her once that a martini "put hair on your chest" - Megan had thought to tell her that she obviously had never had tequila, but decided not to.

A little red in the face from the drink but by no means drunk, she picked up the tape recorder in front of her and started to rewind it. It contained her own voice-recording of what she planned to use in an upcoming criminal case involving a couple of idiots who'd held up a convenience store. She'd written it, read it aloud to the recorder (while pacing around the room and imagining she was in court), and then played it back, making notes on her first draft as she heard the impact (or sometimes lack thereof) of her own words. This would be the fourth revision. Typically she would only do three, the most ever was ten, but she always kept doing it until she was sure that it was perfect. It was part of her insane need to over-prepare for everything, something that she'd had with her ever since grade school. Pre-school, by her mother's words, although she couldn't testify to that herself.

"Ladies and gentlemen of the jury," came her own voice over the recorder, which she was unconsciously mouthing along too. "The defense is likely to try and convince you today that his clients, Adam Bird and Ron Snelgrove, are innocent. This is an insult to your intelligence, to this court, and to the justice system itself." She smiled at herself proudly at that line. "The question is not whether or

233

not these men are guilty. They are unquestionably guilty, and I shall prove that without doubt during the next few days of trial. The question that you should be asking yourselves is not whether or not they should go to jail... but whether or not they should go for the rest of their lives. While their crime, at face value, in no way indicts a life sentence... think of the terror that this act has inflicted on the lives of Mr. Berkhart?" She made a note on the paper that said 'point to berkhart.' "A seventy-five year old man whose wife died last year, leaving only his store to keep himself occupied. How can he go to work now, after years of loyal service to this *community* and not be afraid?" She made another note, point to defendants, "Is that what you went in for? Two hundred dollars... cigarettes... and few dozen beer, maybe some candy bars... and one life? Because that is exactly what you two have taken from Mr. Berkhart... you have taken away his *life*. His ability to not be afraid. Just as it was taken from all of us months ago, by the killer known as Derek Smith..."

"Nice," came a voice from behind her. She switched off the recording immediately, then turned to smile at Nathaniel Summers. Nathan was the head of the firm, and had been for the better part of a decade. He collected antique vases and studied anthropology in the small amount of spare time his job afforded, and he'd always loved Megan's smile. "That's genius, comparing them to Smith. You might as well have called the two of them Hitler in this town. It'll get the jury hating them just by association."

"You don't think it's too much?" she asked, biting her lower lip, tapping her yellow writing pad with her pencil.

"Not at all. It's just right. The 'rest of their lives' thing might be a bit much... just don't overdo it. Say it almost under your voice, like a whisper, and it'll be fine." He entered her office fully and closed the door behind him. He was wearing a grey Italian suit that seemed to have been poured onto him it fit so well, and dark sunglasses that seemed to only cover his eyes, none of the area around him. He had short, slicked-back silver hair and a dashing smile he was never afraid to use in court. It did not surprise her that Nate was one of the best the firm had to offer.

Megan looked at her pad, then nodded silently and made the note. When she turned back to him and went from twenty-nine to sixteen in a heartbeat. "So, what's new, Pinky? Any new plans to take over the world?"

Nathan chuckled at that, taking the seat across from her casually. "Actually, I wanted to talk about you."

She raised an eyebrow.

"This is your day off, Megan. Why the hell are you here?"

She looked shocked, and more than a little hurt, the smile he was so fond of fading away. "I had to work on the opening statement for my case."

"That case doesn't start for another three weeks."

"You know how I like to prepare."

"You're obsessive," he corrected, smiling even though his words were slightly confrontational. "You need to get out more."

"I get out fine. I went out last night?"

"Yeah... where?"

She paused, her mouth open and moving, but no words coming out.

"See?" he said, giving her a look.

She smiled, finally rolling the statement off her back. "I appreciate the concern, Nathan... I really do. But I don't need it right now. Don't want it. All I really want is to work and get my mind off everything else. Can you just let me do that, please?"

Nathan frowned, then nodded, although he made a grunting sound in his throat. It was the same sound he made in court when a judge overruled his objections, something only brave judges did anyway. "I just don't want this job... or me, as you superior... to be a reason for you to regret this, later in life. You're still young, Megan."

"I'm not going to have any regrets, Nathan," she said finally, trying to sound as upbeat as possible. "And if you want to help me, find me a case before this one starts."

Nathan sighed, then started moving toward the door. When he opened it, he was surprised to see someone standing outside it, his eyebrow rising high. "I think your next case just found you."

Megan looked up. When she saw who was there her eyes bulged in shock.

Mike walked Cathy and her sister Trina right to their front door after school, something he and Xander had made a point of doing just to make sure they got there safely. Trina went inside without a word, but a quick smile in his direction let Mike know that she appreciated his kindness. The second that the door was closed behind her the lovers sat down on her front stop together, ignoring the cold of the concrete in favor of the warmth of each other's company, and rare treat for the pair. Their hands linked, and after a moment their lips did as well, both of them sinking into a long, wet kiss that seemed to make their frustrations dissipate into the night air. After several minutes they parted, each one with a smile the other would have described as goofy.

Mike let out a happy breath, leaning back on his hands. "Some times, huh?" he said, almost laughing at the absurdity of their lives of late.

"Mmm," she hummed in agreement, leaning down and resting her head against his chest and curling up close, putting all of her weight on him, both literally and figuratively. He kissed her lightly on the head, one of the subtle gestures the couple had come to give one another in their time together to let the other know it was okay to unload. "It's never going to stop, is it?" she asked, although it wasn't a whine or a plea, more like a general statement.

"Doesn't seem that way, does it?" he heaved, wishing he had a better answer for her.

"I guess I kind of always thought that if we got through this thing, and the next... and the thing after that... and then the *other* thing... that someday we'd... I don't know..."

"You thought we'd win," he finished for her, having known the outcome of the sentence immediately after she'd begun it.

"Exactly," she said, swirling her finger in circles against his chest. "I guess I thought things were going to be the way they were. That we'd be happy again."

"You're not happy?" he asked, leaning his head back to see her face.

She grinned. "I am right now, silly," she chimed, kissing him. "I mean in general, though. Just... no drama anymore, you know? Or at least, *regular* drama. Teen stuff, the stuff we should be worried about."

He kissed her head again. "Yeah, I know."

"So, how do you deal with it? I mean, other than Xander, you see more of it than anyone. Maybe more. How do you deal with how much we've had to change just to survive this world?" She sat up now, looking him in the eye.

"Because I believe it will get better," he said honestly, and she could tell in his eyes it was true.

There was a brief silence, and then she shook her head. "How can you say that, when it seems like everything is just getting worse?"

He reached out and touched the side of her face. He pulled her in for a short kiss, then out again, playing with the nape of her neck. "Because of you," he said finally, stroking her cheek with his thumb.

She tilted her head by way of asking for an explanation.

"There was a time, back when all this started, that I thought the same way you did. That I had to get through this thing and the next and the next... not for me," he stressed, emphasizing his points by touching his chest, then hers, "... but for you. I thought I had to make this world a better place for you, and all my energies went toward that. Then, somewhere along the line, when you and I were apart -- that all changed."

"How do you mean?"

"I used to look into your eyes and want to make the world a better place. To save the world so that it would be a place fit for someone like you to live in... now I look into your eyes, and see the world through you... and I don't think the world needs saving anymore. When I'm with you, everything's perfect. So I know it's going to get better... because the world is, for the most part, a good place. You showed me that."

Her lips trembled, and she leaned in and kissed him passionately. "I love you," she said when they paused, their lips still only a centimeter apart, noses rubbing.

"You'd better."

They kissed again.

CHAPTER ELEVEN: DESPERATE MEASURES

The elm tree's leaves turned from the sun.

No matter how much light it gave they would not take it, hiding instead against the threat of the cold. It burned at them and the shivered back, and the elm lost all its protection from the biting wind. The heart of it became cold with each breeze that slunk through the gaps in the leaves, slicing at it until even the truck forgot what warm even felt like.

ʎ‹›ʎ

Mike closed his locker door and let out a deep sigh that ended in a chuckle and a grin, shaking his head back and forth. He gave himself one last moment to enjoy the memory of the kiss Cathy had given him, then picked up his book bag and slung it over his shoulder. He started to walk down the halls toward smoking section.

He opened the doors and the cool winter breeze hit him instantly, sending goosebumps shivering up and down his spine. "Cathy?" he called out, squinting against the sun's reflection on the snow. "Hun, you out here?"

There was no sound at first, then a small giggle. It sounded like something that would come from a small child. He grinned immediately, wondering what kind of game she was playing with him now. Ever since they were kids, she'd never gotten tired of hide-and-go-seek, only lately his prizes for finding her had become much more rewarding.

"What're you doing out - " he started as he turned the corner, the smile stopping as quickly as the sentence did.

Calla McFadden was leaning against the snow-covered brick wall of the school, her jacket wrapped tight around her as she held her thumb and forefinger up close to her mouth, which was drawn up like a bow, sucking the last few puffs out of the joint that she had meticulously rolled, trying to get as much out of it as possible before it got down to the filter she had hastily made out of the cardboard from a pack of Marlboro's. Her eyes were wide at first, the both of them wondering what exactly the other thought they were doing, but not knowing how to ask. When the shock wore off, Calla's thin eyebrows lowered into a scowl as she tossed what was left of her joint into a snow back, exhaling a puff of blue smoke. She gave him what she referred to when amongst her friends as 'the elevator' (looking a person up and down, usually for the purposes of either checking them out or seeing if you could take them. Or both,) then started to walk past him. She stopped when the both of them were shoulder to shoulder and turned toward him so that her lip was dangerously close to his ear. "You're cute for a spaz," she drawled, snickering a little as she, turned the corner and disappeared, leaving Mike to just stand there bewildered.

Calla walked through the snow with her feet long past cold and approaching numb after standing in it for so long. The door opened before she got to it and Cathy came out, shivering once at the sudden change it temperature. Calla once again gave the elevator, smiled in approval of what she saw, then continued through the doors. She turned before they closed, again giving Cathy the elevator from behind, and again smiled.

Cathy rolled her eyes and blushed, then spotted Mike coming out from behind the smoking area, an expression of shock on his face. "What happened?"

237

she asked, almost giggling as she turned to make sure that Calla was gone.

Mike said nothing for a moment, as if formulating his thoughts, his eyes moving back and forth searching for the answer. Finally, they met hers. "I honestly don't know."

She giggled, then reached down and grabbed him gently by his collar (something she could so rarely do, but her elevation on the concrete step allowed for it) and pulled him up into a kiss. It lasted for well over a minute before she let go of his shirt, and a few more moments after that before she touched her hand against his chest and nudged him away. "What've you been doing all day?" she asked cheerfully, sitting down against the steps.

He moved to sit down beside her, sliding one arm around her shoulder without even thinking about it, pulling her to his shoulder. "Not a whole lot," he sighed, "Went to gym, played doubles with Tommy for a bit, then went with him to get Gatorade. Didn't like physics after that."

"You never like physics after gym," she noted.

"I don't like sitting all sweaty. Even after a shower, it's just not comfortable. Anyway, got bored of that fast. Left class to go to the washroom and didn't come back, hung around with the juniors for a while then got another shower just to make myself wake up and feel human a little, then came out here."

"That's why you smell so good," she cooed, snuggling in.

"That's why I'm frigging freezing out here."

She laughed and placed her arm around him, partly in an effort to warm him, partly just because she wanted to. She paused, just enjoying her lover for a long moment, then spoke. "Have you heard any news today?"

He thought a moment, then shook his head. "Julie called Tommy, they talked a few hours. Nothing major, but she mentioned you and Xander barging into her boyfriend's place a few weeks ago."

Cathy blushed, then turned her face into his chest to hide it.

"Any reason you didn't mention that?" he asked, shaking her shoulder playfully, enjoying her embarrassment.

Xander looked at Cathy as their lips parted, almost laughing. She looked back up at him, her hand still rested on the back of his head. She wasn't laughing.

"This probably isn't a constructive course of action," he chuckled, moving off of her. He felt her hand tighten, and stopped.

"Yes it is," she whispered, pulling him back toward her. Their lips met again as she wrapped one leg around him, pulling his entire frame into her.

"No," she said quietly after a moment, then turned to look up at him, raising her voice so that he could hear. "No reason."

"Hmm. Well, she's doing good now anyway, according to Tom. New boyfriend..."

"Met him. Seems like a tool."

"Not him. New one since him, he said she says he's really nice. Seventeen, looking at a full scholarship next year. Even helping her out, apparently she's been getting As on her last few exams."

"Wow," Cathy said, legitimately surprised. "Never would have thought."

"I know. Tom said she's still having problems dealing with... some things, that's why she wants to stay away. But when she thinks she's ready, she's planning to visit us."

"That's good..." she said, trailing off a little. She looked around, still visibly agitated. She shuffled her feet from side to side, then turned back to Mike. "He's not coming today, is he?"

Mike frowned, then shook his head.

August Styles sat on her back porch, hunched over and in tears again. Her mother was in the kitchen, screaming at someone on the phone.

She was talking about her baby.

She took a sip from her glass of juice even as tears started to come down again, and she tried to make sense of everything. She remembered that Cathy girl, and how nice she'd been. She said that she lost a baby once, too... and even though that would be bad, it would still be all right in the end.

She threw her head into her knees, moisture falling from every hole in her face as she fought the urge to throw up.

"August," came a familiar voice.

She looked up, only to see a man standing at the entrance to their back path. He was tall and thin, with shaggy brown hair and thick, black-rimmed glasses. He had an overbite, and his face and shoulders were covered in acne. His expression was grim and determined, and both his fists were clenched so tightly that they were shaking, their knuckles white.

"...Timmy...." August said, her face full of shock, and just a taste of fear.

CHAPTER TWELVE: ESCALATION

Xander knocked twice on Cathy's door, then opened it. He felt safe doing this. He'd been coming over to play since he could remember, to the point that Mr. Kennessy would get mad at him if he "made him get all the way up and come to the door." He wiped his shoes clean of the snowy slush they'd accumulated, then stepped inside and turned the corner into the kitchen. "Cathy?" he called out, noticing the time on the wall and realizing that it would be getting dark soon.

"Here," Cathy said from around the corner in the dining room, curled up into herself sitting on the table, her feet on the chair at its head. She looked somber and worried, a look usually reserved for when something was happening to either him or Mike.

"What's wrong?" he blurted, immediately thinking of Mike's injuries. "Is he okay?"

Mike stepped around the corner, a phone pressed against his ear, raising his index finger to Xander to indicate he'd be done in a minute.

Xander turned back to Cathy, whose expression (although worrisome) was mostly blank. She didn't know what the call was about either, but it was safe to say that it wasn't good. "Sorry to cut it so close. I know we're going to have to go pray soon," he apologized, tapping her knee to try and break the uncomfortableness.

She smiled. "By the looks of him," she sighed, motioning to her boyfriend, "We might have a long evening ahead of us anyway."

He nodded, a million things flashing through his mind at once as he tried to think of what the call might be about.

"Where'd you go?" she asked after a moment, her hair bobbing as she turned to him.

"To get help," he answered simply and vaguely.

She cocked an eyebrow. "How'd it go?"

"In progress," he grumbled, making a scuff mark on the tile floor with his boot, for the purpose of scuffing it back out.

She nodded.

"Okay," Mike said, speaking for the first time since Xander arrived, raising his finger again. "Okay, thanks. That's good man... and Tommy... thanks, dude. You're the best." He hung up the phone curtly, then joined the both of them in the dining room, putting an arm close to Cathy.

"Tommy?" Xander asked, a little confused by the mention of that particular name. "What's that about?"

"Did he have anything on August?" Cathy chimed, hopeful.

"Not exactly," Mike said, his voice low. "August and that boyfriend of hers, Tim... they both ran away from home tonight. Nobody knows where they are."

"Fuck," Xander grunted, rapping a knuckle against the table. "We've got to find them."

Mike nodded.

There was a silence then, as Cathy looked from one of her men to the other. "Pardon me for saying this but... is this such a bad thing?"

Neither of them spoke.

"I mean, we'll definitely find them, but this might give us the chance we need to be able to help her. Find out if he's the father and exactly what went on, maybe even stop her Mom from going through with the abortion thing. This could work out for us... right?"

Still, neither man spoke. They both looked at one another, knowing they were thinking the exact same thing, their faces a mixture of dread and anger that seemed to switch back and forth between both friends.

"What?" she asked, putting both her hands forward, not understanding. She looked from one to the other in question. She thought for a moment, and it was only when Mike looked at her and she saw the fear in his eyes... and even more in Xander's when he looked, that she really understood what they were thinking. "Oh," she said in a hushed voice, bringing a hand to her mouth in shock, her eyes glistening in terror.

Mike grabbed his coat and slung it over his shoulder, nodding quickly to Xander, who headed toward the door. He gave her a quick kiss as they headed for the door in silence, closing it behind them just as Trina came down the stairs from her room.

Cathy's hand was still on her mouth when Trina approached her, only now she was fighting off tears as well.

"What is it?" Trina asked, automatically concerned when she saw her sister and pieced it with the boy's unusual abruptness. "Oh my gawd, what's wrong?"

Cathy looked at her sister, almost in shock. "Derek's going to kill that girl," she said in a hushed voice.

CHAPTER THIRTEEN: WATCHERS

Jennifer Bradley sat on her living room couch, letting the material fold and distort underneath her as she reached down to the floor and pulled up a brown and orange afghan to wrap herself up in. She shoveled a mouthful of popcorn into her mouth while flipping channels aimlessly, not even really wanting to watch anything. Behind her, her mother stepped in from the kitchen and watched the channels that flickered by for a moment. "Jennifer, did you eat your chicken?" she asked as she dried a dish.

"Mm-hmm," the girl responded, never taking her eyes off the screen. "Wuz good."

"Thank you," the older woman responded politely. "Oh wait, stop there honey."

Jennifer flicked back a channel or two, halting at her mother's requested stop.

"... olice force that was already assembled to look for escaped murderer Derek Smith, have now been forced to divide their efforts, also searching for missing local teen August Styles. Styles and her boyfriend Timothy Brassington disappeared from their Coral Beach homes approximately two hours ago, and have not been seen since -"

"Isn't it just awful, Jen?" she said in a hushed voice, putting down the plate and cloth on a nearby table. "I wouldn't know what to do if that had been you."

Jennifer stared at the screen, its warm glow reflecting off her pupils as the images danced before her.

ᚨᚷᚨ

Mike turned down a nearby alley as Xander followed, looking for anything that might give them even the slightest clue of where the pair might be. "You seeing anything?" he called out, checking a nearby sunken entrance to a Chili's.

Xander frowned. "I lost their scent about three blocks back. Been trying to find it again ever since."

"And?"

"Got a couple of quick whiffs, nothing enough to say for sure it was them... and they were too far apart. I think they must have got a cab or a ride or something."

Mike looked down at the shorter man, becoming satisfied, in a frustrated way, that there was nothing here either. The pair began to walk back down 52nd street and would soon move to 53rd (King Street, as it had been renamed last year), having decided to take a grid approach to their search. "Is it possible that they were... taken?"

Xander shot him a look. "If there's one scent I'm sure I'd recognize, it's his. Haven't caught so much as a trace of him since we started, or I would've told you."

"Fair enough," Mike sighed, running both his hands through his hair. "We've checked everywhere I would go. Everywhere you would go... now we're just walking around, man."

"I know," Xander agreed, reaching for his cigarettes and then stopping himself for the third time, not wanting anything to dull his senses. "But we've got to remember, these two wouldn't think like us. I know they're our *age*, but we can't really get into their heads like we could someone else."

Mike clenched a fist, slammed it once against a brick wall, then continuing his walk as if nothing had happened. "Think. What about the motels? That seems like a good option. It's late, they're going to need a place to sleep."

Xander nodded. "Cathy's been calling them ever since we left. She hasn't turned up anything so far, but if we think they got a cab maybe we should call her and tell her to check the ones in Coral Cove, too."

Mike's eyes bulged as he realized how wide their search area was getting. "We suck. We need new brains. I mean, where would they go? What kind of state of -"

Xander raised a palm quickly, stopping his friend in mid-sentence, raising his head as high as he could, then taking a long, circular breath in through his nose.

"Anything?" Mike asked, hopeful.

Xander frowned. "No. Thought I caught her for a second, but it was gone. The window must have been down in the cab or something, she's scattered everywhere."

For a brief moment, Mike thought of what would happen if Derek found them first, bringing a certain literalness to the statement. He forced the thought out of his mind. "You going to be okay?" he asked. "I want to mind these kids, but if you're starting to feel womb-y, we'll take a time out and bring you to the church."

Xander shook his head. "Even if you did, I'm not sleeping tonight."

Mike nodded.

Xander stopped again, raising his nostrils high and stretching them to their utmost.

"You have a boogy," Mike said under his breath.

Xander shot him a look, as his eyes returned to their normal, human-coloring again. He ignored the statement. "They stopped here. There's a big stain of them here, and then nothing all of a sudden. And motor grease. They were definitely in a taxi."

Mike took out his cell phone and slid it open. His large fingers lumbered on the keys as he typed check local cabs and then pressed send. "Why would they stop here?" he asked, doubtful. "There's no spot to rest or get food within two blocks."

Xander looked all around, surveying the buildings around them, finally stopping when his eyes found something across the street. "I think I'm finally getting into their train of thought," he grumbled, and started to cross the street without further explanation.

Mike turned, looking ahead in the direction he was walking, and sighed. It was a quaint little specialty store, called Baby Bash. He grinned despite himself, then jogged to catch up with his friend as they both reached the entrance. "Of course. They're getting ready. They're kids, they probably don't even realize how far off the baby actually is."

Xander nodded, cupping his hands around his eyes to peer in through the glass door.

"It's closed," Mike said, trying the knob despite himself.

Xander lashed out, smashing through the window with one swift strike that sent shards of broken glass flying in all directions. He grinned at Mike as he turned the latch from the inside, ignoring the blood that traveled down his arm and dripped onto the street below. "I have a key."

Mike sighed even as he opened the door. "You're a tool. I have a key... who says that in real life... I have a key."

The pair stepped in, Mike being mindful of the broken glass.

Xander ignored him.

The shop looked like it had once been a video store, the way the shelves were built and aligned, the 'employees only' section in the back having been the 'adults only' section in its previous incarnation. There were blue and pink stuffed teddy bears and rattles and many items featuring Winnie the Pooh all along the left side of the store, with more practical items like diapers, clothing, and cribs along the right. He leaned back his head and sniffed, his eyes growing wide. "They were here."

Mike shot him a surprised look, even as he picked up a pink bear, squeezing it's tummy to make it produce a squeaking noise. "You weren't sure? Next time, how about being sure before all the breaking and entering."

Xander stepped toward the back room, and Mike followed after only a moment's pause. Xander twisted the knob to the room, finding it to be locked as well. He twisted hard to the right. The bolt inside snapped with a loud crack. He opened the door and continued in as if nothing had happened.

"More breaking and entering..." Mike grumbled, although he had become aware that he was talking to himself.

Xander looked all around the small room quickly, finding what he was searching for quickly on the table. It was a small lock box. He produced a single claw from his index finger, slid it inside the lock, and pulled. The metal shattered into pieces on the floor. "Just don't make 'em like they used to," he said, opening the box and ruffling through the paper inside. He pulled out a large wad of bills, each one separated by a different rubber band depending on their value, and tossed it aside, instead picking up a pile of receipts and fumbling through them.

"What are you looking for?" Mike finally had to ask, eyeing the bills and feeling temptation, which he immediately brushed away.

Xander stopped, taking one receipt out of the box and then closing it, with a loud clang. "This," he said, handing him the large line of paper.

Mike scanned over it, finding there were easily a hundred items on the list, ranging from diapers to toys to a crib. It was timestamped just a few hours before, probably as the store was closing. "And what does this tell us?" he asked, putting the paper in his pocket.

Xander started to march out in much the same way he had come in, only this time Mike was right there with him instead of jogging behind, both men fueled by the fact that they were still on the right trail. "Tells us we don't need to widen our search. Before we were looking for two kids on the run. Now we're look for two kids on the run carrying over a hundred baby items. That's going to make their job harder... and ours easier."

"Makes someone else's easier too, may I remind you."

"You don't have to," Xander said, as the two kept walking down the road side by side, turning the corner onto King Street.

CHAPTER FOURTEEN: DETECT

It was like watching a volcano erupt, or a hurricane grow from a gust of wind into a force of nature.

I curled into Mike and covered my eyes, as if not seeing would in some way protect me from what was going on. His cologne rubbed off on me, and it allowed me a seconds release. But only a second, because that was exactly how long I could look away.

Adam Genblade jumped onto the table, shattering the pitcher of water that had been on it into a million tiny jagged shards. I have a very clear memory of this, the glass falling as water began to pour out, glimmering light as it went. The water hit the floor first, then the glass. It broke and splashed at the same time, and for one instant, I couldn't tell the difference between the two of them. The glass had become fluid, the water hard.

Genblade screamed something as this was happening, I have no idea what. It snapped my attention back to reality, back to him. His orange prison jumpsuit clung to his heavy, muscular body with sweat, and I could smell his BO from the back of the courthouse. He looked dirty and menacing, his teeth that were filed down to serrated edges, his gums bleeding even though he had done nothing to them.

I chanced a look at Xander. I didn't think he could see me from where he was, there were too many people there. His eyes were glued on Genblade, and his mouth was an odd shape somewhere between shocked and enraged. His fists were clenched so tight that his knuckles were pale, and small driblets of blood oozed down them. I had never seen him so afraid in all my life, but I have since it once or twice since. He spoke, and even though it was a whisper, I knew exactly what he had said: "Genblade's free."

ʎ⟨ʎ

Cathy sat alone in the smoking section, her hair a mess and her face conspicuously devoid of any sort of make-up. There were bags under her eyes, and if asked to describe herself, she probably would have said 'road-kill,' or something of the like.

She let out a long, tired breath and stared up at the graying sky. *Don't you dare snow on me,* she thought spitefully, willing the weather to cooperate with her today of all days. It seemed that nothing else was going to.

"Is this a private sulk, or can anyone join?"

She turned her head without parting it from the brick it was leaned upon. She was surprised at how comfortable it was. Maybe it was that it reminded her of Xander, but somehow the moldy old wall had grown on her... although not literally, she hoped.

Tommy smiled, both hands thrust into the deep pockets of his jeans.

She turned away, giving no sign to dismay his presence, which he took as encouragement and sat down next to her. "Have you heard from them?" he asked, getting comfortable as he found a dry spot to lean.

"No," she said blankly, shaking her head. "Not since they called and told me to check the cab companies."

"Same here, asked me to call hotels in Coral Cove. Got nothing. You?"

"Nada," she droned, staring at the skyline. "We're losing them, Tom."

"It's only been a day."

"I encourage you to remember that *last* time we said that about a missing child."

"Wasn't always that way, though. Mike and Xander saved that little boy from Malcolm that one time."

Cathy nodded. "You're right. With those two on it, that girl's got a hell of a chance."

"With those two around, we might have a chance, too," he smirked.

"Nice to know we're appreciated," Xander said, even as he came around the corner, a lit cigarette already between his lips and being inhaled.

"Anything?" Cathy asked. She stood up and hugged Xander without even thinking.

"No," he said, giving her a friendly squeeze before they parted. "Mike's

245

getting some coffee, this wasn't his first all nighter. We got a lead, spent the rest of the night chasing it. Didn't come up with much, but we're going again in a minute... we just came to check in."

She nodded, stepping away from him as the nicotine itched at her nose.

Xander turned to Tommy then, as if only now fully realizing his presence. "You two get anywhere?"

Tommy shook his head. "They haven't been in any motels. I even got..." he paused to choose his words carefully, "... our friend in the Cove to make a few calls to places that aren't in the phone book, but she came up with squat."

Xander nodded. "You tried, that's all that matters."

"What did you find?" Cathy asked.

"One place they visited. They bought something, looks like a direct payment bank card or some shit. We're going to try to use it to narrow our playing field."

She nodded.

"You two get to class," Xander said, tossing his cigarette into the snow.

"You can't just do that!" Tommy protested, his arrogance and anger coming through, something that was rarely seen in him anymore.

"We care about August, too," Cathy added, flicking Xander on the forehead as if to make his brain start working.

Xander looked at her, expressionless. He turned to Tommy, then back again. "I know," he said finally, in an obvious tone of voice, as if he did not know where their attack on him was coming from. "You guys are helping. Most of the best intel we have right now came from in there," he said, motioning up at the school. "Someone in there knows where she is -- or at least knows how she got in her current situation -- and I want to know who."

Cathy nodded, followed reluctantly by Tommy.

"Get to class."

She nodded and walked past him around the corner.

Tommy moved to walk past too, but Xander stopped him, placing a hand against his chest.

"Not you," Xander said simply.

Tommy almost laughed, shrugging the hand away and moving to go past. Xander grabbed him by the arm and threw him to the ground, nearly beating his head off the brick wall.

He knelt down to become on equal eye level with Tommy, who was hissing in sharp pain and clutching his arm. "Not you," he repeated, casually, as if the short burst of violence had not even happened.

"What the fuck is the matter with you?" Tommy glared.

"I want to make sure whose side of the game you're playing on," Xander stated, lighting another smoke.

"What?" Tommy yelled, moving to get up only to be held back by Xander again.

Xander shoved him, hard, and Tommy decided not to try to move again. "You been on the fence for months. Some days it seems like you're with us, some days it seems like you're against us... most days doesn't seem like you care. Truth told, I didn't really care either... but it's different now. Derek's loose, and that means new rules. I need to know where you stand... so *I* can decide whether I stand with you, or if you're just another person I'm gonna put in the ground."

Tommy looked up at him, his face somber with just the smallest bit of spite.

Xander raised an eyebrow as smoke curled around his head, awaiting a response.

"I'm with you. I'm with Mike," he said, and Xander finally released his hold and let him rise to his feet.

"Good!" Xander said happily, slapping his back warmly but forcefully. "Because if you're wondering why you're staying here why me and Mike go do the grunt work... it's because I need someone I can trust to protect Cathy, just in case Derek shows up and decides to go Columbine again -- Can we trust you?"

Tommy nodded.

"Good."

⋏⋎⋏

Putrid black liquid sputtered from a hidden nozzle and splashed into the small paper cup as Mike batted two packets of artificial sweetener against the palm on his hand, trying to loosen the contents within. The machine groaned with effort, the slop it spit out looking less like coffee and more like axle grease. He pushed the thought aside and poured the sweetener in, using a small wooden tongue depressor to stir it. He lifted the cup to his mouth and took a long chug, his face curling with disgust when he stopped long enough for the taste to really set in. "Ugh," he grunted in response to the bitter concoction, then took more.

"How you can drink that, I have no idea," came a calm, soothing voice from behind him. He didn't even have to turn around to know that it was Gallagher.

"As I understand it, you have quite a taste for coffee yourself, sir," Mike said, a little less politely than he usually would have. The lack of sleep was beginning to effect his personality.

Gallagher slid five quarters into the snack machine next to Mike, then stepped back a pace to make his selection. "That," he responded, motioning to the cup, "is not coffee. That is what is left over *after* the coffee is made. It is coffee's refuse, my son. What I have in my office, that is coffee." He pressed the button to make a cereal bar plop down, then reached down to pick it up.

"Agreed. Can't be that different, though."

Gallagher stood back up and smiled mischievously. "Not all on its own of course, no. But if one were in a position to, say, bless the water he used in his coffee every morning..."

Mike raised an eyebrow. "You'd do that?"

"I trust my secret is safe with you, my son?"

Mike chuckled, nodding. "It's Mike... sir."

Gallagher looked at him quizzically for a moment, then nodded. "I am sorry, Mike."

Mike frowned, downed the rest of the coffee, then tossed the cup in the trash. "Not nearly as sorry as I am, sir."

Xander entered the cafeteria. He smiled warmly at Gallagher when he got close and fixed his collar. For some reason being around the holy man always made Xander very aware of how presentable he was. "Good morning, Father."

"Good morning, my son."

Xander shot a look at Mike motioned toward Gallagher. Mike shook his head. Xander rolled his eyes.

"Am I... missing something?" Gallagher asked, quaintly amused by their little charade.

"We were wondering if you'd heard anything about the girl," Xander said, causing Mike to turn and slam his head against the coffee machine. "What?"

"Way to be subtle," Mike groaned, rummaging about his pockets as the need for more caffeine came upon him.

"No, I haven't..." Gallagher said after a moment. He took one last bite of his bar then disposed of the wrapper. "... I was wondering if the two of you were looking for her as well. Have you found anything?"

Xander produced the receipt from his pocket and showed it to Gallagher.

Gallagher glanced over it, then looked back at them. "Where did you get this?" he asked.

"Uh..." Mike stammered, as more coffee droned out of the machine.

"Say no more," he interrupted, raising his hand in objection. "I've just decided I'd rather not know."

"Hear no evil?" Xander smirked, amused.

"Exactly," Gallagher grinned. "Although I don't know how much good this will do you."

Xander placed a hand on Gallagher's shoulder, taking back the slip of paper. "Plenty, with your help, father."

Mike shot Xander a look.

⋏⋎⋏

Xander sat down at the computer in the Guidance Office and made himself comfortable. The desk was small and the keyboard was completely covered with file folders. Xander stacked them on the floor next to the desk and frowned. He turned back to Gallagher, who was pouring up three cups of coffee. "You don't even know how to use this, do you?"

Gallagher started to protest, lost his words, then gave up. "Sometimes I think that machine is the antithesis of everything I have dedicated my life too."

Xander smirked, switched on the monitor, and waited for it to warm up. He squinted to see it as it did, seeing a flashing red exclamation point next to the mail icons. "You do know you've got, like, a hundred unread e-mails from Principal Shnieder in here, right?"

"What?" Gallagher gaped. He handed Mike his coffee and set another next to Xander.

Xander picked it up absent-mindedly, took a long sip, then put it back down.

"Yeah. Something about more student files, electronic ones... they don't have physical files yet, taking too long to print. They're for when you're done with the physical ones."

Gallagher turned to the still-growing stack of physical files that populated his desk and huffed. "I hate that man," he said finally, his shoulders slumping.

"This is amazing!" Mike said between sips.

"There's more," Gallagher smiled, motioning back to the full pot with his mug.

Mike's eyes bulged happily, as his knee started to shake from overdose of caffeine.

Xander shot Gallagher a look that the older man recognized as 'cut him off soon.' He'd learned the look well when holding Easter mass. The cardinals would always give it to him in regard to a particular Bishop that always seemed to overestimate how much wine they should bless and have to drink afterward.

"So what are we doing exactly?" Gallagher asked, leaning in over Xander's shoulder to watch.

"Mmm," Mike agreed, not bothering to take his mouth away from his mug to do so. He sat on Gallagher's desk and got comfortable.

Xander twisted, a tightness forming in his chest as Gallagher got into his personal space, but decided to say nothing. "You know all that crap at the bottom of the receipt when you pay for it with a bank card?" he asked rhetorically, tapping the paper twice. "Well, it's not just gobledy-gook, it's actually a code that's specific to that card. If we can trace the card, we can see if it was used anywhere else, and for what, and try to get a good idea of where these kids are hiding out."

Gallagher nodded, impressed. "I didn't know my computer could do that."

Xander made a side-to-side motion with his hand, even as he opened up the Internet browser. "It can't, not really. But I can use programs on the Internet that can."

Mike raised an eyebrow, finally taking his coffee away from his lips. "Um... I'm a little more tech-savvy, and I'm pretty sure there's no web-site called www. Please enter a interac code so you can track it .com."

Xander grinned. "Remember when my computer melted a few months back?"

"Vaguely."

"Well, I lost everything. All the programs I'd spent years creating and working online with people all over the world to create... pft, gone. So, when I finally got my computer back and started to rebuild, I decided to load everything up onto an ftp site periodically so that it wouldn't happen again... which also means I can access those files from anywhere with an Internet connection."

"Ftp?" Gallagher asked absently, watching in amazement as Xander typed something long and incoherent in the address bar, seemingly from memory.

"File Transfer Protocol," Xander explained, eyes now glued to the screen.

"I almost don't want to ask this," Mike sighed, rubbing his temples. "But since when do you own a ftp site?"

Xander grinned. "I don't."

"Then - "

"I'm using someone else's so that it won't be traced back to us. I'm not going to copy the program to this computer, just activate while it's on the ftp. That way, if anyone -- say, the police -- wanted to track who was entering the banking database without permission, they'd just wind up chasing the owner of the ftp site."

"And whom, pray tell, is that?"

Xander smiled devilishly. "It's located within the FBI server that tracks the illegal hacking of bank sites. They wind up chasing their own tails, and they keep looping on themselves forever, until they give up. I did it the second I figured out Tim White's username and password."

Mike laughed and slapped his knee.

Gallagher raised his finger. "I take it that's not... legal."

Xander stopped, looking from Mike to Gallagher silently.

"I understand. I was never here."

"Yeah, that'd be smart," Xander nodded.

"And practice it more," Mike added, patting the man's shoulder. "You'll be needing that little speech a lot around him."

Xander rolled his eyes. "Three times that happened. Will you let it go?"

The icon in the top right hand corner of the screen spun slowly, then eventually a web site that looked like any other folder filled with files came up. One file was marked 'code-breaker,' another 'mac-clone.' He double-clicked on the icon of a cartoon money sign with a smiling set of teeth on it labeled 'money-mate.' A simplistic program popped up on the screen, with vacant spaces one could type in. The spaces were not marked, something that the creator (a friend of Xander's from overseas) had insisted upon so that if it were ever found, there was a plausible denial for what the program was used for, which there wouldn't be if the program had been labeled with fields such as : 'stick in card number.'

Xander typed in the long string of numbers at the bottom of the receipt, his fingers gliding over the number pad easily. He lost his place only once, recounted the digits, then entered the last five and stopped. He clicked exit.

"What the hell?" Mike asked.

Gallagher shot him a look.

"...heck?"

"It's a failsafe the designer implemented to make sure nobody that shouldn't be using the program could. If you click enter it'll lock your computer and download roughly fifty trojan horses from the net. The commands are all reversed. It's pretty keen, actually."

A dollar sign appeared on the screen and rotated clockwise, eventually stopping when a long list of transactions came up. Xander quickly scrolled to the bottom of the list and began to read. Mike took out a pen and jotted down the locations.

"Okay, after Baby Bash they went to a convenience store at 67 main street and got some milk and eggs and stuff like that. Then they spent forty-six dollars and seventy-two cents at The Candy Shoppe," he said, rolling his eyes. "Then they went to a sporting goods store on Plymoth avenue and got... sleeping bags... and then --" he scrolled down some more. His brow furrowed. " -- they went to two movies... and another one this morning. And that's the last entry."

Mike looked up, perplexed. "What, they didn't sleep anywhere last night?"

"I didn't say this was perfect."

"No, no this doesn't make sense at all. Did you check with their relatives?"

"If you think the police and their parents didn't do that you're high."

"Then where are they?"

"I don't know. Where's Derek?"

Mike glowered.

Xander pushed the keyboard away from him. It clacked against the screen's base.

"No, this doesn't even make sense when you get into their mindset."

"Not that we can."

"No, we can. Think about it. How did they get into a movie carrying a hundred baby items, groceries, *and* two sleeping bags? Where would they have put it all? There wasn't enough time between one and the other for them to have dropped it somewhere else."

Xander's eyes sparked. He closed the bank program and clicked in the address bar again, calling up a mapping web site and clicking on a link that read 'plot points.' Immediately a screen asking for an area code and city name popped up, which he typed in quickly, trying to move as fast as his train on thought did. A virtual map of Coral Beach snapped up with a tiny compass in the bottom left and a small graph for the height of land. "Okay, here's where that baby needs store was," he thought aloud, clicking on the location and marking it with a red dot. "Where was the corner store again?"

Mike looked back through his notes. "Sixty-seven Main."

Xander marked it too, and now a line automatically was drawn between the two locations.

Gallagher watched this intently, intrigued.

"Okay, and the Candy Shoppe?"

"Thirty-six Plymoth," Gallagher stated, causing both parties to look at him. "I have a sweet tooth."

Xander shrugged and clicked on the building. Two more lines were drawn, linking all three together to form a triangle. In a blank field at the top of the screen Xander typed the word hotel. Five blue markers flashed on the screen -- none remotely close to the triangle.

"Damn," Mike cursed, resulting in another glance from Gallagher. He shifted uncomfortably.

Xander raised a finger for pause, even as he deleted the word hotel and put in theatre. Three blue dots flashed on the screen, one close to the school, one across town... and one smack dab in the middle of the triangle. He grinned and clicked on the dot. "The C.B. Cinema. First established in 1972," he quoted

251

proudly as he scrolled down the page.

Mike flipped through his notes. "That's the one they went to all three movies at, all right. I think we just narrowed our search field."

Xander shook his head and highlighted a sentence at the bottom of the document. "I think we just ended out search."

Gallagher leaned forward to read what it said, squinting his eyes. "Purchased after bankruptcy -- five years ago -- by Steven S. Brassington. Isn't that Tim's last name?"

"And wouldn't you know it, it was once an apartment complex that got renovated in the seventies -- still some vacant apartments below the theatre. Wonder if any of the members of the Brassington family members have a key and store stuff there?"

Mike got up from the desk, scuttling his notes into the garbage and downing the last sip of his coffee. "Come on," he said sternly. "It might be day, but that won't stop Derek if he finds them first... or any of the other lunatics in this town, for that matter."

"I'm coming too," Gallagher announced, grabbing his coat off the hook in the corner. "Those children are scared, and she knows me... she may need guidance."

"A guidance councilor that gives guidance... that's a first for this school," Xander said as he closed out of his programs. He glanced at the time as he did so, then bit his lower lip. "Fuck. I can't come," he stated, slamming a fist lightly against the table.

"What?" Mike exclaimed, spinning around.

"You go on without me, I've got something important I have to do," he explained, digging into his inside jacket pocket. "You two go, it'll be fine."

Mike nodded, then turned briefly to Gallagher, and both men headed out the door.

Xander stood alone. He looked up at the wall and saw a cross tacked there carefully, the visage of Jesus being crucified upon it. He frowned at it as the womb-organ within him flared, just slightly. "No rest for the righteous," he said to himself, then started toward the door.

A leaf fell from the elm, and then another.

No longer green, they were deep deep red that penetrated the gaze of all those that looked upon them, dry and arid and cold. They felt like paper and fell apart, with no more consistency than air. More fell, until the elm was bare in the gaze of the sun, everything it once was in pieces at its feet.

Megan sat at the bar of the Rusty Nail, again playing with the spear in her martini, although this time it pierced an onion heart, not an olive. Her hair was down and messy from running her fingers through it the entire day while sorting through files and notes. After an entire night of it, she had decided that Tony had been right -- Jillian Mayer did need to be fired. She vowed to do it at the end of the week. She turned to look around the bar as she took another long sip of her drink, scanning the accumulated masses for a certain face and not finding it. She sighed, cursed, then turned her back.

"Hi," Xander said, holding out a five dollar bill to the bartender. He had been sitting right next to her.

"Fuck!" she exclaimed, clutching at her chest. "If you don't stop doing that, I'm going to put a collar with a little bell on you!"

"It's been tried," he smirked. The bartender took the bill. Xander pointed to the Pepsi cooler. "I try to get it off with my hind legs and wind up limping around for days. Have you given any thought to what I asked?"

She gave him a wry look, glanced him up and down, then took another swig. "I have."

"And?" he pressed. He nodded in thanks as he was passed a cola, then took a long drink.

She sighed. "I can't do it. The case starts *tomorrow*, and I usually take weeks to prepare for one. Not only that, but this would be a slam-dunk case for someone right out of law school, and the Styles mother has hired the best. She really spared no expense in this... I hear she had to borrow money. She really wants this. I'm also not fond of doing a case pro-bono when I'm sure that I'm going to *lose*."

Xander nodded, pretending to consider her points. "Then don't think of it as pro-bono. Think of it as paying me back for saving your life and helping you win the case that made your career."

She growled deep within her throat, glaring at him over her glass.

He sank. "I need help, and you're the only one I can come to," he admitted. He shifted in his chair. "You'll have to help me here, I'm not used to asking for help... and I've had to do a nice bit of it these past few days."

She gave him a sympathetic look, then rolled her eyes at what she was about to say, knowing full well she shouldn't. "I could get Nathan to help me out, I guess. He's a great lawyer, and he loves any chance to get good PR."

"Thanks," Xander smiled, pushing back a strand of her hair with one finger and accidentally brushing against her cheek. "I mean it."

She smiled at him. "One day, I'm going to tell the bartender here just how old you are, and he's going to shit a brick then throw you out on your ass."

"I'm pretty sure I could take him," he replied smugly, finishing his drink before standing.

She grabbed his arm. "One last thing," she said. "It looks pretty bad in this sort of case when the defense shows up to court without a *defendant*."

"Already taken care of," Xander said as he headed toward the door.

She watched him go, and couldn't help but shake her head and smile.

CHAPTER FIFTEEN: LOWER LEVELS

Mike hopped down the last three stairs leading to the basement of the C.B. Cinema, landing next to Gallagher. "You sure we've got the right place this time? I'm not too keen on stepping into another rat trap," he sighed, looking at the chipped purple door in front of them.

Gallagher looked at the post-it in his hand, then at the surrounding buildings. "When one has tried every other venue, whatever is left, no matter how improbable, must be the correct option."

Mike gave him a blank stare, then motioned toward the door. "So... this is it, right?"

Gallagher nodded, heaving a low huff. He reached out and tried the knob, twisting it in one direction and then the other. "This one is locked."

Mike cocked one eyebrow and grinned mischievously. "I happen to have a key," he chimed as he raised a foot high and thrust it forward, just as Gallagher got out of the way. The rusted bolt snapped and sent splintered wood flying in all directions.

"First hacking, now breaking and entering... how many crimes must I commit with you today?" Gallagher spat before composing himself.

"Just a few more, I promise," Mike drawled. Stepping inside, he raised his voice, "Okay kids, party's..." he took stock of the situation. It was just one room and a bathroom. Food and baby care items were stacked and crowded all over the place, along with wrappers and cereal boxes. And in the corner, looking quite terrified, was August Styles... her face staring up in fear, with tears streaming -- and Tim Brassington. Tim stood between she and Mike, both his fists clenched. "Over," he finished, his voice considerably humbled.

Gallagher brushed past him, stepping into August's view. "My child... are you all right?" he said calmly, and even Mike was soothed by the tone of it. It had an ethereal quality.

August said nothing, but turned her head just slightly toward him. There was soot on her face. She burst past her boyfriend and into Gallagher's arms, tears wailing down her cheeks as he patted her on the back, trying desperately to calm her. "They - want - ed - to - take - my - baby!"

"I know, sweetheart... I know," he breathed. He flashed Mike a quick thumbs up.

Mike allowed himself a small moment of relaxation, then turned to Tim, who had unwound his fists. "Hey," he said, presenting his chest and trying to look as macho as possible without actually causing any damage to the frail young man.

"Hi?" Tim responded, backing away just a little.

"I need to ask you something," Mike said, wrapping an arm around the boy's shoulder. "You know what sex is, don't you, Tim?"

"Michael!" Gallagher protested, looking up in anger but still holding the girl.

Mike raised a finger for silence, then met the boy's gaze. "Do you?"

Tim nodded, blushing a little from embarrassment and refusing to make eye contact.

"You didn't have sex with August... did you?" he smiled, trying to look as sincere as he could.

Tim shook his head. "No, she doesn't even know!"

Mike smiled, "Good boy," he released the boy, then started to walk away. "Come on, Rev... we better get these kids back to their - "

"I tried to tell her!" Tim spat quickly, the words all jumbling together.

Mike's eyes went wide, and he turned back to the boy. "I'm sorry?"

"I tried to tell her what sex is," he repeated, still almost incoherent, but slower at least. He spoke like a deaf person would, and Mike was having a hard time understanding him completely. "She said it wasn't true -- she said what I said was something else."

"Really?" Mike smiled, stepping back toward the boy. "And what, pray tell, did she call it when you told her about sex?"

Tim looked more nervous the more Mike paid attention to him. "She called it studying."

Mike processed that for a moment, then nodded. "Thank you, Tim."

He walked back to Gallagher, who stared up at him quizzically. "So, that's it then?" he wondered aloud, more to himself than to Mike, "It's over?"

"Not by a long shot," Mike corrected. "Now the hard part begins."

CHAPTER SIXTEEN: FLASHBACKS

The door to Xander's home wriggled on loose hinges as Cathy stepped in. She slid off her shoes and placed them to one side of the porch before stepping onto the dusty-rose colored carpet. The floor was ice cold. A shiver went up and down her spine. She sighed, then decided to leave her jacket on. "Xander?" she called out, tilting her head to look up the stairs toward his bedroom.

There was only silence in return for a long moment, and then she thought she heard a slight shuffle from the upstairs hall. She raised an eyebrow and began to walk up, stopped, then placed one hand on the banister. She turned. Everything was still and tranquil, like a Norman Rockwell painting. But the air was sticky and thick despite the cold, like wading through half-frozen honey. There was smoke upon it, and since Xander didn't smoke in the house, it was fair to assume that his father had been here not too long ago.

That, or somebody else who smoked.

She turned and looked back at the porch, and remembered a day months ago. The house had been cold that day too, even though it had been mid-September. Sticky, too. There had been a coppery taste in her mouth as Derek had thrown her to the floor. She recalled the feeling of Mr. Drew's gun in her hand as she pulled the trigger, sending a bullet straight through Derek's shoulder and out the other side, spattering blood and bits of flesh everywhere. Mrs. Drew had tried for forever to get the stains out, but if you looked at the wall from the right angle and in the right light, you could still see it. Xander once told her that his senses could even still smell it, the scent of Derek Smith's blood... which meant that if he were in the house, Xander might not notice.

Slowly, she inched her way back down the stairs until she was on level floor again. Keeping one eye trained on Xander's bedroom door she turned and went into the kitchen, fighting to urge to run as much as she could. Running made too much noise, and she'd announced her presence enough as it was. Checking around the corner and the blind spot created by the stove, she avoided the entire area where her confrontation with Derek had been to make her way to the cutlery drawer. She pulled it open and shoved aside spoons and works, rustling about frantically for anything that could be used as a weapon. She found nothing, and had to fight not to slam the drawer shut, moving down a foot and opening up the dishwasher. A foot-long butcher knife with a black plastic handle was perched at one side, jutting up at her like a sword in a stone. She picked it up, still stained with bits of ham, and turned back toward the stairs.

She stopped for a moment and observed a note left against to toaster from Xander's mom, telling him she would be at the hospital with his father for most of the evening. She leaned her head back slightly so that her hair fell back and away from her eyes, then crept her way back up the stairs.

Immediately there was another shuffling sound, followed by a skittering and then a plunk.

Sweat began to drip down her face and chest as the floor boards began to creak, and she bit her lip as she willed them to stop. She reached the top of the stairs and looked both ways, examining all of the doors that were closed securely, taking heart that she should be able to hear if someone came out of one behind her. She headed toward Xander's bedroom door, placed her back flat against it, and brought the blade up with one hand while slowly reaching for the knob with the other...

-BA-RIIING!-

The sound leapt out from her hip and even shook it with vibrations, making her jump nearly out of her skin. She dropped the knife to the floor. It landed blade down and sunk a quarter-inch into the wood. She jolted downward to pick it up as she reached for the cell phone at her hip. There was a noticeable scuffle inside Xander's room, and a moan.

"Hello?" she said in a hurried whisper, backing away from the door a pace or two now.

On the other end, there was only silence.

"Hello?!" she repeated, forgetting to quiet her voice.

"... Cath?" came the strained voice from over the line. If voices had been something physical, this one would have been put through a cheese grater before speaking.

"Xander?" she responded, unsure. She flipped the phone closed and stepped back toward the door, opening it quickly.

Xander lay on the floor, his skin an opaque grey as he stared in dismay at the telephone which lay a few feet from his head, now making an annoying beeping sound at him. His clothes were tight against his frame from sweat and the expansion of his musculature. A pool of black liquid had gathered around his head, seemingly coming from his mouth and nose, and a similar large black stain was on the crotch of his pants. His eyes were once again completely black, but lacked their particular shine, no longer resembling oil but now more that of unpolished coal. His lips were cracked and dry, and the rest of his skin didn't seem far from it. He let out a haggard cough, resulting in even more black liquid. His hands did not have claws on them yet, but instead seemed to be permanently disfigured and distorted to look like claws, his fingers twisting out in all directions. One of his legs was bent back near the breaking point, something she had seen before during his transformation, and seemed to imply that he became double-jointed after a transformation, to allow for the more fluid movement of his alter ego.

"Oh my god," she said, dropping the knife again. He looked amazingly like a steroid-infused albino drowning in tar.

"Don't..." Xander gasped, black blood bubbling from his nose. "You'll need that..." he said, desperately motioning toward the knife she dropped.

"Not likely," she tisked, taking a second away from her horror to debunk his suicidal tendencies. "If I won't let you do that on your own, you're even more stupid than I think if you expect me to help."

He sighed, looking defeated.

"How did this even happen? It's not nearly time for the Womb to come out."

He coughed again. "Been getting tired more often, at weird hours," he said as he turned and pushed off the floor slowly, trying to get to his feet. He found it hard, as if he were chained to the floor. "Like it's trying to make up for all those months of hibernation O'Toole put it in. Like maybe those treatments were never intended to be stopped... stopped --"

"Once they started?" Cathy finished, taking pity on the boy. She helped him to his feet and into the seat next to his computer.

He managed to nod his head once.

Cathy got the distinct impression that had his eyes been visible, they would have been bloodshot. "Actually, I did a wikipedia search on some of the ingredients mentioned in O'Toole's files. I don't think any of them were for the mixture itself, just to make it transmittable by touch."

"So he could easily administer it," Xander agreed.

"Exactly," she smiled, getting a tissue from off the desk and using it to wipe some of the black bile off of his chin. "One of those chemicals was lysergic acid."

"The fuck is that?" he said, reaching for a half-empty glass of orange juice on

257

the top of his computer's tower and literally pouring it down his throat, seeming to get more and more of his strength back the more her presence awoke him.

"It's what LSD is synthesized from."

Xander's eyes went wide, locking with hers for the first time since she came in. "Come again?"

"I think you're having drug flashbacks."

"That's beautiful," he responded sarcastically. "It's like the gift that keeps on giving."

"Mmm," she hummed. She cleaned the last bit of ooze and noticed that his skin pigmentation had returned to normal, but that his eyes remained very dark, only now showing even the slightest sliver of white along the edges. She wondered briefly if it was the Womb or the drugs causing it. She reached into his desk drawer and produced a pair of cheesy eighties-style sunglasses and handed them to him. "Think you can make it to the church?" she frowned, raising one eyebrow.

He nodded, took the glasses, and allowing her to help him to his feet.

"I should," he half smiled. "We've got a big day tomorrow."

The gavel slammed down hard, creating an echo heard throughout the entire courtroom, and all present felt its reverberations.

The room was hot and humid, a stark difference to the blistering cold outside, making the windows steam. It hit all that entered and made them feel even more weight than the mere situation itself presented, as if their physical surroundings were mirroring their emotional ones. The courtroom itself was small and seemed much older than the one that had housed Adam Genblade's trial a few months before, though it was in the same building. The walls and seats were not kept with as much care, and as Xander's enhanced eyesight picked up spots where paint had been touched up and his nostrils inhaled dander and cobwebs from under the seats he recognized as being months old, he worried that he and his friends may have been the only ones taking this case seriously.

Megan brushed a strand of hair away from her face as she stood at near-perfect attention, taking the opportunity to spare a glance back at him and remind him that this was not the case.

"You may be seated," Judge Walton said after a long pause. He was an older man and the fluorescent lights gleamed brightly off of his balding head as he leaned forward to straighten his robe and prepare to sit, the loose skin around his cheeks shaking like gelatin. It was clear that at one point he was not as slender as he was now and that his skin had not yet caught up, making it appear loose and saggy. It belied his age, though he looked over sixty, Xander knew him to be not yet forty-five. His father had played bridge with him when he was young.

Xander felt a tap at his arm, and he turned to look at Cathy.

She was grinding her teeth and giving him an annoyed glance, her eyes widening by the second.

He raised an eyebrow to her at first, then realized that he was the last person standing and took his place. "Apologies, your honor."

"None needed, Mr. Drew," Walton replied in a nondescript fashion, barely even giving the boy a glance as his eyes strained through his bifocals to see the small print of the file in front of him.

The smile Xander had pasted on for the Judge faded as he scanned the room. There were very few people present, on either side of the seating area. Cathy and Mike were there. Tommy had wanted to come as well, but Xander had given him a look and he somehow had known not to show up. Tim Brassington was there with his parents -- probably as witnesses for either side -- as well as a man Xander recognized from his stay at the hospital as a doctor, and a sniveling little man he was sure was one of Tony's psychologists. Principal Shnieder and Mr. Miles and Mr. Calender were there as well, showing their support for the school, though for which side, Xander did not know.

"Why am I here again?" Mike whispered softly, leaning over Cathy to Xander. Their seats were directly behind the defendants booths, where Megan, Nathan and August sat.

Xander frowned, keeping his eyes on the Judge's reactions as he went though the papers, trying to discern from his facial expressions which part of the report he was at. "You're here in case we start to go under. Megan will call you up to testify that when you found August and Tim, they seemed fit and prepared for a child."

"Oh, I see," Mike nodded. "You want me to *lie*."

Xander shot him a look.

Cathy frowned and pushed the boys away from each other and back into their upright positions. "I think he's about to start," she hushed.

Judge Walton looked up from his papers, first at Tony and Martha Styles and then over to August, Megan and Nathan. "Interested parties may rise," he said dryly.

Tony was wearing a dark blue pinstripe suit with a red tie that he seemed to be constantly adjusting. His hair had been sliced back and his face perfectly shaven. He looked almost exactly as he did the day of the Genblade trial, save that he seemed taller, now, somehow.

Martha Styles was about forty-five herself, the same age as the Judge. Her hair wasn't quite yet silver, brunette traces still throughout, giving her a distinguished look. She had a round shape to her body and wore an afghan shall over the shoulders of a business suit that Xander was sure Tony had picked out for her, as it seemed nearly identical to Megan's although in opposing colors. Her face was covered over well in make-up, but it was uneven, and looked like it had to have been touched up repeatedly.

Megan and Nathan wore matching dark grey suits, the only difference being that Megan's shortened into a long skirt, allowing her the range of motion she sometimes needed. Her hair, much like Tony's, looked to have been professionally done no more than a few hours before, and she had made every effort to make herself attractive while still being professional to a point.

Nathan looked smoother than the last time Xander had seen him.

Xander realized that he was wearing make-up as well, to cover up a few facial scars no doubt gotten during childhood accidents. He chuckled.

The only one out of place was August. She was wearing a plain white t-shirt and black jeans with a clip instead of a button, which had probably been the best Megan alone could convince her into. It would not have been so bad had the shirt not gotten stained somewhere along the way. She had not stood at Judge Walton's request, and while he had said nothing toward it, it clearly bothered him.

We're off to a great start, Xander thought, rubbing the bridge of his nose. All at once the Womb flared up and he had to fight the urge to buckle over in pain.

Cathy immediately brought a tender hand to his arm. "Are you all right?" she asked, her voice deep with concern.

Xander nodded. "It's just more of the... the..."

"Lysergic acid?" she finished for him, careful not to be in ear shot of anyone who might have recognized the word.

Xander nodded, though he was beginning to perspire. "It'll pass."

"I would like to begin by stating," Judge Walton began, pausing briefly to clear his throat. "That it is a sad day whenever a matter such as this has to be settled in a courtroom. However, under the circumstances, it has been deemed necessary. With that in mind, I would like to hear the opening arguments, start-ing with Mr. Jones."

Everyone but Tony sat. "Thank you, your honor," he said politely, allow-ing himself a nod that was almost a bow before stepping around his desk. He poured a drink of water, but did not take a sip. Megan rolled her eyes at this, doing her best to hide the impulse from Judge Walton. He shot her a sideways glance, then moved toward the center of the courtroom.

"Your honor," Tony began slowly, clasping his hands together and scuffling his feet, like a car revving its engine before really taking off. "I've been a part of a number of child custody hearings in my day, as I'm sure you have," he paused, waiting for the judge to nod, which he did. "And I'm sure you'll agree with me when I say that they are almost always a gut-wrenching procedure. Fathers and mothers combating over their children, children having to decide between par-ents... or worst yet, cases in which neither parent is capable for properly caring for the child. Situations like these are *crimes* against the children of the world your honor, just like any other crime."

Megan once again turned and looked at Nathan, and then Xander.

Xander frowned, realizing that she recognized where he was going with this, and that it was no place good.

"Last month I was the prosecutor in the rape case upstate, and all I could think was : no matter what I do for this girl, it won't make her un-raped. The same with a murder: you can jail the murderer, but we cannot give that person their life back. We cannot give the mothers their children back, and we cannot give their children their father back. It's a justice system I whole heartedly be-lieve in," he said, actually placing a hand upon his heart to illustrate. "But have no issue saying there are flaws in."

"Objection!" Megan barked, standing up so fast it made the blood rush to her head. "He's comparing having a child to a crime, your honor, it's not - "

"It's a hearing, not a trial, Miss. Greene," Judge Walton interrupted. "There is no jury present. Your objection is noted but unnecessary."

"Thank you, your Honor," Tony said, again doing his mock-bow. "The point is this: a child growing up in an unsafe or unsuitable environment is a crime, just as much as rape or murder is. We have laws to protect these children, but so often they are only enforceable *after* the damage is done. We can only take a child away from abusive parents *after* they have been abused.

"Today, your Honor, we have a once-in-a-lifetime opportunity: we can stop a crime before it happens. There is no way that August Styles can properly care for the child that she's carrying. Her mother is not fit to care for the child that she's carrying, by her own admission. Rather than put this young, innocent life through custody battles, foster homes, abuse and neglect... we can stop the cycle right now. We can end this with one punch. August will survive the terrible ordeal of losing her child. She will heal. She will move on. Her child will not," he paused, turned from Walton to give one last look across the room, finally resting on Nathan. "That is all, your Honor."

"Thank you, Mr. Jones," Judge Walton said. He made one last scribble on the folder in front of him, then turned his attention to Megan. "You have the floor, Miss. Greene."

Megan got up, smoothed the lines of her suit briefly, then smiled at the Judge.

Behind the defense station, the womb-organ flared up again, only to die back down.

Martha Styles whispered something unidentifiable to Tony, who nodded.

"Your Honor, in the past thirty years we as a people have made wonderful strides in how we treat others, specifically the less fortunate. There was a time, not all that long ago, when if a white man got a black woman pregnant, not only could he force her to have an abortion... but he could initiate it himself with his fists.

"Gladly, we no longer operate like that. One of the great foundations of this country is the people's right to choose their own destiny. We have foundations and laws set up now to protect minorities against such treatment... laws which are being ignored here today. Blatantly. If this were any other fifteen year old girl at that school, this would not have even been a question. It is the fact that she had Down syndrome that she is here, and it goes against so many of our society's fundamental beliefs that it is unbelievable.

"Mr. Jones talks about preventing the crime before it happens," she tilted her head to one side, "A promising argument. The problem with it is that you don't know when somebody is going to kill. You don't know when somebody is going to rape. And we do not know that August Styles will be a bad mother. She may have a lot to learn -- every new mother does -- but the point is that her presence here today proves that she is equipped with the only tool a good mother

261

really needs: unflappable love for her newborn child.

"It's true that August was coerced into sexual intercourse. It's true she was convinced to run away from home, though it had crossed her mind anyway. But the fact that she maintains her position on keeping her child even though these same people want to take it from her just strengthens my resolve. She will make a good mother, if we let her." She turned to the Judge. "Someone had to give your mother a chance at some point, right?"

She turned back toward the court, walked to her place, and took a seat. This time she did not even look at Tony.

Cathy smiled, nodding to herself.

"Impressive arguments, both. I'll see first witnesses, starting with yours, Mr. Jones."

Again, Tony stood. "Your honor, I call Mr. Mike Harris."

Mike's eyes went wide and he shot a look at Xander. "Wasn't I subpoenaed for August's side?"

Xander frowned. "He knows you're our trump card. He's taking that away from us."

As Mike rose to his feet, Megan rubbed her eyelids with her thumb and forefinger.

"What does this mean?" Cathy whispered softly.

"Means we need a new trump card," Xander spat.

Mike took the witness seat next to the Judge and felt small for the first time in years, leaning the microphone in close. He glared at Tony as the lawyer approached the stand, smiling wide at the boy.

"Please state your name, for the record," he said politely, fixing his gelled hair.

Mike shuffled uncomfortably. "Don't I have to put my hand on a Bible or something?"

Tony smiled. "Only if a Jury's present. This is just a hearing. It's a common mistake, though," he grinned, and somehow Mike got the impression that it was a shot at Megan for her objection earlier. "Now then, name, please?"

"Michael R. Harris," he responded, speaking as clearly as he could into the microphone. His nervousness seemed to fade the closer Tony got to him, replaced instead with anger.

"Mr. Harris, can you recount for me the events that happened yesterday evening?"

Mike smiled. "I would, but I don't think Cathy would appreciate it. Some things are left private."

"Order," Judge Walton said calmly, hiding his grin.

"Regarding Miss. Styles," Tony corrected.

"Oh. Gallagher and I went looking for her when we heard that she'd run away from home. We found her in one of the basement apartments of a movie theatre owned by a relative of Tim's. We found them and brought them home."

"Why were you looking for them?"

Mike did not notice Xander's repeated attempts to gain his attention, or he might have known not to drop his guard. "I've been helping the police out looking for Derek Smith, and I was worried that the two of them might be easy targets for him."

"How good of you. What kind of state did you find Miss. Styles in?"

"She was crying and scared -- but that was just because I kicked the door in. I actually feel kind of bad, but I wasn't sure if they were there and every other door had been locked, so we kind of had too."

"And what was she doing there?"

"Getting ready for the baby. They had some things bought, it actually didn't look half bad. I've seen worse."

"You found her to be preparing the way any fit mother would?"

"Yes."

"But by your own admission, even with a killer on the loose, she made no attempt to stop you from entering and potentially harming her and her child, had she had one, if you had been him? She ran away, spent all her money, was living below a theatre and could not protect her child against you?"

Mike's face went white. He finally looked at Xander, whose face was buried in his hands.

"No further questions, your Honor," Tony smiled, sitting back down.

"Cross?" Judge Walton asked, turning his attention.

Megan glanced down at her questions. They had been almost exactly the same, except without the negative spin. "No questions, your Honor," she said, sliding the sheet into her folder.

"You may step down, Mr. Harris."

Mike hung his head, walking back down to his seat.

"If you still got that knife, you could just take the kid out yourself," Xander said as his friend shuffled by. "It'd save time."

"Shut up," Mike said, his voice defeated as Cathy rubbed his leg.

"Your next witness?" Walton asked Tony, raising his eyebrows.

Tony smiled. "We call Dr. Robert Gagnon, the state's leading psychologist in individuals with developmental disabilities--"

The sniveling man that had been seated near the middle of the court got up and started walking toward the bench.

Xander slammed his head against the Coke machine in the lobby, not even noticing the change that shook loose when he did so.

"Well, what would you have answered?" Mike asked, thrusting his arms in the air as he paced back and forth.

"Oh, I don't know. Anything besides: they let me walk right in after I burst in the place because they could have been killed by the worst murderer this town has ever seen!"

"*Second* worst," Mike said, motioning in his direction.

"Not gonna work today," he growled in response. The Womb had finally quieted down now that he was outside the courtroom, and he was beginning to wonder if it had just been nerves. "For future reference, when up against a lawyer, anything they don't specifically ask you for: just leave it out. Lying by omission isn't lying in there. It's their job to get it out, but that doesn't mean you have to hand it right - "

"I get it!" Mike barked, slamming a palm against the Coke machine. His hand landed in a sizable dent in its frame, and he suspected that today was not the first day that it had suffered such abuse.

"That'll be enough," Megan snapped, walking toward the both of them with Cathy. "We've only got a half hour recess, and I do not want to spend it with you two testosterone kings at each other's throats."

There was silence between them then.

"He started it," Mike said after a moment, thrusting a thumb in Xander's direction.

"Hey, Tony, the people I'm defending are unfit parents!" Xander exclaimed. "And I have unpaid parking tickets, too! And while I'm at it, if you'll kindly look in my basement, you'll find the body of a - "

"This never goes anywhere between you two!" Cathy yelled at the both of them.

"That's because you always interrupt it," Xander stated matter-of-fact-ly.

"We need a new witness," Megan cursed, sitting down. "Not tomorrow, not the next day, *now*. He's burying us in there. That psychologist was trained in every negative statistic ever. He even cited a case in Canada like this where the mother ended up killing the baby, for the love of Christ!"

Mike sighed, silent. After a moment, he spoke. "Are we sure we're on the right side, guys?"

Cathy glared at him, and it was clear to all that that discussion was over.

"Never mind. It's just, the story Megan was talking about. I never thought of it that way before."

Megan started to chuckle. "That's rich. He's convincing the people that convinced me! That's beautiful. Beautiful. We're done. We need a witness. Now." She looked up at Xander. "What about Gallagher?"

Xander shook his head. "Good guy, but picture the complications with Mike times *ten*."

Mike just turned away.

"Great. Guys! Come on! We need something!"

"We need a father," Xander said finally, drawing gazes from all those around. He turned to Cathy with that driven look in his eyes that made you do whatever he said. "Go back to school. You said there were eight other girls besides you and August that got pregnant this year. I want to know who the fathers were. I want to know the circumstances: was it consensual? I want to know the position, for God's sake -- got it?"

"Got it," Cathy nodded, even as she turned toward the exit.

"Get Tommy's help if you need it!" he called out to her, then turned to Megan. "We call the witnesses now, right?"

"Yeah, but all we really had was Mike. We've got a few professionals. The mother won't say anything in our favor, and I'll be damned if I'm putting August on the stand."

"Call anyone. Call the people present from the school. Call me, for all I care. Just buy us enough time for Cathy to find out something."

"What makes you sure she will?" Mike asked, raising an eyebrow.

"I'm not," Xander replied. "But it's almost all we have at the moment."

"Almost?" Megan asked, hopeful.

Xander shook his head. "I don't want to say yet. Not until I talk to Gallagher first."

"I thought you said he wouldn't be any help?"

"He won't. I just want him here for our new trump card."

Megan smiled. "Which is?"

"If I tell you, you won't do it," he grinned, heading toward the payphones as she and Mike headed back into the courtroom.

"He's frustrating, isn't he?" Megan huffed at Mike without facing him.

"You have no idea."

⋏⟨⋌

The elm stood shivering, naked a frightened in the cold. The remains of her clothes lay at its feet, dead comrades who would never visit again. Her skin was gray and ashen and bitter, her once warm embrace reduced to a bitter boney grasp.

⋏⟨⋌

"Hey, Trace!" Cathy smiled, jogging up beside Tracy Outmore, still out of breath when she reached the school house.

Tracy was a good year older than Cathy. She'd gotten pregnant around the same time, and they'd talked about it in the washrooms once or twice together, even before Cathy had told Mike or anyone else for that matter. She was tall and pretty with light blonde hair, and she'd always treated Cathy like a little sister.

She was as good a place to start as any.

"Hey, Catty," Tracy replied, finished her Coke and throwing it into a nearby garbage as she sat at the picnic table in the school yard, adjusting her stomach, which was just beginning to really show, so that it went under the table. "You look spent."

"Yeah," Cathy agreed. She sat down and wiped a long trail of sweat off her brow, which had formed despite the chill on the air.

"Thought you were going to be over at the courthouse all afternoon?" she smiled, big and bright.

Cathy looked away. "Yeah, um... I don't know. After all the drama I went through, couldn't much take it."

"Totally," Tracy nodded, rubbing her stomach.

Cathy watched her hand move, a twinge of envy coming over her for a moment, and she had to remind herself that what she had just said had been supposed to be a lie. "Yeah... Mike's been so closed off ever since it happened."

"Aww," she whined, but not mockingly, poking out her bottom lip. "I

265

thought you two lovebirds made up?"

In the distance, Tommy spotted Cathy, raised one of his triangular eyebrows, and started to walk over.

Cathy sighed. "We just decided not to talk about it. But I thought after a while he'd be okay to talk about it, and now, I don't know..."

Tommy stopped, his eyes wide with shock.

"Well, you can talk to me, sweetie," Tracy smiled, laying a hand gently over hers.

"I don't know... Mike says it's just between us... that we should forget..." she felt horrible. She explain to Mike later, if he ever found out.

"I won't tell a soul. Come on, it'll feel better," she smiled again, warm and inviting.

"Well -- maybe if you did first. Is your guy acting the same way?"

All at once Tracy's smile faded. "Yeah. Guys are pigs. Listen, Catty, I've gotta get to class," she said, getting up and pasting on a smile that was obviously fake. "But we'll talk later, okay?" She gave a mini-wave with her index finger, then turning to walk away.

Well, that was suspicious, Cathy growled internally, watching the girl walk away toward the school, then stop and sit at another table, behind a tree.

"What the fuck was that?" Tommy asked, walking up behind Cathy and finally making his presence known.

Cathy turned and glared at him.

"Are you bipolar? Why are you saying all that crap about - "

"I'll explain on the way, you little monkey," she hushed, grabbing him by the arm and dragging him in the direction of the school.

"Objection, your Honor!" Tony drawled, thrusting an arm in the direction of Tim Brassington. "Mr. Summers is leading the witness."

Nathan turned to Judge Walton. "Your Honor, the witness's own mother was just up here. She said it to us all. He's very nervous. I'm simply trying to put the questions in a yes-or-no fashion, so that the defendant can answer them."

"Sustained," the Judge said begrudgingly. "If your witness cannot answer your questions than you should not have placed him on the stand, but I will not tolerate you using this boy as a puppet to say whatever you want."

Xander leaned in to Mike. "It looks bad when the Judge insults you, right?" He grunted a little as the Womb surged again.

Mike nodded.

"See that?" Xander continued, pointing to Brassington. "Still a better witness than you."

Mike said nothing, but his nostrils looked ready to shoot twin bursts of flame.

"Mr. Brassington," Nathan started again, running his fingers through his silvery hair. "Did you go to August's house to get her the night you ran away?"

"Yes," Tim said, smiling wide, in his tone-deaf voice.

266

"Good. Did you plan this with her before?"

"No."

"Did you force her to go?"

"No."

"What was she doing when you came to her house?"

"Crying."

"Where?"

"On her back step."

Nathan smiled, leaning against the bench in a relaxed manner, trying to put the boy at ease. "Thank you. Why was she crying, Tim?"

"She didn't want to lose her baby."

"And is that why you told her to come with you?"

"Yes. So she wouldn't be sad anymore."

"Thank you, Tim," he turned to the court. "You see your Honor, everything this pair did, they did out of love for each other and for August's child. I only wish every couple were as well balanced and supportive."

"I thought this was a court of the United States, not Care-A-Lot," Tony grumbled from behind him.

"Hmm?"

"Nothing. Continue, with this... whatever," Tony smiled. "I'm enjoying it. It's like Ally McBeal in 3D."

"Councilor," Walton said flatly.

"Withdrawn," Tony said cheerfully.

"Would you like to cross examine, Mr. Jones?"

Tony almost snickered. "Oh, hell – I mean, not at this time, your Honor. We're good."

Megan's cheeks turned red as she fought the urge to throw he briefcase at Tony. She rose from her chair. "The defense next calls Principal Andrew Shnieder."

In the back row, Principal Shnieder sat up straight for the first time since the hearing began. "Me?" he asked, pointing toward himself.

"Yes, sir," Megan smiled.

Reluctantly Shnieder made his way up the hall, tossing cold stares at Greene all the way.

ᚹᚹ

Gloria Brover was a short, round girl with black hair that had been dyed into two red streaks going down either side of her face. She was a pretty girl, by no means a knockout, but Cathy had always thought it'd do a lot for her self image if she presented herself a little better. Maybe she'd get more dates.

Then six months ago, she'd gotten pregnant.

Cathy sighed as she walked up to Gloria, who was taking a Chemistry book out of her locker. She forced herself the smile and walked up to the girl. "Hey Gloria!"

Gloria glanced in her direction, then back again.

"Gloria, it's me: Cathy!" she smiled again, pushing her hair back.

"Do we know each other?"

"Yeah, you and Mike went out once or twice before we got together."

"Right," Gloria said, smiling now. "How is Mike?"

Cathy's eyes narrowed. "We're fine, thanks. How about you? How are you and Todd doing?"

Gloria frowned. "He left me last month."

Cathy frowned. "Oh, I hadn't heard. Sorry. What a herb though -- leaving you when you're carrying his kid?"

"Yeah, I've got go..." she said, quickly turning and walking away.

Cathy watched her leave, rubbing the bridge of her nose in dismay. *Strike two.*

⋏⋏

"Hey Steph... Dylan," Tommy smiled, lounging up to the both of them as they sat next to the vending machines in the cafeteria.

"Hey, man," Dylan smiled, tapping Tommy once in the arm. "How's it hanging?"

"Pretty good, pretty good..." he rambled, running one hand through his spiked hair around to the back of his head. He scratched idly, clicking his tongue against the roof of his mouth. "Uh... wow, Stephanie..." he started, pretending to just now take notice of her bump. "You're getting huge!"

"Twenty-four weeks," she beamed, even as she and Dylan snuggled into each other.

"Wow," Tommy said, feigning an impressed expression as he tried to mentally calculate how many months that was and failed. "So -- whose is it?"

CHAPTER SEVENTEEN: STUDY HABITS

"Mr. Shnieder," Megan started, holding the last syllable as long as she could. She stole a glance back at Xander as she did. He nodded once, then looked from his watch and then at the door. "You've... started a social aid project at the school to help people in August's position, haven't you?"

Shnieder nodded politely. "It wasn't just me. We had the backing of the entire faculty and the school board, but I helped start it, yes."

"I see," Megan smiled, taking another long pause. "Can you please tell me the reason that you did this?"

Shnieder shifted uncomfortably.

"Is something wrong?" she asked, raising an eyebrow.

He leaned forward, past the microphone in his booth a little. "Why do you keep making those pauses?"

In the back, Tony snickered.

Megan sighed. "No reason, sir. No need to be nervous, just answer the question."

"Ah," he smiled, instantly relaxed. "I did it to help -- well, to help poor girls like August," he said, motioning to the girl, who was playing with something in her chair and avoiding eye contact with everyone in the room. He frowned, then turned away from her and back to Megan, lacing his fingers together before him. "The rest of the faculty and I have noticed an alarming teen pregnancy rate in the last few years. We try our best to educate against it, but it seems the media keeps educating *toward* it. So we set up the foundation to help teens in Coral Beach that we couldn't get through to in time."

"Very good of you. In that respect, would the foundation be providing August Styles with the funds she needs to care for herself and her child?"

"Of course."

"That is in addition to the benefits that she already receives from the state as a result of her disabilities, correct?"

"Yes."

"No further questions, your Honor."

In the audience, Xander bugged his eyes at her for ending it, to which she shrugged.

"Cross?" Walton called out, almost to nobody by now.

"Sure, I'll take this one," Tony said smugly, getting up and walking around the desk.

ʎ⟨ʎ

Nadine Kissinger walked away from Cathy angrily, stomping her heels as she went. Cathy hung her head and began trying to tabulate the amount of work she'd have to put in to repair her social life. She briefly considered that Xander had known that this would happen.

"What the hell was that all about?" asked Wanda Starsmoore, coming up behind Cathy.

"Nothing," Cathy frowned, turning to smile at the younger girl, when she noticed the open pregnancy test sticking out of her purse. "Actually, maybe you can help me..."

ʎ⟨ʎ

"Hey, Kendra," Tommy said dryly and he walked up to the tall redhead at her locker, rubbing his already swollen right eye. "How's it going?"

She smirked at him. "Better than you. What the hell happened? Did you piss Mike off again?"

"You don't want to know," he said honestly. "Can you help me with something?"

"Sure!" she said cheerfully, closing her locker and turning to smile at him. "What can I help you with?"

"Well, your boyfriend Scott told me you were pregnant..."

Her smile slowly faded. "And?"

"And he asked *me* to ask *you* if you if there was anyone else who could be

269

the father."

The girl's eyes went wide, and she drew back her hand.

"Principal Shnieder," Tony smiled, addressing the educator formally. "Does August's mother receive compensation from the government because of her child's disabilities?"

Shnieder looked bewildered, then shrugged. "I would assume so, yes."

"And she works as well, yes?"

"I believe."

"So while they are by no means well off, she has the means to care for her child. There have never been any sort of investigations as to whether or not August is in good hands."

"No -- she's a good mother."

"But even a capable mother, in full control over herself like my client, can't watch their child constantly, is that correct? Otherwise this wouldn't have happened?"

Shnieder sighed. "Yes, I suppose that's true."

"So it's fair to assume that, although she would have the funds to support her child financially, August would have an even harder time, especially with an infant... correct?"

"In my opinion... I suppose I would have to say yes, reluctantly."

Tony smiled. "No further questions, your Honor."

Judge Walton smiled. "You may step down, Principal Shnieder. I'll see you and your wife at poker next Thursday?"

Shnieder nodded.

Walton's smile faded as he turned back to Megan, his cheeks shaking as he moved. "Do I dare ask if you have another witness, Miss. Greene?"

Megan turned back to Xander, who again looked back at the door and around the room, then shrugged. She sighed, rising to her feet. "The defense calls Mr. Alexander Drew."

A murmur fell over the courtroom, even as Xander got up and Mike lowered his head to between his knees, unsure if this was amusing or terrifying.

The true womb surged as Xander walked past August and up toward the stand.

"Hi, Skyla," Cathy sighed, sitting down next to her.

Skyla raised an eyebrow, then rolled her eyes.

"What?"

"Don't even bother," she said, adjusting her sweater to better cover her bulging mid-section.

"I'm not sure I understand?" she asked, shocked.

"Nadine Kissinger told me you were going through some sort of Postpartum thing, asking all the pregnant girls about it and all that, well you can forget it," she said, turning away. Cathy just stared for a moment, until Skyla turned back to her. "You can go now."

ʎ〉ʎ

"State our name, for the record," Megan asked.

"Adam Evensong," Xander said, his smile spread from ear to ear.

Megan huffed. "Xander, state your *real* name, for the record."

"Project # 08276."

"That's enough, Mr. Drew," Walton barked. "And this nonsense is not helping your case."

"As my Dad used to say, your Honor, you can't kill a dead horse."

Somewhere in the back, Mike snorted.

"Alexander Drew, state your name!" Walton bellowed.

"You just said it, what's the point?"

"Just do it, sir."

"I object!" Xander yelled, slapping the bench and leaping into the air.

Judge Walton took a long sip of his water... then another. He looked at it evilly, as if he wished it to be something stronger. "Mr. Drew, stop this right now."

Xander glanced at his watch, then held it up to show the Judge. "Honestly, sir, just a little bit longer."

In the back, Gallagher entered and took a seat next to Principal Shnieder. He waved at Xander.

"No further questions, your Honor," Xander said, turning a smiling at the Judge.

"I believe that to be Miss. Greene's line, young man," Walton reminded him.

"Right. Megan?" he said, turning to her expectantly.

Megan stared at him emotionlessly for a full twenty seconds, her face growing as red as an apple. "No... further questions, your Honor."

"Cross?"

Tony snickered, then held up his water and toasted Xander with it. "Aw, hell no."

"Excuse me?"

Tony coughed, composed himself, then stood up straight. "The prosecution rests, your Honor."

"Get the hell down," Walton cursed. Xander happily hopped over the bench, crossed the room in two large bounds, then sat down next to Mike.

"Have fun with that?" Mike whispered to him, tears of laughter in his eyes.

Xander leaned in. "More scary than when I fought Zakron. Plus I took your place as worst witness."

Mike smirked and patted his shoulder.

"Defense," Walton plead, holding out his withered old hands to Megan. "Please tell me that was your last witness?"

Megan smiled. "Just one more, your Honor. The defense calls August

271

Styles."

August's eyes went wide as Nathan tried to coax her out of her chair and to the stand.

"Jennifer," Cathy huffed, her arms crossed as she stood firm behind the girl.

Jennifer's blonde hair was short and she was wearing a tank top that exposed her belly. Heels made her look much taller than she actually was.

"Cathy?" Jennifer asked, raising an eyebrow as she clicked her mirror shut.

"Listen, I really need your help. I'm through playing around, now. August's in trouble. I lost my baby once, and she's terrified that she's going to lose hers now."

"I don't know what you're..."

"I wasn't finished," Cathy snapped, reaching out and grabbed the girl's arm and digging her nails in before she could get up. "Think of what would happen if you lost your baby. Think of how much it would devastate you."

Jennifer's eyes turned downward, and she seemed to open up to what Cathy was saying.

"Now -- think of my boyfriend reputation in this school, and realize that that is what is going to happen to you if you don't tell me exactly what the fuck is going on here," she spat.

"I don't have to listen to this," Jennifer stammered, making a bee-line for the exit.

Tommy stepped in front of her, his arms crossed. Even with her heels, he had considerable height on her. "I really think you do," he said calmly.

Cathy came up behind her again, Jennifer now sandwiched between the both of them. "Tell me... every... last... detail."

"My son," Gallagher whispered. He had moved up and sat down next to Xander and Mike as covertly as he could as Nathan helped August to the stand finally. "Why was it so urgent that I come here so quickly, if you do not intend for me to speak?"

Xander leaned in. "You're a counselor. I think August's going to need that after this."

"What makes you so sure?"

Xander frowned. "I'm counting on it, father."

Gallagher and Mike exchanged confused looks, then turned toward the front to watch.

"State your name, for the record," Megan said, walking up to August.

August said nothing and lowered her shoulders. She averted her eyes from everyone and tried to pretend she wasn't there.

Megan huffed and turned back to Xander.

Xander lowered his brow and shook his head at her.

She paused, then smiled and turned back to August. "That's all kinda silly, huh?"

272

August's eyebrows rose and she turned to Megan, then looked at everyone else in the room, all looking back at her, and began to curl back again.

"Them?" Megan asked, motioning to the people, and then to the Judge. "Just pretend they're not here. It's just you and me, sweetie. My name is Megan Greene," she beamed, extending a hand to the girl. "What's yours?"

August took Megan's hand, shook it briefly, and then let go. "August Styles."

Xander smiled, nodding.

"Nice to make your acquaintance, August," Megan said, taking a pace back from the child. "Are you going to have a baby, August?"

August nodded.

"I need you to answer, sweetie."

"Yes. I'm gonna name her June."

"What if it's a boy?"

August paused. "Then I'll name *him* June."

Megan chuckled, along with several other members of the court, including August's mother. "How silly of me. Are you going to love your baby, August?"

August nodded, then remembered, and spoke. "Yes. Just like my Mom loves me."

"And are you going to take care of June, August?"

"Yes."

"Forever and ever?"

"Forever and ever and ever."

Megan smiled. "Good. I'm sure she'll love you very much." Megan turned to the Xander, and then the Judge. "No further questions your Honor."

Gallagher furrowed his brow, motioning toward the stand. "That was it?"

"Give it time, father," Xander smirked, assuring him with a touch on the shoulder. "We're just breaking the ice."

"Cross?" Walton called.

At the prosecution table, Tony frowned, making no effort to hide his glare at Megan this time. He stood up straightened his overcoat with both hands, and approached the bench. "Your honor," he started, addressing first the Judge, then turning toward Megan and Nathan. "I want it stated for the record that the reason I did not call August Styles as a witness myself was that I wanted to avoid the following unpleasantries, but Miss. Greene has left me little choice."

"So noted."

Tony walked over to August, making no effort to smile at her. His gut flipped when he saw her cower back into her ball, but he kept his resolve.

Xander reached out and touched Megan's shoulder, motioning forward toward August.

"August," Megan called softly from her chair. "This man is going to ask you some questions now. His name's Tony, and he's a friend of mine."

August straightened back out, smiling wide at Tony.

He turned to Megan, raising an eyebrow to her.

"August, how do you know when baby milk is too hot?" he asked, as emotionlessly and as loudly as his drill captain in cadet camp always had when he was a teenager.

The question took August aback. "I don't know," she said honestly, her smile faded but not yet gone.

"Where does baby's milk come from?"

"I don't know."

"What do you do if your baby is crying?"

"I... don't know," she whimpered, her smile gone again, and she was beginning to retreat back into her little human ball.

Tony did not stop. "What do you do if the baby's coughing? What do baby's eat? How do you change the baby's diaper? What if the baby gets a rash? What do you do if her lips are *blue*? What do you do if she falls out of her crib? What do you do if she drowns in the tub?" he slammed his hand against the bench in front of her. "What do you do if your baby is *dying*? What do you do?"

"I don't know!" August wailed, tears streaming down her cheeks now, her face half-hidden by the stained white shirt she had pulled over it to hide from the scary man.

"And what do you do if we decide in the courtroom," he asked, stepping back and spreading his arms, as if to encompass the room. "Right now, that you, August are not fit to be a parent? What if we decide to take your baby from you before it's even born. What will you do then?"

"Wait."

Tony turned and pointed an accusing finger at Megan at the outburst, then stopped. She was just sitting there, smiling at him. He turned toward his desk, where Martha Styles sat, tears streaming down her withered face, as she looked up at her crying daughter. "Martha?"

"I'll do it," she said in a hushed voice, then slowly smiled up at August. "I'll help August look after the baby. After June."

Tony's arms fell to his sides, and once again he turned to Megan, who just shrugged and thrust a thumb back at Xander.

Mike grinned, patting his friend on the back. "Good play, man. Good."

Xander nodded, beaming proudly. "I rather thought so myself."

CHAPTER EIGHTEEN: PAL

Xander drank his cola, taking half the can in one long gulp before coming up for air. The Womb had finally stopped flaring up, but had left him oddly thirsty, and he took a long gulp of the liquid as Mike grinned at him.

Megan looked over, breaking off from her conversation with Judge Walton, Principal Shnieder, and Tony and walking over.

Mike smiled, then got up and strolled a few steps away.

"You knew, didn't you?" Megan grinned, waving her finger at him. "You knew right from the start."

Xander shook his head. He looked down into his cola and then back again, playing with the tab. "Naw," he admitted. "I knew what we had to do, but I never dreamed it would work out like this. It was what I had planned, more or less, but... naw, I didn't think I was winning this one."

"Still, you pulled some pretty risky moves there for the team. If you learn how to stop giving lip to Judge Walton, you might make a pretty good lawyer someday."

Xander smiled. "That's your battlefield, not mine."

She chuckled, squinting at him, "You sound so old sometimes, you know that?"

He laughed. "Feel that way too -- but this one time, I'm glad to say -- no regrets."

She smirked, leaning in and giving him a peck on the cheek. "No regrets," she reciprocated.

⋏⟨⋏

"August," Gallagher said in a soothing voice, still inside the closed court-room. "You did very well today, but we aren't quite done yet."

August was still in her little ball. "You aren't going to yell at me, are you?"

Gallagher smiled warmly. "No, my child. Never. But, the other day... Tim mentioned studying... can you tell me what studying is?"

August furrowed her brow, then looked away.

He sighed.

"It hurts," she said finally.

Tears welled up in Gallagher's eyes. "Yes, angel, I know. But what else?"

"He... said it would hurt. At first. He said that was how you learned. And then when you learned, it didn't hurt anymore. And studying is how we learn."

"I suppose," he soothed, reaching out and stroking the girl's hair, ever so gently. "But who said that?"

"I saw him - - *studying* - - with the other girl, Jennifer. He asked if I wanted to study too. He said I could learn just like she did. But... it felt funny. Funny and hurt. And he said that if I told anyone, it might make me hurt more, because I would forget. And then, he reached out and..."

"I know child, but *who*?"

"It was..."

⋏⟨⋏

"Xander," Cathy whispered. She was out of breath and Tommy was just a few feet behind her.

"Can this wait?" Xander asked, pointing to Megan.

"We found it out. We know who the father is."

Xander's eyes went wide. So did Megan's. "What the hell? I just didn't want you in the courtroom when Tony cross-examined August."

"You mean I got beat on by two girls for nothing?" Tommy yelled.

Xander ignored him. "Well, who is it, Cat?"

275

Gallagher grabbed Mike by the shoulder and spun him around. "My son -- Mike -- we must find Xander and the authorities. Young August has just told me who her assailant is."

Mike's grabbed him with both hands. "You're sure?"

"Positive. She said it herself. The girl can omit truths, but I do not believe she is capable of fabrication."

Xander walked up to Gallagher and Mike with Megan, Tommy and Cathy in tow outside on the courthouse. "You know?" he asked Mike, weighing the expression on his face.

Mike nodded.

"Well, my boy," Walton smiled, waddling up to Xander and patting him on the back. "Tony was just telling me what a hand you had in this case. Aside from the attitude, good work."

"Yes," Principal Shnieder smiled, extending his hand toward Xander. "Excellent work. Though I must admit, I'd rather you had been in class during school hours."

Xander glared for nearly half a second, which was a second more than he had wanted to wait. He thrust out both of his arms and grabbed Shnieder by his shirt collar, then pushed him back and pinned him against the wall of the courthouse. "You insignificant little weasel..." he bellowed, his voice just having a touch of the Womb's. "I'm going to rip you..."

"My son!" Gallagher protested, pulling Xander back off Shnieder. "Violence is never the answer!"

"Thank you, father," Shnieder gasped, composing himself.

Gallagher spun around on his heels, slamming his small fist into Shnieder's nose and sending him to the floor with blood gushing from his face.

"It may not be the answer... but it doesn't hurt the situation any."

"What is the meaning of this?" Walton asked, waving over the bailiffs. "Arrest these - -"

"Yes," Megan interrupted, stepping forward. "Please, arrest him," she said, pointing at Shnieder.

"What are you talking about?"

Megan grinned. "I had August's fetus tested for signs of Down syndrome... the trump card I never told Xander about."

"Hey --" Xander balked.

"How much do you want to bet that the baby's paternal DNA matches yours?" she asked coyly, handing the file to Shnieder, then turning to August and her mother.

Shnieder smiled, getting up. "You'll never make this stick. I'd never touch --" he looked August up and down with disgust. "-- that! It's absurd!"

Tommy smiled. "What about Jennifer Bradley?"

"Or Wanda Starsmoore?" Mike chimed.

"Wanda Starsmoore?" Tommy echoed. "Really? Wow. Way to go Shnieder."

"Tommy," Xander said sharply. He leaned in toward Shnieder, even as the bailiffs approached. "You're missing the point, Shnieder."

Shnieder just glared, not saying a word.

"Besides the fact that all eight girls you got pregnant are under the age of sixteen... meaning that your teaching career is over and you'll have some very nice prison time ahead of you... once you get out, you will owe *each* of those eight children..." he paused.

"Eighteen percent," Megan chimed.

" -- Eighteen percent of any paycheck you earn for child support."

Shnieder's face went white, and he started to sit down, but the bailiffs helped him back up and began reading him his rights.

As the whole group watched them carry him away, Megan leaned in to Xander:

"Now, that's what you had planned all along... right?"

Xander smiled.

CHAPTER NINETEEN: BEGINNING OF THE END

K - click!

"Make sure they're tight, Cathy," Xander reminded her, craning his head back to see her as she rotated the key until it snapped in solid. "We don't want me getting out."

Cathy gave him a droll look, then reached over and tussled his hair. "What makes tonight different than the last few nights?" she asked idly as she checked and then double-checked the bonds.

Xander looked downward.

She turned to face him then, finally taking it seriously. "Hey, what is it?"

"It's the Womb. It was acting funny today in court."

"More flashbacks?"

"No..." he corrected. "No, I've felt like this before, around you. When you got pregnant. It's the same way it reacts to Genblade or Black Heart..."

She moved slowly for a second, taking that in. "Do you think the Womb's going to attack August?"

He lowered his head again, his eyes becoming visibly tired, then raised it and nodded.

"Aw, Xander..." she tisked sympathetically, putting her bag down. He lowered his head again, and she put both of her hands on his chin to try and raise it, but he wouldn't budge. "Look, there's a reason that *you* transform into the Black Womb and not the other way around. That they need to drug you and mess with your head to get it to do what they want," she smiled. "It's because you're a man with a monster trapped inside, not the other way around. And it's the man that Mike and I love, you can't ever forget that. We can beat this, together. We *will* beat this together."

He still hadn't looked up, and she thought she felt tears running down his face.

"Xander?"

His head jutted forward suddenly, already partially transformed. His razor-sharp teeth dug into the soft flesh between her neck and left shoulder even as they protruded from his gums.

She screamed, long and loud, as he began to thrust against his restraints feverishly, their clangs echoing throughout the church walls and back again. "Xander!" she yelled, hitting him with the arm that would still move over and over again, even as it locked in the iron grip of its jowls, still pulling on the re-strains.

"You see?" Spider laughed, deep within his subconscious. "It is as I've told you..."

-SNAP!-

Xander's wrist shattered under the immense force of his own tugs, letting his mutilated hand slide free. Instantly it was covered in black blood that started to swarm over his body, making his fingers into claws that grabbed onto Cathy's shoulder for support, making escape impossible. As his legs turning into muscular, powerful things, he brought one up and slashed at her with it as his teeth gnawed, much like a cat, barely missing cutting her right through her if not for her down jacket, which was now spilling feathers everywhere. Gaining the extra leverage, as the ooze almost finished enveloping him, he wrenched his arm free of the second bond and let her drop to the ground.

She fell limply, slumped into a heap with a -flump- sound that, for some reason, did not echo. The creature looked down at her, her jacket and shirt torn open, revealing her smooth stomach. Her shoulder gushed blood onto the floor and her chest. It leaned over her, licked its lips of her blood, and took a long whiff of her, closing its aqua eyes to enjoy the scent. When it spoke, it almost did so in retaliation to the kind words she had said to Xander against it:

"Black... Womb lives."

The creature spun on its balled heels, then leapt toward one of the boarded windows and crashed through it, sending splinters of wood along with it.

For a moment, all was silent.

"Fuck!" Cathy cursed, sitting up and applying pressure to the wound that had been dangerously close to her neck. She examined the blood on her hand, then put it back again. "Fuck!" she repeated, reaching into her pocket and producing a cell phone, quickly pressing speed dial one and putting it to her ear. "Mike," she said quickly. "Code Black. I'm fine, I'll make it over to St. Claire's alone. Fine, I'll call a cab. Just get after him. He might go after -- she's not? Oh, okay. Just find it, its been going stir crazy, no telling what it might do. Love you too... bye." She pressed end and slid the phone back into her pocket, still holding her neck tightly. "Fuck," she said again, as she started to limp toward the exit.

Officer Aaron Munroe walked down the corridor of Coral Beach Penitentiary, watching the moon rise to its highest through the cells that he passed. He clicked his tongue against the side of his cheek aimlessly as he did so. He took one last look down the hall toward the New Fish cell, smirked, then turned to head back toward the office.

"Urk!" he exclaimed, looking down at his chest. There was nothing there at first, and then he saw spots of blood forming. It was only just before he passed out that he realized they were from his own mouth.

Black Womb dropped the body and stepped over it, then stepped up to the bars of the empty cell he had been next too. It took a long whiff, its triangular nostrils flaring, catching onto a familiar scent.

It opened his eyes again, its almost-invisible pupils searching the darkness of the cell left and right. Finding nothing, it howled widely, then turned around...

... coming face to face with Shnieder, cowering in the back of his cell.

The Womb stepped forward until its nose was touching the bars, then pivoted its body and began to slide through the bars, the wet snap of its bones breaking and then resetting themselves as it made its way in the only sound it made.

"Please..." Shnieder begged, tears running down his face onto his orange prison jumpsuit. "Please, no -- I didn't mean too -- I never will again..."

The Womb -- through the bars now with its left leg snapping back into socket -- walked forward calmly. It never once took its unblinking eyes off of the man.

"I'll never... please..."

With one sudden motion, it jutted its hand forward and stuck its un-clawed thumb into Shnieder's left eye socket.

Shnieder screamed, the sound becoming more a more moist a sound as blood gurgled from the socket and down into his mouth.

It slammed his head against the concrete wall, its thumb still in his eye. Then again. And again. And again.

Its mouth finally opened into something that could have been described on anything else as a smile.

Shnieder finally stopped screaming, his body growing limp, blood splattered on the wall behind it.

And then it started to slam again, faster and harder with each one until finally letting go. It drew back its hand swiftly, sending long, slender trails of muscle and brain tissue spattering against the far wall. "Black Womb lives!" it bellowed, howling at the moon outside. It turned toward the exit... then stopped.

The cell door was open wide now, the security camera just outside it sparking with exposed wires and tape. The lens was shattered. It turned its head slightly to one side, confused, then felt the bat alongside it's head.

"Son of a bitch!" Mike yelled as the Womb hit the floor, not letting up for an instant, swinging the bat around again and cracking it in the face. The Womb tried to get up but Mike kicked its legs, then started wailing on it with the bat again. "I'm sorry, Xander," he said, letting loose another blow that sent black ooze spraying against the walls of the cell. "I really am. This has got to end. Not tomorrow, not next week... now. Now I love you, Xander, but... this is it." He punctuated each sentence with a blow. The Womb raised its claws but Mike again lashed out, successfully snapping one of the talons off. It grunted in pain, finally stopping in its attempts to get away, just recessing into itself. "You hear me, Womb? You're the one going down, not us! This is the last stand -- either smarten up, or get extinct -- you hear me?"

The Womb looked up and Mike stopped pounding. For a second, he thought he saw tears in the Womb's eyes. Then, all at once, the blackness lost its ability to stay together, splashing down off of Xander Drew's naked, shivering body as if it had never been there to begin with, leaving only a thin layer of blood behind.

The tears had been Xander's, and he shed them even more now, pounding his fist against the concrete. "Don't stop..." he pleaded, so low it was almost inaudible.

His face still a mask of rage, Mike didn't realize what his friend meant at first... then looked down at the bat in his hand, the top half of which was covered in black and red. The anger melted away to pity, and the bat dropped to the ground.

Reluctant at first and shaking from the cold and the blood still seeping from his eyes, Xander shot into the arms of his friend and fell to his knees, letting the tears mix with the blood all around him.

"It's okay, buddy," Mike said, ignored the congealed bodily fluids and stroking the back of his friend's head.

But somehow, both men knew it wasn't.

Nor would it ever be.

CHAPTER TWENTY: DOORS

The elm stood in the dark, the wind moaning through her dead branches. They cracked and broke until all that was left of her was her core, tattered in snow and clinging to life as she watched the horror of winter all around her without breath or reprieve or hope of either.

"Do you think this'll be enough?" Cathy asked, motioning down toward the frozen dinner she held in her hands.

Mike smiled warmly at her, her kindness never ceasing to amaze him. "A crumb would be enough."

"Still," she pouted, looking down at the plate of turkey and mashed potatoes and gravy she had taken from her fridge when they'd passed by her house. It was covered in wrap and looked as though it could have used some heat, tiny droplets of dew clinging to the inside of the plastic. Before getting it, she had hoped bringing food would help alleviate her guilt, but it did not. She'd spent her lunch hour writing, and couldn't help but think at least some of that time could have been spent going to the church to let Xander out of his chains.

He smirked at her. "Did you make it?"

"No..."

"Tell him you did. He'll love every bite."

She smiled. The smile in and of itself was nothing, the expansion and contraction of a few key facial muscles, but the feelings behind it was nothing short of spectacular. For the two of them to have come so far in just a few months, to not forget their mistakes but to build upon them and learn from them, it meant everything in the world to her. Right then, looking down at the plate of thin turkey slivers, she couldn't imagine herself being with anyone else. But then there was Xander. Her smile began to fade away again as her thoughts became more complicated.

"Did I say something wrong?" he asked, looking down at her with concern.

She forced the grin back into its place, but it wasn't quite the same. Like a lithograph of the Mona Lisa, something just wasn't right about the fake. "Never."

"I'll remind you you said that the next time you try to tell me the contrary."

She laughed and slapped his arm. He pretended to stumble backward into the snow, balancing on one foot and holding the offended arm as if in deep pain. Smirking devilishly, she gave him a tiny shove and sent him toppling over for real.

"Hey!" he yelped. He grabbed a pile of snow into his hands and began to walk toward her menacingly.

"Mike, don't you dare!" she scolded and giggled all at the same time, backing away a few paces down the sidewalk and put a hand outward in a vain attempt to halt his progress.

He said nothing, shaking some of the snow off of his head and taking another step forward, and another, quicker each time.

"Mike!" she screamed as she turned as laughed, running down the street as fast as she could without dropping Xander's dinner, causing peas to loosen from the saran wrap and fall to the ground all the same.

He was gaining on her, and all at once he hurled the large snowball he had made, splashing it against her back. The snow traveled in all directions, a fair portion of it going down her coat and onto her back. He stopped, snickering wildly at her and twisted back and forth, trying to wriggle the snow out.

"Mike, I swear, I'm going to fucking - - "

"You kiss your mother with that mouth?" he jeered, stepping closer to her and grabbing her arms gently but firmly.

"Oh, shut up."

He laughed again when he saw her cheeks, red and livid with anger, her mouth pouting a little and her eyes drawn down in a scowl. He leaned in to kiss her.

"Not likely!" she protested, jerking her head back and wiggling some more, reaching up the back of her shirt and coming out with the last bit of snow. "You jerk."

She leaned in to kiss her again, and this time she let him, both of their eyes closing as they sunk into it. All of a sudden Mike's eyes went wide and he jumped back a pace, beginning to wriggle himself. Cathy smirked at him as he tried to get the snow out of the front of his pants without calling attention to himself, trying to by shaking his right leg. His was hissing from the screaming cold coming from every one of those nerves. "That was vulgar."

He tapped him twice against the chest, as if punctuating her victory. "Don't forget who always comes out on top."

He smiled, shooting her a look.

"Ugh," she sighed in disgust, slapping his arm again. "Why must all men have such a one track mind?"

"We're devoted to that track. We think of it all the time, and we love it. In some ways, it's very romantic."

"Sure," she beamed, pulling him forward and kissing him again. She turned out of the kiss, and noticed for the first time that they were there.

It jutted out of the snow as if it had been grown there. Staring up at its height compared to the buildings around it, it was hard to believe that it had been built by man at all. It's twin towering, pointed peaks seemed to pierce the moisture-saturated clouds that loomed overhead, hiding the crosses that had once adorned both. One had fallen down recently, and was still stuck in the ground bottom up, about five feet from the west end of the church. The church was simple grey brick on the outside, with no extravagant statues or sculptors like in the movies, the bricks seemed to make faces that stared back at you until you looked right at them... like the faces that one sees in the trees. A single stained-glass window added color to the front. It had long since been shattered in by rocks, but the top of Mary's head was still plainly visible, the last pieces hanging onto the frame for dear life.

"I hate this place," she stated, her hair caught in a sudden and timely stiff breeze as they both stared up at the church.

"I know," he said, trying to comfort her but not giving her his full attention as he looked around to make sure no one was watching. "It'll be okay."

"I still can't believe we chain him up in that horrible place."

He turned back toward her, confident that there was no one about. There never was here, really. This part of town had belonged to the Tee gang until not too long ago, and people still didn't wander around the streets too much. "It's a church, Cathy."

"An *abandoned* church, Michael," she said, using his full name as a way of emphasizing her point, "You know what my grandpa said when Trina asked him why this church was so creepy?"

"What?"

"He said that the devil's greedy. He said when God moves out of one of his houses, the devil moves in."

He laughed a little, picturing Cathy's grandfather (who did not look unlike the devil himself, bushy eyebrows and triangular face) telling such a story to the girls. He wondered if his teeth had been in at the time, or taken out for effect like when he'd told them vampire stories as children. "I think your grandfather was pulling your leg, Cat."

She glowered at him, and he stopped laughing. "Say what you want, but it's a bad idea anyway. It's like a band-aid on a tumor, chaining him up here. It's not actually fixing the problem, just putting it out of sight."

At this he nodded, even as he started to walk toward the doors, motioning for her to follow. She did. "I know," he admitted finally.

He reached out and grabbed the brass loop on the door, a few flakes of its rusted surface scraping at the insides of his fingers as he lifted it to the sound of creeping hinges, took one last look at the street outside, then opened it.

Light splashed into the church, casting their shadows long and thin in front of them. No matter how many times they opened it, Mike would always think that the light seemed wrong here. Cobwebs and tattered curtains blew in the air, covering the holes in the walls the way he covered his hands covered his eyes when his mom turned on the lights when he was sleeping in. Sometime since it closed the church had gotten used to the dark, and now hated its passing.

It smelled like week-old vomit mixed with baking soda and mold, and every particle of dust that floated about, catching the sun before their eyes, carried it.

Mike took a step forward toward the curtain which blocked their view of the main hall. Cathy moved to follow him, then stopped. "Something's wrong," she said, again stating it blatantly as a truth rather than an insight.

Mike turned and looked at her. "Nothing's wrong."

"No, Mike. His hearing. His *special* hearing. He should have heard us even when we were out in the street, why isn't he calling out to us or anything?"

Mike rolled his eyes, then resumed his walk toward the curtain, pushing it aside and making a cloud of dust.

When it cleared, the long hall stretched out before them like a black and white sketch with no focal point. It looked like something they used mirrors to make of television, a hallway that went on forever. Row on row of pews, many of them broken of burnt, lined it on either side; and at the end was a large brass cross. Chained to it was the Black Womb.

Not Xander Drew.

The creature rose its head. Light shone in from a hole in the building's brick, and they could see that a few millimeters of dust had collected on his scalp. His mouth was invisible when it was closed like it was now, but to anyone who had seen it before the memory of it was enough, with row upon row of razor-sharp, serrated teeth that moved freely at the creature's whim, each tooth joined to the jaw at its own joint. The small, round, black scales that covered his body from head to toe rippled up and down, changing color to dark blue and then back again. It was subtle, but Mike had a theory that this was what it did when it really wanted to get a good whiff of something, soaking the scent in through every one of its pores. His chains were red and black with his blood. The talons on his toes were extended, too, which was rare. There were spikes in those chains,

Xander's idea. They went right through his ankles, like Oedipus'.

"Told you," Cathy whispered, taking a step forward past her lover.

"Cathy!" Mike hissed, grabbing her by the arm and spinning her around and almost making her drop her plate.

She stopped, looking at him with a confused look.

"You can't go near it. Big sign. Don't feed the bears," he huffed, motioning toward the Womb and her plate of food at once.

Behind her, the Womb made a low growling sound.

"Something's wrong with him," she said, her voice full of empathy as only hers could be. "There's no blood on the floor. He didn't become Xander then come back or something, he's been like this since we left him last night."

He glanced over her shoulder at the floor around its feet, and sure enough, she was right. "Still, that doesn't mean..."

"I'm going to see him," she stated, and he let go of her arm and walked forward with her.

"Just be careful," he said, gingerly caressing her left shoulder where the Womb had ripped into her. "You know what he's capable o--"

"Yes, I do."

"Can I get a sentence o - -"

"No, you can't," she cut off again, but this time she grinned at him playfully. But she didn't turn toward him. To do that she would have had to take her eyes off the Womb, and that was something you never, ever did. If you had and you were telling about it, then you should go buy a lottery ticket.

As they both got closer they could hear its deep breathing. It reminded Mike of when he learned about Pavlov's dog, the way it drooled whenever the bell would ring, excited at the idea of food. The Womb was panting out of sheer, blood-lust-driven excitement, its eyes still transfixed on them like opaque lenses.

It stank like sweat and semen.

Cathy got as close as she dared, with Mike right behind (his hand clasping hers both in encouragement and in case he needed to pull her back) and stared directly at the creature, staying as silent as she could while still breathing.

The creature met her gaze for less than a second before turning away and huffing quickly, as though it were uninterested. It was like the way a dog broke its gaze with you when you were staring it down. It continuing to look to one side for a moment, then glanced back into her pupils, seeing she was still there, and looked back again.

"Xander," she said, firmly but patiently.

"Rakk!" it barked, turning quickly back toward her at the sound of its alter ego's name. Its mouth opened for the first time since they'd come in, showing those teeth she'd been envisioning moments ago and snapping them shut right in front of her face, its mouth disappearing again, as if to say: *don't push it, lady.*

She blinked but held her ground as Mike tried to pull her back.

"Wmmmmbbb..." it growled in defiance, the sound emanating from deep inside of its throat as resonating against her. She could *feel* the sound, the way one felt very loud music or the vibrations a car motor makes when it starts. It looked away again, and this time she grabbed it by the chin and forced it back. Mike made a fearful hissing sound when she did this.

"We could just stab him," Mike offered. "It means his bloodlust will probably triple tonight, but given the circumstances..."

Cathy ignored him as he trailed off and eventually stopped, realizing that this was not an option for her. "Xander," she repeated, in exactly the same tone as before.

"Wmbbbb..."

"No," she said patiently, if not a little patronizingly. "Not Womb, Xander."

"Black Womb lives!"

"Yes, yes he does. Black Womb lives. Black Womb smash. Black Womb the strongest one there is. But I want to talk to Xander now, okay sweetie?"

Mike raised an eyebrow, unable to believe what he was hearing.

"Xnnndrrr..." the Womb growled, low in his throat, as the aqua starting to drain from his eyes and turn red.

"Holy shit," Mike said, taking a step closer. "It's working."

"Like trying to wake up somebody who overslept," she whispered, smiling to herself. "You don't just walk in and start shaking them, you just nudge them a little until they wake up."

The scales that covered the Womb's body began to shiver then, joining with each other like two drops of water placed too close to one another and becoming one. They did this all over, the ooze becoming less and less solid and more unstable, beginning to drop from his body as he shook and spasmed in what appeared to be a seizure, his claws slowly retracting into his hands. The Womb's mouth opened in what looked to be a scream, but instead of long teeth, the face and Xander Drew peered out, eyes closed and teeth clenched in pain as the darkness finally lost all of its cohesiveness and fell from of his body in one big splash. His body went limp in their chains and he began to breath hard, a thin layer of blood covering his entire body now.

Cathy bent down and touched his matted hair. He jerked back, as if sensitive to her touch.

Mike began unlocking the chains, and as each limb was freed it fell to the floor with no life in them at all. He curled on the floor in that pool of his own blood and bile, staring up at the cobwebbed ceiling with blank, emotionless eyes. In this form his body seemed to be nothing but skin and bones, his stomach concaved like a famine victim.

The wind outside picked up again, and he shivered when some of it reached his bare skin. Cathy grabbed a wool knit blanket her Aunt had made years ago. It was full of different earth-tones like evergreen and dirt-brown, and looked completely natural on him. It almost made him look alright. He blinked hard, and when his eyes opened again, they were almost normal. Now, at last, he was finally awake. He looked around at his surroundings, scared and confused a little at first, and then his eyes rested on Cathy. He looked a little surprised, as if she had just appeared there in his line of sight.

"I didn't hurt anyone, did I?" he asked, his voice hoarse and raspy. It wasn't even really phrased as a question, like he expected to answer to be yes.

"No," she smiled, stroking back his hair, big globs of congealed blood sticking to her fingers. "No sweetie, you didn't hurt anyone."

Mike watched them silently, his eyes focused on her hand on Xander's hair as he collected his clothes, folded neatly on a nearby pew. He hoisted them up, quickly grabbing the socks as they started to roll off the top, and brought them over to the pair.

Xander reached up to grab the underwear once, winced, then tried again and succeeded, sliding them on from under the blanket.

CHAPTER TWENTY-ONE: UTERUS

Calla McFadden stopped in the middle of the hall, staring at a bumper sticker that had been stuck on a locker that read: horn broken, watch for finger. She giggled to herself, then erupted into a full-blown belly laugh. After a moment she forgot what she had been laughing at, saw it again, and giggled once more before walking past it. She felt like maybe the sticker reminded her of something, but wasn't sure. But she was so sure. She felt like the answer was just in front of her, but that her mind was surrounded by a thin fog that she couldn't see through. If she concentrated, hard, it would begin to clear and she could see her train of thought clearly -- but she didn't really care enough to try. The entire reason she'd lit up again was so that she wouldn't have to concentrate hard on anything.

The sound of squeaking sneakers and bouncing balls coming from just down the hallway seemed miles away, the girls volleyball team practicing hard for the next week's game. As she walked past she glanced in at the girls diving for the ball, skidding their knees off the spongy floor, trying hard to keep the ball on the other end of the court. Off to the side, some girls that were waiting to play were bouncing their balls off of the gym wall in lieu of an opponent. She smiled as she watched them, watching one in particular as she wiped sweat off of her brow with her arm, trying to do so without taking her eyes off of the game. It was Samara, her cheeks red and her hair was up in a bun to keep it out of her eyes. Calla briefly put her hand on the door and started to push it to go in, then reconsidered, turning around instead and walking across the hall to the stairwell, sighing to herself only briefly before her smile returned. She started to giggle again as she remembered the bumper sticker.

The silence was broken by the smallest of sounds. It reminded her instantly of the sound that Cindy-Lou Who made in the old Grinch cartoon she loved as a child. *Like the coo of a dove.* But sadder somehow, and longer. It was a sound that grew until it was a dull moan.

Raising one eyebrow, she turned the corner to look down the next flight of stairs and saw him. He looked tiny in comparison to the room around him, curled up into a little ball sitting at the bottom of the stairs, sobbing into his knees. His shirt was dirty, his jeans filled with holes. He didn't look old enough to be going to school here, like he should be in grade five at the most. If he did go to this school, he had to be in grade seven. His skin was a little dark, like coffee with just a little milk in it, and she thought briefly that if he cleaned up a little and bought new clothes he could be quite the ladies man when he got older. She took a step forward and opened her mouth, then stopped herself, unable to decide on what to say, and a little worried that the child would know that she was stoned. She turned to leave the way she came, then back again. "Hey," she said finally, rolling her eyes at the stupidity of it.

The boy looked up, startled, his eyes full of tears. He said nothing, just stared at her like a deer in the headlights.

"What, uh, what's your name?" she asked, inching a little closer, trying not to scare the boy.

"Jaden Mal," he stated, his voice small and squeaky. He sniffed back a large string of mucus, then wiped his nose with his shirt the way children do.

"I'm Calla," she said, forcing a smile as she sat down next to him. They stayed there in silence for a full minute, which seemed a lot longer to her. "So -- what's wrong?"

He looked away, staring blankly at the knob on the door leading to that floor as his eyes welled up again. "Nothing," he said after a second, then started to cry outright.

Calla sighed, clenching her hair. "Listen, don't do that. I'm really not good with this sort of thing, maybe you should talk to someone else. I think Reverend Gallagher is still in..."

Suddenly the child started to cry even more, a loud wail escaping from his open mouth, and she could see that a few teeth were missing, one with a large cavity in its place. "Oh, hey, I'm sorry -- what, uh crap -- we can talk to someone else. I'll talk to you, just tell me what's happening?"

He turned to her, opening his mouth to speak. It took a moment for the words to come, and when they did, a fresh spring of tears came with them: "Reverend Gallagher is touching me."

Xander stopped dead in his tracks where his walkway met the sidewalk, staring silently ahead at the bright red front door to his house. After a moment his legs began to get rubbery, and he braced himself against his mailbox for support.

Cathy stopped a few steps later, turning back to face him.

His face was as white as a ghost and his free arm slumped loosely by his side.

She crossed her arms in front of her. "You have to come in," she reminded him, clicking her tongue against the roof of her mouth.

He stared at a rock in the walkway a few feet in front of him, mostly obscured by snow. He recalled having tripped over it once or twice, and vividly

287

recalled the time Sara had hit her knee off of it after falling off a skateboard, and then another time when Julie had stubbed her toe on it. He stared at it until the whole world became blurry except for it, then shifted his focus so that the world was clear and it was blurry, then back again.

"Xander - -" she moaned, her hands falling to her sides as the pity she had been trying to keep in check began to overtake her.

"Where'd Mike go again?" he asked finally, still staring at that spot in the path.

"He had to shower sometime," she said glumly, taking a single step toward him.

She was now obscuring his view of the rock, and he blinked twice before looking back up at her. His eyes were bloodshot and puffy, the way someone looks after they'd spent a long time crying... only she knew that he had not. His hair was a matted mess, and she chided herself for not remembering to bring a comb or brush again today.

"And he doesn't like the bathroom at either of our places," she continued, feeling that she had waited long enough for him to speak, as she had assumed he would have. "He's a bit of a germaphobe."

Xander was still looking at her, then his eyes went to one side in their sockets, and finally, slowly, he nodded. His head lolled to the left until it was looking at the house next to his, the one with Johnson marked on the mailbox. There was a big **FOR SALE** sign hammered into the snow next to it, and all of the lights inside were out. "When did her parent's move?" he asked, almost as if he were saying it to himself and she wasn't even here.

"A month ago," she sighed, taking another step toward him. "It was right after the thing with Circe and... and Mandy. I don't think that had anything to do with it, though. Her dad had been looking for a new job out of state ever since --" she trailed off, knowing better than to finish that sentence.

He stared at the house a moment longer, then chuckled, turning back to her. "You remember that night?" he asked, finally making eye contact with her. He seemed almost relaxed now.

She shuffled from foot to foot, unsure of what to think of his sudden lividity. "The night Sara..."

"No," he said, raising a hand to cut her off again before she said the word. "Do you remember the night that Derek escaped?" He was still smiling, but now she could see through it, see that it was entirely superficial.

She stared at him for a moment, a dumbfounded look across her face, then she smiled a little. "Yeah, of course."

"I was going to give up fighting. I thought I was in control of the Womb and that I was going to catch one last killer and then call it quits. Ride off into the sunset," he chuckled, reached for a cigarette, then stopped himself. "But it was me, I was the killer, and Derek got loose... and I guess I've been thinking..."

"That when you catch him you can get control of the Womb again, then finally start your life?" she finished, finally closing the gap between then by touching him on the cheek and making him turn toward her.

288

He nodded.

She tisked him. "You're going to. I know it. More than that, I feel it. You're going to get control -- and whether or not you catch Derek isn't a big deal, just so long as he stays out of our hair and stops killing the people we love. He's gone now, and we'll probably never hear from him again."

He snorted a little at that, his attention more normal now that she was the only thing in his field of vision. "Yeah, because we're that lucky."

She patted him twice on the cheek playfully, then started to walk toward his front door. She stopped again and back toward him, and this time her smile was gone. "About... about what else happened that night, when we found out Derek had - -"

He raised an open palm quickly cutting her off. "It's okay. Not your fault."

"Xander, we both --"

"No, I was just caught up in the moment. I'd..." he trailed off, looking away for a second and then forcibly making eye contact with her. "... I'd never be able to get with you, anyway. I think it was the excitement and the last of O'Toole's tampering and the Womb acting up and a crap load of other things. But, yeah... maybe nobody's fault, but not anything to write home about either."

"Yeah," she said, somberly at first, then smiling back at him. "Thank you."

He nodded curtly, and they both started toward the door together.

He reached out and grabbed the knob, but waited to turn it. For a long moment he just stood there, arm outstretched, as if waiting for something to happen. His brow furrowed after a second, willing something to happen.

"Some people turn those things," Cathy reminded him, raising an eyebrow from behind him.

"Yeah," he agreed reluctantly. "I... I'm just - -"

"Waiting for the Womb to flare up and tell you that Derek's inside, because if we were talking about not finding him, that's just when he'd show up like in some slasher film?"

He turned back toward her, blushing a little.

She laughed. "Come on. Open the damn door."

He did, and they both stepped inside and started kicking the snow off their boots.

"Xander," came a voice from his immediate right. He spun on his heels to face it, almost extending his claws. Cathy brought up a hand to stop him, grabbing his wrist with speed that surprised even him, until he thought back and realized he'd actually been more than a little slow.

Xander's mother looked back at him, her eyes as red and puffy as his had been a few moments ago, but the rest of her face looked pale and withdrawn, and even a little sunk back, somehow. Her short, curled hair seemed to fall limp somehow, but her shirt was bright and happy, with flowers and Hawaiian colors tie-dyed all over it. It reminded him of the wolf from Little Red Riding Hood, trying to look nice but hiding something horrible.

In the background, his father glared at him through eyes that were wetted by tears, both of his fists clenched until his knuckles were white, and a little blood dripping from one of them. There was a hole in the wall next to where he stood, little bits of drywall still crumbling from it. A few feet t his left there were two more.

Now the Womb twitched.

"Xander, honey," his mother began again, fresh tears dribbling down her face. "We have to talk."

Cathy sat in the middle of Xander's bed, his pillows propping her up as she tried not to eavesdrop of the raised voices downstairs. There were screams and there was crying. She heard a loud thud, and thought that Mr. Drew must have just put his hand through the wall again. She closed her eyes tightly, as if that meant she couldn't hear; then so tightly that she began to see brightly colored spots. Sighing, she opened them again and reached for Xander's phone. She picked it up and started to dial Mike's number, getting four digits in before she pressed the disconnect button and tossed the phone back onto the bed. She fell backward onto the pillows again. They were stiff and uncomfortable, and smelled too clean. They had not been slept in since the last time they had been washed, and if she curled into them and breathed deep she could still identify the particular brand of fabric softener.

There was another hard, loud sound from downstairs, and she thought she recognized that one as Xander. She remembered reading once that in World War II, snipers had learned to recognize the individual crack of each other's rifles. She was sure it wasn't *that* specific, but right now, she was quite positive that the last fist to crash into the drywall had been Xander's.

She reached out and grabbed her book bag and hauled it up onto the bed with her. She began to thumb through it, finally producing a wire-bound exercise book with a bright red front and the letters BW etched into the front with a sharpie. There was a mechanical pencil shoved down into the metal binds that held the pages together, and now she opened it to about three-quarters of the way through. She surveyed the remaining pages quickly, hoping that there was another blank notebook in the bag just in case she got in a good groove and ran out of room in this one.

Making a couple of clicks with her pencil to get the lead out, she propped the paper up against the legs and began to write.

I wasn't there for most of it, but Xander and Mike told me the rest. They told me how- -

She stopped and scribbled out what she had written until it was all black. A voice from downstairs seemed to be crying again, Xander's mom, and for a brief second she debated knocking on the floor and yelling to them that she was trying to write. Burying that thought down deep, she took a deep breath and started again.

"But, why would start a rumor like that about Xander yourself?" I had said, and I felt like just slapping Julie Peterson right upside the head. I didn't feel like *asking* her about this, I felt like *demanding* it, and maybe I was, just a little. I could feel my frustration with her giving way to anger, as the redness in my cheeks wasn't just because of blush anymore.

"Well, y'know..." she started, her eyes gazing off to one side like they always did when she was trying to justify something unjustifiable. It was as though this was the first time she'd actually thought about what she'd done and how it could affect others, and it was dawning upon her how stupid it was. "I just thought, like, if enough people thought we'd been together, it might make Alex want to actually be together. Just so it wouldn't be a big lie, y'know?"

I felt for the girl a little, though I wasn't sure why -- not then. Now I know that while I would never try something so stupid, that we were all capable of acts of stupidity in the name of love; each and every one of us. "Xander's not like that," I stated bluntly. After a moment's pause, I realized who I was talking too, and decided I might need to elaborate a little. "He's complex. And he's been through a lot more than you or I realize. He keeps so much of it inside, trying to be brave. But what he doesn't get is : he doesn't need to be brave. It comes naturally to him. Everything he's been trying so hard to be, he keeps thinking that it's just one step away. That if he tries hard enough, he'll be a good man. What he doesn't get is... he was there ten steps ago. He's never going to stop trying to be better. To do what's right. And that's why he'll always be good. He's not just going to jump into bed with you. I'm not saying anything against you, it's just... he has old fashioned morals. He's going to do what's right. For him to get serious with you, in his mind, that would be him 'cheating' on Sara. And he'd never do that. No matter what people say, I'll never believe - -" I stopped and noticed the enlightened look in Julie's eyes. As if the girl just figured out something that had been on the tip of her tongue for a long time.

Her mouth opened, and when the words came out, they sounded true, even to me : "You love him."

She stopped writing, rubbing her hand a little from the strain it put on her wrist. That was how the conversation with Julie had gone, she thought, for the most part. At least that part she could mostly get from memory. The fight with Black Heart a few pages before had been completely fabricated, made up of half-truths from the news reports and what little Xander had told her about it. What she had said to Julie was true: at that point, he had been bottling everything up, even more than he did now. The whole trip to L.A. seemed like such an odd chapter of their lives now, like it hadn't really happened. Maybe that was just because it had been all the way across the country, or maybe it was just because of the weirdness that had surrounded the whole ordeal.

She rubbed her eyes and tried to think of where to go next. After a moment she smiled, then started to write again. She started by writing Later that night... even though it had been at least a week between one event and the next, but she thought that added some immediacy to the tale.

Later that night my phone began to ring. As I opened it and rummaged for the talk button, I remember thinking that it was Mike. That the Womb had come out during the night and done something to him, killed him, that I'd lost the person I love just as Xander had a month before. "Hello?" I asked, and my voice felt raw and unused.

"It's me," came the voice from the other end of the line. It sounded hushed and deep, and there was a lot of static in the background. I felt like I had just gotten a call from Deep Throat.

It took me a moment to place the voice, then finally it slid together in my brain. "Xander?" I groaned, pressing my free hand against my free ear to try and hear him better, even though all the static and noise was on his end, I was sure. "Are you okay? Is Mike okay?"

I heard the silence through the line and recognized it. Somehow, I could picture him making his hurt face, those puppy-dog eyes turned upwards. I hadn't said 'did you hurt Mike,' but I may as well have.

"I'm sorry," I spat, fully awake and trying to get my apology into his head before he had a chance to really absorb the pain I'd just caused him, even though I knew it was too late from that the moment I had said it.

"It's okay. I understand," he said glumly, and the sad part was that he did understand, completely. It's one thing to think those things about yourself; but for me to vocalize them like that had just been wrong. "It's just the rain, it's making me irritable."

I reached up and pulled the window shade aside, kneeling on the edge of my bed and looking out. "It's not raining here... Where are you? What town are you in?"

She continued on writing. She wrote about how they'd first met Mandy on a trip to Coral Cove, and how she'd decided to come back with them. She wrote about Randy and Tommy and Sud for a little, but as little as possible. It left a bad taste in her mouth when she thought of the events leading up to the day that Sud had been shot, and she did not like it at all. Finally, she got to Xander's first real confrontation with the Tees. She sat up in bed and snatched her Cherry Coke out of her book bag, opening it and taking a long swig before starting again, her hand flying over the page at a mile a minute.

He crashed through the skylight that sparkled moonlight down into the warehouse that the Tees used for their headquarters, spraying large shards of glass and black blood everywhere as he fell. Time seemed to slow down, and all ten Tees looked up in awe. And in the center, little Amanda Peterson looked up as well, clutched into herself tightly. The glass spun around the falling black form and sparkled in the low light, catching it and making it shimmer and shine. It made it look like wings, like he were flying to earth instead of falling to it. Deep inside her heart, Mandy felt the desperation melt away and filled with hope.

He finally landed after what seemed like an eternity. He stayed crouched from the impact for a few moments, then arose. The thinness of him made him look taller than he was, all sleek and oiled with long, taunt muscles. His eyes opened, large and radiating red, and the Tees had just enough time to fathom what was about to happen to them before it did.

She stopped, huffing as she reached the end of the last page, then quickly pulled another notebook from her knapsack and opened it to a clean, white page and continued.

Xander - -

She stopped immediately, crossing out her friend's name and starting again.

The Womb reached out with his hand full of razor-sharp talons and grabbed the closest Tee around the neck, making four tiny slits as he did. As he pulled forward he bent backwards, using the momentum of the movement to hurl the Tee back over his head and crashing into another, both men tumbling into the darkness that surrounded the moonlight.

The Womb righted himself again, his scaled form serving as a barrier between them and the girl now, and it eyed each of them carefully, its claws dangling at its sides. One of them lunged at it, spinning a chain around his head with one powerful arm and thrusting it in the heroes direction. The Womb raised its arm quickly but calmly, and the chain hit it and whipped, typing itself around even as the demon gave it a solid tug, bringing the Tee with it. It extended its fist and the Tee's face flew into it. The thug fell into unconsciousness.

"Never knew I was that cool," Xander said, leaning against the door behind her.

She turned, startled, then smiled a little. "That's not how it went?"

He chuckled, wiping his eyes a little. They weren't red or puffy anymore, but now she got the distinct impression that he had been crying for some reason. It occurred to her how little she'd seen him with his parents. "Not quite," he answered finally, sitting down backward in his desk chair.

She turned and looked back over what she had written, raising an eyebrow. "That's how I see it happening. She called you the Black Angel, so I figured I'd play it up."

Xander nodded, but did not respond verbally. He had that same faraway look in his eyes that he had had outside, leaning against the mailbox.

"Bob the Squirrel..." she sang musically, putting down the notebook and waving her head in front of him comically, trying to cheer him up.

He raised a hand for her to stop and she did.

"Were your parents mad about you being out all last night? You should tell them it was my fault, somehow, it's really the truth - -"

"My mom has cancer," he said, and his eyes started to well up again. His chin crumpled up toward his mouth as it always did when he was about to cry. But he didn't.

Her mouth went slack, and for a moment it just hung there, unsure of what to say.

"She has cancer," he repeated, running his fingers through his hair. When they came back with blood on them, Cathy realized that his talons had been out and grabbed him by the wrists.

"Don't!"

"Cancer. This little shadow..." he chuckled giddily, then thrust his head back in a full laugh. "She has this little dark spot... on her uterus, Cathy." He chuckled again, but the tears were coming freely now. "She has a black womb."

Her eyes went wide with fright, and without even thinking about it, her hand went to her own abdomen.

He noticed, and the chuckling slowly died down. "Everything coming together and falling apart, all at the same time," he said finally, and even though it didn't really make sense, she nodded in agreement.

"How did this happen? I mean, how can she know so fast?"

He squinted and his mind raced as he remembered something.

He climbed in through his bedroom window, still drenched in blood and bile, landing on his floor with a thud. He was glad that the car wasn't in the driveway, that meant his parents were not home. This was the last thing his mother needed to see.

Xander turned around and looked up the stairs. "Mom?" he called upwards to no reply. He sighed and looked onto the kitchen counter. There was a plate of chicken covered in plastic wrap waiting for him. Water vapour clung to the outside of it, and it was frigged cold to touch. Next to it was a short note: Alex, Gone over to the hospital to see the Kennessy's. Eat some chicken, and go to bed at a decent hour. We'll be home late. -Love, Mom.

He looked through the bathroom garbage, pushing aside bits of tissue and empty toilet paper rolls, and a few used prescription bottles, then finally found what he had been searching for...

"Actually, I think it's been happening for a while," he said quietly, snuggling into Cathy's shoulder. He hadn't even realized that she had started holding him, but that was all right as far as he was concerned. "I think we just didn't notice."

"This doesn't mean anything," she said, pulling back so she could look at him. "This wasn't you, it couldn't have been. You know that, right?"

He said nothing, didn't move. Didn't even breathe, as far as she could tell. She thought that maybe he was in shock, but didn't know how to tell for sure. "I should call her," he said after a long moment, reaching for his cordless phone and depressing the receiver. There was a clicking sound, followed by another, and then the dial tone hummed to life.

"Call who?" Cathy asked, looking down at the phone quizzically. When he didn't answer she watched him dial. He got three digits in and he realized that the person he was calling wasn't in Coral Beach. "No!" she yelled, moving to grab the phone from him, but he jerked it away, finishing the number sequence with his thumb. "You can *not* call her!" she ordered, falling to the floor as she again made a grab for the phone and missed, banging her knee off the wheel on his chair.

The ringing stopped, and Julie Peterson's voice rang out over the line. "Hello?" she chimed, sounding chipper.

Xander's face went white and he just sat there, listening to the sound of her voice.

"Hello?" it came again, more annoyed this time. "Is anyone there? Hell - low - oh?" Finally she disconnected the call, and Xander's ear was once again graced with the low hum of dial tone until he turned the phone off again.

Julie stared at him, her face deadly serious. "What you really love more than anything. You love death Xander Drew... and as long as you do, death will keep following you."

"What was the point of that?" Cathy asked, rubbing the knee she had banged.

He looked at her, really at her, for the first time since he had told her the news, and started to cry again, retracting his claws and burying his eyes into his palms. He sat there on his knees in the burned carpet of his bedroom and cried like a newborn. She reached out to hold him but he swatted her away.

She hit him and then moved to embrace him again, and this time he complied.

Gallagher opened the large wooden door to his chapel just a crack and peered out at who was knocking, then opened it completely and smiled warmly. "Hello, kind sir," he said, adjusting his white collar, more out of habit than of a need to. "And what can I do for you this evening?"

Officer Adrian Extol glared at Gallagher from under the peak of his uniform hat, the smallest twinge of sympathy for the man floating in his eyes briefly, then leaving again. Behind him, another officer leaned against their squad car in the parking lot, its lights flashing blue and red intermittently. He heaved a sigh, then finally spoke. "Robert Gallagher?" he asked, tipping up his hat.

"Yes, I'm *Reverend* Robert Gallagher," he said, correcting the man, but trying not to sound pretentious.

Extol pulled a pair of handcuffs from his side and snapped one loop around Gallagher's wrist, and it snapped shut quickly and tightly. "Not no more, you ain't."

"What is the meaning on this?" Gallagher bellowed, a look of shock overcoming his face as the policeman finished.

"You have the right to remain silent. Should you choose to waive that right, anything you say can and will be held against you in a court of law. You have the right to an attorney. If you cannot afford..."

But Gallagher wasn't hearing it anymore. His face was pale and his eyes were blank as he was helped into the squad car and carted off to the precinct.

"Want to run that one by me again?" Cathy asked, raising an eyebrow as she clutched the phone tightly to her ear.

"Gallagher just got arrested," Mike repeated, his words filled with just as much astonishment as hers, even he was the one delivering the news.

Xander lay on the bed rubbing his eyes with his thumbs, hard. "And today, we continue a long tradition of Guidance Councilors in Coral Beach," he mumbled before plopping his hands down against the mattress and using them to brace himself up. "So, what are we going to do about it?" he asked, loud enough that Mike could hear him, too.

Cathy didn't speak, and there was silence from Mike's end of the line too. "What do you mean?" she said finally, breaking the silence.

"Yeah," Mike agreed, his voice muffled a little as he spat out toothpaste. "Mystery solved, man. Bad guy already in cuffs, good cops probably having a beer already. Not everything has to be a huge drama, man."

"I guess," Xander said, slumping down into himself. "It just seems too easy, is all."

"Tell that to that poor kid," Mike tisked, disgusted. "I never liked that guy."

"I thought he was okay."

"Me too," Cathy said, placing a hand on Xander's shoulder. "But this is too much, Xander. This is beyond even the thought of forgiveness."

"I know," he sighed, then snatched up the phone and brought it to his mouth. "I know," he repeated into the mouthpiece, louder and clearer than the first time.

"What?" Mike said innocently, raising his eyebrows from the other end.

"I heard what you said."

"I didn't say anything."

"Super. Human. Hearing. Don't make me say it again."

"You're a knob," Mike grunted, and there was a soft jingle as he put his toothbrush away.

There was silence then from Xander's side, and Cathy motioned for him to give her back the phone. He ignored her.

"You're gonna wanna talk to him, won't you?" Mike heaved, the frustration in his voice evident.

Xander nodded. After a full minute of no response from Mike, he said "Yes."

"Fine," Mike spat. "But don't act all depressed when this turns out bad. Because I guarantee you, this will turn out bad."

"Yeah, yeah," Xander drawled, smiling out of the corner of his mouth and before handing the phone back to Cathy.

"You coming over again tonight?" she asked, the former subject closed as far as she was concerned.

"Um, no," Mike replied dumbly. "I think your mom would cut off a few parts of me that I'm rather attached to."

Cathy giggled, then turned and saw Xander staring at her with one eyebrow raised. She coughed. "What are you doing, then? Can I come over there?"

"Actually, I think I'm going to be staying over with Xander tonight."

To her side, Xander shook his head wildly, waving his arms back and forth in negative response.

"Xander thinks that's a great idea," Cathy smirked, winking.

Xander slumped, then mumbled something incoherent.

"Love you too, hun. Bye." She pressed the receiver to disconnect the call and looked smugly at Xander.

"You enjoyed doing that, didn't you?"

"Yes," she chirped, then sat back at his desk to write some more.

Mike put the phone back on its cradle and smiled, the echo of his lover's voice still ringing in his ears. He gave himself one last quick look in the mirror, then rubbed his hand across his chin to see if he'd gotten all of the stubble. He smacked his face then walked out of the bathroom and into his bedroom.

He opened the drawer to his nightstand and started to ruffle through it, pushing aside candies and school papers that should have been passed in days ago and saline solution, even though nobody he knew wore contacts. Finally he withdrew a small scrap of paper, beaten, torn, and worn around the edges, the numbers on it were faded but still very visible.

Megan Greene = 555-5428 ext. 308

He pressed down on the big button in the center of his phone (the numbers on it having long since been scratched off, probably by him while very bored one night when there was nothing on television) and dialed the digits, then waited as the phone rang four times before someone on the other end picked up.

"Hello," came Megan's professional voice from the other end of the line.

"Hi, Miss. Greene, it's Mike..."

"You're reached the law firm of Mayer, Summers and Soul, the office of Megan Greene. I'm not at my desk or working on an important case right now, so please leave your message at the sound of the tone and I'll get back to you as soon as I can... -BEEP-"

He sighed, knocking the receiver against his forehead once before bringing the phone back to its rightful position. "Hi Megan, it's Mike -- Mike Harris," he said, his voice sounding tired and mechanical. He hated talking to machines. "I'm just calling to... to tell you that if you hear from Xander in the next few days, just say no, okay? Really, it's just for the best. I think he's having a hard time and... anyway, it's nothing. Just, don't listen to him if he calls."

"To save your message, press one. To re-record it, press two. To delete, press three."

Mike looked at the phone for a moment, then finally pressed three. He tossed the phone onto his bed, then pulling on his hair until some of it came out.

In her office, Megan looked at the phone with one eyebrow raised, her hand still clasping the pen she'd been using to finish her notes on the Styles case file.

"Message not saved," her answering machine informed her coldly, as she leaned back in her chair and tapped her pen against her mouth thoughtfully.

CHAPTER TWENTY-TWO: JUSTICE

It was three in the morning and Cathy was still at her computer, typing away at what she had begun to call 'her manuscript' in her head, her fingers pounding against the keys furiously. She had considered transcribing what she had written in the notebooks onto the computer, then decided against it when she realized where she was in the story. Even though the subject disgusted her while making her want to cry, the words flew out of her like nothing else, each one exploding onto the page with a burst on emotion.

I thought an explosion had gone off next to my head, and a big slab on concrete slammed into me, making me buckle over. For some reason, the first thing that crossed my mind was Genblade. That almost seems silly, now... but not really. Up until that point, he had definitely been the most nightmarish thing I had seen in my life... *up until that point.*

It towered over me, filling the entirety of the hole it had created in the side of the school. It looked human, just larger, but I quickly realized that it wasn't. It had no lower jaw, its mouth just joined with its chest in a maw of teeth and blood red gums. It had the parts of a human, the arms and legs and head; but they swirled and distorted of their own conviction. It was like someone made a sculpture of a person in half-formed Jell-O and it was baying in the wind.

Its claws were massive each easily the size of my hand, one on each of its three fingers.

Twirling, churning tendrils swarmed around it everywhere, each one making spikes and then retreating them, like a lizard sticking out its tongue to sniff the air. Its face turned toward me... not its head, just its face, as through the skin wasn't attached to the bone, and it bellowed, long and loud: "Zakron!"

I felt fear wash over me, replacing blood in my face as it all drained out. It lashed out with one arm and hit me broadside. The bruise was there for over a month, and I felt the brief sensation of flying.

When I woke up three hours later, I wasn't pregnant anymore.

She stopped writing, rubbing her abdomen tenderly and looking down at it. In her mind's eye it looked as though there were a basketball under her shirt, the way she would have looked by now had that not happened. She took a deep breath and waited for tears. When they didn't come and she was sure they wouldn't, she continued.

Her name would have been Amora Jasmine Harris if she had lived, I think...

Mike woke up the next day with the church roof leaking on him, a small puddle having formed in the nape of his chest. He groaned and rubbed the bridge of his nose as he picked up his copy of 'The Lord of the Flies' from where it rested against his groin and laid in down on the floor next to the pew he had slept on, wondering what time it was.

"Let me out," Xander said simply, taunt forward as much as he could be in his chains, looking at his friend with grim determination.

Mike arose, blinked twice to adjust to the dank church, then grunted and scratched his chest. After a moment to compose himself he turned and looked at Xander, who was still lulling the bindings as close to him as he could. "How

298

long have you been awake?" he asked, his voice monotone and achy.

"Two hours," he responded curtly. "Let me out."

"No rush, man," he assured his friend after a quick glance at his watch. "We've still got plenty of time before we have to get to school."

"Not going to school. Not right away, anyway." He gave his left chain a good tug and made it rattle. He was soaked in his own blood again, the black ooze on the floor having long since dried and become crystalline, as if someone had just tarred the floor of the confessional.

Mike rolled his eyes, his arms falling to his sides and away from the keys that hung at his belt. "You're not seriously going where I think you're going, are you?" he asked, even though he already knew the answer.

"I have to know. I need to be sure that Gallagher is guilty."

"This may be hard for you to believe," Mike drawled as he removed the keys from his belt loop and fumbled through them, finding the correct one and sliding it into the left arm shackle. "But there was a justice system *before* you became the Black Womb."

Xander looked at him flatly, but did not speak.

"I'm just saying."

"Yeah, well. Feel free to stop doing that anytime you want."

Mike shot him an annoyed look as he finished unlocking the last shackle.

Xander stepped forward a pace or two, stretched, then moved to pick up his clothes.

"You're feeling better today," Mike noted, noticing the bounce in his friend's step.

"Mmm."

"Is there any way I can convince you not to do this?" he pleaded, hands out before him.

"No."

"You're going to kill again," Mike finally said, making a fist as he said the words he had desperately not wanted to. "That's the only way it ever ends with the Womb, you know. Somebody bleeding and dead on the ground. That's its idea of justice. It'll either be Gallagher or that kid or Calla - -"

"Calla?" Xander repeated as he slid into his dark green t-shirt, turning his head and acknowledging that Mike was speaking, finally.

"Yeah, this girl at school. She was the one who convinced the kid to go to the cops."

"She the one that was smoking pot?"

"I never told you someone was - "

"I can still smell it on your clothes."

"I changed."

"On your skin then."

"I showered."

"Then you didn't do a very good job," he mumbled as he put on his black hiking boots, lacing them quickly as he sat on the hard wooden pews. "Let me do this, even if you don't help. Worst case scenario, I find out the cops were right

299

and then let it be."

"That *isn't* the worst case scenario when the Womb's involved," he reminded, pointing a finger to the right side of Xander's gut.

"It's taking my mind off things. Off my mom..."

Mike stared his friend in the eye, then finally relented. "Fine. Go. Be Sherlock Holmes for all I care, just don't do anything that I'll have to stab you for."

Xander saluted, then turned and started to head for the door. Mike watched him go for a second or two, then looked up and the monument of Jesus on the Cross and followed.

The buds of the elm opened and her leaves looked up and saw the sun, but never forgot the cold of the winter night. No matter how warm it got, the winter was in her now.

Cathy looked from side to side at the mostly vacant cells, her nose twitching from the smell of dried sweat and urine as she stared past the bars. One very close to her had blood in it, the little press-on label just to the side of the cell read: Shnieder. She averted her eyes from it as quickly as possible, realizing that Xander was a few steps ahead of her and quickly moving to catch up.

"Hey," came a voice from her side, and she turned quickly to see who it was. A man leaned against the bars of his cell, his hairy arms hanging out of it casually as he looked at her, his eyes darted up and down her body, then ran one hand through his thinning black hair. "My name's Malcolm, what's yours?"

Her eyebrows lowered as she took a cautious step back from his cell, and finally noticed that he was touching himself. One of his hands had been slid down the front of his prison jumpsuit, and was rubbing vigorously.

Cathy balked in disgust and she gagged. She thought that she might throw up.

"Why don't you come here a - - Shut up, Bitch!" he yelled, spinning around quickly and yelling at the toilet, which did nothing to respond to his outburst except drip a little onto the floor. "If I've told you once, I've told you a million times to just shut up! She wants it, there's nothing *wrong* with that!" He turned back toward the bars quickly, pressing his body against them and thrusting his arms out at Cathy, as if trying to squeeze through.

- tap tap -

Malcolm turned to the side of his cage, where Xander leaned against the opposite side of the bars, tapping one slightly raised talon against the metal to get his attention and smiling. Malcolm nearly jumped out of his skin, stumbling backward and slamming his rear end onto the floor. "Christ!" he yelled, then scurried under his bunk and stayed there in silence for a moment, then he mumbled quietly. "Shut up, you bitch."

Xander chuckled a little, then his smile faded as he turned to Cathy. "You okay?"

"Yeah..." she said, still staring at the man under the bed, then finally tore her frightened eyes away from him. "Yes. Isn't that...?"

"Yes, it is. Don't dawdle. Not here," he cautioned, cocking his head toward the far end of the hall and then heading in that direction, followed quickly by Cathy.

She tried not to look after that, but her eyes still strayed from side to side, mostly to the name plates on the empty cells that had yet to be removed. She was surprised at how many of them she recognized, then realized that she probably shouldn't be. Char's name was there, and so was Owchar's. Then, no matter how hard she tried not to see it, was Smith. Derek Smith's old cell.

A shiver ran down her spine and she walked a little faster, until she was side by side with Xander. "Why did I have to be here again?" she asked, getting as close to him as possible without actually latching on.

"You weren't friends with Gallagher," he stated, keeping his eyes straight ahead.

"Only met him a few times."

"You're not biased. I am. I want him to be innocent, I'll find a way to believe he is."

Cathy stopped, and after a second, so did he, turning to look at her. "What? Don't you think you should talk to the kid instead? No matter what, Gallagher's going to say he didn't do it, Xander. Innocent or guilty, he'll say he's innocent."

Xander gave her a look that made her heart go out to him, and then they both continued walking without a word.

"I hate this place," she said after a moment.

"I think that's the point," Xander mused, smirking at her just a little.

He stopped, turned to his left and staring through the bars of the cell they'd arrived at. At first, he'd thought maybe he'd gotten the number wrong, the man inside looked nothing like Robert Gallagher. His balding hair was sticking off on either side of his head, and an orange prison jumpsuit with numbers stamped across the left breast replaced his black suit and white collar. Then the slight breeze inside the penitentiary changed, and Xander got a good whiff of him. Of the fear that rolled off him like a fog, and knew he was at the right place.

"Father?" he asked, and Cathy raised an eye to him. His voice was softer when he spoke to Gallagher, more child-like. She hadn't heard anything like that come out of his mouth since Sara died. Maybe even before that.

Gallagher looked up, his face drawn down in an exaggerated frown and bags under his eyes. He looked like his face was melting, and the tears only helped toward that illusion. "My son?" he asked, squinting and rubbing his eyes as he sat on the edge of his cot, then finally stood up and started to walk over to the bars.

Cathy stepped back half a pace.

Gallagher looked at her, hurt, then forced a warm smile in her direction. "Miss. Kennessy," he said in greeting, giving her a little nod.

Xander reached up, holding a bar in each hand and looking through them. "How are you?"

Gallagher sighed, and his heart raced for a split second, then slowed again. Xander struggled to hear, and the Womb surged inside him to help, making every footfall of every rat in the building become as clear as day to him. "I'm fine. That awful man down the hall seemed to take an unhealthy interest in me at breakfast, but then he began to yell at someone who wasn't there and wandered off."

Xander nodded. "Tell me if he gives you any trouble."

There was a silence between them then, as both men could only think of questions that they did not want to ask. Finally Gallagher broke it, his heart skipping a beat. "You think I did it, don't you?"

Xander listened, and the man's heart rate was still steady. "I don't know what to think, Father. That's why I'm here."

Behind him, Cathy rolled her eyes.

"And what about you, Miss?" Gallagher asked, raising his head to see over Xander's, getting a full look at the girl's troubled face.

Xander listened, his beat was still regular.

"You don't want to know," Cathy replied honestly. "But I hope you're innocent."

The heart sank, its beat slower again. Depression, Xander labeled it.

"Father, I hate to ask..." Xander sighed.

"No, I certainly did not," Gallagher protested, his cheeks flapping in outrage before calming again.

Pulse was mostly steady, except for the anger. "I'm going to be a part of this, sir, just like I was with August. Is there anything I should know now?"

"No," Gallagher sighed, eyeing the boy. He looked even more depressed than a moment before, somehow. "No, there isn't, Alexander."

His pulse skipped twice there, once around each time he said no. Xander furrowed his brow and shot a pained glance back at Cathy before looking back at Gallagher. "I want you to know something," he almost whispered, mindful of the guards at the end of the hall.

Gallagher perked his ears, his smile clearly fake.

"If I'm in this, I'm in it all the way. If I prove you're innocent, that's great. If I prove otherwise... well, let's just say you'll see a side of me you never have before." He turned on his heels without saying goodbye and marched back toward the entrance.

Cathy stood, eye to eye with Gallagher before turning and running to catch up with Xander.

"What do you think?" he asked the second she got close enough to him.

She gasped, trying to catch her breath between words. "I think he showed a lot of empathy during the Styles thing that I'm not seeing here, and that's got to mean something." She paused, taking another lungful of air. "What about you, Mr. Super-Human-Hearing, what's the verdict?"

"I don't know," he stated angrily as he shoved open the exit into the main hall with Cathy in hot pursuit.

"What do you mean you don't know?" Mike yelled, thrusting his arms out, his blonde eyebrows shooting upward comically. Xander sat on the snow-covered picnic table in front of him, rubbing his own knotted shoulders rhythmically, wondering why the healing factor didn't take of such things for him. Cathy was standing between the two, her arms folded in front of her and staring downward, watching as her foot made concentric semi-circles all around her. Mike took off his jacket, suddenly deciding that he was sweating, and tossed it on the table. It hit Xander. "Super. Human. Senses," he said in a mocking tone, flapping one palm open and closed like a puppet. "Who was it that kept saying that? Was it you, yeah, I thought so. How could you not know?"

Xander looked up, running his hands over his face as he did, stretching it out. "He responded differently to two different questions. He said he did nothing to the kid, and his heart beat was steady, means he's telling the truth."

"So?" Mike said, looking confused. "There's your answer, isn't it?"

"Then I asked him if he did anything to the kid I should know about, he said no twice, his heart did a double-beat both times."

"Means he's lying," Cathy said absently, remembering an episode of some television show where they had the characters hooked up to a polygraph machine, the little marker waving back and forth jaggedly on the page as he lead character lied.

Mike sighed, kicking a snow drift and sending large clumps flying in every direction. Cathy reached out once to touch him, then rethought it.

"Will you calm the fuck down?" Xander said, irritated. "I really don't need it right now."

Again, Mike's eyebrow's rose. "Again, just don't come crawling to me when this one blows up in your face, because it has disaster written across it in bright shiny letters, man."

"Noted," he said, keeping his eyes on the back entrance to the school a hundred or so feet in front of him as he reached into his inside jacket pocket and produced a cigarette, pinning it between his lips and then lighting it.

Cathy coughed, even though the smoke was nowhere near her yet. He gave her a droll look, and she smirked.

"So, what's your plan now, hero?" Mike teased, jabbing his friend in the arm.

Xander took a short drag then removed the smoke from his mouth, motioning toward the door with it. "Already in action," he said, as if that explained all.

Both Mike and Cathy turned toward the door and watched it for a second, then back to Xander. "What?" Cathy said finally, taking the word out of Mike's mouth.

"Hold it," Xander said, smiling wide. "I can smell it. She's coming now."

This time only Mike turned, waited a little longer, then back again. "You having another fever dream, man?"

"Wait for it. Three... two... one..."

Calla McFadden opened the back door and stepped out, glancing behind her quickly, and then reached into her pocket and pulled out a metal case and headed for the smoking section, where the brick wall met the fence.

Xander smiled, his eyes following her until she disappeared behind the cornerstone.

Mike turned back to him, no small amount of panic behind his eyes. "No," he said, and it came out as an order.

"What?" Xander smirked, throwing his smoke to the ground.

"You are not going near that girl," he said in the same tone, folding his arms and stepping up toward his friend. His chest was level with Xander's head, and he used it to try and exert dominance over him, and tactic he'd used many times in their shared youth.

"It's not a good idea, Xander," Cathy agreed, taking a step toward him herself, but still behind Mike. "Gallagher's not worth that."

Xander shot her a look.

"Come on, you know what I mean. Phillips, O'Toole, now him... it's a little too convenient, don't you think?"

"Everything about this is too convenient," he mumbled, then got up from the table and started to walk over toward the smoking section.

Mike stepped in front of him, still towering overhead.

Xander looked up at him, almost having to crane his neck to do so, flaring his nostrils slightly. He stepped to one side and started to walk again, and this time Mike made no effort to stop him, placing his head in one hand and shaking them both.

Cathy sighed, standing on her tip-toes to give her lover a kiss. "Watch him. Make sure he doesn't do anything stupid. I'm going to go find that kid, hope that cooler heads prevail."

"That's likely," Mike cursed, returning the kiss and watching her walk toward the school, then turning to follow Xander.

ʌ⟨ʌ

"That smells like feet," Xander said, causing Calla to twist her head uncomfortably in his direction. She had been in mid-puff and almost dropped her joint. "I could smell it from over there."

The shock wore off her face as she looked him up and down, and became a sly smile. "Want some?" she asked, handing the joint to him and sticking out her tongue, revealing a small pink stud in it not far from the tip.

Xander took the rolled up paper from her and watched the smoke rise from its tip for a moment before handing it back. "No, thanks," he said as she took it.

She shrugged, then brought it to her lips and took another draw. She held it in as long as possible before letting it out. "Your loss. This is some kick-ass stuff."

"I'm sure." He patted his jacket for his smokes and realized that he just had one and stopping himself.

Again her eyes danced over him, sizing up every square inch of him. This time he felt it, and repressed the goosebumps it invoked. "You're Xander Drew, aren't you?"

304

Xander regarded her with an amount of curiosity. "I don't know you, but you know me."

"I'm Calla," she smiled, but did not extend a hand, just stayed there in her relaxed stance against the wall. She took another puff, quicker this time. "I was in Evan and Mandy's Lit class. Didn't do so well last year so they let me repeat for credit."

"Huh," Xander grunted, noticing the red streak in her hair.

She smiled at him devilishly. "Wondering if the carpet matches the drapes?" she laughed.

Xander stared at her until he finally got the joke and smirked. "Cute," he said finally. He found himself comfortable around her, but couldn't place why.

She brought the joint to her lips again, and it was getting down to the butt now. She looked over the rising smoke at him. "Sure you don't want any?"

Xander did not respond, just waved his hand once to dismiss the idea. He saw it now. She reminded him of Julie.

She took a last puff, then tossed the roach into the snow and turned back to him, standing to face him now. "So, what do you want?"

"I just want to ask you something about that kid you helped," Xander said honestly, appreciating her forwardness.

"Hmm," she half hummed, half-laughed, coming even closer to him. He almost wanted to back up a little, but didn't. "Can you ask me them in bed?" she asked, again flashing him her tongue ring.

"Excuse me?" Xander asked, perplexed.

"You know -- pillow talk. Can you ask me the questions... afterwards?" she asked, her eyes locked onto his as she reached out and touched him on the arm, gently at first, then grabbing at it.

"Okay, that's enough," Mike said, coming out from around the corner and grabbing Calla firmly by the arm. "That's enough chocolate for you today."

"Hey," Calla protested, her cheeks livid with anger as Mike gave her a polite shove toward the door. "I was - -"

"Just leaving." Mike finished, saluting a wave to her. "I know. Bon voyage."

Calla huffed then cursed loudly, stomping her way through the snow toward the door.

"Thanks," Xander chuckled when Mike rejoined him, there was already a smoke between his lips. "Weird girl, huh?"

"Yeah," Mike smiled, sitting down next to his friend and leaning his head back against the wall, the first time he'd really been relaxed since waking up. "She reminds me of Peterson."

"Which one?" Xander asked, smoke curling around his head.

"Take your pick," Mike shot back. They both laughed.

There was silence for a few moments as Xander smokes, and he ended it as he doubted it. "Listen, man, I'm sorry about..."

Mike smiled, and it stopped him in mid-sentence. "Me too. But we're supposed to butt heads. It's what we do. Don't worry, I think everything's going to be fine."

Xander shot him a look. "You really believe that?"

"No, but it sounds nice."

Xander nodded, then looked up as Cathy came around the corner to join them, her face pale white. "Did you find the kid?"

"Um, yeah," she said, crumpling her brow.

Silence.

"And?" Mike asked, gesturing his hands in a rolling motioned, trying to coax the words out of her mouth.

"He said that Calla McFadden's been touching him."

CHAPTER TWENTY-THREE: FLESH

Cathy flipped the page of the file folder, letting a long breath out from her puffy cheeks. The library smelled like the oddly comforting mixture of stake old book and fresh, newly printed ones, with one scent overtaking the other depending on which section one sat it. The smell of Mrs. Grimes' rose oil perfume was also unmistakable, even though she was all the way across the hall at her desk. "You sure we should be doing this in public?" Cathy asked, glancing at the large stack of file folders they'd swiped from Gallagher's desk before coming in.

"It's not public, it's the library," Xander said, running a finger over the page in a way that he was told helped with speed-reading. "Besides, if she catches us, what's she going to do? Send us to the Guidance Councilor? Or maybe the Principal?"

"Good point," Cathy conceded, turning the page again. "Who is this Nick Carry kid anyway? I don't remember him."

"Dropped out," Mike mumbled, taking a sip of his coffee but never once taking his eyes off the page. "Some said he transferred, but he dropped out."

"Looks like he had it rough," she sighed, closing that file and laying it aside with all the others they'd already checked through.

"Did he get crucified?" Xander asked, almost completely under his breath.

"No..."

"I win."

She rolled her eyes, then grabbed another unmarked file and opened it. "Hey, I think I got one," she said excitedly, standing up out of her chair.

Xander and Mike both moved to see as she lay the folder flat against the table, a photo of Jaden looking out at all of them, and large toothy grin across his face.

"Says here he said one of his teachers touched him a year and a half ago..." Mike mumbled, pointing to the information as he found it.

"He said Phillips did, too," Cathy chimed in, disgusted.

"Yeah, but he didn't," Xander said angrily, hoisting up the file he'd been reading. "And a few months later this girl said the same thing about Phillips, and they dismissed it citing that kid."

Mike craned his head to see the folder Xander was talking about. From inside, a picture of Greer Donaldson looked back at him sweetly. She had been one of Phillips' victims, and was still in a coma to this day. He cursed.

"Again," Cathy said, having flipped to the next page and pointing near the bottom. "When he was in Kindergarten. He said it was... his parents."

Mike cursed again, slamming his fist down against the table. "Dammit!"

Xander rubbed a hand through his hair, looking down at the kid's file. "What if it's not true? What if I read Gallagher wrong? I mean, the little boy that cried wolf got eaten at the end -- right?"

Mike nodded. "Sad thing is, he probably was abused at some point, maybe even before he can remember, and now all this is just... ugh."

"Transference?" Cathy offered, touching his hand lovingly.

"Thanks, honey," he smiled, rubbing her thumb in response.

Xander again tugged at his hair, then observed the both of them, his face devoid of emotion. "We need help," he said finally.

⚬⟨⟩⚬

"Hello. You're reached the law firm of Mayer, Summers and Soul, the office of Megan Greene. I'm not at my desk or working on an important case right now, so please leave your message at the sound of the tone and I'll get back to you as soon as I can... -BEEP-"

"Megan?" came Xander's rough, scratchy voice; and Megan immediately turned toward the machine, her pen dropping from her hand and rolling along the floor. "Megan, it's me. Pick up."

Her hand shook just a little as she reached for the receiver, then she stopped and frowned. She let out a heavy sigh, then retracted her hand and took another pen from the clay dispenser next to her paperweight rather than picking up the one she had dropped.

There was silence on the other end of the line for a moment, but the machine did not beep, so she knew he was still waiting for her to pick up.

She pretended to look over her case notes on the Bird and Snelgrove trail. She twirled her hair around her fingers, the words on the page becoming one big blur to her.

"Hey," the voice from the telephone said again, a little short this time. "You don't have Mimosas this time of the week until eight, and I know you're not home. Pick up the phone."

She bit her lower lip hard, her teeth playing clear contrast to her red lipstick. She clenched her fist so tight that her nails dug into her palm, but she did not reach for the receiver.

There was a sigh on the other end of the line, and then the sound of the caller hanging up their phone. "-BEEP - message not saved," the answering machine said in its cold, mechanical voice.

She smiled, wiggling a little in her chair to shake off the call, and then turned her attention back to the file. The appeal yesterday had gone well, and she thought that the jury was on her side, but one of the defendants had the mitigating circumstances of his father's recent death and was a single parent - -

RIIING!

She cursed, slamming her pen back onto the desk and turning to glare at the phone, her eyes wide with rage. She was tempted to unplug it, or maybe forward all the calls to her machine at home so she could get some work done, but decided that Nathan would kill her if she did.

"Hello. You're reached the law firm of Mayer, Summers and Soul, the office of Megan Greene. I'm not at my desk or working on an important case right now, so please leave your message at the sound of the tone and I'll get back to you as soon as I can... -BEEP-"

"Hey," came a male voice, albeit a different one. This one was deeper and clearer, none of the scratch of the last one, and sounded more masculine, without the telltale squeak of adolescence. "It's Mike, Mike -- will you shut up?" he said suddenly in a whispered voice, and there was a muffled sound that she recognized as a caller placing the mouth of the phone against his or her shirt to avoid being heard. She raised an eyebrow. "I'm telling her, just -- I'm sorry, okay? I was -- fine, you're right just -- shut up and go have a smoke, you damn idiot." There was a huff at the other end of the line, and the muffled sound of fabric stopped as the caller returned. "Mike Harris," he continued, as if the middle part had never taken place. "I don't know if you got a message from me yesterday, I didn't think I saved it. Anyway, whatever it said -- I was wrong, I guess. Maybe. Just, if you hear from Xander..." again, the muffled sound, and his voice became hushed again. "This is stupid, if she could hear you and she can hear me, why are we being so -- oh, that's nice, man. You can sit on that and spin - - BEEP- message not saved."

She laughed a little at that last bit, trying to imagine what the conversation would have looked like had she been there to witness it. She laid down her pen and rested her chin on her hand, waiting patiently for the phone to ring again.

RIIING! "Hello. You're reached the law firm of Mayer, Summers and Soul, the office of Megan Greene. I'm not at my desk or working on an important case right now, so please leave your message at the sound of the tone and I'll get back to you as soon as I can... -BEEP-"

"Pick it up," said the rough voice again. "Don't make me put Cathy on the phone."

She reached out and pressed the speaker button to open the line and smirked to herself, picking up her red pen and making a small notation in her line of questioning for tomorrow as she did so. "Hello, Mr. Alexander Drew. And to what do I owe the pleasure of this call?"

"Cute," he chuckled, and she could have sworn she heard the crumpling and cracking of that disgusting leather jacket he wore as he leaned in closer to the phone. A pay phone, she thought. "You always screen your calls?"

"Only since I met you," she mused.

"Hey, you're my lawyer."

"To my recollection you have never paid anyone a dime in legal fees, so that would mean that you don't have a lawyer, Mr. Drew," she said, pretending to make her voice as fake as the machines as she finished one last note, then closed the folder and slid it to one side, clasping her fingers together and addressing the phone as she would a client. "Now, what can I do for you?"

There was a pause, then. "I hear a hum."

"See a doctor, not a lawyer."

"No, I mean -- do you have me on speaker phone?"

"Yes."

"Take me off, please."

She looked at the speaker on the phone oddly, weighing the sincerity of his voice. "There's -- nobody else here. The walls are soundproofed."

"Megan, take me off speaker phone, please."

She reached out and picked up the phone and placed it to her ear. "There. Now, what's so important. If it's about August, let me assure you that everything's fine."

"No, I need your help. It's about Reverend Gallagher - -"

She grinned, leaning her chair back until she almost slipped, then righting herself. "I heard. You have nothing to worry about. Tony's on the case, and he's going to made sure that guy never hurts another child again, okay? Mike's right. You should stay out of this one."

"No, no," Xander interjected, and she could hear that grin on his face. It was the same one he'd used on her during the Genblade trial and when they'd caught Shnieder. She called it the 'I'm about to drop the bomb on you' grin. "I think Gallagher's innocent. I know he is."

Megan sucked in a long breath of air, then let it out as slow as possible. Her head started to hurt around the eyes in a way she had begun to associate with his requests. "You can't be asking what I think you are. Even if I had the time --"

"Make time," he said bluntly, and she knew that he had shrugged as only a fifteen year old boy could.

"I can't, Xander. I have an important case..."

"Ask for a continuance, or something."

"This *is* my continuance!"

"This is important."

"So is the seventy-something year old man looking to get justice on the two assholes that broke into his store months back. I don't think he can take much more of this trial, Xander..."

"Suppose I could take care of that?" he said musically, even a little whimsically.

She rolled her eyes. "You don't even know what I'm talking about."

"Ron Snelgrove and Adam Bird, right? Convenience store heist, about three months back?"

She sat in her chair, bewildered. Almost falling again, she decided her high-school teachers had discouraged against leaning them for a reason and stopped. After a moment of sitting there slack jawed, she said "How did you...?"

"Grapevine. Small town, you know how it is. Was going to check on the old man, but when I heard you were involved, figured you had it covered. But I can handle that, you handle this... cause I can't."

"Xander," she plead, digging her nails into her scalp, wishing for it to be five so she could have a drink with this conversation. "It's not a case I can win. They *are* going to make an example of Gallagher. They *are* going to massacre him on the stand, and that kid's testimony is all the judge is going to need to hear to start the trial that'll put your friend away for the rest of his life."

"Testimony?"

"What?"

"You just said something about a testimony?"

"Yes," Megan said, grabbing her coffee and taking a long slug of it. "The trial's not for a little while, but the kid speaks to the judge with the prosecutor and the defendant tomorrow, along with the arresting officer. They want the kid's story on the record so that he doesn't have to appear at the trail. The kid's been through enough."

Xander was silent for a moment, and she could hear him tapping his lip in thought.

"Xander?"

"Be there, tomorrow. Call your boss, Tony, the Judge... I don't care. You're Gallagher's defense, just in case I can't work out something better."

"But my case --"

"You owe me," he said flatly, losing some of his good nature, but not all. She got the feeling this was him without the smiles and lace he put on around her.

"No, I don't. I *did* owe you for the Genblade thing."

"The August case, which you won with my help. The case you did pro-bono, giving your firm no end of good publicity and putting you in your bosses good graces. What's his name again?"

"Nathan Summers."

"Right. Seems nice," he said, and there was a hint of connotation in his voice.

"Yes, he is."

"Good. It's nice that he's so nice."

She paused, and this time it was her turn to put the phone against her shirt. She bit her lip until it hurt, then brought the phone to her ear again. "Fine. I'll be there, Xander. But only tomorrow, and if it looks bad, I'm removing myself from the case entirely, and that'll be the last I have to do with it."

"Thanks," he said honestly, if not a little glumly.

"Don't thank me. It's not going to go well. The second that kid tells the Judge what he told the police, it's over for Gallagher, and you know it. I in no way expect to even get the chance to *speak* at this thing tomorrow, let alone do anything to help. It's over. If you really want to do something to help Gallagher, buy him a cake with a file in it."

"Thanks anyway, Megan. I'll come by the bar sometime and have a drink when things wind down a little. We'll catch up."

"Sure. I've got to go. I should be working on my cases. That's plural, now."

"Thanks again. Bye."

"Bye," she said, placing the phone back on its rest and looking at it for a moment. She put her hand back on the Bird and Snelgrove file and slid it toward her, opening it, then closing it again. Getting up from her chair for the first time in hours, she grabbed her blazer and headed for the door.

She suddenly needed a stiff drink.

🦇

Calla stared out the window of the school, watching as Mike, Xander and Cathy walked out the back entrance and out into the world outside the school. She sighed, laying a chubby cheek against her fist as she sun beamed down on her, illuminating her face in a heavenly glow. She turned away from the trio, opening her desk and taking an envelope out of it.

"Hey," came a voice next to her, and she turned to see Tommy leaning in her direction from one seat ahead and to the right. "Can you see where they're goin' from here?"

"What do you care?" she remarked snidely, curling her nose as she looked at him.

"I don't know. Just feel left out is all."

"If you feel left out, it's probably because you *were* left out," she remarked, turning her attention to the sealed envelope on her desk. It was the pure white of any paper right out of the pack and never exposed to the sun's harmful rays, but the edges of it were worn and the corners beaten, like it had been stuffed away in her desk for quite some time. It did not have an address on it, nor any kind of markings whatsoever. She picked up her pen to write on it, then stopped, tapping it against her desk rhythmically as she thought.

"Whatcha got there?" Tommy asked again, nodding his head toward the letter.

"Don't you ever shut up?" she yelled, slamming an open palm against her desk.

Tommy's eyebrows shot up and his head tilted back in shock a little. The outburst drew the attention of Mr. Calender, who stopped writing on the chalk board and looked up at the pair with his hands on his hips. "Is there something you'd like to share?"

"No," Tommy said nonchalantly, beginning to write what he had missed from the board.

Calla shook her head, then put the envelope away again.

🦇

"Feel better?" Xander said, throwing Cathy a look as she came around the back corner of The Factory, sipping on a Cherry Coke through a straw.

"Much. Mike's inside, he was hungry. I don't think he's eaten in days. He said his brain needed food."

Xander nodded, trying to remember the last time he'd eaten and deciding it was irrelevant. He sat on the large, circular stone that pressed up against the edge on the building, now just big enough for two as the snow covered it in.

311

After a moment she joined him, resting the Coke in the middle of her legs between sips. She turned and looked at the big, grey building behind them, which looked kind of like a warehouse from this angle, its siding covered in the mold that the damp of winter brought. "Can't believe this place is closing down next week."

"I killed the owner. It's a miracle her family's kept it open as long as they have," he said, his shoulders sinking.

"You didn't kill Joan."

"We're fairly sure I did. From what Mike found, and all the other craziness that was going on that day... yeah, I killed Joan. I even think I remember it, but I'm never sure. Could just be I've thought about it so much that I imagined remembering it."

"No," she said, touching him on the knee and leaning toward him. All her hair fell to one side, outlining her china-white face with its black, and she looked beautiful. "I meant, *you* didn't kill Joan. The Womb did."

He shot her a look, laughing a little through his nose.

She was silent then for a moment, realizing that he no longer saw much distinction between his two halves, and her body quaked at the thought. She thought back to a time, years ago it seemed now, when they'd both been sitting on this same rock. It had been spring, she thought.

"Oh, look Xander." Cathy said, schooching to the edge of the stone.

"What?" Xander said, grinning as he turned on his heels to see her.

"A squirrel," she replied, her lower lip pouting slightly at the cute sight.

"What?" Xander repeated, a puzzled and sceptical look passing over his face. He thought this would be another of her made-you-look gags, but turned his head anyway. Sure enough, there was a little baby squirrel, no more than a few weeks old. "Oh."

"Oh my gawd, he is the cutest thing," she said, like a child that wanted a toy she knew she could never have. She turned and hit him on the chest suddenly, so excited that she blurted all her words out at once. "Let's name it!"

"Okaaaaay." Xander sighed, pretending to be too mature for her antics. "How about 'squirrel'?"

She tisked and gave him a little slap on the arm. "No! A real name."

"It's a squirrel, Cat. That's why it doesn't have a real name. If your brain is the size of a pea, you don't get a name. It's in the Bible."

"Then why do you get one?" she shot, brow furrowed angrily. "You're just saying that because you can't think of a name anyway."

Xander rolled his eyes, taking a single step forward cautiously until they were shoulder to shoulder. "How about Alvin?"

"It's cliché."

"So's Cathy."

She shot him a look. "Besides, Alvin was a chipmunk."

Xander opened his mouth to respond, then closed it and nodded.

As suddenly as before, she turned and backhanded him across the chest.

"Ow." he winced, though she didn't notice.

312

"Let's name him Bob." she blurted.

"Bob the squirrel." Xander stated bluntly, raising an eyebrow at her.

"Yes. Bob the squirrel." She smiled at him with her big brown eyes and ruby red lips. She knew he was way too uptight to actually get the joke there, which just made it that much more funny. The squirrel gazed up at them, and in the blink of an eye was down on all fours, examining them. "Oh, you little cutie. Come here, Bob."

"He could have rabies." Xander said in caution, gently grabbing Cathy's shoulder to keep her from getting closer.

"Ew. I didn't know squirrels could carry scabies." she said, crinkling her nose as she recoiled from it a little.

Xander burst in laughter, frightening the little animal, although it didn't run.

"What?" Cathy smiled.

He kept laughing, turning his face away from her as he tried to stop.

"What?" she demanded again, pinching his sides to get the answer.

"I said rabies, not scabies." He said, laughing through the words.

"Oh." she said quietly, her face losing all expression for a moment as she filed that away. She shrugged, stepping in close to Bob again, "I don't care about that."

Smiling warmly and making little clucking sounds with her tongue, she reached her hand out slowly and tried to pet him on the head. It looked up at her with large, black eyes as though it were trying to figure her out just as much as she was it. It inched closer to her, its nose twitching and whiskers turning this way and that until finally it turned and bolted back into the woods as quickly as it had appeared. "Oh." She said sadly, as if she'd just lost her best friend. "Bye Bob."

She turned and looked at him, and in comparison to the memory, it was hardly even the same person. So much of the light and innocence had vanished from his eyes, and he always looked tired now. Always looked sad. Quietly, she leaned over and gave him a peck on the cheek.

His eyebrows shot up and he turned toward her, narrowing his eyes in a confused plead. "What was that for?" he said, and he almost seemed frustrated.

Out of the corner of her mouth, she frowned just a little, then ruffled a hand through his bangs to mess them up. "Just wanted to see something," she said, taking another sip from her drink then quickly changing the subject without making eye contact with him again. "Have you figured out what you're doing about the Jaden kid yet?"

"No, I haven't."

"We could talk to his parents, maybe. See what they have to say."

"Kid lives with foster parents. Been in and out of different homes since he was three."

Cathy rolled her eyes. "Wonder how he got molested to begin with."

"Mmm. I don't know, this just isn't the type of thing we're used to. Ever since the thing with Circe and Genblade, it's like there hasn't been anything tactile for me to hit."

"There's no big evil behind it all, it's just evil people."

He groaned, then nodded. "It's just hard is all."

Mike came around the corner, a far-off look in his eyes, as if he were sleep-walking.

"Hey," Cathy chimed, smiling over at her lover.

He did not respond, just stood next to the old rock and looked dazzled.

"What is it?" Xander asked, brow lowered as he got up to face his friend. "What's going on?"

Mike finally woke up, looking for Xander to Cathy and back again. When he spoke, his voice was cracked and dry, and it was as if the taste of them made him sick, his face turning white. "I just had a really bad idea."

It's probably the worst thing we've ever thought of collectively, and the fact that it started as Mike's idea makes me hate him a little, wrote Cathy, sitting at a one of the booths in The Factory. She'd written about the whole Circe thing, and then Xander's relapse into the Black Womb, and she'd just finished Derek's escape and the search for him. She'd slowed down considerably at the end, and now was close enough to date that she could write things as they happened, and found she liked it. After we figured out how we were going to pull it off, Mike had suggested coming into the Factory, to try and enjoy it a little before it closes.

Xander shook his head, mumbling something about 'paying a debt' while glancing at the sun as it got lower in the sky, taking one of those awful cigarettes out of his coat and lighting it. "You guys go. We'll meet up at the place after dark. Until then, try to relax." He didn't look at me while he was talking, but I didn't feel left out. I suppose one could argue that it's because I'm his friend and he cares for me, and he was afraid of what he might see in my eyes if he looked in them after what we'd just talked about. If that's the case, then he'd been right not too, because he would have seen sickness and disgust.

He walked away without a word, the way he's been more and more prone to doing lately. It's like his only concern is with doing the job. Really, he's just the type of person who needs something to be obsessed about. Before all this it was Sara. Before that, his computer. Before that, Thundercats... the list goes on and on.

Mike slammed his hands against the buttons on the game machine, teeth clenched and sweat pouring down his face even though The Factory is very drafty tonight. He's disgusted with himself, as well he should be.

For the first time, I think that Xander was at least half right. Maybe the lines between him and the Black Womb aren't as clear anymore... but maybe the lines separating us from our darker halves aren't so clear either.

She finished off the last of her drink, put down her pen, closed the book, and started to cry.

A minute later Mike noticed and came over with her.

The Womb landed in the snow ten feet inside the alleyway, its legs buckling backward from the impact naturally, righting themselves almost immediately.

Its mouth was open wide, revealing two long rows of jagged teeth and a slender serpent-like tongue. It stood full from the crouched position it had landed in, turning its head hard to the right side until the bones in its neck popped satisfyingly. It stopped then, standing almost completely still, and waited.

Inside the shell of flesh that made up the Womb, Xander Drew could feel the organ in his right side twitching, pumping more of its black blood into its ears, straining them to listen harder. The entire street was pitch black, the moon blotted out by the clouds, but the creature could see just fine.

Further down the alley, something fell, making a soft clanging sound. An empty can from an overflowing garbage bin, perhaps.

The Womb's face turned, then its head. It bellowed long and loud, displaying its teeth once again, and the pair it had been chasing jumped with fright, making their forms clearly visible at the alley's dead end.

"Ron Snelgrove!" it yelled in a voice like broken glass scraped over sandpaper. "Adam Bird!"

The two men shivered beside a trash bin. One, an obese man with a tattoo of a snake covering almost all of his left arm, was covered in soot and grime from where he had fallen trying to outrun the demon a few blocks back, and had landed in a puddle full of butts and garbage. The other was average sized, but his blonde hair was long and straggly, tied back into a pony-tail with a dark blue elastic.

"What do you want?" the fat one (Bird, Xander thought, although he wasn't quite sure) screamed, not trying even though his eyes were glossy with the tears that wanted to come.

Inside the creature, Xander smiled. On the Womb's face, the grin was sickly and menacing, like the way a cartoon skeleton smiles. "Justice," it said, but it came out sounding more like *just this*, which was just as effective as he took a step forward toward the men, springing his claws for the first time since he'd begun chasing them.

Both men's eyes went wide, and now Snelgrove was crying too, his lip blubbering up and down like a child.

Two hours and ten minutes later the Womb landed in the snow again, this time having vaulted off of a lamppost and landing next to Mike and Cathy. He landed on all fours and looked up at the two of them like a dog. "You guys didn't have to come," he said, craning his head in all directions as he spoke, looking out for spectators even though they were well within the cover of darkness.

"Yes, we did," Cathy said, her eyes cast downward.

"I can handle this on my own. I don't really need your support."

"It's not about supporting this, because I don't," she corrected, and she couldn't help her upper lip curling just that little bit in revulsion. "It's about sharing the responsibility for this."

Mike nodded once in agreement, but said nothing.

The Womb finally rose to his feet and looked at the house they were standing next to. They were facing its back end, the odd little dirt road that went along the backs of houses on this street so that dump trucks could collect the garbage without going on the main drag. He turned his slanted red eyes toward the door, two deadbolts located just above the knob. One looked freshly installed, a consequence of life in Coral Beach. There were three windows on this side, two with their lights off, one with it on and the window cracked just a little to let air circulate. The very top of a shower fixture told him that that room was the bathroom. "How long since the lights went out?" he asked finally, never taking his eyes off the house.

"About twenty minutes for the one on the left. The one on the right was off since we got here."

"That's the one, then."

"Safe bet, yeah." he said, clenching his fists. "We could still find another way to do this."

The Womb turned and regarded him emotionlessly. They stared at each other for a long moment, and finally Mike nodded. He turned to Cathy then, who would not meet his gaze. Retracting his claws, he reached a hand out to touch her cheek... and she jerked back immediately. He held his hand there in mid air for a moment, then let it fall, turned, and walked toward the house.

His leap over the fence took him three-quarters of the way through the yard, and a few seconds later another leap put him on the roof. Silently, he leaned over the eve and slid the bathroom window the rest of the way open, then disappeared inside with one fluid movement.

"Heaven help us," Cathy whispered, burying her head in Mike's shoulder.

Jaden Mal lay in the bottom bed on the bunk beds in his room, his warm covers pulled up and around his body tight and his head laid between two fluffy pillows. The last foster kids that the family he was with had taken in had been twins, so now he alternated between beds, even though his foster mother repeatedly told him to just pick one and stay with it so she wouldn't have to do so much on laundry day.

Batman wallpaper lined the wall and if you looked at the images staring at the door and moving your eyes across until you were at the door again, they told a story of Batman fighting the Joker. Except for a dresser with a few cheap toys on the top of it (hand-me-down Transformers that weren't even real Transformers, just Go-Bots) the room was almost completely bare.

Jaden opened his eyes and looked around, a car passing by and its headlights illuminating his room like a flashlight swept across it. Everything was just where he'd left it, just where it should be, and then the light went out again, leaving him in darkness. He turned his head back into his pillow smiling, and closed his eyes.

- Creeek!-

The sound of the floor board bending echoed off the walls quickly, and was gone as soon as it started.

Jaden's eyes snapped open and he whirled around in the bed, his eyes scanning the night frantically. After several seconds of silence that felt like forever, there was another, similar sound, but quicker, like the foot being removed from the board it had stepped on. His heart began to pump fiercely, as if trying to escape from his chest, and beads of sweat began to dot his brow and grow, tumbling into his eyes and making them itch.

There was a small, skittering sound that his mind could not identify concretely, but made many guesses at. It could have been the sound of a rat scurrying across the fake hardwood floors, the sound of claws scraping against a hard surface, the sound of a few marbles falling and then rolling across the room...

A giant millipede clattering across the floor.

The sound stopped, and was followed by a slurping, and that one was unmistakable. He knew of nothing in his room that could make that sound, on its own or with his help. He clutched his covers tight against his chest, wanting to pull them over his head to hide but too terrified to. Too terrified to move.

Outside there was the telltale engine roar of another car turning to come down the street outside his house. This one was accelerating, the low hum growing louder with every mile it went up. The lights hit his window fast, and he barely had time for his eyes to adjust when he saw it. Hunched in the corner, its back turned to him, was something that might have been a man covered in black scales, only the arch of its back and its feet clearly visible. It turned its head as soon as the light hit it, and Jaden saw that its eyes were large and red, and they glowed in competition with the headlights.

Jaden let out a small yelp, and the creature was gone before the light had even left, disappeared in a quick flash of movement as if it had just evaporated.

Jaden was breathing heavily now, his shoulders rising and falling dramatically with each breath. He could feel his heart in his throat and felt like he was going to choke on it, as his eyes again searched out the darkness for some sign of whatever he had just seen.

There was nothing for a long time, maybe five whole minutes. No scratching, slurping or creaking, and no movement from the dark that enveloped his bed. Building up his courage, Jaden closed his eyes and bit his lip... then stepped down from the bed, his feet gradually finding their place on the cold floor, sending chills up and down his spine. He looked around the room again carefully, squinting at every dark shadow or place that provided any shelter, then turned around to face his bed.

There was a sigh from the darkness and he froze, his entire form becoming as rigid as a corpse. He thought he felt hot breath on the nape of his neck but did not turn around, did not make a sound except to swallow dryly, his mouth feeling like a desert. After another minute of nothing, he bent down and looked underneath his bed. There was nothing there, just dust bunnies and a comic book. He arose to his feet again. He reached to his left and fumbled for the light switch. He thought he felt his hand brush against something that ought not to be there, but the sensation was gone after a millisecond, and his hand finally found the switch. The lights came on all at once, startlingly bright and fixtureless, and

317

he had to close his eyes a second even though he didn't want to.

When his eyes opened, he gazed all around his room. There was no closet, a fact for which he was suddenly very grateful. He checked everywhere, his eyes digging like a prospector for any sign of motion or danger, but found nothing. He smiled, then reached for the light, stopped, and decided it was better to leave it on as he curled up into bed again, this time facing the room. After several long minutes his eyelids started to get heavy again and began to close as he drifted off to sleep.

- squeak!-

It was soft, ever so soft, and he had no idea where it had come from. It seemed to have come from everywhere all at once, and again his eyes feverishly scanned every nook and cranny in the small space he called a bedroom for some sign of where it could be coming from. He tried to tell himself that he was dreaming, but he knew that that wasn't true. He'd never seen anything scary enough in his life to make his imagination dream up that thing, whatever it had been. The memory of it, still fresh in his mind, came to him, and suddenly his eyes were not tired anymore.

There was another sound, a kind of frumping noise, and this time it was all too clear where it had come from.

The top bunk.

The slurping sound came again, and he lowered his head into his covers just enough so that only his eyes stuck out. There was a growl, and then a mumble, and the voice sounded like it was a bear trying to say human words, rough and inhuman.

- squeak-
- squeak-
- squeak-

Each sound was stretched out as long as it could go, like nails on a chalkboard, and there was a slight pause between each one. Their close proximity to each other worried the child, whose pillow was now soaked down with tears.

- squeak-
- squeeaa - -

The room plunged again into darkness, and there was a loud smash that made Jaden almost leap from the bed onto the shattered glass. He realized too late that the creature had been unscrewing the light bulb.

There was another frumping sound, then again (shorter, though), and then silence.

Jaden sat up in bed, his eyes wide, waiting for the motion the creature would make when it jumped from the bed. There was none. There was no doubting its presence now. Anything could have made the sounds, and his imagination could have been responsible for the quick flash of black mass he had seen, but there was no scared thought so powerful that it could unscrew a light bulb.

He stared into the darkness as it slowly grew, the light fading from his memory until all he saw was black. He watched it for a full six minutes, a few more tears and lots of perspiration washing over his cheeks, and then let out a small whimper and turned toward the wall, bringing the covers up close to his nose again.

Red eyes opened suddenly, centimeters away from his. They were so bright they were blinding, and so close that they completely overtook his field of vision. He opened his mouth to scream, and immediately felt a cold hand over his mouth, the creature's claws dragging along his cheek but not cutting it as it rolled in one unbelievably swift motion, stratling the child's chest. Its weight felt enormous, and its hand smelled like molded bread.

As Jaden watched, eyes bugged out so far he felt they might explode, the creature bent down toward him and opened its mouth, exposing bright, glimmering sharp fangs and a long tongue that came out and touched the boy on the tip of his nose. Tears were coming out of his eyes faster than he could make them now, like a dam had exploded inside their sockets.

The creature took a deep breath, then bellowed "DO YOU KNOW WHO I AM?!?"

The boy said nothing. Didn't move, didn't breathe.

The creature brought its other hand forward, a single talon extended, and slowly closed in toward one of Jaden's pupils with it. "Do you?"

Jaden nodded frantically, and the claw retracted just before it would have blinded him.

"Who am I?"

It removed its hand, and the child did not scream, and he had to struggle to get the words out. "You're the Boogy Man."

The demon smiled, showing that its teeth went back at least six inches further than a human's would. Then the smile left and it lashed out with both hands, nicking the boy's earlobe and drawing blood. "Do you know what I'm going to do to you?"

Jaden shook his head, clasping his hands together in a prayer at his chests. His tiny, chubby knuckles had turned so white that they looked like bones.

It slammed its hands against its own chest, digging the claws in deep and then retracting them after only a second. Eight tiny holes were in it, slowly closing before Jaden's eyes, and the creature leaned in until its chest was hovering over his head, letting the one or two drips of black ooze that came out fall onto the boy's cheeks. "I'm going to eat you. I'm going to eat you one piece at a time until there's nothing left."

Jaden shook his head no, but it wasn't an answer, it was a plea.

"Do you know why?"

Again the boy shook his head, the teardrops mixing with the black ooze on his face and dribbling down his cheeks onto his pillows, making mascara-like stains of his face.

"Because that's what happens when you don't tell the truth. Because that's what I do to little boys that lie. Do you know what I'm talking about?"

Jaden nodded, and his tears weren't silent now, they came out it pained little wails because they weren't just fear anymore, they were clouded by sorrow and guilt. When the creature heard them, he leaned back, just a tiny bit. Then it came forward again, extending a claw to its fullest length and lowering it toward the boy's chest...

"I'll do it!" Jaden squealed, closing his puffy red eyes tight so he wouldn't have to see what was happening to him. The words were barely distinguishable, distorted by pain and fear and his wailing. "I'll tell the truth I swear I will just don't hurt me, please don't hurt me please please please please please..."

He opened his eyes and found the creature no longer there, even though he was sure the weight of it was still on him. He looked around, moisture shaking from his scalp with each direction he turned in. After five minutes it occurred to him that the creature had left, after ten he was sure of it. At one point he thought maybe it had been a nightmare, but the glass on the floor and the black smudges on his pillow were all the proof he needed.

He would find no sleep that night, nor the one after.

Again something landed next to Mike and Cathy, and this time it was Xander, not the Womb. Cathy had fully expected him to be in tears, but he wasn't. To the contrary, there wasn't anything on his face at all.

Mike opened his mouth to speak, then stopped. He looked down and cursed under his breath.

"Did..." Cathy began, then stopped as well.

"It's done," Xander said flatly, and started walking away from the house without a word. They followed him and walked in silence all the way home.

They did not chain Xander to any cross that night. He assured them it would be a sleepless one.

CHAPTER TWENTY-FOUR: NOTES

As I lay awake that night, my thoughts kept going back to the boy. Could he have been reasoned with? Could the courts have been convinced with the same evidence that convinced us? Was this the only way to do it?

I kept reminding myself that it was pointless, now. That the damage had already been done, and that no amount of speculation was going to undo it. But every time I dispelled my doubts with that argument, the same recourse came to mind: what happens next time? How far are we going to have to go the next time something like this happens?

As hard as I tried not to think about it, it kept coming back to me.

CHAPTER TWENTY-FIVE: SILENCE

Mike jogged along at a brisk pace, finally catching up to Cathy and Xander as they headed to school. They were early for once, not having to make a detour to unchain Xander at the church. He huffed from lack of breath, his face sweaty even though the air had a biting cold wind on it. "Hey," he said, taking a moment to compose himself.

Neither of them said anything in return, they just kept walking in silence. After a moment, so did he.

As the school came into view, Cathy finally broke it. "We did the right thing, right?"

"No," Xander said, without a moment's pause. "We did the wrong thing for the right reason. There's a difference."

She paused, considering that. "We did do it for the right reason -- right?"

He did not look at her, nor did he answer.

"We'll see when Megan calls us after the meeting with the kid," Mike said, touching her hand gently.

"So, what? The end justifies the means? Is that our new team slogan?"

Again, silence.

"Maybe it always has been," Xander said, his face glued to the icy sidewalk in front of him. "Maybe now we're just growing up enough to realize it."

Cathy sighed, joining him in his staring contest against the road before them. When she looked up again they were at the school. There were almost no cars in the parking lot.

Mike opened the door for both of them and then entered himself. "What do you have first period?" he asked Cathy as they neared the corner to go to her locker, trying to change the subject any way he could.

"Chem, I think," she said, rubbing her temple. "My brain won't work. I didn't get any sleep last - -" she stopped in her tracks as they turned the corner, her mouth open wide.

Xander and Mike turned toward the source of her shock, and Mike's expression changed to watch. Xander's remained constant, silently regarding the horrific scene presented before them.

Calla McFadden hung from the ceiling, a rough noose made from what looked to be one of the big white sheets for Home Ec. Class tied around her neck. Her head was jerked awkwardly to the right, and there was a red ring around the edges of the sheet. Her mouth was open but here eyes were closed. Her arms dangled at her sides and she swayed in the breeze from an open doorway down the hall. Next to her was a toppled over chair. On her chest a white envelope had been pinned, and there were several names on it but scratched out, the end result being the letter was addressed to no one.

Cathy turned a threw herself at Mike and began to cry again.

Xander took one cautious step forward, noticing the urine stain on the front of her pants and the small puddle on the floor from when she had lost control of her bladder. He closed his eyes and listened, trying to get any sense of a heartbeat, or of any smell except that of death.

He found neither.

"State your name, for the record," the Bailiff said, and each word was followed by the clacking of keys as the stenographer in the corner dictated all that was said.

The small room just to the side of the main courtroom was dank and drafty. When the other areas of the courthouse had been renovated and redesigned in '86, this one had been left out, as it was so rarely used. There was an old oil portrait of Richard Nixon on the wall behind where the Judge sat at the far end of the table, and it dated the room considerably. Dust was everywhere, making Megan cough every time she took a breath. Nathan had patted her on the back in support the first time, but after that didn't see the point. The room was small, with the large oak desk taking up most of it. Even with one's belly pressed against the table, your back still wasn't too far off from the wall.

"Judge Miriam Pike," she said, crisply and clearly, without bothering to look up from the file before her at the man taking down every word spoken. She was pushing fifty at least, but her curly blonde hair tumbled over her shoulders and down her back and made her look fifteen years younger. Her eyes were big and blue, with long lashes. She had full, pink lips and a tight chin.

"Anthony Jones," Tony sighed under his breath, his hands clasped before him on the desk. He was wearing a grey pin-striped power suit, his hair slicked back and his face so cleanly shaven it might have been waxed. No matter what the case, it seemed, he went all out to dress to impress.

"Megan Greene," she said, trying to sound involved but with her eyes were firmly glued on the boy, who sat between Tony and the Judge on the opposite side of the table. Pushing the sides of her dark red hair behind her ears and wishing she had worn it up, she glanced back down at the few frantic notes she had made after Xander's call.

"Nathan Summers," Nathan stated, his arms folded around the bulking chest of his grey suit, which almost matched the color of his silver hair. He was by far to tallest in the room, and even sitting he came very close to the height of the short, stocky bailiff.

All eyes turned to the boy. His eyes and cheeks were still red and puffy, and his lower lip quivered as he surveyed all the faces watching him meekly. He looked terrified, and had ever since he got out of the car out front. Tears seemed ready to spring forth from him at any moment, and Megan drawled a sigh at the sight. With a face like that, her case was six feet under before the child had even spoken. "Jay - - Jaden Mal."

"Thank you," Judge Pike said, smiling at the boy as politely and warmly as possible, trying hard to put the child at ease with his surroundings. She turned toward Tony and gave him a nod.

"Jaden," Tony coaxed, leaning in to face the boy. "I need you to tell us what happened three days ago, when you were in the Guidance office with Reverend Gallagher."

The boy was silent. He stared blankly at the file Tony was leaning on. It had his name on it.

"Jaden?" Tony said again, coughing discreetly into his sleeve and throwing a quick look to the Judge, then to Megan. In the corner the stenographer typed away.

"I have to tell the truth," Jaden said, his voice far away and tired, as if he wasn't even aware of where he was.

Megan shot Nathan a confused look, who returned it.

"Just tell us what happened," Tony repeated, his hands open palmed in a sort of pleading gesture now.

"Nothing," Jaden said finally, looking from Tony to the Judge. "Nothing happened. He just talked about my foster family and how things were going. He didn't do anything."

Tony's eyes went wide. He looked to the Judge, who had an eyebrow raised to him.

"Jaden, if you're scared..." Tony coaxed, leaning toward the boy, placing a hand on his shoulder in support.

"I am scared. I have to tell the truth, that the man didn't touch me. It told me so."

Megan leaned in, her ears perked.

"It?" Tony pressed.

"The Boogy Man. He told me I had to tell the truth. I should tell the truth."

"Uh-Huh," Tony sighed, watching as Megan took out her notepad and started to scribble down what was happening. "And... who is this Boogy Man?"

Jaden looked confused, turning from Tony to the Judge, as if the question had been obvious. "It was black... and slimy, and it had scales and black blood. And it had red eyes and a red mouth with lots of teeth and it came into my room last night after I went to bed and told me I had to tell the truth."

Megan looked at the child, her brow crumpled, her mind taking in what she had just heard and filing it away.

"Your Honor," Nathan interrupted, standing to his full, empowering height as he finally spoke. "Is this serious? Because my firm has other cases it's supposed to be handling right now. We are doing this, without cost, because we believe in Gallagher's innocence. If the child says that's true, than..."

"That will be enough," Judge Pike said, motioning for Nathan to sit back down.

"Thank you, your Honor," Tony nodded, sweating a little.

"From *both* of you," she corrected, pointing her pen at Tony.

"Your Honor," Megan said, raising her hand without looking up. "In light of the child's testimony, I move that all charges against Reverend Robert Gallagher..."

"Will be dropped," Pike finished, nodding as she closed the folder before her, tapping it twice against the desk. "We'll process his release immediately. You may leave, Miss. Greene. Mr. Summers." Megan and Nathan rose and began to head for the door. Tony rose as well, but the Judge turned to him and waved him back down. "Not you, Mr. Jones. Your client and I have a bit more to discuss."

CHAPTER TWENTY-SIX: NO REASON

Mike and Cathy sat on Xander's bed, their backs against the wall. Cathy's legs were curled up into her breasts, her chin rested on her knees. Mike looked depressed, occupying himself by tearing loose material from his jeans, staring at a spot or stain on the bedspread. Xander sat backward in the swivel chair at his desk, facing both of them but not looking at them. School had been cancelled, and for good reason. Most of the student body hadn't even made it there by the time word had spread, hadn't even seen the body.

"What did the note say?" Mike asked, forcing himself to find his voice. It came out squeaky and uneven.

"Nothing, really," Cathy frowned glumly, her voice muffled by her pants. "That's what that cop you're were friends with said, anyway. It was three pages long, but it didn't say much of anything. There was no... reason. And the date. It was written three months ago, but the date she killed herself was right there on it."

"She knew all this time?" Xander asked, raising his head off the back of his chair. "She was planning this? There had to be something that set it off."

"No," Cathy sighed, her lips pursed. "She was just depressed, I guess. She just... decided she didn't want to live anymore. She even said sorry to anyone she hurt or for anything she did, that she was going live her last few weeks however she wanted."

"Why are you doing it here?"

Calla looked down at the clumpy green substance in the baggie, then back up at her friend, an annoyed and comically exasperated expression on her face. "Because when I do it at home, my parents get mad."

"What're you doing out - " he started as he turned the corner, the smile stopping as quickly as the sentence did.

Calla McFadden was leaning against the snow-covered brick wall of the school, her jacket wrapped tight around her as she held her thumb and forefinger up close to her mouth, which was drawn up like a bow, sucking the last few puffs out of the joint that she had meticulously rolled, trying to get as much out of it as possible before it got down to the filter she had hastily made out of the cardboard from a pack of Marlboro's. Her eyes were wide at first, the both of them wondering what exactly the other thought they were doing, but not knowing how to ask. When the shock wore off, Calla's thin eyebrows lowered into a scowl as she tossed what was left of her joint into a snow back, exhaling a puff of blue smoke. She gave him what she referred to when amongst her friends as 'the elevator' (looking a person up and down, usually for the purposes of either checking them out or seeing if you could take them. Or both,) then started to walk past him. She stopped when the both of them were shoulder to shoulder and turned toward him so that her lip was dangerously close to his ear. "You're cute for a spaz," she drawled, snickering a little as she, turned the corner and disappeared, leaving Mike to just stand there bewildered.

The shock wore off her face as she looked him up and down, and became a sly smile. "Want some?" she asked, handing the joint to him and sticking out her tongue, revealing a small pink stud in it not far from the tip.

Xander took the rolled up paper from her and watched the smoke rise from its tip for a moment before handing it back. "No, thanks," he said as she took it.

She shrugged, then brought it to her lips and took another draw. She held it in as long as possible before letting it out. "Your loss. This is some kick-ass stuff."

"It was happening the whole time," Xander mused quietly. "We just didn't notice."

They sat in silence for a minute and considered that, and Cathy couldn't help but think of when she'd found Xander's gun when he'd tried the same thing, and failed.

"There has to be a reason," he said hoarsely, his eyes welling up finally and drawing the attention of his friends. "This can't be it. This can't be all there is. I terrorized a young boy, I've killed more people than I'd care to count, risked my life more -- and this girl just decides she doesn't want to live anymore for no reason? Spends the last three days crying out for help to deaf ears and then does it... for no reason? It can't be, there's got to be more --"

"But there isn't," Mike said glumly.

Xander looked up to meet his friend's steady gave, a single teardrop traveling down each cheek.

RIING!

Xander moved, picking up the phone and wiping his eyes with his sleeve, as if the person on the other end could see them. He sniffed back hard once to compose himself, then answered. "Hello?" he was silent for a moment, then smiled just a little. "That's great. Yeah, sure. Tonight's fine. Bye," he hung up the phone and turned back to them.

Mike raised an eyebrow to him. "Hot date?" he said, trying for lividity, but his voice was still far to sombre for it.

"We won," Xander said, then leaned his head back on the chair.

There was several minutes of silence then, as all three considered the validity of that statement.

"Yay for us," Cathy said finally.

CHAPTER TWENTY-SEVEN: CONFER

Megan Greene sat alone at one of the booths at the bar across from the offices Mayer, Summers and Soul; attorneys at law. She sipped her margarita casually, keeping one eye on the yellow legal folder next to her as she scanned the room, waiting for her guest. She did not know whether or not he would be late, as he had always shown up to meet her of his own discourse, hardly ever by something prearranged. She was still wearing the power-suit and grey skirt she had been in the meeting with the boy, but the suit was unbuttoned now and so was the top button of the white blouse underneath, making her much more relaxed. Covertly, she slid her right foot out of its heel and stretched it. After the meeting she'd spent the majority of the day processing and running back and forth from the Bird and Snelgrove case to the office, and her feet were killing her. She ate the olive from her drink then took another sip, hoping the pain would subside soon.

"Hey pretty lady," Xander said, his voice devoid on the usual upbeat twist it had in these meetings. He said the words as though he were reading lines from a script, rather than feeling them.

"Hey," she smiled, motioning to the beer she had ordered for him at the seat across from her. "I guess that's three I owe you."

"We'll call it even for the beer," he smirked, bringing the bottle's long neck to her mouth and taking a long drink, the smallest bit of it dribbling out of his mouth.

"Sorry I doubted you before. I think this was the easiest case I ever worked, subject matter aside."

He did not respond, except to peel the label off his drink.

She coughed uncomfortably. "Well, Gallagher was released a few hours ago, and the charges should be officially dropped by the end of the week. He should be getting home right about now, actually. The Judge ordered the boy taken out of his foster home and admitted him into psychiatric care, pending further examination. They're worried that one of his other caretakers abused him and caused this whole mess."

Xander nodded, still not looking up, and took another swig.

"They'll find out who, I'm sure."

Again, he nodded.

"I meant to ask -- what made you so sure Gallagher was innocent to begin with?" she pried, trying hard to draw him into the conversation.

He looked up finally, but his eyes were twin black holes. It was like looking at a machine. He tried to speak, then closed his mouth.

Something inside him was broken, she could tell, and she reached out and touched his hand, wanting to help him badly.

"It was his permanent records," Xander replied, finally finding his voice. "Anyone who had cared to look would have seen it. He'd cried abuse so many times it probably would have been uncovered anyway, if the prosecution hadn't rushed so much."

Jaden closed his eyes and tried to go to sleep, the image of the black man still burned into his eyelids. He shuddered. This time, the room was completely bare, nothing but the bed and the walls around it, no windows except the one in the door the hospital had locked after the lights in the rooms had been turned off remotely.

"I thought so," Megan nodded, frowning. She paused and clicked her tongue against her teeth, then took another drink as she decided exactly how to phrase what she was about to ask. "How much do you trust Gallagher?"

That got Xander's attention. He looked at her, eyebrows raised and pupils sparkling. "What?"

"I'm just saying," she sighed, laying her hands out as if to display her points. "*You* looked through the kid's records and found out that he'd said it before, and knew that he was probably lying. Like you said, we would have probably found this out too, but not before the legalities had ruined Gallagher's life. But didn't he have access to the files too? Couldn't he have seen them, known someone would assume the child was lying, and do this?"

The lock to Jaden's room door snapped to with a crack, and the door slowly opened on creaking hinges. There was a man in the doorway wearing a uniform with brown hair that went down past his ears and thick braces, smiling wickedly to himself as he took one last look around outside.

"I trust Gallagher completely," Xander said, but his voice lacked conviction as he thought back to when he had spoken to Gallagher in the penitentiary, and how his reading hadn't come out quite right. It was like Gallagher had been holding *something* back, without outright lying.

"Okay," Megan sighed, forcing a smile and raising her glass to him. "To another victory for team Drew / Greene."

Xander paused, still considering what Megan had said, then raised his bottle as well.

The orderly sat at the edge of Jaden's bed, sliding his hand underneath the covers.

"No," the boy said, starting to cry. "I'll tell. I'll tell the truth. The man said I have to tell the truth..."

The man snickered, his voice high and nasal. "Go ahead," he laughed. "The more you tell them someone's touching you, the longer they'll keep you in here -- with me."

-clink-

Their glasses touched briefly, and they shared a moment of eye contact that made them both smile. Even though they both had so much on their minds, and they were so different in age and background and... everything, really; they found solace in one another's friendship and drank to it, both of them finishing their beverages.

"You did good work today, Xander," she said, smiling warmly at him.

"No, I didn't," he corrected. His voice was gruff but there was an honest smile on his lips. "But I'll do better tomorrow. Maybe that's the important thing."

"Cheers."

He straightened his jacket, obviously getting ready to leave, then stopped. "How'd it go with the Bird / Snelgrove thing, anyway?"

Megan looked up at him, raising an eyebrow suspiciously. "Curiously enough, they admitted to all wrongdoing at the hearing today. They're going to pay all damages and will be serving at least six months apiece."

Xander smirked. "Somehow, I thought they might," he got up now, touching her hand briefly as he did. "I got to go. I have a previous engagement with Mike and Cathy, and I don't want to keep them up too late. Keep the peace, okay?"

She smirked at him. "See you later."

"Not if I see you first," he said, then turned and headed for the door and out into the night air.

Megan watched him go, then opened the file that had been at her left side the entire time, and took out two sheets of paper. The first was the stenographer's report from the meeting with Jaden and the rest earlier today.

Jaden Mal: The Boogy Man. He told me I had to tell the truth. I should tell the truth.

Anthony Jones (prosecution): Uh-Huh, And... who is this 'Boogy Man'?

Jaden Mal: It was black... and slimy, and it had scales and black blood. And it had red eyes and a red mouth with lots of teeth and it came into my room last night after I went to bed and told me I had to tell the truth.

She frowned and motioned to the bartender for another drink, then picked up the second sheet, examining in carefully. It was stamped as the official stenographer's report from the trial of Adam Genblade.

Megan Greene (defence): Mr. Genblade,

Adam Genblade (defendant): Please, Adam.

Megan Greene: Adam, do you know the man seated behind me?

Adam Genblade: His name is Xander Drew.

Megan Greene: Correct. And how do you know him?

Adam Genblade: We studied together.

Megan Greene: Really? Where?

Adam Genblade: At the Church of Smoke and Mirrors, of course.

Megan Greene: But how do you know him, really?

Adam Genblade: He is the Black Womb.

Megan Greene: Of course he is. And what is that exactly?

Adam Genblade: A manifestation of a genetic disorder which resulted from meticulous breeding for decades by Engen's top scientific minds.

Megan Greene: What does it look like?

Adam Genblade: It covers your body in a dark, black film with red eyes and mouth.

Megan Greene: Why can't we see it?

Adam Genblade: It exists inside him until blood loss or lack of consciousness or emotional stimulation forces it out.

Megan laid the sheet down carefully next to the first, then looked at them side by side. Black, slimy, red eyes and mouth. Black, filmy, red eyes and mouth. The bartender laid her drink down next to her and she immediately took a long gulp, looking at the door that Xander Drew had just walked through.

CHAPTER TWENTY-EIGHT: LAST

The night air was cool on Julie Peterson's skin, and made her shudder as she stepped out the back porch, realizing she hadn't taken the clothes off the line as her Aunt had asked her to hours before. To add to the chill she was only wearing her yellow tank top and grey pajama pants, and the wind cut through them as easily as though she was wearing nothing at all. Her auburn hair was still a tangled mess from the shower and draped around her freckled face, she huffed as she looked at the long lineup of clothes pinned up before her.

One by one she started picking them in, bending over every now and again to lay them in the clothes basket at her feet.

He watched her intently, especially when she bent, her long legs moving as if she'd been poured into her clothes.

In the kitchen the kettle started to whistle, and she turned back to it, several pins stuck between those thick, ruby lips.

He chuckled softly to himself from the bushes, a high-pitched and whiny sound.

Another gust of wind came, and this time she cursed as it not only nipped at her already freezing skin, but took a shirt clean out of her hands and into the snow below the step. She growled at it, then turned and went back into the house.

He lost sight of her for a moment, beady eyes searching the various windows frantically, pushing away the leaves he stood behind and his own long brown hair aside for clarity. She came into view through the kitchen window.

She took the kettle off its burner, then turned it off, shivered, and walked out of the room.

Again he looked for her, scanning each window within sight.

She appeared in her bedroom, taking an old sweater out of the closet. She started to pull off her tank top to change into something that would protect her better.

He watched her undress, his smile undeniable, but his pulse steady.

When she was done she went back downstairs, then through the kitchen, and finished taking in the clothes. Her mother came in from the living room, and the both of them sat at the kitchen table and sipped tea for thirty-two minutes.

He watched the entire time, trying to figure out what they were saying while watching their lips, often being distracted my Julie's, sweet and supple.

After that they went upstairs and to bed, and he watched her change a second time, and finally she turned off the light.

Derek Smith rose to his feet out of the bushes, smiling to himself as he continued to watch the window, then licked his lips and turned to walk back into the forest.

EPILOGUE

Reverend Gallagher was reinstated as the school's Guidance Councilor, all the charges against him were dropped. I don't feel like we can call that one a victory. The school isn't assigning students to go see him anymore, and very few will willingly. There's an odd logic to it, I suppose. Like, where there's smoke, there's fire. That once someone's been accused of something so hennas, even if proven innocent he shouldn't be trusted again. Still, it almost seems a shame not to count it as a win for our side... we've gotten so few over the past few months.

You can see the hurt in the man's eyes now, too. Xander said it's all natural, that everyone has their own natural healing factor for things like this, as he does for everything else. That the human soul has an infinite capability for regeneration. He said it, but he doesn't believe it. His actions are louder than his words, and every day, more and more, his actions spell defeat. Looking at him now, I think maybe the opposite is true. That maybe our bodies can heal, but our souls can't. That maybe the first stab comes at birth and we all spend the next eighty years bleeding to death spiritually.

Some of us don't even take that long.

When Mike and I chained up Xander for the night, there was that look in his eyes as he slipped into delirium. Somehow, even though his eyes were only just beginning to turn black, it seemed like he was already the Womb. Like the transformation matters less and less, like now that's just who he is. I looked at him, sweat dripping down his brow, and somehow I knew he was seeing things that weren't there.

"Mike?" I said, tugging on his shirt. "Mike, I think he's hallucinating."

Mike finished snapping the chain tight around Xander's hand just as tiny enamel claws began to poke their way out, just breaking the flesh. He turned toward Xander emotionlessly, squeezing his friend's chin to make him look up at him. "It's hard to tell. I think maybe his eyes are rolled up into his head."

"Is he in pain?"

Mike looked at me. His eyes were filled with pity, but not toward Xander. It was like I wasn't getting something that he was, and he felt bad for me. The way you feel bad for mental patients who just can't help that they don't understand. "I don't think he notices it anymore, sweet heart," he told me earnestly. "You go now. I'm gonna stay with him a minute until he transforms."

I turned to go, then stopped. Instead, I planted my feet squarely in front of him, looking into the pools of tar he called eyes.

"Hun, you don't have to..."

"I want to watch," I said, cutting him off. I'm sure I'm making myself sound much more determined and righteous here than I actually was. Maybe.

"Cathy,"

"I want to watch!" I said again, turning to chide him. When I looked back, the ooze had already begun to slither over his body. I use the term ooze only because that's the way he describes it. To me it's more like gel, and I always thought it went over him the way a slinky goes down stairs, tossing itself forward over his body and then pulling itself up, then repeating. Watching it like this, it wasn't hard to see it as a living thing, completely separate from Xander.

But I wasn't looking at the black gel, I was looking right into his eyes. They say the eyes are the gateway to the soul, and I wanted to see if it changed. When Xander became the Womb, did his soul change as well? I thought I'd gotten my answer months ago, when he'd first revealed the Womb to Mike and me, but lately... I just needed some reassurance, okay? Let me do what I want, I'm damaged.

His eyes may have been black, but his face was still his. It made it easy to see how much pain he was in. He turned away from me and mumbled something that I think was in French, which was odd, since Xander didn't know French. I paused for a second to translate internally, and it was something about a blonde.

When he turned back to meet my gaze, I knew. He was thinking about Sara. That was it, that's what he was seeing... and yet it wasn't really. That was part of it all right, but not all. Suddenly it was like I wasn't looking into his eyes anymore, but seeing through them. That's the best way I can explain it, I know it's not coming out the way I mean. I could see what he was seeing, and it wasn't just Sara, it was Julie, too. And Mandy. Poor, sweet Mandy. Kerri Walker was in there too, her tiny corpse rigid and frozen when they found her naked in the woods. For the briefest of instants there was Megan Greene, and Jaden Mal, then his mother, and then there was me. He spent a good long while on that thought, and for the first time I saw myself the way he must see me all the time, and it made me want to cry everything out of me right then and there. Then, at the end, there was Calla McFadden. A girl who had spent her last hours on this earth calling out to all of us for help, and we just wouldn't listen. Who, even through whatever it was she was going through, had stopped long enough to help a young boy crying out himself, astute enough to see something of herself in him.

The gel was almost covering him now, and the place where I was looking wasn't even so much his eyes as dents in his face. I blinked and the link between us, whatever it had been, was gone. I looked around at the old abandoned church we were in, and at the cross behind him that supported his chains, and suddenly it all seemed very fitting. I wondered if the church he'd been in as an infant had looked anything like this. The church, the cross, his background with the foster home and Engen -- suddenly it all made sense with what I had seen in his head. It was Catholic guilt, twisted somehow so that it was his own. I got a mental picture of what Xander's mind must be like. It was just a hallway filled with doors. Like the old lady and the tiger trick, only he's waited too long. There's a lady behind each door, and the tiger's already gotten to them all. No matter what he does, he always feels he was too late. And then, right at the end, he realizes he was the tiger all along.

Two long red slits formed across the two dents I had been looking at, as if they had been cut there, then they opened and revealed themselves to be eyes. Long, curved, triangular eyes. I swallowed hard, then looked into them. The Womb made a shallow purring sound that I recognized as what it did when it did not want to be noticed by its prey. I don't think it realized I could see it just as it could see me. No wonder, not many things would look at it so closely without running in terror.

"Cathy..." Mike started again, but I ignored him.

I stared into those red puddles until I saw what I wanted to see. Somewhere, behind the cat-like corneas and the cones that took in all of the light in the room, I saw it. It wasn't quite Xander, but then I wasn't really expecting that. What it was... was guilt. It was thinking of doing things to me, and somewhere inside it, the Black Womb felt guilty for what it was dreaming.

I felt a smile spread over my lips and leaned in, pressing them hard against him. It tried to open its mouth to bite me, but I wouldn't let it. My mouth caressed his the way it had Xander's not so long ago, its flesh warm and wet against mine. Its flesh felt scaly, and it reminded me of kissing Mike when he had been trying to grow a mustache (something I'm glad to say he gave up on quickly). I cut the inside of my lip against its jagged teeth, then reached up and ran my hand over his bald scalp. I kept my hand there as our lips parted, and I finished my child-hood crush on Xander Drew. Somehow, it was over now. I loved him more than anything, but in that moment, I had gotten everything I ever wanted to.

I turned to Mike as I stepped out of the Womb's biting range, expecting him to look mad or bitter, but he just stared at me with a knowing look in his eyes. He knew what it had been about, and somehow the kiss had made him feel even more secure. At least, I know that's what it did for me. I told him I loved him and asked him to come over to my place when he was done, just as we had the night this all started. It seemed like a life-time ago. Like my soul had bled buckets since then -- and maybe come out better for it.

As I walked home I started to think about the differences between Xander Drew and Black Womb, and as I did, I couldn't help but comment on the differences between good and evil. Lately that line had gotten blurred, to the point where everything was just grey now. Someone had told me once that when you mix black and white you get grey... and no matter how much white you stir back in, you'll never get anything but grey. What we'd done to that boy in the name of good... did a good ending justify a horrible act? By that same measure, does an evil act nullify a million good ones? They say the road to hell in paved with good intentions, and it makes me wonder what the road to heaven is paved with.

Somehow I think I don't want to know.

Cathy hit save, then closed out of her word processing program. The file stared at her from her desktop and Mike looked at it with her, leaning over her shoulder. "That's really good, baby," he said approvingly, kissing her lightly on the side of the head.

She said nothing, just stared at the file. BW.doc looked back at her, each of the capital letters like a pair of eyes staring her down, seeing which of them would blink first. Of course, she did. She brought her mouse pointer to the file and clicked down on it, holding it in her digital grasp as she brought it to the recycle bin and dropped it in.

"What are you doing?" Mike asked, but made no motion to stop her.

She right-clicked on the trash bin and clicked empty. A message came up asking if she wished to permanently delete the file, and she clicked yes.

"I thought you wanted to document everything, so that people will know everything that we did in case something happens -- so that the truth can be known."

She turned around in the chair, looking at him glumly. "Some things are better left not said," she said, not meeting his eye.

He frowned at her and stroked the side of her face with his thumb, then leaned down and kissed her. "I love you," he said, then started to walk toward the bed. He had a feeling they were in for another long night of talking. She seemed to have a lot on her mind.

Even now her brow was furrowed, the way it was whenever she was in deep thought. She bit her lip and stood, walking toward him as he lay down on the bed and started to pick up his DS again. "Promise me something?" she said, and her voice was right there and far away at the same time.

He lay the game back down and looked into her eyes. "Anything."

She lifted the edges of the loose shirt she used as a pajama top over her head and let it fall to the floor. She looked at him calmly, bare breasted in the moonlight. "Hold me afterwards," she said as she walked toward him, pulling a cover over them both. She kissed him before he had a chance to answer. She'd already known what it would be.

What happened next was many things.

It was a expression of the love they had both felt since meeting one another.

It was proof that they could overcome anything that this world threw at them, together.

It was a search for something good and right in a world that had proven to be the anything but.

It was a symbol of their devotion and trust in each other.

More than anything, it was a door... a door that led only to the future.

ABOUT THE AUTHOR

Matthew LeDrew holds an Honours Degree in English from the Memorial University of Newfoundland with a minor in Anthropology, and studied Journalism at College of the North Atlantic in Stephenville, Newfoundland. He was honoured to be a jury member of both the 2018 NLBA awards and the 2020 Arts and Letters Awards.

He has written twenty-four novels for Engen Books: the ten book Coral Beach Casefiles series, *The Long Road, Cinders, Sinister Intent, Faith, Family Values, Fate's Shadow, First Aid, Jacobi Street, Touch Your Nose, Infinity, The Tourniquet Reprisal, Exodus of Angels, Garden of the Eighth Circle, and The Rats of Refraction* the latter five of which with his co-author and wife Ellen Curtis.

He lives in Chapel Arm, Newfoundland.